W9-AVI-749
NORTH MINCH
CH
LOCH CARRON
STROMEFERRY
SCOTLAND
N
W
E
S
NORTH SEA
GLASCOW
LAND
MULL OF KINTYRE
KIRKCUDBRIGHT
RNE
GUS
FAST
WHITEHAVEN
IRISH SEA
LIVERPOOL
ENGLAND
WALES
BRISTOL
LONDON
PLYMOUTH
ENGLISH CHANNEL
LAND'S END
FRANCE

Aug '95

For

Dorothy Lunt.

A member of a great, great American family.

Best wishes

Tom M'Namara

Henry Lunt & The Ranger

Tom McNamara

NUVENTURES
PUBLISHING
La Jolla, California 92038-2489

Henry Lunt & The Ranger

Published by NUVENTURES® Publishing. First Edition 1991.
Ellen McNamara, Editor.

Library of Congress Catalog Card Number 90-061642
ISBN 0-9625632-3-4 $18.95

NUVENTURES® and its logo are registered trademarks
of NUVENTURES® Consultants, Inc.

NUVENTURES® Publishing is a division
of NUVENTURES® Consultants, Inc.
SAN 200-3805

In Memory,

George Henry McNamara

George P. Lunt

Donald Z. LaRue

Tom McNamara

has also recently co-authored the critically acclaimed non-fiction:

"AMERICA'S CHANGING WORKFORCE -
About You, Your Job, and Your Changing Work Environment."
ISBN 0-9625632-1-8 $12.95 Trade Paperback
NUVENTURES® Publishing 1990.

Prologue

Eight men rowed in the darkness towards a rocky beach they could only hear. Crouched at the bow of the longboat sat a ninth man whose small frame was enveloped by a greatcoat, his tricornered hat was fitted snugly down over his brow so it would not be lost in the turbulent sea. His vigilant eyes were focused ahead into the blackness. They searched for information about the water surrounding them and the shape of the beach ahead.

Close overhead soared an English gull, whose wings silently cut the chill night air. The bird tilted his head to one side in order to observe the strange men and their boat tumbling up and down on the dark surface of the sea. The gull did not raise a cry, for instinct had conditioned his species never to prematurely alert intruders that there might be a nesting place nearby. Instead, the gull raised one wing to circle silently back towards the rugged cliffs above the beach. It was April, hatchlings must now be silent if there was going to be danger.

To the men in the longboat, the roar of crashing waves intensified. A boy from Vermont shivered and tried to suppress his fear. In thc darkness he glanced at his fellow oarsmen to judge their reaction to the engulfing sounds, which were bringing mounting waves of terror and dread to his own being.

Sensing the collective concern of his men, the leader cupped his hands to his mouth to better channel the sound of his voice. He faced his crew and shouted in a deep, commanding voice that was only barely audible above the enveloping din of surf and spray, "Ready anchor."

He shifted to one side to allow the larger of the lead oarsmen to perform that duty.

For an uncertain moment longer, the small vessel continued to be carried like a leaf bobbing on the rim of a maelstrom. Above, a thin schism opened among the oppressive dark clouds to allow the faintest of nocturnal light to fall upon the rocky shore ahead.

From his position near the bow, the leader now had a hint of the conditions ahead. A towering rock cliff rose straight upward into the night air. At the meeting place of land and sea there was only the narrowest of beaches. The sea between the longboat and that margin of shore appeared like a cauldron of boiling white sea foam. They were only a few boat lengths from the edge of a barrier reef. As each ocean wave struck the submerged shoulder of that reef it exploded with a great roar. Following each collision, some of the spent white water continued to flow over the reef towards the shore.

The leader had only a moment to decide if there would be a sufficient depth of water within that flow to carry them safely over the reef, or whether they should seek another landing site elsewhere in the darkness. Another place might ultimately be more dangerous, and they had only a few hours in which to complete their mission.

The leader removed his right hand from beneath his wool greatcoat and clasped the shoulder of the man who held the anchor line. When the large man leaned back, he shouted resolutely into his ear, "Over the side now. We'll be going in stern first."

The man nodded. The drag anchor splashed only slightly as it descended quickly below the dark surface. The stout chain to which it was attached began to play itself out through a vent at the bow.

Moving swiftly over the benches among his oarsmen, the leader shouted directions amid the thrashing sound of dying waves, "Pull to larboard. Pull hard, men! Oars down to starboard, drag deeply on the starboard rail."

The longboat responded by changing its heading

relative to the shore. It rose and fell on the crest of each incoming wave just seaward of the submerged reef.

Just as the boat achieved a heading exactly parallel with the shore, there was a sudden dip in the constancy of the ocean's overall surface. Its abruptness brought alarm to each man in the longboat. Stomachs churned as they descended rapidly into a trough. Glancing out to sea, the leader could only sense the rising presence of an ominous wave, one which could shatter them against the ragged shoulder of the reef, now left exposed by the sudden displacement of water. They were most vulnerable in this broadside position. The wave would be upon them in an instant.

"Pull harder, men!" he screamed to his larboard oarsmen as they pumped frantically to alter their orientation before the wave struck. The longboat continued to descend into the dark channel forming between rising wave and reef.

The leader screamed towards the bow, "Give a yard or two more anchor rode, be quick!"

The vessel responded to the urgent strokes of its oarsmen by almost completing its turn away from the shore just as the leading face of a enormous wave slammed against the bow of the vessel. Great quantities of salt water erupted into the night air as the vessel found a path of least resistance, cutting straight upward onto the face of the rising behemoth. As the longboat climbed, the men inside were pitched backwards. They clung tenaciously to their positions at the oars while their feet frenziedly sought any solid fixture beneath or in front of them. Falling about them came great quantities of cold sea spray. The crest of the great wave carried them up over the top of the reef, again covering it with water.

The man tending the anchor rode now slowly and delicately played out more and more line as the vessel backed stern first through the boundary of foam that marked the turbulent region where shallow water rushed over submerged rocks. His judicious control of the anchor line limited the violence with which they might encounter obstacles, but would only endure so long as the anchor continued to bite into the ocean floor.

The men used their oars to keep the longboat in its outward facing orientation as it continued to back over the reef. Occasionally, its hull thumped against an upcropping, but succeeding wavelets and deft control of the anchor rode gradually brought the small vessel into a safer region, where the waves lapped gently against a hull that relaxed in the company of spent waters.

Moving about the boat, the leader patted his men's shoulders in appreciation of their seamanship. "Well done, lads!"

Leaving the greatcoat in a cubby beneath the bow, the leader was the first overboard into the calf deep water. Pulling his short officer's sword from its scabbard, he looked up at the towering, rocky cliff that they must now scale to reach the plateau above.

The voices of aroused English gulls began to screech threateningly above the leader, their echoes reverberated in ever increasing protest to the invasion of their shore. In an attempt to frighten the men away, they dived off by the hundreds from their small cliff face nests to whirl in the darkness above the beach.

Undaunted by the shrill harpies soaring above him, the leader turned back to glance at two of his men who were still gathering up the remaining muskets, broadswords, and grappling lines from beneath the oilcloth which had been tightly secured to the bottom boards of the longboat during the perilous approach. The remainder of his men already stood with him on the beach.

Over the high pitched protests of gull voices, he gestured with his sword towards the sheer cliff and commanded,

"Forward, marines!"

1

Empire

The glistening, four lanterned, mahogany coach catapulted past the pillars of Whitehall, and then swerved at break neck speed down the last stretch which would bring the vehicle to its destination. It was well past midnight, an hour at which normally the affairs of the British Empire had been thoroughly discussed, digested, and then retired for the evening. It was the season of endless evenings of elegant candle lit dinners attended by white wigged influence peddlers and power brokering politicians, their wives, their mistresses, and a sprinkle of senior military, whose majestic uniforms gave each affair its needed sense of grandeur and empire. It was the season of Parliament.

The breaths of the six black horses punctuated the chill April air as they propelled the elegant carriage. The air was thick with dew and the warm sweating bodies of the steeds shimmered in the cold as they roared past the polished glass street lights of the capital district. The marine adjutant leaned over to advise his driver to arrive in front of their destination with a flourish. The whip was applied with a resounding crackle, just as the beasts pressed around the corner and into Admiralty yard.

A squad of royal marines were barked to full attention as the brakes of the carriage squealed in torment and the driver hauled in on the reins, straining to bring the black beasts to steadiness. The carriage's sole occupant threw open his own door and stepped down into the yard before anyone could give him assistance. The tall, lean man held the rank of Rear Admiral in the Royal Navy. As he walked briskly forward, he made minor adjustments to his uniform, wig, and sword. He had left his greatcoat inside the coach.

As he ascended the steps into Admiralty House, the great door at the entrance opened in anticipation. Light and warmth spilled out into the cold yard. A voice from inside announced the Admiral's presence. Just as he reached the top step, a second squad of impeccably dressed royal marines rushed out to form a line on either side of the doorway.

"We'll be using your carriage, Hugh," said the first officer to emerge from the doorway. The Rear Admiral quickly stopped mid stride and saluted the imposing height and great girth that was the Earl of Sandwich, First Lord of the Admiralty. The Rear Admiral kept his breath measured, and his demeanor reserved as two columns of royal marines were barked through a special series of gestures reserved only for Lords of the Admiralty. Three other Admiralty Lords filed out.

"Good of you to get here so promptly, Hugh. You see, the Prime Minister is in a bit of a frenzy. Hopefully, we'll be able to use your presence to assure him that something will be done immediately."

"I don't quite understand, Sir."

"You will shortly."

He was urged to turn around by one of his seniors, accompanying them back into the carriage he had just departed. At the side of the carriage, the Admirals collected together to allow themselves to enter the carriage in a very precise sequence. The carriage door was closed firmly, but soundlessly, by the Adjutant. A group of four mounted marines preceded them in a canter as the carriage again headed through the regal streets to the Prime Minister's residence.

"We were ordered to come over when we had a solution," said Lord Spencer as he withdrew a box of snuff from his coat pocket.

"Yes, Hugh," said another, "you are the solution."

"Or at least a convincing demonstration of the Admiralty's ability to respond rapidly to the pressing needs of His Majesty's government," corrected the First Lord.

The carriage roared along, preceded by the sharp clatter of the marine escort. The Rear Admiral strained forward in his seat, fearful that he would miss something very important amid the jostling environment of traffic and half spoken words uttered as the carriage tilted unnaturally to one angle and then another, as it made a series of rapid turns through the London streets.

He had been summoned at great urgency away from his fleet at Plymouth, and had just spent the last thirty tortuous hours in a succession of carriage rides. Now was he going to be paraded before the Prime Minister without a hint of the matters at hand? Enough was enough. He held up his hand.

"Please, your Lords, I know not why I have been summoned or what solution I might represent. I am a fighting man, not a politician. I pray that you will give me a hint of what has transpired or I fear that ignorance might cause me to respond improperly in the presence of the Prime Minister."

Lord Spencer drew in a large pinch of snuff and inhaled. His eyes seemed to water slightly and then he began to speak, "You see, the King has lost some wine."

"Am I to understand that I have been summoned here with the utmost urgency because the King has lost some wine?" quizzed the Rear Admiral, in a sense offended at the triviality of the matter, but yet relieved that its solution must be equally as simple. He let out a sigh of relief and rested his hitherto rigid back against the jostling carriage frame. He listened attentively as the Lords of the Admiralty continued.

"The concern, of course, is not the wine itself, it's how he lost it," said Viscount Palmerston, adjusting his white wig, which had become dislodged during the most recent turn.

"Let me explain, Hugh," spoke Lord Sandwich to his

left. "You see, for years the King has had a certain penchant for French wine."

"Bordeaux, isn't it? A red," commented Spencer.

Lord Sandwich waved off the interruption. "Since we are always either at war with the Frogs or at least in a state of agitation, close to war, as we are today, the King understandably does not want to bring attention to his little vice. Bad politics, you know." As the wheels careened over the uneven streets, there was an undercurrent of chuckling in the carriage.

"Every couple of months for the past few years, an Irish merchant over in Wexford arranges that a delivery be smuggled over from France. Then, he in turn smuggles over to England a few cases of the King's delight at a time. The local authorities have been told to leave him be. Sometimes even a low grade navy collier provides him an informal escort, that is, if the King is particularly concerned about his wine arriving in time for some special occasion. At any rate, it has always been transported with some regularity across the Irish Sea to Bristol, from where it is delivered by coach to wherever the King is in residence at the moment."

"And?" quizzed the Rear Admiral.

"Well, a few days ago, the little merchant skiff was captured."

"Captured? By whom?"

"Some damnable pirate. What's worse is that the pirate sent the King a message inside of his wine case."

"How was that allowed to happen?"

"The pirate apparently promised the Wexford merchant that he'd spare his ship, or his wife, or his dog, or something of value if the man delivered the box as if nothing had happened. The matter is very hush, hush. Don't suppose we'll ever get the full story. The merchant has been detained indefinitely for questioning by the Beefeaters. The whole matter is being kept under wraps."

"Damn fool," stammered Lord Spencer.

"Well, the wine arrived a few mornings ago, and the

King himself was standing by as the wine case was opened,"

"Who would have ever anticipated that the King would ever personally witness the opening of a case of wine."

"That's what the Wexford merchant had presumed, that the servants at the castle would intercept any insult. However, it seems that His Majesty was longing for a Royal snort." Mild laughter filled the coach.

"Better not be frivolous," advised the First Lord harshly. "This has become a matter of state. Heads will roll if the Prime Minister feels the Admiralty is not on top of this one. Ah, we're almost there."

"Can I ask what the insult was?" inquired the Rear Admiral.

"Seems the pirate was an American," said the First Lord.

"In the Irish sea?"

"Yes, the scoundrel filled the wine case with dirty canvas rags and rocks then resealed it to look as if it had never been opened. Removed all but one bottle of wine which he apparently drank half of himself, and then left the King the remainder as well as two glasses, one dirty and one clean. Tied to the bottle was some claptrap letter inviting the King to share a toast with him to American Independence."

"So, you see what is in store for us this evening, and you now know your mission, Hugh."

"Yes, find the pirate," answered the Rear Admiral with a nod. His mind raced ahead to a rational plan he could formulate and describe to the Prime Minister in the minutes he had left.

"Here we are," announced Viscount Palmerston, preparing his cane for egress.

The carriage rounded one last corner and jerked to a halt with a sudden screech of brakes. Its momentum sought to drive the full carriage forward, but was held in check by its leaf springs. In reaction, the carriage rocked from side to side for a time, while its occupants gathered up their belongings.

The First Lord smoothed out his uniform after exiting the carriage, and then continued speaking to his Rear Admiral. "You're aware of Pitt's emotional speech a fortnight ago, advocating the recall of the army from America. What with the former Prime Minister teetering on his crutches at death's door, it caused many in Parliament to be swayed by emotion to his viewpoint. And now with rumors flying that the French have signed an alliance with the colonials, we could have a world war thrust on us very soon." The Rear Admiral nodded to indicate his familiarity with recent events.

Lord Sandwich continued, "Well, on top of all this, the Prime Minister has had a tough go in Parliament just today. Seems that Edmund Burke chap offered a resolution to permanently alter the status of the American prisoners from traitors, subject to hanging, to mere prisoners of war. He also advocates a naval prisoner exchange. Feels it will speed up the likelihood of a negotiated settlement. This could be a long night."

"Burke, ah, you mean the arrogant Irishman. Never should have allowed him to sit in Parliament. The man is a travesty," scoffed one of the departing Admirals.

"They had to do something with the Americans in rebellion. The Irish agitators might be tempted to start a disturbance or two of their own. Never know what those people will do. I can see that the Prime Minister had to make some concessions. Ease up a bit," advised the First Lord.

As the five Admirals approached the door of the residence, the two guards on station at the front door jerked to attention. The Admirals noted with displeasure that the usual marine honor guard had been replaced by Army Hussars. The door was opened by the Minister's familiar manservant.

"Gentlemen, he is awaiting you in the study."

Lord North sat at his desk. He wore his favorite green silk smoking jacket. At this late hour his beard had assumed an appearance that made him look gruff and unfinished. He stared with favor at the map of the British Isles which had just recently been painted on his study wall. The artist, loaned to him by the geophysical scientists at Greenwich, had performed impeccably. He did not yet fully understand all of the notations made at the borders of the map about the relative position of the sun in various months. Mathematics had never been his forte. His particular special attribute was people and controlling them. But the whole map effect gave his office a needed aura of scholarship.

North tapped his fingers impatiently as the five Admirals saluted. Before him was the epitome of the system of Tory patronage. Each Lord before him had achieved his high position through well rooted political connections, rather than seamanship. As North looked at them, he was only able to pick out one of their number who had ever really commanded a ship of war. They were bureaucrats, effective at engineering paperwork, not ships. At least the First Lord had had the presence of mind to bring one legitimate naval officer to this meeting. The Admirals looked about for convenient seats.

"I did not invite you to sit, gentlemen."

North studied each man's reaction to his deliberate rudeness. When his eyes met the Rear Admiral's he tried to look deeply into them. He only remembered him slightly from past meetings. The man looked tired, but he had just been through one horrific carriage ride.

He asked the group at large, "How many warships are on the ready worldwide in His Majesty's navy?"

The Admirals looked at each other. After a silence, Viscount Palmerston spoke up, "Probably a little over five hundred, Sir. Counting the ..."

"No probably, there are precisely five hundred and thirty-one," snapped the Prime Minister, and then continuing, "and how many are in the British Isles, including everything from ship of the line to armed sloop?" Lord North looked from man to man. His preparation had caught them off guard.

They would worry that he might be studying the numbers in order to make reassignments in the Royal Navy. It would keep them on their toes.

North knew that none of the Admirals had the precise figures on the tip of their tongues. He exploited his knowledge further, "There are three hundred and five."

North stood up and pounded the table fiercely. "Fine ships, bought with the money I have procured for you through the Parliament. I have funded all the fancy ships you have ever requested for the defense of this realm, including some of those albatrosses you talked me into with a hundred guns. Seventy-fours would have been quite enough."

North's voice lowered to a snarl, his demeanor was visibly unhappy. "When I found out that we lost three merchant ships in the Irish Sea, I called over to the Admiralty, only to discover that not a single vessel of the Royal Navy had been deployed in response." He pounded the table again with his fist. "Shocking, gentlemen, outrageous!"

The Prime Minister continued, "This is not about a few bottles of wine. It is about these," North pointed to a pile of newspapers at one corner of his desk. "Don't you read gentlemen?" Lord North continued, picking up the top paper and unfolding it. "From Liverpool, 'Yankee Pirate takes the Dolphin'." North picked up another, "From Holyhead, 'Revenue cutter H.M.S. Hussar narrowly escapes Yankee Pirates'." North took the remainder of papers from his desk and flung them to the ground at the feet of his Admirals.

"This man gets more ink than I do," he quipped.

North left his desk and walked to the windows to look out. "This afternoon at Lloyd's, ship insurance for cargo vessels passing the Irish Sea has doubled. Tomorrow, that will make headlines in the London dailies. And tomorrow I must listen to more rubbish from that damn Irishman with the silver tongue. Wait until he hears about the American privateer off our coasts -- if he hasn't already. It will give him even greater ammunition for his despicable suggestions.

Like Pitt, he advocates making peace with the Americans."

Lord Sandwich spoke up calmly and deliberately, "Sir, may I remind you that each of us has had to spend every day of recent weeks appearing before the committees of Parliament explaining the progress of the American War, and our current preparedness should we also have to stand against the French if it comes to war in Europe. And in the evening we have been required to make the rounds at those endless dinner parties. I apologize for all of us for overlooking the events of the past week; though goodness knows why First Secretary Stephens did not call the matter to our immediate attention."

"The man's had a death in the family, been off all week," interjected Lord Hawke.

Lord Sandwich cleared his throat and continued, "The Rear Admiral has been brought here to take action at your direction."

"Very well." North turned around and spoke directly to the officer, "The vessel I am told is called the Ranger. She is of the corvette class. A little over a hundred feet in length, but bears the outward appearance of a commercial vessel. She has been seen flying both the Lowlands flag, or a combination of the Lloyd's commercial ensign and the Union Jack. They say you can recognize her because she has a bright gold strip painted along her freeboard. This decoration, I am told, makes the gun ports difficult to detect, until she is on top of you and puts up her real colors. Bears eighteen or twenty guns, probably six pounders. The vessel was American built last year in Portsmouth, New Hampshire..."

Viscount Palmerston interjected, "Knew we should have torched that place."

"Then, why the hell didn't you?" screamed North. "Do you need me to tell the Admiralty its every move? Your charter, gentlemen, is to defend England, and to clear the seas of her enemies. How you pursue that mission represents details I do not need to get into. For if I do, by God,

I'll start making some reappointments in the Admiralty; notwithstanding the political influence I know it took to get each of you to where you are. I remind you, that if this particular Tory government falls, gentlemen, you all fall with it. If the King himself feels that his navy is inept, all the political influence you can muster elsewhere will not save your positions."

North looked back at the Rear Admiral, "The Ranger's Captain is named John Paul Jones." North looked down at notes he had transcribed onto two sheets of paper, the only papers now left on his desk. "The man is a bit of a mystery. I thought that we had a record of every influential officer in the rebel's navy, but this man has come out of nowhere. One of the newspaper accounts said that he spoke with a Scottish accent."

"Perhaps a Jacobite remnant," quipped Spencer.

"Would be a bit long in the tooth, by this time," corrected Viscount Hawke.

"But maybe a son of one," interjected Lord Sandwich. "Likely knows the Irish Sea like the back of his hand, if he is Scottish."

North turned towards the Rear Admiral. "What are you going to do to relieve our home waters of this pirate?"

"Sir, before I left to come here, I ordered every ship in my fleet to stand ready to sail immediately upon my return. Within 40 hours from this moment, I will have seven, possibly eight, vessels under sail from Plymouth. We will proceed directly northward up the Irish sea from Land's End to the Hebrides. The flotilla I propose will be centered around H.M.S. Stag and Vengeance, each with 64 guns. I can also dispatch a message to Waterford to have H.M.S. Boston, with 32 guns, ready to meet us. If a dispatch rider can be sent immediately to Glasgow, we can seal the top of the Irish Sea at the North Channel with the Thetis, a frigate with 36 guns. Then there will be no possible escape for the pirate."

The Rear Admiral noticed the Prime Minister's newly

painted map of the British Isles and strode over to it. Enthusiastically, he pulled out his sword to point out positions. North cringed a bit at the thought of the sword point damaging his masterpiece, but decided to trust in the man's good judgement. He listened as the Rear Admiral spoke, the man's lean frame and his weather-beaten visage giving creditability to his proposed plan.

"Depending upon visibility, the two men of war will sail a parallel course between twelve and eighteen miles distant, right up the center of the Irish Sea or as near to center as the wind will allow. I'll have three sloops of war assigned to crisscross the prescribed course of each man of war, and then extend their patrol outward in a particular pattern which best conforms to the land contour of either coast. They will have general orders to explore the outer fringes of any channels or harbourages where the pirate might be lying at anchor. The simultaneous assistance of the army from the land side would be most appreciated. We will have it timed as to when each vessel should intercept our course up the center. If any of the smaller sloops are substantially late in the planned rendezvous, we will all render assistance in that direction."

The Fleet Admiral pointed towards Waterford and drew an imaginary path into the center of the Irish Sea. "H.M.S. Boston will meet us about here. We will also pick up a few other vessels as we proceed north. Possibly the Heart of Oak at Liverpool. Perhaps, the Drake at Belfast. No vessel of the description you have given me will go unchallenged."

"How long will this take?"

"Depending upon the wind, four to seven days after we weigh anchor from Plymouth. I will allow no Yankee pirates to be left behind our fleet after we pass. As soon as the Thetis seals the North Channel between Ireland and Scotland, there can be no opportunity for escape left to the north. We will have them."

Viscount Palmerston had stooped to pick up one of the

papers on the floor and was reading it. "This Jones was very well informed in his choice of vessels. He has taken very selective booty for a hit and miss operation. Do you suppose that he knew about the King's wine shipment, being that he was likely outfitted in France?"

A dark thought entered the mind of Viscount Lisburne. He put his hand on his chin, trying to remember some papers which had passed his desk a fortnight ago. He started to speak up, "Do you suppose...?"

North cut him off, "We've had enough supposing, I want action."

North cleared his throat and walked over to the map beneath which the Rear Admiral still remained, sword in hand. He put his head beside the other man's, and spoke softly and discretely so that the Admiralty Lords could not overhear, "This is a bit delicate, but it must be said for your ears only."

North looked around to see that the others had not approached. "This man must be hung for piracy. We don't need or want a public trial at the Bailey. I don't need Mr. Burke defending the rogue. The newspapers are making a hero out of this man. I don't want to have to reexplain our policy of selectively raiding American seaports. It would certainly come up as part of his defense in any public trial."

The Rear Admiral spoke softly in turn, "The Yankee pirate will be dead, Sir. One way or another. I understand you perfectly."

North stepped away and looked first at the Rear Admiral, "You have your mission." As the man saluted, he turned to his Admiralty.

"Gentlemen, I will need the rest of you available at my office in Parliament early in the morning. There will be a lot of explaining to do. Get some rest. God save the King."

As the Admirals departed, Lord North contemplated what actions he might take to prevent any further exploits of this pirate from seeping into the English newspapers.

2
Rescue

Lunt stretched out his legs and then quickly withdrew them under his horsehair blanket. His bare feet had protruded for just a moment out into the cold dampness which permeated his cell. During sleep, he had forgotten for an instant that it was an evening in which he had taken off his boots, rather than have his feet accumulate a damp sweat all night.

During the past winter the cold of Plymouth's Mill prison had been so penetrating that he could not endure being without some kind of covering on his feet. Now that he had been transferred for road building to an isolated village jaol in Wales, his feet still retained their acquired sensitivity to cold and dampness. He wondered if he would ever have warm feet again.

In his cell, one of the other inmates coughed briefly in his sleep. Lunt was wide awake. Since they had been transferred, their guards had frequently been too few in number to permit them much time out of their cell. The public works detail, for which they had relocated, had been delayed because of some dispute among the local authorities. So for the past six weeks, each day had dragged into each succeeding monotonous day. Sleep was succumbed to with increasing irregularity. At any given moment, whether it be day or night, some of the cell's occupants might be awake.

Lunt's gaze fell upon the cell floor, and the crude chalk board he had drawn on the floor of the cell, and the flat pieces they had made from torn cloth.

"Thank God for chess," he murmured.

The endless tournaments among the cell mates had kept

their minds active for at least a few weeks. But now even that game had become tedious. It was difficult to get anyone to play any longer.

In the dark of this particular evening, Lunt observed that he seemed to be the only one awake. Briefly, he rose from his hard bench cot and walked over one prostrate figure towards the solitary high window, whose sill he could just touch if he stood on his tiptoes. Lunt stared up at the window. Where was the benefactor this evening? He jumped and caught his fingertips and then palms on the sill. Placing his toes on the wall of the cell, he chinned himself upward to peer into the recessed window cavity. No sweet cakes or bread this evening. They had faithfully been set there every night for weeks. They had left notes for whomever was leaving the breads, but there was never any answer. Finally, they had just become accustomed to the treats and accepted them. But suddenly, tonight there were none. He missed them, as would the others when they awoke.

Lunt released his grip on the window sill and dropped back to the ground. When they had first arrived, he and the other cells occupants had surveyed every inch of their confined area. There was going to be no easy escape. The confinement cottage had been well chosen. The walls were made of reinforced mortar and stone. They were almost an arm's length in thickness, judging from the long recess of the window sill which stretched that distance in order to reach the outer wall of the jaol.

In the first few days of captivity, one of their number frequently would peer out the window in an attempt to see more clearly where they were situated. In order to do this, it was easiest for the observer to use another prisoner's shoulders to gain access onto the high sill, and then someone had to push his feet while the would-be observer wiggled into the increasingly narrow recess until his face touched the four iron bars which were at its farthest end.

Only three of the eight prisoners were narrow shouldered

enough to succeed in getting their bodies compressed sufficiently to get their faces right up to the bars. Jonathan Harken, the very slightest, could actually squeeze part of his face between the two center most bars and get a better perspective than anyone. From his observations they found out that their window was only two feet off the ground from the outside and that the back of the jaol stood buried into the slope of a hillside. This explained the persistent dampness of their cell.

After Jonathan succeeded in becoming more experienced at getting correctly positioned into the window cavity, he had reported that immediately ahead of the window there was only a view of several bushes and the upward slope of a hillside. However, after straining and straining, Jonathan became aware that one section of the hillside to the right fell away a bit more sharply than the other. There was just a glimpse of a panoramic view.

Through constant vigil, by the end of their second week of confinement, Jonathan had been able to report that he could just discern a few cottages about a mile distant and that their jaol seemed to be isolated on a high grassy plateau. When the wind blew strongly one evening near twilight, it had displaced enough shrubbery so that he observed two of their guards walking down to the village below.

With careful listening, the occupants of the cell came to agree that there must be at least one other cottage in close proximity to the front of their building. If everyone was silent, they could hear the door of that other building creak open, followed by the crunch of boots across the ground between, and finally the opening of the wooden door to their cell. The inner door was simply an iron barred grate with a small trap at the bottom for the passage of food underneath and the removal of their toilet bowl. Since both doors had the trap, it was possible for the guards to pass food in and out without ever seeing their prisoners.

One morning after their evening meal, Jonathan had

been lodged in the window crevice for over an hour, his feet sticking straight out over their heads like an manikin amputated from the waist up. Suddenly, they heard the approach of boots upon the ground. In whispered voices several of them tried to warn Jonathan to get down. He did not respond.

The outer door of the cottage opened and feet strode rapidly across the floor of the ante room.

Still Jonathan did not seem to respond to their urgings. Another prisoner, Joseph Woodbridge, had jumped upward and slapped one of the protruding legs violently. Yet again there was no response. Finally in frustration, Lunt jumped upward towards the dangling feet of Jonathan and, after seizing them, he and the full body of a shrieking Jonathan fell backward onto the cell floor, just as the trap opened.

"Thought you might like a spot of tea, lads. We're sorry to keep you all confined so long. Things will get better in a bit. Once they get the funds straightened out, you'll be out every day," a Welsh guardsman's voice reassured them in a sympathetic tone, as he pushed the tea through both trap doors.

After the outer door closed, Lunt removed his hand from Jonathan's mouth, whose chin was visibly scrapped from his violent withdrawal from the window cavity. Lunt whispered, "Why didn't you respond?"

Jonathan rubbed his chin, and looked at the blood on his hand. He looked around at everyone else in the cell and said, "Guess I fell asleep. It got to be comfy up there."

The occupants of the cell roared with laughter and joined spontaneously in the song they always came back to:

Father and I went down to camp,
Along with Captain Good-in,
And there we saw the men and boys
As thick as hasty pudd-in.

Yankee Doodle keep it up,
Yankee Doodle dandy,
Mind the music and the step,
And with the girls be handy...

From outside in the anteroom, the occupants then heard in a Welsh accent, "'Fraid I don't understand yer song, lads."

"Neither do we," shouted one of the men, and they laughed and laughed. Lunt smiled in remembrance. Things were better now than during his first months of captivity as a prisoner deep within the bowels of the British Man of War, Reasonable.

Over a year ago, he and his cousin, Cutting Lunt, had been crew on the privateer Dalton. It had been his third ship in Continental service, and his most unfortunate. After the Dalton's surrender, he had spent nearly two months on the Reasonable confined with sixty men in a space no larger than his cell of today.

They had lived in the perpetually dark holding area beside the anchor chains, and just over the bilge cavity into which they had no where else to relieve themselves. For two months they ate half rations, and could see nothing in the continual darkness as the vessel cascaded relentlessly against every wave in the dark Atlantic. Seven men died in that confinement, and every Sunday a British lieutenant would come below and offer any of them pardon, if they would renounce the rebellion and agree to serve above in the Royal Navy. No man in their company had ever accepted that offer. Instead they sang patriotic songs, and lived over the stench of the gurry with the rats.

Plymouth's Mill prison was better; more room, more humane, but dreadfully cold. Escapes were frequent, but punishments were severe, if you were caught. Unless, of course, you were part of a guard controlled escape scam.

The British government offered a standing reward of ten quid for the recapture of escaped prisoners. If you were allowed to escape and were soon caught by the guards, or their designated friends on the outside, they would split the reward with the prisoner. But if you were let escape and did not allow them to recapture you, they would normally kill your two closest friends. On the night of the planned escape, they would tell you who they would be. Few men could accept that burden on their conscience.

But generally, the guards were stupid and lax. They had poor accounting of who was there. Lunt was pleased initially when he learned that he would be transferred. He felt a smaller location would offer a better opportunity to make a real escape. But, with having to remain in their cell all day, there was little hope for the present. They had talked about trying to dig out of this cell, or work the window bars free, but unanimously concluded it would be very difficult.

Ultimately, they all agreed, 'wait until we get out on a road gang, near dark, we'll overpower the guards, and then steal a ship and sail across the Irish Sea to Ireland'. His old ship mate O'Mally had said that most of the Irish hated the English, and that they'd help.

O'Mally, where was he now?, thought Lunt. He rested his head back against the cold mortar wall and allowed his mind to wander again with thoughts of O'Mally and of the first time they had met. His thoughts became filled with sweet remembrances of Newburyport, and of his wedding day. He had married Sarah Orcutt on the third Sunday of July, 1775. At this moment, that seemed a thousand years ago.

Henry could picture the brilliantly white clapboard edifice of the Old South Church and the towering steeple that was the building's outstanding external feature. The combined clock and watch tower was the highest structure in Newburyport. It had been constructed to encompass a winding iron staircase whose top step emptied onto a viewing platform which held as many as twenty people at a time.

Just above the platform, the steeple narrowed again into a cone, at whose very top was perched a twirling gold weather vane in the shape of a rooster.

The elaborate steeple had been built for the benefit of the many sea captains who were patrons of the church. They frequently climbed up into the tower where they could view the weather seaward of Plum Island, and also be kept aware of the comings and goings of the many ships which populated the Merrimack River and gave the Massachusetts town most of its livelihood. With the view, the wind direction given by the vane, the barometer which was kept by the foot of the staircase constantly filled with the proper amount of colored water, it was natural that the church attracted a high proportion of sea faring families as its parishioners.

Henry could remember with perfect clarity the scene on his wedding day. As the Lunt wedding carriage first rounded the corner, he could see his older brother, Ezra, standing there smiling in his bright blue uniform, with its red lapel and piping at the sleeves. Gracing his Continental Army Captain's uniform, he wore a black leather belt and a scabbard, from which hung a dress sword. On his left chest was pinned a solitary blue ribbon. It had something to do with the Battle at Breed's Hill down in Charlestown, across the harbor from Boston, where he had commanded a company just the month before.

There was another officer with Ezra, a smaller, darker man, who during the wedding ceremonies was introduced as an advance member of General Washington's personal staff, a Lieutenant Aaron Pardee from Delaware. After attending his brother's wedding, the two officers were planning to travel from town to town in northern Massachusetts to recruit soldiers for the gathering Continental Army under General Washington.

Outside the church, several carriage loads of well wishers had formed, many of them Lunts. As always tended to happen, the men and women congregated into their own separate groups. But from among both groups, furtive glances were stolen at the two handsome Continental officers. The men tended to admire the bright blue uniforms, which many of them had never seen before. The women, and especially the young bridesmaids, admired the men themselves. The two officers had been peering into the Gazette window, across from the church, until the Lunt carriage arrived. Both were savoring winter pears they had picked from the small orchard behind the Old South.

The isolated groups broke up when Henry arrived with his father driving the family carriage, and his mother whose dress was decorated in bright ribbons. The applause had sounded first from one group, and eventually filled the entire street as well wishers crowded around the tightly packed open carriage with a covered honeymoon hansen in its tow.

Henry's mother, formerly Jane Moody, was as charming as always when she expressed to the gathering crowd, with arms raised in an expression of sheer glee, "I'm so happy." Then glancing across the street, she saw her other son for the first time in weeks and exclaimed, "Ezra, you were able to get leave...," and she descended to the ground in order to give her approaching soldier son a welcoming hug.

As his beaming mother left the carriage, Henry remembered looking downward because the presence of so many people had caused him to blush with embarrassment. It seemed everyone he had ever known his entire life was there among the crowd. He pretended that it was the glinting sun which caused him to look downward, rather than his actual embarrassment at being the center of attention. Only after he had shaken a couple of dozen hands, had he become used to the attention enough to be able to look his friends directly in the eye and return their smiles. After awhile, the clamor of voices died down, and the original groups of male and female began to reform.

Just then, unwilling to be subjected to another round of boring talk about where the ladies had each purchased their ribbons or how many stitches were needed to maintain a tight pleat, Henry's eleven year old little cousin, Micajah, piped up loudly with the question which at least every man in attendance wanted to hear an answer to, "Uncle Ezra, are you going to tell us about the great battle?"

Everyone turned around to see Micajah hanging playfully on Ezra's red trimmed sleeve. Glancing down at the boy, Ezra smiled, "Perhaps a bit later."

Before the small groups of conversations could be resumed, Henry's father, Matthew, announced in his gentle but persuasive tone, "The Orcutts are arriving, let's make them room."

As carriages were moved up and down the road to accommodate the bride's family, his father whispered in his ear, "It's time to go inside, you know it's unlucky to see the bride early."

Henry thumped his head backward regretfully against the damp stone wall wishing that he could relive that wonderful moment when beautiful blue eyed Sarah had walked down the narrow aisle of the church amidst the congregation, all joined in song. She was the most beautiful girl he had ever seen, with raven black hair, that fell across her shoulders and down onto her back.

For a solid two hours, the Presbyterian congregation had struggled to politely endure a rather lengthy sermon by Jonathan Parsons, whose tremendous white hair flowed down from each side of a full face. At the center of that face there sprouted a lean Anglican nose, which thrust out over an open mouth that spouted continual wisdom about the righteous meaning of life.

By the second hour of that warm July afternoon, the tything rod had been used twice. The feather end was placed tactfully under the nose of poor old Mrs. Bragdon, who was hard of hearing at any rate, and consequently most of the Reverend's wisdom was lost on her regardless of whether she was awake or asleep.

Later on, one of Henry's boyhood friends, James, cried out in surprise as the butt end of the rod knocked him flying from the end of his family pew. Many of the congregation had to work hard to suppress their laughter because of the sudden surprise squeal. Henry particularly remembered hearing the sound of his cousin Micajah's boyhood laughter amidst the congregation. Jonathan Parsons continued on with his sermon undaunted by the failings of the mere mortals which composed his congregation.

After kneeling at the altar rail for over an hour, Henry's eye lids also began to become heavy. But when his hand was squeezed tenderly by Sarah, they exchanged glances and smiles full of hope, which he would never forget.

And then, just as Jonathan Parsons was about to begin his third restatement of the meaning of life, suddenly the succulent smell of roast pig began to fill the air. Someone had started the fire and must have been turning the pig on the spit outside. Jonathan Parsons was among those who succumbed early to the temptations of his worldly stomach, and it was not another ten minutes before the marriage vows were exchanged, and the bride and groom were outside busily shaking hands with their guests.

Out behind the church in the pear orchard, his mother and the Orcutts had prepared a sumptuous feast. They had laid three long tables together in the shape of a crescent. At the center were several vases of yellow roses, Sarah's favorite. To the left and right of the flowers were stacks of wooden plates. Guests had been asked to bring their own utensils, but a limited supply was on hand for those who had forgotten. Above, the sky was as blue as possible, without a cloud.

His father had hired a fiddler to play a happy note in the church yard. First, well wishers congratulated the newlyweds, and then proceeded to pick up the wooden plates prior to stuffing them with steaming, well buttered mashed potatoes, bright red carrots, and sweet corn. At the end of one table was a pail of freshly steamed coahog clams, a favorite of Henry's, taken that morning from the ocean side of Plum Island, not more than a few miles away from the church. Behind the center table was the suckling pig rotating on the spit; his cousin, Cutting Lunt, was living up to his name as he placed choice pieces on all wooden plates presented to him.

After eating, Jonathan Parsons excused himself to visit a sick parishioner who lived on the other side of Newbury. Soon thereafter someone broke out a small jug of fine white corn whiskey and set it under a distant pear tree, to give the men all the courage they needed to ask the ladies to twirl across the green grass immediately behind the church. Henry recalled that the Lieutenant who had accompanied Ezra took quite a shine to one of Sarah's bridesmaids. They danced together all that day.

Soon members of the Lunt family began to propose toasts between the dances. A fine spiked punch allowed the ladies to keep their own pace. Finally, Matthew Lunt stood up in front of the center of the table before the yellow roses and announced, "I have a special treat. A fortnight ago, I was able to help a young man from Ireland who would surely fall into the hands of some Redcoats, if I had not taken him onto my ship. He had not much money, but he offered to work for his passage, and upon hearing of my son's wedding, he also offered to sing here. All of you who know this Yankee skipper, know that he never gets the flat side of very many bargains."

There was some background acknowledgement at the remark, and with a welcoming gesture, Matthew Lunt held out his hand and stepped aside, "Mr. O'Mally, if you please."

Out from among the crowd there pushed forward an almost impish looking man in his late thirties with a bright smile upon his face. He was smiling so fully and sincerely that the entire assemblage started to giggle at his demeanor. The man raised a conspicuous eyebrow and with his left hand slowly reached up to remove the oversized tricornered hat which had been placed with much exaggeration over half his head. The assemblage literally gasped as he removed the hat to reveal his bright red hair.

O'Mally pointed first at his bright red hair and then gestured backward at the plate of carrots which rested close to the roast pig, "I had to keep it covered until after you ate. I was afraid to be mistaken for one of yer vegetables."

The impish man bowed over laughing at his own joke along with the crowd, creating an ever increasing atmosphere of infectious merriment. The Lunts, the Orcutts, and all their friends were putty in his hands.

For the next quarter of an hour, O'Mally told joke after joke to the delight of his audience of usually rather somber Yankees. At one point he grasped hold of the hands of both Sarah and Henry's mothers and proceeded to tell several well meaning mother-in-law jokes. The crowd roared, and the two proud mothers could do nothing to spoil the merriment. Finally, O'Mally left hold of the red faced mothers of the bride and groom, and walked over slowly to the yellow roses on the center table.

"Are these your favorite, Sarah?"

Henry's bride nodded.

"They remind me of a song of my home land, which like yours is not yet free."

And then the mood of the assemblage changed from one of humor, to one of respect. O'Mally gestured towards the bride who he had positioned beside her choice of yellow flowers, and proceeded to sing. From out of the highly freckled face of the impish little man with ridiculously bright red hair and perpetual smile, there came the most hauntingly beautiful voice that anyone in the congregation had ever heard, singing, "*The Rose of Tralee.......*"

After their wedding, his father had arranged for them to spend a honeymoon near the Ipswich dunes. Henry savored the recollection of their first night together as man and wife, and his surprise that the act of love was as eagerly sought by Sarah as it was by himself. For the first two days they had remained in the crude straw filled mattress bed, which literally dominated one of the two small rooms of the cabin. They made love so many times that they both lost count, when trying to recall it during one morning's walk together on the beach.

Besides the moments of passion, Henry Lunt's fondest memory of that all too brief honeymoon week was of the mornings Sarah and he would sit together on top of the Ipswich Dunes and stare out to sea at the sunrise. He loved the sea more than any other gift of nature.

Lunt's tranquil reverie was suddenly interrupted as he thought he heard a footstep outside the cell window. Perhaps it was the mysterious benefactor who had been pushing sweet cakes through the bars of the high window every night. For a few minutes he listened attentively, but heard nothing more. Likely it had been only a sea gull which had landed in the courtyard and was walking about.

* * * * *

As the coach thundered along the road towards Liverpool, Hoche, the spy, feinted sleep to let the annoying English woman believe that she was not being heard. He was tired of verbal fencing with the busybody. Several hours worth of her infernal questions had wearied him.

His coach was running at least a half day late. It was supposed to have arrived in Liverpool by midnight. It was well past that now, and they were not even close. Hoche was becoming concerned that the coach was not going to make it to Liverpool before the packet left for Belfast in the morning. On the supper stop, Hoche had given the driver an extra five quid to persuade him to agree to press on to Liverpool that night. Some of Hoche's fellow passengers had not wished to travel at night. Hoche had had to state that he was on urgent Admiralty business to get them to agree to the all night passage. This had opened Hoche up to questions. He expected some, but the woman across from him had been insatiable.

Hoche was not concerned about being detected. His papers were quite in order to substantiate any lie. It would take several days for any suspecting authorities to send a message to London and for them to receive a reply that he was not whom the papers indicated. Most local authorities would not have the courage to detain a possible member of the Admiralty staff for that length of time.

The supper stop had been cut short by a half hour to the complaints of many of Hoche's fellow passengers. New horses had been hitched. For an hour or two after they had resumed the passage north again, there had been a noticeable increase in the pace of the horses. Now the beasts were becoming tired again and had slowed. Upon questioning during the last stop for water, the driver had simply said it was too dangerous to travel much faster in the dark. They might break an axle or a wheel, and then they would not get the coach into Liverpool that morning, but might be another day late. A little slower and little more cautious was better, the driver had concluded. Hoche resigned himself.

If he missed the morning packet, it might be another two days before he could arrange other transportation across the Irish sea to Belfast. Alternatively, he would have to take one of the daily packets over to Dublin and then get a coach up to Belfast. But, with his forged credentials, that might be a tricky business. By protocol, any official visitor to Ireland, especially coming through Dublin, should call at Government house and present his papers to the Governor General's staff. However, if Hoche arrived directly in Belfast by boat, the neglect in protocol might be understood by the Royal Navy. After all, it was to be a Navy matter anyway. They might not want the Governor General made aware of their plans.

On this mission, Hoche would be operating in disguise

as a civilian employee of the Admiralty, a Mr. Robert Shaw. His letter of introduction had been written on stationery taken from the desk of Secretary Stephens. It bore the official seal of the Admiralty. Stephens had been absent for a week on a family emergency and the cleaning person had an unusual opportunity to peruse through some of the Secretary's papers.

Stephens was not a trusting man and so not one of his staff had the combination to the Secretary's large walk-in safe, which he personally sealed each night. Stephens was ordinarily a man who never missed a day of work, processing the paperwork and details of the Admiralty. But now in this unusual period of absence his staff had not known what to do, so they simply left all the pending papers of the week on top of his desk, awaiting his return. After all, they reasoned, letters would be safe inside Admiralty House.

The letter in Hoche's coat pocket was an exact duplicate of one which had lain on Secretary Stephens' desk overnight, along with hundreds of others requiring his signature. The original letter had been borrowed with a few others, taken to Hoche's embassy, and then returned later that same evening. The man going in and out of Admiralty house was a low level civil servant, who chatted with the Royal Marine guards on a first name basis. Someone had to clean the offices, and the English, with their penchant for servants, were very vulnerable in having to put their trust in people from the lower classes.

For months, the military observation group which composed much of the Ambassador's staff had been on the lookout for new developments. This one letter matched another piece of information known to have crossed the Ambassador's desk during the past few weeks.

The Embassy maintained a network of operatives about the British Isles looking for intelligence. Just a few days ago they had heard from one of their very best agents, via coded message, that the agent needed immediate expert help in assessing the importance of a new piece of Royal Navy ordnance. The operative believed that something was developing which might profoundly affect their country's ability to wage war with England.

Hoche was regularly on staff at the Embassy. His routine function was to continually assess information on England's naval preparedness for war. His was normally a paperwork shuffling job, but since the message from the Belfast operative was decoded, Hoche had been put on alert. The letter authorizing a Mr. Robert Shaw to travel to Belfast on behalf of the Admiralty to observe ordnance testing was a perfect fit with the operative's request for help. After this overt mission, Hoche could no longer be posted in London. The possibility of someone in Belfast later linking his face with that of the ambassadorial staff was a chance they could not take. It might bring about a premature war.

Hoche had missed the earlier coach to Liverpool because he had spent most of the previous day packing his possessions so that they could be shipped home from his London flat during his absence. He now regretted taking the later coach. If he made the morning packet over to Belfast, he would be seven days ahead of the real Mr. Robert Shaw; if he did not, his time would be reduced to five days -- no more. He had done everything he could. It was all in the hands of God now.

* * * * *

It was later in the same sleepless evening and Lunt's daydreams shifted again. One Sunday in April, 1775, just after the Lexington and Concord battles, his brother, Ezra Lunt, had called for volunteers after services at Old South. Henry had wanted desperately to join up and to go with his older brother's company. But his father had forbidden it. Afterwards, Matthew Lunt had taken his disappointed son to Plum Island and together the father and son climbed the high elm which their family had nicknamed "the Climbing Tree" and upon which generations of Lunts had sat and discussed their problems amidst an unsurpassed vista.

From that high tree, they could see both the Atlantic and the Merrimack River. They could even see the steeple of the Old South. After some trivial talk, his father had said to him, "Son, I stopped you this morning because of something I felt in my heart was best. You are to be married in just three months time. I promised Sarah that I would keep you safe until your wedding day. After that, because of your age and temperament, I have no doubt that you will do what is right, and that you will stand up against the oppressors. But when you choose what you are going to do, remember, the Lunts are sea faring men. Ezra may have drifted away from it a bit because of his coaching business, but I know in my heart that you will best serve the cause at sea."

On a day, not two full months after his wedding, O'Mally and he were working at the chandlery when his cousin, Cutting, rushed through the door of the shop. He had a notice from the Gazette asking for seamen to serve on the Alfred, a privateer of 440 tons register. That evening, Henry spoke of the opportunity with Sarah, who was not shocked but had expected it. She only said, "Do your duty, Henry, but come home to me as much as you can." She placed no burden of guilt on him.

Two days later, O'Mally, Cutting, and he were off to begin the greatest adventure of their lives. As he gave Sarah a parting hug she presented him with the leather vest he now wore. Remembering, he now felt and smelled it. It was no longer the same garment, but he had become accustomed to it. It had been through nearly three years of war and imprisonment with him. He would never stop wearing it entirely.

Lunt's reverie was suddenly interrupted by a sharp thud, which seemed very close to their jaol. Next, came the sound of troubled, surprised voices still half asleep, followed by the sound of a brief scuffle. And then silence again.

Lunt listened. It was unnaturally quiet. The usual chorus

of nocturnal bird, cricket, and toad voices outside his cell window were all silent as well. He almost sensed someone moving outside in the courtyard, but then the feeling of a nearby presence subsided. Again, there came almost a deliberate silence.

Lunt listened intently. He concentrated beyond the level of breathing bodies within his own cell. Something was afoot. It reminded him of the game of hide and seek which he loved to play as a boy. His greatest pleasure was to go undetected and then to spring out on someone who had not sensed his presence.

Lunt rose from his bench and placed his ear against the cell door. He could not tell what was going on.

If something was going to happen, they must all be ready for it. It was better than to be taken unawares in their sleep. He crouched over and started to place his hand over Jonathan's mouth. But a hand was held up to save him the time. Jonathan was awake and had also been deliberately silent to concentrate on the strange sounds outside.

Then there was a sudden and immediate sound of the clash of steel upon steel. Lunt and Harken instantly knew the sound of a broadsword making contact with opposing metal. Broadswords had an unmistakable metallic tone that reverberated through the thick blade. The harder they struck another surface, the longer the resonance continued. Lunt had become accustomed to hearing that sound aboard the Alfred, and later the Providence when they had boarded another ship and resistance was encountered.

Suddenly, there was the sound of flaring of a pan of gunpowder, always the prelude to a shot being fired. The inevitable sound came sharp and loud, piercing the night like a screeching eagle on a dive downward towards prey. The report would be heard for miles. Then there was a momentary lull followed by the sound of men's feet running on gravel. Lunt moved across the cell quickly, shaking any of the men who were still not awake.

For a moment they heard the feet going away in another direction. Indistinct voices questioned each other and then the noises came closer again. Lunt heard the bracing of bodies against the outside door to their jaol. Once, twice, and by the time of the third effort the outer door crashed open. Lunt felt all the occupants of his cell rise behind him. They could see a light from beneath the crack of their cell door.

The outer, wooden door opened. Lunt and his fellow cell mates were confronted with the blinding sight of a ship's lantern held high in the air. Initially, they could not see anything but the bright light at which they winced and turned away briefly. Gradually, their eyes adjusted and they realized that several uniformed men were looking at them through the bars. One held the lantern very high. Beneath it was a short, unusually handsome officer in a tricornered hat; he held an officer's sword in one hand, and a pistol in the other.

The man spoke in a deep resonant voice, which seemed to be incongruous with his smaller stature. He was surrounded by figures fully a head higher.

"Be ye Yanks?"

Lunt gaped in amazed disbelief. He knew the man who confronted them almost as well as his father or brother. He had served with him aboard the Alfred, and again under his command aboard the Providence. He had been Lunt's immediate superior for almost two years. Still speechless and dumbfounded, Lunt heard Joseph Woodbridge shout out from behind him, "Stick a feather in your cap, and call it macaroni."

Lunt watched the officer give a broad smile in reaction to the familiar phrase, and then turn away apparently intent on other duties. Had he not seen him? The handsome, piercing blue eyes had rested on his face for an instant, but they seemed to show no glimmer of recognition.

Someone shouted, "Break the lock and get them out of there."

A mountain of a man in a green and white marine uniform motioned for the others to stand aside. He made a couple of light taps with the butt of his musket to determine the location of the locking mechanism. Then, holding the butt and stock of the weapon in each hand, he drove the butt of the weapon with great energy into the lock. The sound of impact was deafening. It was followed by a chattering as each bar of the cell door shook in protest to the hammering.

Six more times the giant struck the lock mighty blows with his musket as another soldier continued to hold the lantern high. Within the cell, the prisoners' brief sense of euphoria was being dashed with each battering. It collectively entered their thoughts that if the giant hammered the lock into a molten mess, it might just jam shut and they would be locked in their cell forever.

All these fears were set aside, as the next thundering blow was met by the telltale snap of metal from within the lock. The barred door reverberated one last time and then opened slowly inward with a mild creaking. They were free. They instantly rushed to leave the cell, shouting and hugging each other.

As they passed through the door, a uniformed man said, "Line up outside, Captain will want to talk with all of you."

Lunt found himself third from the end of a line of his cell mates. On each end of the line a uniformed man held a ship's horn lantern high. As best they could, each of his cell mates found the strength to stand at attention, despite the aching muscles which had been for so long confined.

In front of them they could see another cottage, and a light from within one of the windows. Out of the door and across the courtyard came the man in the tricornered hat. He stopped directly in front of them, with his hand on his hips. In his right hand he still loosely held a sword. He was dressed in a dark blue coat with red lapels under which a white blouse shone in the lantern light.

"You're all American sailors?" he asked.

Each man in line nodded or responded with an, "Aye, sir."

The officer stepped up to the first in line. He motioned for the light to see his face. A head shorter than most of the men in line, he peered up at each man in turn. When he came to Lunt, he paused for a long moment before saying anything.

"Is that you hiding under that bush, Henry Lunt?"

"Yes, sir. I thought you were not going to recognize me. How are you, sir? I am mighty happy to see you. But how...?"

"Later, Henry, we'll have much time later for remembrances, but now time is short. That pistol shot may bring unwanted guests."

On the officer's collar Henry noticed the symbol of a segmented serpent, in glittering gold. The Lieutenant of the Alfred, and Captain of the Providence had always liked the "Don't Tread On Me" symbol, hadn't he.

In front of Jonathan Harken, the officer stopped, "What ship did you sail on last?"

"The Revenge, sir."

"You were put up in France for a long time then?"

"Yes, sir."

"Did ye like it?

"Aye, sir."

"What I really meant was did ye like the ladies?" the liberator asked with a grin.

"Aye, aye, sir," said a smiling Harken more enthusiastically as he recalled some long forgotten adventure.

The officer then strode up to the center of the line and looking directly into all of their eyes, he said, "My name is Captain John Paul Jones." Lunt concentrated on the man's words coming to him in a deliberate deep, resonant tone. It was a speech pattern he remembered. As an undercurrent to Jones' speech was the definite burr of a Scottish accent.

"The Brits are calling me and my men the Yankee pirates. We are an embarrassment to them, and that's exactly what I mean us to be. For a fortnight we have been capturing their ships, one by one, right here in the Irish Sea. One of the reasons I came to get you men is because we have taken so many prize ships that I'm now a wee short of crew."

"Beg yer pardon, sir, how'd ye know we were here?" asked Woodbridge.

"A fair question," said Jones. "One of the crew of a merchant vessel we captured yesterday reported that there were some Yankee seamen held in an old poor house here on these Welsh heights.

"I'll not mince words with ye," continued Jones, as he in turn looked directly into the eyes of each of the former prisoners, "My crew and I are about to sail into very great danger."

Captain Jones paused, and traced his sword in the dirt in front of him. "I abhor the taking of men into ships against their will. I'll not take any man with me under those circumstances. Each of you is free to leave here now and try to find your own way home."

The prospect of trying to escape as wanted prisoners into the Welsh countryside, without a hint of understanding of their customs or language, seemed futile.

"What kind of ship have ye, Captain?"

" 'Tis good ye should ask," Jones eyes sparkled pridefully in the lantern light. "I've a sweet ship. She be called the Ranger in honor of Colonel Robert's men. She's nearly a hundred and ten feet and she's fast. Some French officers boarded her at Nantes and called her, 'un parfait bijou' - a perfect jewel." Jones looked around at his listeners and could see that he was catching their imagination.

Jones continued in a deep, prideful voice that seemed to emanate from deep within his viscera, "We have eighteen six pounders, positioned with good interval for close action. I've also five swivels that can be positioned on the rails where we need them. She's a New England built vessel out of Portsmouth, New Hampshire. I've taken her across the Atlantic. With my own hands I've refitted her with new sails and a brand new sail plan so that she can sail closer to the wind than any other vessel I've ever known. Into a crisp breeze no one will ever catch us. Off the weather she moves over the water like a princess on a polished dance floor, yet she packs a good wallop when she gets angry."

Jones looked down, at first a little embarrassed at his hyperbole, then he looked straight in the men's eyes, "Are ye with me?"

A couple of the men scraped their toes into the earth in hesitation. It had only been ten minutes or so since they were forgotten men confined in an isolated village jaol in Wales. Now they were free men who could run away and take their chances in the night.

The Captain's phrase of "great danger" bothered each of them. He looked and sounded like a man who meant it. One of the group spoke out for the rest,

"Sir, just what did ye mean by great danger?"

Jones replied swiftly, "The Admiralty has many vessels. With the end of the French Wars, over half of those vessels are here somewhere in the British Isles. The Ranger is the only American vessel commissioned, at the discretion of her captain, to operate in these waters. We cannot possibly defeat the entire British fleet, and it would be suicidal to try. I'm not daft. Yet I have succeeded thus far in taking the enemy by surprise. I have plans for more mischief before we leave these waters."

Jones drew a breath and then continued, this time more philosophically, "Think of the Ranger as a hornet and the enemy as a great lion. The hornet cannot kill her enemy, but she can give him a pesky sting he'll not soon forget. That's all I'll tell you until you're aboard my ship.

"Be quick to decide now, there is no more time for discussion. Are ye with me?" Jones looked into their faces. As each in his turn indicated agreement, Jones gave him a strong handshake and said, "Welcome to the Ranger."

He turned to the giant blond haired man in the green and white uniform, "Sergeant Miers, organize everyone and get them down the cliff. I'll take two marines and Lunt with me."

Coming up close to Lunt, Jones whispered, "Feeling chipper, Henry?"

Lunt nodded. He was handed a broadsword and pistol by Sergeant Miers. He gazed down at the weapons. The feel of the metal sword and the smell of gunpowder that emanated from the flintlock gave him a sense of power and personal freedom he had not had for a long time.

When Lunt looked up to thank Jones, he saw that the Captain had moved away to squat under the light of one of the signal lanterns. Jones was closely examining a piece of paper he had just drawn out of his uniform jacket.

Jones then rose and proceeded to lead his party of four away from the main group, and down along the village road. But as an afterthought, he turned back to the prisoners and spoke, "And by the way, 'tis not exactly true that I came in search of just any American seamen. I have sailed with several of you before. Our coming here tonight was very deliberate. I just needed to say that, in the off chance that some of you chose not to join us."

"Sergeant Miers," Jones shouted, "Lead these men down the cliff on the lines we've rigged and take care. They'll likely be a bit out of shape.

"Let's go, Henry."

3
Reunion

Lunt, Jones, and the two marines made their way down the dirt road which led from the plateau to the small village below. Lunt shivered in the cool air. He gathered his mildewy leather vest about him tightly, almost able to double it over by an additional third. This was in sharp contrast to when it was new and had fit him perfectly. Prison life had not been conducive to gaining weight. Momentarily, the cold air made one part of him wish that he was back under the warm horsehair blanket.

After they had gone only a few hundred yards, Jones ordered the two marines to stop and position themselves as lookouts for the entire rescue party. If they saw anyone coming up the road, they were to retreat to the top of the cliff and warn the rest of the group of the coming danger. Under no circumstances were they to follow Jones and Lunt. The marines saluted and took a position behind a large group of boulders at the side of the dirt road.

After a few hundred yards, Jones remarked that apparently no one was going to respond to the lone pistol shot which had gone off when one of the English guards had attempted to shoot him. Sergeant Miers had deflected the discharging weapon with his broadsword.

"Apparently everyone in the village has slept through the fracas." After a moment Jones added, "Or they're too damn scared to come up here and see what happened."

Looking at Lunt, Jones observed, "You're still as silent as ever, Henry. Did you have a good visit with Sarah and the baby after you left us over a year ago?"

"Yes," replied Lunt, "it was a good visit home."

"Was it really worth it, seeing it got you captured and imprisoned for over a year? By the way, I was in Newburyport last summer during the time I was assuming delivery of Ranger. Your parents are fine. Your brother's company fought with distinction at Saratoga. No concern, he is well. I did not have time to meet your wife and young son. They were at her parent's farm. But when your parents said you sailed out on the Dalton, I had to tell them that you were very likely a guest of King George.

"You had a little cousin, Ma.. Mica..."

"Micajah," responded Lunt concerned, "has something happened to him?"

"Only that he has followed his older cousin's footsteps, and ran away from home one night, and joined a privateer. His parents got a letter from him just about the time I arrived. Very young is he?"

"He'd be only fourteen," said Lunt, not at all happy about this bit of news.

As they walked along Jones continued talking, "By the way, Ambassador Franklin has been trying to negotiate a naval prisoner exchange. I've a feeling the Brits may finally agree to one this summer." Jones looked over towards Lunt, "If they don't, we'll have to take something of theirs that will give them renewed incentive to make an exchange."

Jones cleared his throat, and announced, "We're there by my reckoning. It's that farmhouse there." He pointed down into a meadow at a thatched cottage from which a tendril of chimney smoke drifted into the night air.

"Stay here and warn me if anyone comes up the road. It'll take a half hour to get all those men down over the cliff safely in the dark. I'll be back to this spot in a quarter hour, or you come after me and drag me out." Jones looked at Lunt and gave an exaggerated imitation of someone hauling someone else out of a hole. Lunt nodded.

Jones trotted down to the farmhouse and pounded sharply on the door. Slowly and cautiously it opened, revealing a woman's shape against the background light of a fireplace from within. Lunt saw the two embrace and, after a female sigh of ecstacy, he faintly heard the word "John" as the two passed inside.

Lunt turned away in disbelief, but kept his eyes on the village. While he waited, Lunt had a deja vu of another evening almost two years ago in Brest when a certain Lieutenant had asked Lunt to give up half the inn room they shared for the night, while he brought the wife of a lumber merchant to their quarters. Was his new Captain up to his old escapades while his men were dangling down a cliff, high above the sea?

Just as Lunt was about to walk down to the farmhouse to see if his worst fears were true, out came the Captain. Two hands held onto Jones' arm from within, which the Captain had to firmly shake off. Then, as he backed quickly away from the doorway, Jones bowed and gave a grand sweep of his tricornered hat to its occupant who was obviously extremely sorry to see her John depart so rapidly after such a brief visit.

Lunt looked down the village road, still no one was coming. By the time he looked back, Jones was beside him. Lunt turned his face back up the hill. A scowl beneath Lunt's hawk nose was obvious. Jones was still tucking part of his shirt into his breaches as they hurried up the road together.

"Don't give me any of your Puritan sermons, Lieutenant Lunt. Did you like the sweet cakes delivered every night to your cell window? Do you believe you just happened to be rescued from that God forsaken hell hole?"

Lunt turned to listen to the other man, whose methods were so different from his own. Jones continued, after drawing a fresh breath to replenish his obvious exertion of the past quarter hour, "Remember, I sailed these waters for twenty years before this damn war. I've been making love to that widow woman off and on for most of that time. It makes her feel good, and it usually makes me feel good. I am a single man. What harm is it?"

Lunt shook his head at his companion's logic, and then noted, "You said 'Lieutenant' Lunt?"

"It's fitting that if you were my mate when I was a lieutenant, then you should become my lieutenant when I made permanent captain. You would have had that promotion already, if you had gotten back to France aboard the Dalton.

"And there's another reason, Henry. It'll be a good ten minutes more before all your cell mates can be transported by the rope chair down onto that beach. Let's sit down a moment and have an old shipmate's gam while we are still alone."

Jones continued, "Henry, how would you like to be in command of a ship, a fine ship, when every blasted time you issue a major order, your crew goes below and votes on whether they want to do it or not?"

Lunt listened as Jones explained further, "Over half my crew are from Portsmouth. I took them aboard in good faith last summer. I was unaware of this town meeting business.

"A few days back we were in Belfast Lough. The Spymaster had provided me with a list of the permanent stations and size of Royal Navy ships in the Irish Sea."

"Spymaster?"

"Henry, I need to take someone else into my confidence but, before I begin, the word Spymaster is never to be repeated again, except when we are alone."

"Agreed," said Lunt, "but who is the Spymaster?"

Jones smiled at his Lieutenant's directness, "Henry, that is the greatest secret in Europe. Only a handful of people know the identity. Only a handful more know that someone with a high degree of competence is directing the American intelligence effort here in Europe. Enough, let me get to what will concern you the most."

Jones cleared his throat and doodled in the dirt as he spoke, "The Drake is a sloop of war about our size, sail plan, and firepower. At the outset of this voyage, Ambassador Franklin gave me extraordinary orders to go anywhere I chose to cause mayhem to English commerce. The British Isles were my own choice because of my knowledge of local conditions here. I had taken Ranger through some pretty extreme weather after refitting her in France this winter. I know what she can do. Ambassador Franklin informed me that there could be tremendous political advantages resulting from our being able to conduct a few actions which would bring this war into the British homeland. Instead of exclusively fighting far away on American soil."

Lunt attentively listened as Jones continued, "About a week ago I located H.M.S. Drake, at anchor off the deserted Irish castle of Carrickfergus. Some fishermen told me her exact location. She was among one of a possible list of locally based Royal Navy warships of equivalent size to Ranger. So, I let the crew know that my plan was to take the Drake with minimal damage to all in the darkness.

"You know what these men from Portsmouth said, after they had one of their meetings? They came to me and simply said they wouldn't do it. That it was too dangerous and that as crew of a privateer they preferred to get prizes that were worth real money. They did not want to waste their time on British war ships that could fight back, and that had little potential monetary value represented in their cargo."

"Why didn't you just throw them in the brig?" asked Lunt.

"How do you throw two thirds of your crew in the brig and carry on this voyage?" retorted Jones. "These men don't have a spark of patriotism. They're simply in it to get the greatest privateering share each, at the least personal danger."

"So what did you do?" inquired Lunt.

"Well, I talked them into a try at the Drake, and it took more than a wee bit of persuasion," said Jones. "Mostly I emphasized that we could take the Drake with very few casualties, if they followed my plan."

Jones continued, "We closed all gun ports. We hoisted the Union Jack and even displayed the Lloyd's commercial flag. There were at least five other merchantmen anchored off Carrickfergus. So just after midnight we came in attempting to look like a merchantman who had just made port. We deliberately anchored up current in the flood and pretended to be settling down for the night, only two cables from the Drake. There appeared to be only two guards on her quarterdeck. It was the opportunity of a bloody lifetime. Imagine it, we could take a King's fighting ship, while the crew slept.

"We anchored about an hour. I had the entire crew armed to the teeth. They squatted out of sight behind the rails. We slowly turned the capstan to weigh anchor so that we could drift into the Drake. I went below briefly to discuss the boarding objectives with Marine Lieutenant Wallingsford and to see to the arming of grenades. By the time I returned to the quarterdeck some damn fool had pulled the capstan retainer loose, and lowered the anchor again so that we snagged the bottom a bit and our orientation changed. By the time I figured out that the anchor had been lowered, we were 20 paces forward of the Drake's bow and well past her. Our anchor line had even fouled in one of hers. And there wasn't a spot of wind with which to maneuver.

"Being down current we would have little opportunity to get back to her without tipping off our purpose. With no wind at all, they were broadside to our bow with 10 guns pointing down our deck. All we could have returned was musket fire. It could have been a disaster, a bloody disaster," Jones rolled his Scottish burr for effect.

"The Drake's watch were even hailing us to ask if we needed assistance, and were offering to wake up their crew so that a couple of longboats might be sent to help untangle our anchor lines."

Looking down, Lunt shook his head and said ironically, "Just what you wanted!" He then looked at the Captain, and asked "What did you do?"

"I took an ax myself and cut the damn anchor rode. We drifted off into the night like a cur with its tail between his legs. It took us most of the night to work our way out of that harbour. I'd say we should never allow ourselves again to get deeper than the bend opposite Carrickfergus. The lough is very shallow at points. A ship could be very well trapped in there during the wrong conditions of current and tide. The men of Portsmouth were right about that. I've conceded that to them."

"Hadn't we better go now?" asked Lunt.

"There's one more complication. We've just been ordered to take the Drake. Without further delay," said Jones.

Lunt stared in disbelief, "Just ordered?"

"Here, Henry, read this message when it gets light and then destroy it. It is intended to be for my eyes alone. It's from the source I told you not to mention."

"Isn't that the paper I saw you with earlier?" asked Lunt.

"No, that's a different piece of paper." Jones produced a second piece of paper from his pocket, "Read the one you have as soon as it gets light and then destroy it, without fail."

"Where did you receive this message?" asked Lunt.

"From the widow at the farmhouse, of course." Jones turned to look at Lunt, "Did ye think I went there just to make love to a lonely widow while my men were in potential danger? You don't know me, if you did," quipped Jones.

At that, the two men got up and hurried towards the two marines standing at the side of the road. No one had come up or down the road in the half hour since the rescue had begun.

* * * * *

"Damn that Simpson!" Lunt heard Jones curse under his breath.

The longboat, filled with both rescuers and former prisoners, was bobbing about alone in the Irish sea. The visibility was still poor. The packed longboat had struggled through the heavy surf, but had made its way safely over the reef, towards the direction where Jones had left the Ranger anchored. They had rowed a little more than a quarter of an hour in the darkness. With ten oarsmen on the return they should have made the mile out to Ranger easily in that time.

Jones said, "I know my sense of direction. They've lifted anchor. I told Simpson to remain where he was at least until dawn. That's two more hours."

Lunt reflected and then whispered back, "There's not much wind, they could have only drifted from here. Was the tide higher or lower than when you came ashore?"

"Lower, we're in a flood," replied Jones. "We had much more difficulty clearing the reef on the way in."

"To the south," the two men said in unison as they nodded to each other. Jones gave the command to his marines pointing, "Row this way as if Lucifer was after you. Aye, he might be the lesser of two evils, if an English patrol boat catches us adrift in their pond," shouted Jones.

With the Captain's inspiration the longboat picked up speed. A few of the marines were spelled by the former prisoners. Jones asked everyone to shift to the rear of the vessel as much a possible so that the bow of the longboat would ride higher in the water, helping the now heavily laden vessel cut through the water with less resistance.

As they moved along on a southerly course in the pitch black night, they began to experience a slight following sea. At times, the rolling waves slapped into the stern of the longboat, sometimes drenching the men at the stern, especially Joseph Woodbridge who, acting as coxswain, worked the rudder carefully so that the greatest forward effort could be converted into speed.

For over an hour the vessel was rowed at its maximum

hull speed. Each man poured his heart into the effort, encouraged by the willingness of the two officers to take shifts with the men in order to keep the longboat moving. They all adopted a sense of urgency. To larboard, they gradually began to see the outline of mountains as a hint of morning light announced the coming of a new day.

"We'll see her soon enough, when lights up," encouraged Jones. "Put your backs into it, lads."

In another ten minutes the first of the morning's light provided them a sight of Ranger still further to the south. Her sails were just being rung out as in preparations normally taken to weigh anchor.

Jones exclaimed, "Well, they may claim they didn't see us but, by God, they'll never be able to say they didn't hear us!"

Jones reached under the thwarts of his oarsmen, and yanked out one of their muskets. He momentarily checked the powder and prime, and then the flint. The weapon was still loaded from the rescue mission. Jones pulled back the cock and, pointing into the air, he fired the piece. The sound assaulted the dawn's stillness with a sharp crackle. A squadron of birds flying in tranquil formation all altered course abruptly.

"Hand me another, Sergeant," and Jones disrupted the morning silence again. Just as he was about to fire a third round, one was fired from aboard Ranger. A command had obviously been given to brail up the yards. The vessel awaited them.

Knowing the longboat must now be under observation, Sergeant Miers directed the marines to assume all oars. Their strokes appeared long and crisp as they rapidly cut the distance to Ranger.

Lunt's eyes took in the vessel as they approached. She was a beauty, long and sleek. Her hull was unusually close to the water for a vessel of her length and class. But with less freeboard above the water, there would be less wind resistance and greater speed. He wondered, would her lower gun positions give Ranger as great a range against an equally fortified vessel?

Ranger had three masts. From her broadside aspect, Lunt could discern that her fore and mizzen masts were each considerably shorter than the main. All masts appeared to be raked backwards. Each carried at least two or three crossing spars for rigging traditional square sails downwind. Lunt observed that rigging was in place to support a series of high topgallants should they be traveling for some time away from the wind. Other lines from fore mast to bowsprit revealed that a series of staysails could be rigged to provide lift for the bow, otherwise her square sheets and topgallants would tend to drive Ranger's bow too deeply into the water while running before the wind. The bowsprit lifted above the water at an increasing angle as it jutted proudly out over the ocean.

As they approached, suddenly the heading of Ranger began to change. It was obvious that the anchor had just been lowered all the way to the ocean floor. For as it took hold in the southerly current, Ranger's bow swung around to face them as the vessel responded to a now taunt anchor line. Hitherto, the anchor rode must have been hoisted, as they first saw the vessel from broadside at the break of day.

Lunt looked across at Jones, who had also seen the telltale shift in position. They nodded to each other.

By the time the longboat was only about two hundred feet from Ranger, Lunt's attention was fully enveloped in the details of the carved figurehead below the bowsprit. It was not the traditional figure of a maiden. Lunt stared up at it as they passed under the bowsprit to reach the larboard side of the vessel. The figure was a very intricately carved likeness of a Colonial soldier. His coat was navy blue, with traces of red trim. His shirt was white and he wore a tricornered hat. In the figure's hands was clutched a long musket which merged into the bowsprit at the muzzle. Ranger was a tribute to the men of the Continental army, and to their predecessor, Roger's Rangers, who had defended the frontier in decades past. But to Henry Lunt, the figurehead immediately took on another significance. It reminded him of his brother, Ezra.

"Do you like her?" inquired Jones.

Lunt looked at him, and nodded approval, while providing an enthusiastic, "Yes, sir."

As they rounded close to the larboard side, the shrill boatswain's whistle could be heard, first low then high and finally a return to the low pitch, signaling for all aboard that the Captain had returned. A Jacob's ladder was thrown down from the gangway. Seizing it instantly, Captain Jones lifted himself up onto the netting and began to move up the rope ladder with obvious intent. Lunt followed closely behind, stepping over a marine who was still trying to attach the lowered end to the longboat so that the rest of the party could ascend in safety.

As he reached the top, Lunt heard Jones addressing his second in command mockingly, "Lieutenant Simpson, are ye just a wee bit surprised to see me?"

As Lunt climbed onto the gangway, Jones was standing in the center of the gun deck and was screaming in rage at two lieutenants who stood at attention before him. Taking the blunt of the tongue lashing was a tall lanky man in his late forties, who obviously resented the raging temper which was being unleased upon him in front of the entire crew. As the Captain got angrier and angrier, the two lieutenants backed up towards the center line of the vessel with the Captain's boiling red face pursuing them. Then Jones wheeled to face a nearby marine lieutenant, "Lieutenant Wallingsford, you were left in command of the deck, including the disposition of the capstan?"

"Yes, sir," the man in a green and white uniform shouted a response to his captain. To Lunt he seemed like a man who was unaware that anything was wrong.

Jones pressed him, "And how did we go adrift? I left Ranger securely anchored, and went directly inshore. We rowed for a quarter hour. When I returned we came back the same route, Ranger was not where I left her. She's now four miles to the south. Who raised the anchor?"

"Absolutely no one, sir," said the marine lieutenant holding his ground. "Captain, I've been on this deck every moment since you left. Inquire of my marines, sir. We have not allowed anyone to willfully move this ship. After it turned light, Lt. Simpson did suggest that we could have drifted a bit. We were not intending to leave this area. Just before we heard your shot, we had already decided to hoist sail and attempt to get sufficient wind to sail up current in search of you. Only after we heard the report of your musket fire did we set the anchor deeper."

A great body of the ship's crew had gathered around the heated discussion of the four officers. Many of the men were obviously unhappy at the rage which was erupting from their Captain. As Lunt watched, the circle of crew was closing threateningly about Jones and his officers.

"If I may make a comment, sir," Lunt spoke up loudly.

"Who's this?" commented the senior Lieutenant after looking up with the rest of the crew to find that the speaker was a very unclean looking man with a hawk nose, long, greasy blond hair, and an equally long beard which flowed down over a tattered white shirt. About the man's body hung a loose fitting leather vest which sprouted a visible layer of green mildew. From where Simpson stood he could smell Lunt, who looked to him like the worst sewer rat he had seen in any port city on the continent. Just after Simpson spoke, Lunt's liberated cell mates came climbing through the gangway. Most of the men were quite emaciated and frail, yet from them effused a sense of strength and resolve from their recent triumph over a desperate situation.

"Gentlemen," said Jones to all the crew, "may I present

to you, Lieutenant Henry Lunt, and his long suffering cell mates, whom this mission has just liberated, and then came close to losing because this ship was not where it was supposed to be. They have agreed to the last man to join our crew."

Behind the Captain there rose a tremendous spontaneous applause joined in by all the crew, including the officers, who seemed to be in imminent danger of being thrown into the brig by their Captain. Jones' mood was also uplifted by the genuine reception. He put up his hand, and the crew was again silent. "Proceed, Lieutenant Lunt, speak your mind."

"Sir, there is a place off Cape Ann, in Massachusetts. It's called 'False anchorage.' A lot of ships stop there, because it's in the lee of a headland. Under certain conditions, the currents can change between tides, and there is a narrow shoal rising to 15 fathoms. If the anchor has been set at the edge of the shoal it can be dragged off as the current turns in the other direction. The surrounding bottoms drop to over 80 fathoms. Many a ship has been set adrift without it being immediately apparent to the ship's company, especially on a dark night. It's possible the situation was repeated here."

Lunt continued, "Unlike the situation you described to me concerning the attempt to take the Drake, where it takes only one man to accidentally lower an anchor, to weigh anchor it takes a great many men to turn the capstan, perhaps eight, or ten at a minimum." Lunt stopped and looked about, his intelligent eyes and solid logic immediately gaining respect among the crew.

Inside Jones' head, there raged a conflict. After his weeks of frustration with the older Simpson and his Portsmouth town meetings, he sincerely doubted Lunt's explanation. Yet he did trust Marine Lieutenant Wallingsford, so it was possible that the anchor had been pulled off a ledge of some sort. Lunt's "false anchorage" tale did allow everyone on board to save face; himself and the men from Portsmouth. And he still needed them to run the ship.

Jones spoke up, "From now on, Lieutenant Wallingsford,

a marine is to be stationed to sit atop the capstan at any time this ship is at anchor, be it day or night. If the capstan turns unexpectedly, the soldier on watch is to call this to the immediate attention of the officer of the watch and this captain. If the marine does not feel the matter is getting proper and immediate attention, he is to fire his musket into the air. Understood?"

"Aye, aye, sir," shouted Wallingsford with relief, happy that the issue was being resolved in this way.

"Men, these former prisoners have endured a great deal of hardship. Let's welcome them to Ranger. Mr. Whitson, bring up a keg of rum. We will celebrate their return to an American ship. Purser, give them all new boots and clothing. And for God's sake, half a bar of brown soap each. Forenoon watch and all marines, save those who participated in this rescue, are to abstain until the wind is up and we are under sail."

General revelry broke out on deck. Lunt and his comrades found themselves surrounded by well wishers. From behind, someone said timidly, "Beg yer pardon, sir, but Captain's orders," and emptied a bucket of cold sea water over his head.

As Lunt shook his head and then placed his hands to his eyes to wipe away the salt water, a very familiar smiling, freckled face was the first thing he saw. The man's bright red hair startled him into familiarity. "Beg your pardon, sir, can I give you a hug?"

O'Mally stood in front of Lunt, and in one hand he held a huge piece of ham bone with well cooked meat hanging from it. In the other he held two flagons of rum. He pushed the ham leg into Lunt's right hand and then proceeded to wrap both arms around Lunt's thin middle, spilling rum all over him. The two embraced. Lunt shouldn't have been surprised to see O'Mally aboard Captain Jones' ship, but he was, nevertheless. Over the course of the next hour or so, O'Mally explained how he had been with the Captain much of the time since Henry had taken leave to visit his wife. Now over a year ago.

Jones took one tankard of rum with his men, and personally supervised the sail set as performed by the men of the forenoon watch. After a half hour, he retired from the poop deck and entered his cabin to go to sleep. He did not speak to Lieutenant Simpson again that day.

* * * * *

About mid afternoon Lunt awoke. There was someone in the small quarters he had been assigned, sifting deliberately through his dirty clothes. Lunt sat up sharply. The man sensed his movement, and turned around to face him.

"Beg your pardon, sir. I'm David Smith, attached to the purser. Was wondering which clothes you wanted to launder and which to discard. I didn't want to wake you, after what you've been through, but I've brought you your uniform, all pressed. It was a spare one of Lieutenant Hall. He's about your size." The man had an Irish accent.

Smith pointed to a lieutenant's uniform, that had been hung neatly on a hanger over the foot of Lunt's cradle. Lunt placed his hand down under his blanket to check something, and then replied, "You can throw out everything but the vest. I'd be very appreciative if you can clean it up a bit. Maybe put some good oil into it afterwards. It's special to me."

"Be glad to, sir. It'll be good as new, sir. If there's anything else you should require, David Smith is the best man to get it for ye. You get some sleep now, sir. Sorry to have disturbed ye."

Lunt waited until the man was gone and then reached under his body to pull out a folded piece of paper he had placed there before going to sleep. He got up and went to the porthole to read the handwriting more closely.

April 18, 1778

JPJ

H.M.S. Stag and possibly as many as six or eight other vessels are being readied to sail from Plymouth in a few days time. Likely you are the reason.

You must take the Drake. You must take her whole. There is something of the greatest possible importance aboard her. Destroy this.

Lunt looked with intense curiosity at the symbol of the diamond backed serpent wrapped about the telescope. Was this the stamp of the person whom Captain Jones had told him to be cautious about mentioning, or was it just a note from a friend?

After a moment's further reflection, Lunt torn the paper into tiny bits. One at a time he tossed the tiny pieces of paper out of the small porthole over his cradle. He could just see the sun hit the paper as it fell rapidly out of sight behind Ranger. It was midday or a little later, and Ranger was moving at a good clip to the west. Lunt returned to sleep.

* * * * *

There was a rapping at his door. Lunt sat up. From the failing light in the porthole, Lunt could tell it was near dark.

"Beg your pardon, Lieutenant Lunt."

Not accustomed to being addressed this way, Lunt did

not respond instantly, but then answered, "Yes?"

"Captain requests your company for dinner in a half hours time. Full dress." The footsteps went off towards another part of the vessel.

At the foot of his cradle, Lunt observed his new uniform pridefully. It was a shade of blue very similar to that he had seen Royal Navy officers wear aboard the Reasonable, but it lacked some of the gold embroidery. The uniform jacket had two simple rows of gold buttons, each embedded with 13 stars, and lapels of a lighter shade of blue. On one side of the stiff, gold trimmed collar, also in gold, was the 'Don't Tread on Me' symbol. Two crossed gold swords were on the other. It was not quite the same lieutenant's uniform he had seen aboard the Alfred and the Providence, but it was similar. Lunt guessed that Captain Jones had had it made in France to his own specifications. Beneath the hanging uniform and two pairs of white breeches, there was a light blue neckcloth and two folded bleached white blouses. The latter were designed to be pulled overhead and buttoned up from the chest to the collar.

On the bench beside his cot were a set of off duty clothes, several pairs of woolen stockings, and a pair of brand new leather boots, with extremely pointed toes.

They must be the French style. The crew had shown the boots off during their celebrations on deck. Apparently, someone from the French government had donated boots, a pair for every man on the Ranger. Some of the crew liked them, others did not. Lunt remembered that he had told the man from the purser to throw everything out except the vest. Beside the clothing there was a straight razor, soap, a pitcher of water, and a pan. The intention was obvious.

Lunt was soon dressed and pulled open the door which gave his compartment privacy. He found himself facing the base of the mizzen mast and a series of cabinets which had been fashioned along the center line of the vessel. Off the narrow corridor were the other officers' quarters. The ship lunged momentarily as it settled into a wave. Lunt instinctively moved his body for it to remain centered above his feet. To his right, the corridor immediately made a left turn around the mizzen. Lunt pulled the cabin door closed behind him and stepped in that direction.

Lunt found himself face to face with a fully armed marine, who immediately snapped to the ready in a salute with his musket. Without Lunt having to say anything, the marine instantly opened the door behind him. Lunt passed by the man and stooped to enter into the great cabin. Jones was staring at the door as he entered. He stood up and acknowledged the new Lieutenant's salute with a genuine smile and a handshake.

"You're sure a lot fresher looking than when you came aboard, and you smell pretty too," said Jones. "I also slept a bit longer than I had intended. Let's go on deck while there's still light, I want you to see my ship before you have to leave. Later, we'll have a sumptuous repast in my quarters."

"Leave, sir ?" quizzed Lunt.

"Aye," said Jones. "You read the message and have destroyed it?"

Lunt nodded affirmatively.

"Incidentally, I have something here for you." Lunt's eyes followed his Captain to a lazaret which he opened with a key drawn from his pocket. Jones reached inside and withdrew a sword and leather scabbard.

"Every lieutenant should have his own sword."

"Why, thank you, sir," replied Lunt enthusiastically to the unexpected gift. Lunt examined the weapon, drawing it out of its sheath. It was a short sword, but had good balance. Near the throat, the blade was wide. One face of the sword bore a long ridge almost forming a third edge. The back side of the blade bore a long grove along its face.

Jones touched his fingers to the blade to emphasize the groove. "Helps let the blood out freely. The blade's ideal for repelling boarders in close combat. That should be the only time in a sea battle when an officer has to fight hand to hand."

Jones took the sword from Lunt's hands. "The most effective motion for this weapon is the thrust." He suddenly lunged forward with the sword stabbing into empty air. "This blade will pierce through bone and gristle, flesh, even light armor. Don't try to use the weapon as a broadsword, 'tis a different weapon."

Lunt nodded, still admiring the gift.

"You can look at that later, leave it here, and follow me," said the Captain who strode past him. Lunt remembered one thing about his friend from their past voyages together, Jones never seemed to walk anywhere. Lunt returned the sword to its scabbard, and placed it on a chair in the Captain's cabin, before he followed, racing after his liberator.

Lunt donned his hat as he strode out the doorway onto the quarterdeck. As he straightened into his full height, he looked into a glorious setting sun toward which Ranger was racing at a strong beat. Lunt took in a deep breath as he saw the vessel under full sail.

Each mast carried a full compliment of staysails which were larger and cut differently that any Lunt had ever observed on a previous vessel. From just below the doubling joint of the main, a huge trapezoidal staysail stretched almost to the deck, its larger leading edge luffed occasionally with slight changes in the wind direction. The leading edge of the staysail was held to the main mast by a series of rings which passed through the sail itself. From the sail's foot hung a boom attached to the sail by a series of lines. From the foremast to the main, the same type of gigantic sail plan was propelling the vessel to windward. Some of the sails had a yellow tinge, which Lunt suspected might have been caused by a manufacturing flaw in the greening of the canvas.

The vessel tipped several degrees to starboard in response to a puff.

"Mr. Cullan, loosen the staysail sheets half a foot,"

ordered Jones. Further orders from the sailing master caused a dozen men to move across the deck and up into the rigging to make the required sail adjustments.

Lunt continued to concentrate his gaze skyward. High above each staysail was rigged a similarly cut topmast staysail. From a platform at the doubling, men were loosening the sheets via a series of deadeyes.

Lunt turned his face toward a distant landfall directly to the west. He moistened his finger and placed it into the wind. He judged that the true wind was coming from the west. Yet Ranger was on a tight northwesterly course. Lunt strode to the compass bowl to check the reading. It confirmed his suspicion. Ranger was sailing closer to the wind than she should have been able.

Lunt turned to face a smiling Jones. "Aye, it's something that Doctor Franklin and I have worked upon. He did the design and I made it work with the rigging. We spent the winter refitting her at Nantes. We took out the Portsmouth rigging and the New England masts and substituted them with Kauri timbers from the Southern Continent. The wood is stronger, and allows a thinner and more resilient mast.

"We restepped the masts backward some four feet each. When going to weather they can be raked backwards even further by removing a brace at the stepping point. See how each of the masts are raked," pointed Jones proudly to the backward angle of each mast.

"Want to see it up close?" quizzed Jones.

"Yes, sir," responded Lunt whose eyes had scarcely left their observation of the sail plan.

"Light's a fadin', let's go," said Jones. Together they descended the quarterdeck stairs and moved across the gun deck, which pitched slightly to leeward in response to another puff of wind which blew firmly as the two officers made their way forward. As they proceeded across the busy upper deck, Lunt noticed that lashed between the masts was an additional supply of yards and even two spare mast lengths.

Members of the crew moved aside and then stood at attention to make way for the Captain, who nodded to several of them. Jones stopped at the base of the main and checked a line which descended from the leading edge to the staysail and was lashed to a belaying pin. He untied the line and together Lunt and he put their full weight behind it so that it was several inches tighter. Behind them came the Sailing Master, on the run.

"Just the Captain tinkering, Mr. Cullan," said Jones over his shoulder.

"Aye, as you wish, sir," said Cullan, obviously a little disturbed with the officers making adjustments without talking to him.

Jones moved away, and spoke to Lunt, "I think you'll enjoy the foremast view the best, Lieutenant Lunt."

Jones resumed his course forward, but now proceeded up the slanting deck toward the weather side. With one hand he turned to Lunt while holding on to one of the foremast's lower shrouds.

"Up ye go, Henry," said Jones.

Lunt started to take off his brand new jacket before making the climb, but the Captain spoke up, "'Tis a wee bit nippy in the tops, this time of day. I recommend ye leave your uniform jacket on but ye might tuck yer hat away in a cubby."

Lunt followed his Captain's recommendation and placed one foot of his new boots on top of the gun barrel just below the shrouds. Hatless, he started to pull his body up into the shrouds when he noticed something peculiar about the gun mounting. He stopped in the midst of his pull upward to stare at the mounting.

From behind Jones offered, "I'll explain the peg tackle mounting later. Let's climb the shrouds before the sun sets."

Lunt swung through the space between the ratlines and proceeded upward along the rope stairway taking a new rung with each step. When he was thirty feet above the deck, he was pitched forward rather suddenly as the list of the vessel heeled in response to another gust of evening wind. Flattened against the shrouds, he let his gaze fall to the deck below. It seemed every member of the crew was on the gun deck, watching the Captain and him make their ascent. On the quarterdeck, Lieutenants Simpson and Hall stared upward with their arms folded. Lunt wondered what they were thinking.

Was Captain Jones as hated by his men as he believed, or was Simpson simply more of a cautious man, who disapproved of the recklessness of his younger Captain? So far, they had both been kind to him personally. Lunt found out that it was Simpson who offered up his cabin for Lunt to get some sleep after he boarded, and that Second Lieutenant Hall had suggested his spare uniform to the purser so that Lunt could be in full uniform immediately after he awoke.

Below him, he felt the weight of Captain Jones pull on the shroud that supported his right leg. This compelled him to continue his assent past the fighting tops to the uppermost lookout platform which was another twenty feet above his head. Hand over hand he climbed, still a little shaky and weak after his long imprisonment. For just a moment, a little nausea passed through his stomach as Ranger pitched him forward in response to another puff. It caused him to feel like an insect trapped on a spider's web in a stiff breeze, excepting that he had no sticky residue to help him cling to the ratlines. One slip and he would fall fifty or more feet to certain death, or worse, lifetime confinement as a cripple. Instinctively, his muscles tightened to grip the swaying rope ladder with firmer resolve. He continued upward.

He came now to a point where the spacing between the vertical shrouds was less frequently interconnected by the ratlines' cross structure. Again Ranger shifted, it seemed now, with the extreme heel of the vessel, that if he fell he would plummet right past the leeward deck into the sea itself.

Filling his vision past the tautly stretched staysails, the sea hissed below him as a white foam formed at the bow wave. He glanced upwards and, in doing so, temporarily lost footing so that the pitch of the vessel caused his body's momentum to drop him between the gaps in the shrouds. For just an instant most of his body hung freely over the deck.

From behind, he heard, "You all right, Henry?"

He nodded at the voice from behind and pulled himself back through the gap in the shrouds as the vessel resumed a less extreme heel. After hooking his leg firmly around the shrouds, he noticed that Captain Jones was on the same level and that his hand had hold of his stiff collar, ever so lightly. The Captain had been watching him very closely. For an instant, Lunt looked directly at him. There was a glimmer of recognition. Then Lunt understood, 'this was a trial run to see how fit I am. He's testing me,' he thought.

Lunt's pulse quickened. He summoned all his strength and pulled his entire body, hand over hand, up towards the last ten feet without use of the ratlines, higher and higher towards the platform which was fixed to the doubling point where the lower mast and the beginning of the upper royal mast joined. As he groped for the top of the observation deck, he felt his wrists being seized by strong helping hands. Having achieved the platform, he found himself in the company of two uniformed marines. Behind them, supported by an iron ring, were six extra long muskets and containers which presumably housed powder and shot. Was this one of Captain Jones' methods of retaining command of his ship? He glanced back at the two other masts to find that the highest doubling platforms, as well as the lower fighting tops of each mast, all held a healthy complement of marines.

"Evening, sir..." and then correcting himself, the corporal said, "sirs."

Jones said, "Would you two like relief? 'Tis almost the end of your watch."

As the two marines descended, Lunt was enraptured

by the unparalleled sea gull's view of sunset over a far away landfall. Jones came to his side and the two stared forward for over a minute as they swayed together in the rhythm of the ocean's surface far below. The orb of sun started to fall behind the land, and the sky became increasingly red. Below and in front of the two men, the bowsprit's fore and aft sails split the twilight air.

"That's Ireland?" asked Lunt.

"Aye," said Jones, "the greenest place on earth, you'll see."

"What do you want me to do there?" asked Lunt.

"Find the Drake and report to me why she has refused to face my challenge. I'm going to let you off at the south entrance to Belfast Lough. You should be able to hitch a ride into the town. There's always potato men pulling their produce on carts into the Belfast market. It should be time for new potatoes - the young ones. They're a great delicacy. Try them."

Jones continued, "Two nights after this, just before dawn, I'll have Ranger at Carrickfergus. You must be there. In the off chance that Ranger does not make it to Carrickfergus, you should proceed to a village called Larne. I'll be further north outside of the harbor along the North Channel. I'll have a longboat at the very tip of the point on the following night. If we also fail to make that destination, at least you'll be better off than you were yesterday."

"Sir, you said you have challenged the Drake since the anchorage incident. Can you relate the details?" asked Lunt, still looking into the sunset which was now turning the sky blood red. The narrow platform took an unexpected sharp tilt to leeward as the last breath of a dying sun drove a breeze across the water. The first real chill of the evening came with it.

Jones pushed his right hand through his curly, rust colored hair and faced Lunt. "The Drake has moved to anchor deep within Belfast Lough. I can't easily sail in there. I sent a challenge via an Irish fisherman to her captain's flat. Twice. The last time was two days ago. Either there is something wrong with the Drake, or her Captain Burden is afraid to come out and meet us."

"Are you certain that these messages were delivered?" asked Lunt.

"As certain as it is that I'm standing right here," retorted Jones, mildly irritated that Lunt would question him.

Jones continued, "Because of her Captain's seeming reluctance to meet us I had given up on the Drake, until I received last night's order. The men of Portsmouth are right, in that a sail deep into Belfast Lough without good information, would be very foolish indeed. The currents, winds, and shallow waters could trap us."

"Do you know why it is so important to take the Drake, in particular?"

Jones shook his head and, clasping his hands on the red lapels of his uniform jacket, he continued, "This message has changed our mission's priorities. But, I am still going to pursue our other objectives, while you identify whether the Drake is incapacitated, or if there is any possible way to capture her and get her out of the lough. As a possible substitute, if the Drake can't be coaxed out of her warren, it may be fitting that we selectively burn a few English commercial vessels anchored in the lough.

"Therefore, I want you to appraise all vessels as alternative targets and be able to direct me to every one. But remember, the prime objective is still to find me a way to get the Drake, intact. You know how little time we may have left. Once I see the sails of those bloody men of war, I'll be obliged to beat it north, out of the Irish Sea for the Hebrides and places beyond. But, I can't be taking the risk of venturing deep into Belfast Lough without good intelligence. The recent near disaster proved that. That's your mission, Henry."

"Can I ask what you plan during the next two days?"

inquired Lunt.

"Since John Bull has seen fit to burn American ports, I thought we might burn one of his, or at least the shipping. And maybe we'll capture a Lord or two. With two days to sail along the English coast with me loyal lads below, the opportunities are endless." Jones chuckled at some private thought, and then continued, "Now, let's go below and have a fine dinner. I've had the galley prepare a leg of mutton, and I've a bottle of good Bordeaux." Jones turned to lower himself off the platform.

"Wait, sir, you know I've never been to Ireland. I don't speak, ...uh, Gaelic?"

"I've been there many a time, lad, ye won't have any trouble. Just don't speak a lot with your Yankee accent...not a problem for you, Henry," Jones laughed, as he descended hand over hand, down the shrouds barely using the ratlines for a footing. His voice carried for a moment above the platform and then it was lost. Lunt drew a deep breath and glanced towards Ireland. He felt very alone. Unlike any normal mission, if he were caught scouting out Belfast harbour the British would surely hang him. Captain Jones had neglected to mention that.

After descending to the gun deck, Jones was waiting for Lunt. "Lieutenant, you asked about the guns. You, above all, are responsible for what I have done. Remember aboard Providence, we had long talks about finding a way to correct in the midst of a broadside, instead of blowing off an entire misaimed volley into empty water. We mused many a night about how much better it would be if you could adjust your aim and make a corrected hit with the second half of the volley, while you still have good boat position relative to the target."

Lunt nodded and Jones continued, "Well, I've done better than that. I took the original twelve pounders off Ranger and exchanged them for lighter sixes. It made Ranger faster, and, of course, the gun barrels can be moved about more easily. These guns are all mounted on rolling carriages, which can be fit temporarily in specific places on the deck through these pin holes. 'Course, the wood dowels break off during recoil but they are a small price to pay compared to the increased speed received, versus trying to use knots on a training line.

"You see the pin holes here," Jones pointed down, Lunt followed his finger. "We can shift the angle of the gun barrel relative to the mid line of the vessel. If the first three rounds land forward, the gunnery officer can order one to five notches back on the next three. If the result is too far backward, the officer can order one to five forward on the final three rounds. On these wheels, two men can make the adjustment in the flicker of an eye. We've used it and it works. 'Course, each gun captain has to still make his own judgments according to the peculiarities of his individual piece."

"What about elevation?" questioned Lunt.

"Coded shims. Sixteen hundred paces is the maximum range of a six pound ball, with two flannel bags of powder. But for most targets you need to be closer than twelve hundred paces to do much damage. I've had the shim sets painted red, yellow, and bare wood. Red is full powder, yellow three-quarters, and plain wood is half a charge." Jones rolled his r's, "Each shim is marked for the number of yards it will carry the ball at that powder charge. Every gun on deck has their own set of shims, each marked and placed in order on the rack in front of the gun," Jones pointed to the slot in which each gun had a shim set.

Lunt was pleased with the details of the gunnery, but still very uneasy about being put ashore in Ireland. Captain Jones had not even asked him if he'd do it. Was this why Lieutenants Simpson and Hall were less than enamored with their Captain? Lunt was distant and deep in thought as he strode across the deck. He was conscious of the entire crew staring at him. Did they think of him as a pawn of the

Captain? What about Sarah, he needed time to write her a letter.

The two officers went directly to the great cabin, where they were joined by Lt. Wallingsford, Lt. Hall, Midshipman Hill, and the surgeon, Ezra Green. All of these officers were obviously privy to the adventure. Lieutenant Simpson was on watch and had thus, indirectly, been excluded from the repast. Lunt's mood was solemn, but he allowed the steward to pour Bordeaux in his glass.

Captain Jones stood up. Protocol required the other officers to do the same. Jones held his glass out and toasted, "Gentlemen, to American Freedom and the triumph of Ranger."

Jones swallowed half a glass before sitting, while Lieutenant Wallingsford took only a small sip. Lunt touched his lips to the rim of the glass and sat down after his Captain.

Noticing that he was not imbibing, Jones spoke up, "Really, Lieutenant Lunt, you must try this wine. It is very good. You might even say it was fit for a King." The table of officers roared at some joke that Lunt did not understand.

"Aye," continued Jones, "one of the benefits of being a Yankee pirate, is being able to acquire some very good wine. But I'll not be happy until we take a few drums of Scotch." Jones and Wallingsford laughed together. Lunt stared at his plate while a large portion of fine smelling mutton, stewed tomatoes, and potatoes were served.

"You'll be going ashore to find the Drake?" inquired Wallingsford.

"So I've been told," replied Lunt as he cut into his first piece of meat. When the taste hit his palate he savored the pleasure of the meat flavor so much that he almost convulsively began to swallow it. For the next few minutes Lunt's full attention was directed towards the meal. He had not eaten since the impromptu banquet when he first arrived on deck early that morning. Within a short time he was on his third serving of food.

Finally, Jones spoke up, "Look's like we'll have to put another two marines on to row Lieutenant Lunt ashore tonight."

Lunt retorted almost spontaneously, "Sir, you could send a lighter man."

Jones, obviously enlivened by his wine, pounded the table in a fit of temper. "Lt. Lunt, there is no one else to send but you. Each of us at this table has a prescribed regimen of duties to perform aboard the Ranger. You are still in an unofficial capacity here." Jones brought his third glass of wine up before his eyes and swirled it within its container, the red fluid casting a tint to the sides of the container. He lowered his voice to a more civilized level.

"You see, you have a unique advantage over the rest of us, if you are caught you can just claim that you escaped from Wales in a small sailboat. Your Welsh guards were deliberately led to believe that some of the crew did not choose to go with their captain. If you are found in Ireland, just two days after an escape from Wales, they will never believe that you are doing anything other than pursuing an escape. If it's one of my rostered officers, they could be hung as spies. We have had prisoners off and on this vessel in the past week who could later identify this crew, especially the officers. The Admiralty would like nothing better than to hang one of John Paul Jones' lieutenants. But we will not give him the pleasure, will wc?

"Lieutenant Lunt," said Jones from the head of the table, "all I want you to do is to observe the enemy, and to give me your best advise on how to proceed. It is not necessary for you to engage the enemy in any way. Look, and observe what is going on. Simply walk the perimeter of Belfast Lough, count ships, and make note of where they are. Find me some targets that I can burn, if need be. Make sure that they are British, not Irish, that's important. We have a number of Irishmen on this vessel - they want a piece of the King, but won't relish our attacking local commerce. The whole journey from where we leave you off will be a distance of less than forty miles. But remember to be at Carrickfergus in two evenings time. Ranger will be anchored just a half mile seaward of the deserted castle with the round turret."

Lunt said nothing, but decided to drink the glass of wine before him. After a swallow, it did make him feel better. "Sir, I repeat, can you spare an Irishman to go with me? I don't know the language and, if I have to talk, my accent will reveal my origin to the authorities."

"Yes, that's easy, one has volunteered this very evening, suspecting that since we were on a course to Ireland that he could be of service. He's a very amiable chap, always eager to help. Name's David Smith."

"He is with the purser?" asked Lunt finishing the wine.

"Aye, you've met him then," said Jones.

"Sir, when do I depart?" asked Lunt.

"In about two hours," responded Jones, who was leaning back in his chair, watching Lunt carefully.

"Then, sir," said Lunt, "I request permission to leave your table." He stammered a bit, then looked directly at his Captain. "I'll need to write my wife a letter."

"Certainly," said Jones. Lunt rose from the table and started for the door, when Jones spoke up, "But, you'll be posting that letter for yourself, Lieutenant Lunt. I'll merely be holding it till you get back."

Before going to the cabin to write Sarah a letter, Lunt walked out onto the quarterdeck to get some fresh air. There was so much to think about. He saw Jonathan Harken leaning on a rail, and descended to the gun deck to ask his old cell mate's opinion of something. They spoke a few minutes and then Lunt went below deck with Harken to the crew's berthing area.

* * * * *

The same longboat, which had brought Lunt and his

fellow prisoners to Ranger just the past evening, was now going to deliver him to Ireland. Eight marines and the giant Sergeant Miers were already in the craft. David Smith was standing by with Captain Jones.

Lunt came up from below deck, followed by O'Mally.

"Sir, may I have a word with you," asked Lunt.

"Of course," said Jones. The two walked away from the rail.

"Sir, I'd rather take Mr. O'Mally with me. He has volunteered. He has a sister living in Belfast, who is married to a victualler. That would give us a safe harborage tomorrow night. O'Mally knows Belfast well and I understand that Mr. Smith is from another part of Ireland. No offense, but since this is my mission, I'd like to choose my own men," said Lunt. "I'd also like to obtain some weapons, just in case."

"If I were you, Lieutenant Lunt, I'd not bring a weapon. All I want you to do is take a long walk with your eyes open. But suit yourself, it is as you say, your mission. I'll inform Mr. Smith that his services will not be required."

"One other thing, sir."

"Yes?" said Jones, impatient with the last minute changes.

"O'Mally has asked that he receive half his share to give to his sister. I think it's reasonable," offered Lunt.

"Better than Smith wanted," quipped Jones, "I'll see to it."

Lunt departed with Lieutenant Wallingsford to secure arms. Jones walked over to the purser's assistant and informed him that he would not be going. The man seemed to protest animatedly, but Lunt heard Jones say, "I have another, more important mission tomorrow night. I'd be very privileged to have your help then."

Lunt went with Lt. Wallingsford to the arms locker. When he returned later to the deck, he carried a fair sized seaman's canvas bag. Lunt was now dressed in common seaman's attire that had been selected for him by Lieutenants Wallingsford and Hall. Lunt's dress included a white shirt, brown breeches, and his leather vest, which Smith had cleaned for him earlier in the day. Despite the recent attention, the vest still had a very worn look. Lunt felt it would not be conspicuous in what O'Mally had called 'one of the poorest countries on earth'.

Captain Jones approached, "What's in the bag?"

Lunt replied, "Some provisions, sir."

Jones remarked, "Suit yourself, but if it were me, I'd still take nothing other than a fast pair of boots."

"I have that too, sir," replied Lunt who glanced down at the shoes that the purser had given him earlier. Lunt and O'Mally saluted and then departed over the gangway to descend the Jacob's ladder into the longboat which waited in the darkness below. Jones had a standing order never to bring a lantern directly on deck while Ranger was close to shore.

As all sign of the longboat vanished, and even after the sound of oars striking water could no longer be heard, Jones continued to stare off in the direction of the departing vessel. Finally, under his breath Jones whispered, "Godspeed, Henry Lunt. Come back safe and bring me the Drake."

4
Contact

Lunt and O'Mally quickly departed the longboat and ran up the beach hurtling over a dozen or so seaweed clumps that lined the first thirty feet of shore. The waves had been light and the longboat had no difficulty bringing them right onto the beach. They ran together for several hundred yards and then dropped onto the course sandy beach to rest and observe their environment. In the darkness, there was nothing but the sound of light surf behind them, and a few insect noises. They seemed to have landed undetected.

"Thank you again for agreeing to come with me," said Lunt, "I really felt that I needed an Irishman along for this one."

"You did," confirmed O'Mally, "I only hope, for both our sakes, you've chosen the right one. I warned you that some time ago I had a bit of trouble in these parts," said O'Mally.

"Yes," said Lunt, "but your past might just provide us with contacts or knowledge we could use in an emergency."

"By the way," said O'Mally, "I do want to thank ye for coaxing a half share out of the Captain. As you...."

"Let's get moving," said Lunt, who stood up to avoid a long conversation. "You say that we'll likely be able to catch a ride on a farmer's potato cart?"

"We call the two wheeled ones, traps. That's what it might be, a trap." O'Mally restrained a chuckle as he sensed Lunt's instant disapproval of his pun. He apologized softly, "Pardon."

O'Mally stood up, heaved the canvas bag over his shoulder, and followed Lunt. There was a lull in the conversation while they hiked inland in the pale moonlight, each taking turns with the canvas bag which weighed its bearer down in the course sand.

After another few minutes they came to the edge of a well worn dirt road that seemed to parallel the harbour.

O'Mally spoke up, pointing animatedly with his finger, "This road sweeps all the way around the lough, into Belfast and back out to the north. There'll be no getting lost, just keep the water over your right shoulder the entire way. We want to be going this a way," O'Mally pointed to the right.

"How long will it take us to get into the city?" asked Lunt.

"We'll be there before the morning dew is off the heather, especially if we can catch a ride part of the way," concluded O'Mally, shifting the canvas bag for emphasis.

"The Captain did advise us to carry nothing," Lunt raised an eyebrow.

"Aye, but surely the good Captain doesn't know Ireland like I do. First off, there's a lot of desperately poor people here. If we look just a little bit prosperous we could have trouble. That'll be why I advised you to have Lieutenant Wallingsford provide us with a few pistols and grenades from the arms locker. And the second reason is that here in Ireland a few weapons like these can be much more valuable than mere coin," O'Mally chuckled in reference to something only he seemed to understand.

Lunt let the comment go uninvestigated, and instead asked, "I don't look especially prosperous, do I?" Lunt tugged at his old leather vest.

" 'Tis in the eye of the beholder, Henry. You've never seen poor people in your life like you are going to see when the sun rises," O'Mally said, with a straightforwardness that seemed out of character.

Lunt glanced over at him, a bit in shock at O'Mally's sudden familiarity.

O'Mally sensed his irritation and spoke up, "Don't let

that new rank go to your head, boy. This is the same O'Mally that worked in the chandlery those months with you and that sang at your wedding. It's the same O'Mally who shipped out with you to parts unknown in a tall ship to fight for a country he did not know. It's the same O'Mally who consented to land here with you this night, because I knew how easily you would get into trouble here. After all that, I figure you shouldn't mind if I keep calling you Henry, like I always have, seeing it's just you and me together alone. We wouldn't want to let the word 'Lieutenant' slip out in the vicinity of the wrong ears. Would we?"

O'Mally blew a bit of breath on his knuckles and brushed them on his own chest. In his unique Irish way he was sending the signal that he'd won the point and there was no need to argue further.

Lunt had an inkling that O'Mally seemed a bit more in charge of things than ever before. Lunt had slept just two hammocks away from O'Mally in the Alfred, along with his cousin, Cutting, who was likely still in Mill Prison. The three tended to share the same duty watches. O'Mally had never before seemed particularly firm or strong about anything. Lunt tended to think of him as just a good natured companion, who was an incessant talker.

Lunt did not like the familiarity which O'Mally had decided to take. In the day or so since his promotion, Lunt had begun to like the feeling of being an officer. He had to admit it. He liked having the marines come to sharp attention when he came down from the foremast with Captain Jones. However, in the interest of getting along on this mission, Lunt decided to permit O'Mally the harmless pleasure of using his first name, for awhile.

The two made progress along the road easily. There was little traffic upon it. Here and there they passed close to groups of people. Some were obviously families with children who seemed to dwell only in lean-tos along the side of the road. All wore dark clothing, which at night made it difficult for Lunt to distinguish the men from the women. As they passed along the way, almost everyone who was awake asked them for money, usually first in a highly accented English, and then in Gaelic, which Lunt found incomprehensible.

Lunt knew almost immediately that he would never be able to imitate the Irish version of spoken English without it being obvious that he was not from Ireland. As they walked along, he had O'Mally coach him on the pronunciation of a limited vocabulary that he might have to employ during their mission. He practiced saying, "Yes, sir," and "No, sir," in a very Irish way.

After an hour or so on the Belfast road, they had encountered no potato carts. Lunt began to become uncomfortably conscious of his feet. Almost every rock along the roadside seemed to drive his toes forward, further into the narrow pointed tips of his boots. By the time they reached Belfast, Lunt knew that his feet would be very sore. Perhaps, he would find a hot tub to soak his feet at O'Mally's sister's home.

As they continued on their nocturnal journey, increasingly they encountered groups of people sleeping along the side of the road. Lunt wondered aloud where they lived in the winter. Surely they couldn't live there all year?

When they were out of earshot from any group, O'Mally explained, " 'Tis the homeless. They've been turned away from their land 'cause they can't pay the rent. Imagine being required to pay rent to farm the homeland of your ancestors."

Lunt listened in sympathy, and was silent as O'Mally went on for over an hour about the Irish, and the English, and the right to own land only if you took the pledge to the Church of England. According to O'Mally, if you were Catholic and practiced your faith in Ireland, you were doomed to a life of everlasting torment, poverty, and hunger.

O'Mally explained that the only way to become prosperous in Ireland was to become a land owner, which, of course, you could not do if you were a Catholic. It was against the law. The prevailing practice was for each person who owned land to divide up their property and then rent the portions. In turn, some of the renters of larger bits of land then rerented smaller parcels at an even higher rate to make a profit. Often the English aristocracy, who had traditionally been deeded the property by the Crown, had never been to Ireland. They hired overseers to manage their holdings who subsequently subdivided the properties into even smaller parcels for which they charged more per given area. This, explained O'Mally, was why the farms Lunt would see in Ireland were so tiny.

O'Mally continued, "What's left at the bottom of the system is the actual farmer having to pay more for his rented land than he can ever possibly earn from it. It is impossible, with the crowded conditions, for most families to successfully work the land. The price of potatoes simply will not pay the high land rent.

"So evictions of renters are very common in Ireland and there's always militia about to enforce the evictions and protect the land owners and overseers. Many of the people you see by the sides of the road have been evicted countless times from their land. They live here by the wayside until another overseer agrees to let them rent a parcel again. Ultimately, they will be doomed to failure in the new attempt but in the meantime they have a place to live."

Lunt asked, "Then, if the price of potatoes will not pay for the land, why not grow corn, or tomatoes, or raise pigs, instead?"

"I guess the people see it as an English plot. You see, the English are always pushing to have Ireland diversify. Every year, since I can remember, they send a fancy commission over from London, or from some damn University." O'Mally spat on the ground to emphasize his disapproval. "They get to the cities, but they never get the word out to the people. It gets in the newspapers, but the common folk can't read or write, and they're always suspicious of any English plan, no matter what its merit."

"How could they get the people to listen?" asked Lunt.

"By getting the priests to tell the people. 'Tis the only way it would be believed by the Irish people. Most people can't read or write," O'Mally reemphasized.

"Then why don't the authorities use the priests to get the word out to the people?" asked Lunt innocently.

"Because there are no priests," said O'Mally, then to correct the misunderstanding he could see forming on Lunt's face, he explained further, "Priests are outlawed, the practice of the Mass is illegal. In truth, just to defy the English, more people probably go to Mass every Sunday than would normally."

O'Mally continued, "They hold the Masses in the strangest of places: at the undertakers, in barns, on the beach, in people's homes, and in the woods. The priests have these little traps. They keep their little relic of a saint nailed to the bottom. They'll stop the cart in a wood, throw a wrap over their shoulder, haul out some bread and wine, and they're ready for the Lord's business. People come. Sometimes that little piece of bread is all that they get to eat that day. When the priest is flush, it's a banquet rather than a communion." O'Mally chuckled, and then continued.

"But the people come. I think it's too, a little bit of the danger that makes them come. They want to defy the English, just to feel they've done a little something. Sort of a bit of courage to start the week off with; a Mass, and maybe, a wee bit of whiskey."

"You drink at this Mass?" questioned Lunt. "Don't you listen to what the priests say?"

"You can't understand what it is they say!" corrected O'Mally. "They speak in Latin. Who knows what they are saying? It's between them and God, and the rest of us are thinking about who we made love to the night before." O'Mally laughed irreverently and then continued.

"I don't want you to get the wrong impression, you being a protestant yourself. That's what I like about America and why I'm serving on this ship. You people really don't seem to care what religion a man takes."

"We have a few problems," corrected Lunt.

"Ah, but not on the scale of dear old Ireland," concluded O'Mally.

After a few minutes reflection over O'Mally's philosophy, Lunt observed that O'Mally seemed to be laughing to himself. Lunt nudged him to explain what was so amusing.

"'Twas thinking of me father's day. Over in Galway, and the moving Mass."

"The moving Mass?" asked Lunt

"Aye, 'twas a moving experience." O'Mally slapped his knee and dropped the canvas bag with a thud onto the dirt road.

After getting control of his laughter, he continued, "You see, it was very dangerous in my father's time to be caught at a Mass. You might be killed right on the spot. Now things are a bit better. Not economically, but at least politically.

"'Twas in a time of intense English raids on several Masses in the area. This priest, Father Jamie Reilly, got the idea of a moving Mass. Now that's not that he was moving us so much spiritually, but that he was physically moving the little trap that was his altar. Someone would drive and he would sit on the back and speak to us in that bloody Latin. The rest of them would walk behind, pretending to listen attentively.

"It got to be a very popular thing with the men. They soon found out that they could drift back away from the ladies and get a little freedom. The ladies tend to practice the religion a bit more sincerely than the men. Unless we're dying, then we all tend to take it seriously.

"Ah, but back to the moving Mass," continued O'Mally. "Sooner or later, one of the lads would fish out a jug of poteen from beneath his jumper, and they would pass it about. Some of the less religious lasses would fall back too. Soon the bunch in the rear would get to singing. It could get quite loud. Finally Father Reilly, out of fear of his life, had to stop the moving Masses. There was no secrecy at all. You could hear the Mass ahead on the road for miles." Lunt smiled at the picture which O'Mally's words had painted in his mind.

Lunt nodded and O'Mally continued with his discourse, as they trudged down the road with no sight yet of a potato cart, and the relief from their burden that it would bring. Another hour passed and Lunt developed a slight limp from the blisters he had raised from the friction caused by his boots. "Don't the French have toes?" he murmured, in irritation to their impracticability.

As they walked, they began to encounter a large sweeping bend in the contour of the road as it shifted gradually westward. Here and there were large ruts gouged in the uneven roadway. Lunt surmised that they were evidently caused by a diurnal flow of heavily laden potato carts, punctuated by a fair amount of rainfall.

During one of the few pauses in O'Mally's conversation, Lunt inquired, "Why has there been such trouble aboard Ranger? The Captain told me about several near mutinies."

"Aye, 'tis the men from Portsmouth and Lieutenant Simpson. The heart of the matter is they're afraid. They expected, after the refitting in Nantes, that they would just patrol the mid Atlantic and pick off a few merchant vessels, and bring their share of the prize money home. Just like you did to Sarah, Henry, after the voyage of the Providence."

O'Mally continued, "You see, our old friend Captain Jones is sort of a strange man. His now having his own ship, and the rank of captain have made his eccentricities more pronounced. He has no wife or child I've ever heard him speak of, and he really believes in this Revolution. You remember how he was always reading the crew the Declaration of Independence aboard the Providence." Lunt nodded in remembrance.

O'Mally expounded, "The Revolution has almost become his religion, if you know what I mean. You know there's patriotism and then there's Patriotism. Well, Captain Jones is a sincere, true patriot. Of that there is no doubt. Since he's had command of the Ranger he has become a driven man. And because of the things he does, he has pushed the crew to the edge more than once.

"A lot of the trouble started a few days out of Portsmouth, at the very beginning of the voyage last summer. Ranger had a southerly breeze and a good lift to France. You know, a natural smooth ride, a few swells, but nice. Well, Captain Jones says he's going to see what the ship can do. That's to be expected with a new ship, but in the minds of the crew he went to the extreme."

"Jones turned Ranger on a southeasterly beat and ordered all sorts of sail changes, from dawn to dusk for days. The bloody crew was out on full shift for every hour of sunlight. There wasn't a bloody sail that the Captain didn't have out. He had Ranger tested at every conceivable tack, and he took notes on foolscap about the Ranger's speed and the sail trim for every possible angle and position. It went on for days and days," O'Mally reemphasized.

"Then he had the sailmaker cutting off and adding bits of canvas on this sail and that. By the time we got to France all thc sails looked like patchwork quilt. The men just viewed the whole exercise as a lot of needless work but, all in all, during most of the crossing the men took it pretty well. They figured that the Captain was just trying a little too hard.

"Until that day Lieutenant Simpson let the Captain's notes blow out of his hands and fall overboard. I'm told no one ever saw the Captain so mad. He called Simpson about every name in the book. It was the worst tongue lashing that I've ever heard. It went on in front of the entire crew for nearly a half hour. Lieutenant Simpson is almost fifteen or twenty years older than Captain Jones and he just stood at attention and took it, but the Captain lost a lot of respect, especially with the men of Portsmouth, and that was about the entire crew on the passage over."

"Why didn't the Captain just relieve Simpson?" asked Lunt.

"He can't. There was some sort of an agreement made about Lieutenant Simpson's position when Captain Jones got command of Ranger. You see, at the beginning Simpson was supposed to have been Captain of Ranger, and then Jones showed up from France, via Philadelphia or someplace first. The Marine Committee of the Continental Congress issued orders for Captain Jones to take command of Ranger, but the shipbuilders of Portsmouth, who had actually put up the money to build Ranger, had a different feeling. They wanted a local man to command Ranger to ensure that the ship would bring back a good bounty to make them rich in return for their investment. It's all about money, at the heart of it."

"It frequently is," observed Lunt.

O'Mally continued, "The Ranger should have sailed early last summer, but there were all sorts of disagreements. It took many weeks to get it all sorted out.

"In a way the crew was right to be a little resentful of the situation."

"How so?" asked Lunt.

"Most of the men signed on under Simpson, with the promise that there would be good prize money from the voyage. Instead, they now find themselves in the middle of the British Isles, going who knows where, for purposes they don't understand. Prize money is not a high priority of Captain Jones.

"Anyway, right after the notebook incident, that's when the town meetings started. Simpson, Hall, Cullan, and the rest. First, they objected to there being two marine officers on board Ranger, a captain and Lieutenant Wallingsford. They said it diluted their share of the prize money. Nearly the whole crew signed a petition that was presented to Captain

Jones. A lot of the crew were praying that Jones would take the two marine officers and leave Ranger, and move to another ship as soon as they arrived in France.

"Anyhow, from then on, when the Captain issued an order, Lieutenant Simpson would call a town meeting and the next day he might flatly refuse to do what Captain Jones wanted. The men of Portsmouth mustered behind Simpson when he spoke. Simpson always confronts the Captain on deck, where he has support of his men. On the voyage over, Jones didn't have all these marines you see now. They were picked up in France this winter. You know that big giant marine sergeant, the blond haired man named Miers?"

"Yes, he smashed in the door to our jaol. I'll never forget him," said Lunt.

"Well, Miers is one of the new marines. Like me and about a third of Ranger's crew, he's not an American at all. He was, until recently, a Lieutenant in the Swedish army. He showed up one day at Ambassador Franklin's residence in Paris asking to serve the American cause. When Franklin was brought into the dispute between Jones and Simpson, he simply exchanged Miers for the Marine Captain. Jones had a second marine leader to take charge while Wallingsford was off duty, and the men of Portsmouth did not have to give up another officer's share from their prize money."

Lunt looked about him as he walked. In the darkness, there appeared to be large hedge rows bordering the road. The individual farms were hidden behind these hedges.

O'Mally talked further about the Ranger and its crew. "At the heart of all of this is also the Captain's Scottish accent. Every time he speaks, the Yankee group make fun of his accent behind the Captain's back, pretending they did not understand. The truth is they resent taking orders from a Scott, or any foreigner. They talk about Miers, Ryan, Fitzgerald, and me in the same way, I'm sure," mused O'Mally. "Then, there's the Captain's women..."

Lunt changed the subject, "What about Smith, the man

the Captain wanted me to take, before I insisted on you?"

"Can't figure him. He attends the town meetings and talks a lot. At times, he supports the crew below, then at other times I see him up brown nosing the officers and marines, giving them things from purser supply. Couple of times I tried to talk to him about Ireland and he always found something else he had to do," reported O'Mally.

After a few minutes, O'Mally offered a few more insights into Ranger's difficulties. "One day before the Ranger arrived in France, when the men of Portsmouth were especially slow in carrying out his orders, the Captain called everyone out on deck and read them that Thomas Payne sonnet, you know the one about the Sunshine Patriots. The men did not like their patriotism being questioned. There would have been a mutiny that evening if they hadn't spotted a sail at dusk. The Captain guessed its destination and an hour after dawn we were just 800 paces from her. It was a good prize."

"Has it been a profitable voyage?" asked Lunt.

"Not bad, since we left Nantes," said O'Mally, who took out a small bag and shook it with sufficient turbulence to produce the telltale sound of coins jingling. "Thanks to your talking the Captain into letting me have half my share to this point, I've a few guineas to pass on to my sister. I've never given her anything but trouble before. A little nest egg will be very welcome, if she don't fall over dead from shock. Wish it could have been more, but the Captain kept the other half of my share in his safe. Said it'd strengthen my resolve to come back on board."

"Will it?"

O'Mally turned and looked at him. They both stopped and faced each other. Lunt again felt that different side of O'Mally of which he had felt traces of all evening. The expression in the man's face changed. He straightened himself very tall and looked directly into Lunt's eyes from less than an arm's length away. "Henry, you can be sure of one thing, if I can help capture an English fighting ship in an Irish harbour, it will be the pride of me life. Believe that."

The doubt was there. O'Mally might elect not to return with Lunt to the Ranger. Lunt needed him now, or his mission was going to be very difficult. He decided to deal with this possibility later, rather than cause a confrontation. They resumed walking along and O'Mally returned to explain even more about the Ranger and her difficulties.

"You should know what happened after Ranger and her prizes got to Nantes," continued O'Mally. "The first thing that Captain Jones did was to give Lieutenant Simpson orders to take down all of Ranger's rigging entirely. Masts too. Every bit. He wrote the order down and then made Simpson sign it. Then Jones left for Paris. It wasn't two hours before Simpson was off to Paris himself. Apparently, they had a big argument in Paris at Doctor Franklin's house."

O'Mally continued, "Anyway, Lieutenant Hall, and David Cullan, the Sailing Master, and the crew got the rigging completely taken down as Jones had ordered. Not knowing what to do, Hall gave about a third of the crew leave at a time. It was six or eight weeks before any of the crew saw either officer. A lot of the crew went to Paris during that period."

"Did you?" asked Lunt.

"I was already there. Remember, I did not come over with Captain Jones, I am new to the Ranger as well. All of what I have told you is based on what I've heard from the rest of the crew. After the Providence landed in France, over a year ago, I departed with my share and have been enjoying the sights and sounds of gay Paree for most of the winter. Found a cute little charmer who likes my red hair," bragged O'Mally before he continued.

"I was asked by Dr. Franklin's secretary to serve on Ranger. You see, what Franklin and Jones have done is to gradually lower the concentration of Portsmouth men now aboard the Ranger. Sort of as a way of defusing the home town strength, Dr. Franklin reassigned some of the Ranger's original crew to another privateer. You see, there are lots of Irish expatriates living in Paris who will do anything to get a crack at the English.

"Another thing, every time that Jones takes a prize on this voyage, the prize crew leaving the ship is always completely filled with Portsmouth men."

"I see," said Lunt.

"Anyhow, I wasn't there at the time, but one day this past winter, Dr. Franklin came back in a coach with Captain Jones and Lieutenant Simpson. After they transferred about 20 of the Portsmouth men to another vessel, they let nearly the entire crew have leave for two weeks. Then Dr. Franklin and Captain Jones, and even Simpson, walked the deck. They made plans to completely modify the vessel. Simpson was left in Nantes to set up a receiving station for new rigging, sail, and ordnance supplies. Jones and Dr. Franklin returned to Paris."

"This was at the beginning of winter," guessed Lunt.

O'Mally nodded and continued, "During that time Ambassador Franklin introduced Captain Jones to the French court. Overnight he became their darling. Especially with the women."

Lunt nodded in affirmation. He could imagine two or three women fighting over their rights to the company of the dashing Scot.

"So Jones made great friends with Madame de Chaumont, her husband heads the French Government supply agency. Within a few weeks there were wagon loads of sail, line, new cannons - the six pounders, swivels, and those fancy Kauri wood masts from the Southern continent," commented O'Mally.

Lunt stopped a moment, and kicked the heel of his boot into a rock to relieve the pressure on his compressed toes. Then, he caught up with O'Mally, who continued his narrative.

"In December, Jones returned and ordered all of his crew back. I joined Ranger at that time, right after Christmas.

He made a lot of changes. Anyway, he then began to work everyone twelve hours a day, sunrise to sunset. First, we set the masts, then all the stays. Then Mr. Johnson, the Sailmaker, had us stitching canvas. I did it for days. Me hands were really bloody, the awl never goes through right. It was a horrendous job. Everything was changed on deck - everything. By February, we thought it was finished. Then Dr. Franklin arrived again and we took Ranger out for a test sail."

"You met Dr. Franklin?" inquired Lunt, who had not met the famous man, but was eager to.

"He signed my copy of the Almanac," said O'Mally proudly.

"Well, Dr. Franklin spent several days aboard. He talked about things I've never understood, but I've heard Captain Jones repeat them since the Doctor was aboard. Words like wind vortexes, center of effort, tension, pressure, vacuum funnel. He and Jones even talked about seeing the wind and did it."

Lunt listened very attentively. When O'Mally paused to take a breath, he interrupted, "How did they see the wind?"

O'Mally continued, "Did you see those yellow marks on all the sails? Looked like the greening had gone bad when the canvas was prepared."

Lunt nodded, and O'Mally continued, "It was Dr. Franklin did that. He had Sergeant Miers and some of the marines mount a burning sulfur pot on the end of a long pole. Smelly thing it was too. We took Ranger out and for three days at sea, Dr. Franklin and Captain Jones saw the wind."

"I don't really understand," said Lunt trying to piece together O'Mally's description.

"The smoke, the wretched smoke. They watched the smoke. Ya see, Dr. Franklin and the Captain put a marine up on the foremast tops, where the Captain and you were standing last night. This was how they saw the smoke."

"You mean while the vessel was moving?" quizzed Lunt.

"Aye, they watched the wind, and the smoke it was carrying, go through the sails. The marines used a very long pole to hold the burning sulfur pot out so that Dr, Franklin and the Captain could make drawings of the wind coming through the sails at various tacks. Anyhow, Dr. Franklin took the notes back to Paris; there were pages and pages of them, and a couple of weeks later he sent a notebook of rigging changes for the Captain to follow. The Sailmaker had to recut all the sails again. By the time this was over, it was February."

"And I had been moved to Wales by then," offered Lunt.

O'Mally continued, "Then Captain Jones takes the crew out in two different storms to test the rigging. Can ye imagine deliberately going out in a storm, and they were howlers too. Luckily I missed the second, a group of us were in Paris to get some supplies.

"Anyhow we had just about to set sail, when the Captain takes off again, back to Paris. I heard Lieutenant Simpson tell Lieutenant Hall that it was probably to have a last go at all his women. Anyway, I doubt it because within a week he returned with the special orders from the Marine Committee. Rumor was that it was a carte blanche charter to take Ranger anywhere Captain Jones wished. Often on this voyage, Lt. Simpson has said that the wording was vague. He feels that the writer meant for him to go anywhere to merely test the vessel.

"Captain Jones has personally gone ashore three times since the beginning of this voyage. A lot of the crew think he is picking up some kind of a message when he does that. He never takes anyone to the final place he goes. Did he ever go off by himself when he came to rescue you? Do you know?" inquired O'Mally looking at him.

Lunt said, "It was a confusing time during the rescue. It was dark. Anyone could have gone off anywhere."

O'Mally accepted it and continued his observations.

"If the Captain had forewarned the men that he intended to raid the British Isles, few of the Ranger's original crew would have remained aboard. Nantes is not a bad town, and the French coast is beautiful. Did you ever get to Belle Isle?"

Lunt did not answer.

They had been walking now for approximately three hours. They came to a stream which flowed down from a meadow and across the road on its path to the sea. There was no bridge, they would have to ford the shallow stream to continue on their way. Beyond the stream, the road had started to curve towards the southwest. From his memory of the map which Captain Jones had shown him before evening dinner, Lunt knew they were now deep into the lough. They would easily be in Belfast, or very near it, by sunup. Across the water, Lunt believed he could just see lanterns burning among the streets of the city.

At the small stream, they both knelt and took water with cupped hands. Just as they did, the air seemed to turn a bit damp. Lunt felt suddenly very cold. Beside him, he could feel O'Mally tighten up. In the distance, upstream, they could hear a woman crying. The noise seemed to come at them anonymously, its clear direction was distorted by the creek which gave off a gurgling sound. The wail of the crying woman seemed to permeate the air above the flow.

Lunt sipped water. As he crouched, he thought momentarily of trying to help the woman but O'Mally cautioned him not to get involved. The possibilities were too great that they might become distracted from a mission that they had only two days to complete. Just before he prepared to cross the stream, Lunt carefully washed off his new boots, cursing them under his breath for their tightness.

Over the hours that they had walked, Lunt had heard quite a few sounds from the numerous people who lived by the roadside. The sound of children crying, two brothers arguing about who was going to repair their lean-to in the morning, and even the sound of a couple making love. But this sound of the crying woman was different; it was commanding. Suddenly, as if in reaction to the sound, O'Mally stood up and began running across the creek to the other side. Lunt followed him and the two resumed their progress.

For some time the sound of the woman's unhappiness seemed to hang in the air, but eventually they were far enough away that they could no longer hear it. Lunt still wondered about her plight and then his thoughts turned again to his own affairs. For a time, O'Mally was strangely silent. Each man had his own thoughts.

Lunt thought for awhile of Sarah as he stared at the partial moon which lit the landscape and gave it an ominous glare. He wondered if later this same night, she might also look up at the moon, and see the same white orb whose darkened patches gave the hint of a face. Does the face of the moon look the same in Newburyport as it does here in Ireland? He wondered for some time, would he ever see her face again, or anyone's face he knew, for that matter? If he were caught and the British found out that he was a member of Ranger's crew, they would hang him as a spy for certain. After all, he was.

After another hour or so they came to a road which intersected the coastal road. It descended from a group of hills. Midway along the road way they saw a number of small carts descending.

"They'll be the potato men. Our ride," said O'Mally, reaching into his pocket for a small coin with which to bargain with the nearest driver.

* * * * *

Lunt's head nodded off and bounced off a few of the potatoes he had strategically aligned in the bed of the compact, four wheeled cart to give his head support. The smell of potato dust came in with every breath. O'Mally was sitting up with the cart's owner and conversing in Gaelic. The road was bumpy, but Lunt was so exhausted that he had managed to sleep for some time. It was still dark, but a lightening sky gave hint of coming daylight.

Looking toward the rear of the cart, he glimpsed the presence of a hand that seemed to slither very quietly over the edge of the filled potato cart. The hand found a good sized potato and then was gone. Lunt watched as a dark shape fled off into a thicket with its prize clutched beneath its cloak. He said nothing to O'Mally or the driver. He did not want to reveal his accent, or to make trouble for a person who must have needed the potato desperately. Lunt did momentarily check his sail cloth bag which was buried beneath the potatoes. Satisfied that it had gone undisturbed, he reshuffled the potatoes into a more comfortable pile and aligned his head to obtain a better view of the sunrise which would be upon them shortly.

The sunrise prompted him to think of his mission for the day. He would have to plot the position of each merchant vessel, and of the Drake and any other armed ships in the harbour. Also the position of any on shore batteries, shore boats, or other means that might cause resistance to Ranger. Would the Captain really take Ranger this deeply into Belfast Lough and burn all the shipping? Was that his intention? Lunt doubted it. Jones wanted the Drake, just as the message had ordered. The sky was brightening quickly. Lunt sat up, turned, and looked towards the city. It was still some three to five miles in the distance. Most of it tended to be on the far side of the harbour, across the water from his vantage point. There seemed to be a bridge at the extreme end of the lough. And there was a profusion of ships' masts everywhere, however, most were not large enough to represent an appropriate military target.

The sky brightened again, and Lunt was awe struck by the beauty of the landscape, and particularly of the green grass which stretched all over the high hills surrounding the city and bay. It was a shade of green, quite unlike any which Lunt had ever seen before. It seemed painted rather than real. For a while he wondered if so vivid a color was an illusion caused by the early morning light. But as the sun pulled upward into full view, the impression of green became more and more vivid. Lunt could also smell the vegetation, particularly the small purple flowers which grew everywhere.

Lunt glanced down at the farm land in the foreground beneath the green hills. As O'Mally had said, all of the flat areas were divided by stone fences, or in some places by high hedge rows. Lunt was astounded by the small sizes of the land divisions. Each was filled with neat rows of leafy green sprouts which Lunt recognized as young potato plants.

Many of the farms were only a hundred to two hundred paces on a side. Almost all of them had a tiny one room stone cottage built into the extreme corner of the land, with two of its sides being part of the fence itself. This maximized the amount of land that could be used to grow potatoes. Some of the cottages even had potatoes growing out of sod which had been placed on their roofs.

On the stone side of the peasant cottages there was often a lean-to. Occasionally, Lunt saw a pair of sleeping feet poking out from their partial covering. Lunt was struck by the number of people about. During their walk, O'Mally had said that tiny Ireland was the most populated country in Europe. Despite the statement, Lunt was unprepared for the large numbers that seemed to be living in each tiny square of land and along the sides of the road.

Lunt began to look into the faces of the people. Curiously, they seemed happy and he began to exchange waves with many of the children. Until they came abreast of one lean-to against a boundary hedge, where a mother with an especially gaunt face stood clutching her children. All were shoeless and covered in dark rags with obvious tears of hunger flowing. They all trembled in the morning dew. Lunt sat up and exchanged a long glance with one of the children. He was overcome with a feeling that these were perhaps the poorest people he had ever seen in his entire life.

Lunt glanced quickly over his shoulder at O'Mally and the driver, who were seemingly engrossed in a spirited conversation in Gaelic. Lunt reached his hand into the pile of potatoes and, finding the two biggest within his grasp, he put his finger to his mouth in a symbol of silence, and then silently tossed the two potatoes from the cart. The children broke from their mother's grasp and, in a fit of squealing, they dove onto the two potatoes with fervor. Reinforced by the righteousness of his deed, Lunt tossed another lone potato into the hands of the mother, who, after quickly tucking the potato into the rags which hung about her body, placed her hand to her forehead and then moved it in a ritual fashion across her body. It was a gesture which Lunt had seen his Catholic crew mates perform before, especially during a big storm.

Suddenly, Lunt felt the collar of his leather vest being tugged backwards, he jerked his face around to find his hawk nose just inches from the face of the old man who owned the cart. The hood had fallen off the old man's head to reveal a shock of fine white hair which blew in all directions about the ruddy red face it enveloped.

"Don't be so free with another man's potatoes, lad. They're the work of three families, who struggled hard to plant them, and to dig them up, and paid a lot of rent to the Earl for the right to grow 'em on the land. It doesn't pay in the end to start tossing 'em at the pitiful. Pretty soon those who work the land wouldn't be able to get down the road at all, because the beggars would be demanding a potato apiece. There'd be none left to sell at market. Then, the working people would soon be living by the side of the road too," emphasized the old man.

Lunt reached into the vest and pulled out a wrapped cloth. The old man stared at the cloth curiously as Lunt unwrapped it. Inside were five coins worth a schilling each. Lunt took one coin and passed it to the man. Both knew that it was worth more than the value of all of the potatoes Lunt would be likely to toss from the cart. Lunt pressed the coin into the man's hand.

"Who are ye, spending money like that?" asked the old man, looking directly into Lunt's expressionless steel blue eyes. O'Mally broke up the potential exchange by saying something in Gaelic and tugging at the old man to look at the road, lest his mule turn off in an unwanted direction. Occasionally the old man glanced over his shoulder to observe the passenger who silently tossed a few potatoes at a time to the homeless. This continued for several miles. The old white haired man shook his head but smiled faintly, as he drove the cart onward to market. O'Mally kept him somewhat busy with a constant chatter.

Lunt's attention was drawn to an increasing background rhythm of strong hoof beats, which began to overcome the calm patter of their slowly moving mule. The sound continued to increase in tempo, indicating that many riders were approaching them. Lunt turned to see three red uniformed dragoons riding towards them. He let his latest potato offering fall from his right hand and grabbed instinctively for the sail cloth bag. He reassuringly found it. His hand closed through the canvas on the butt of one of the pistols inside.

The lead rider wore a highly ornamented cap and a scarlet red uniform trimmed in white and gold. On the man's sleeves were bright gold chevrons, he was a sergeant. The rider's horse was a majestic brown beast with small white freckles across his chest. As he came closer, Lunt could see that the rider had a very muscular, square, bony face. Beneath a large black mustache, his mouth had formed into a cruel snarl.

Lunt's mind raced, what had they possibly done to alert the authorities? Had someone reported his innocent potato tossing, and somehow alerted the British garrison that there was a mad Yankee on the Belfast road tossing potatoes to the natives? Lunt knew his thoughts were absurd, but his heart still pounded at the potential threat of imminent detection this early in his mission.

"Off the road, you beggars. Make room for yer betters!" ordered the onrushing Dragoon. Lunt felt almost instant relief, until a few paces from the front of the mule, the Dragoon raised a huge horse whip which had been in his right hand and waved it threateningly at the driver. The old man stared at the soldier, but did not respond. Not seeing an attempt to move the cart, the mounted soldier let his whip fly. The whip struck the mule's face and back with a sharp crack. The animal shook himself to relieve the sudden, senseless pain imposed by the man. The cart became unsteady as the animal sought to back up to avoid further pain.

Lunt immediately looked off towards the side of the road that the Sergeant was indicating. He realized why the old man had not responded immediately. At this point on the road, the only way off was down a very steep dirt grade. The Dragoon's request was unreasonable. If the old man were to move there the cart might tip over, or push the animal towing it into a fall. Lunt turned his attention back to the mustached man, who was recoiling his whip, preparing for the perverse pleasure of another strike at the occupants of the potato cart. The mule whinnied in fear seeing the whip being readied for another strike. The old man slowly shook the reins trying to coax the cart off the road. The old man seemed reluctant to get off his cart and lead the mule on foot. Lunt, and then O'Mally shifted their positions so that their weight would help keep the high end of the cart from tipping over. As the cart settled into a steep sidewards angle, some of the man's potatoes began to roll off the side of the cart and tumble down the steep grade.

Lunt gave some consideration to grabbing the whip should it fall again on the cart or its occupants. He looked up at their tormentor. Two other dragoons were pulling their horses to a stop behind their Sergeant. Several hundred paces behind there seemed to be forty or fifty riders who were riding at a more casual gait. Human heads appeared in the distance to rise up and down above the cloud of road dust their horses' hooves were stirring. If Lunt did anything to arose attention, he would be immediately seized and questioned. Nevertheless, his right hand still clutched the pistol butt through the canvas bag.

Sensing the other riders approaching nearer, the Sergeant let lose the whip downwards at the driver. Part of its biting coil caught the old man on the shoulder, while the whip's tail crackled through the air, exploding into Lunt's cheek. Lunt jerked back his head in pain and impulsively his right hand extended deeply into the canvas bag below him to retrieve his pistol. His hand locked over the pistol butt and was about to draw the weapon, when suddenly he felt the weight of O'Mally's hand over his own, restraining it from further movement.

The Sergeant bellowed, "Off the road, now," and then readied his horse for an immediate gallop into the midst of some black figured pedestrians standing further along the road, gaping at the stricken potato cart. As the Sergeant passed the potato cart, through tears of pain Lunt caught sight of his well polished boots and sleek leather riding gear which gleamed in the sun.

Holding his cheek with his hand, Lunt's gaze continued to follow the Sergeant as he moved away. The powerful horse's freckled flanks pushed off, as it galloped towards the next group of helpless victims its rider had chosen to torment. Dust kicked back from his horse's hooves, as their metal shoed bottoms were exposed momentarily to the morning sunlight.

The two other dragoons trotted closer to the wagon. One placed his hand on the old man's shoulder but the man shifted to avoid his touch. "I'm sorry, old man, the Sergeant Major gets a bit carried away sometimes, but you will have to keep your cart entirely off the road 'till they pass. It's orders, you know," he said apologetically. The old man nodded and urged his mule to pull the cart further forward and downward. Lunt and O'Mally looked at each other. Lunt was struck by the thought that many men were not enamored with their leaders. He could almost tell O'Mally was reading his thoughts. The two dragoons galloped off after their Sergeant who was again applying his whip with relish further down the road.

Lunt felt the welt that had risen on his left cheek and touched it lightly to find it was bleeding. "Who are these people?" Lunt questioned O'Mally about the contingent of riders for whom they had been forced to the side of the road. "Who are they? What makes them so important?" he asked again.

"I'd say it 'twas just the gentry going to a fox hunt, by the look of it," guessed O'Mally, who had seen many such road clearings over the years.

As the faces and forms of the approaching riders drew closer and clearer, Lunt became aware that the form of one of the lead riders was a woman. There seemed to be many uniformed men in the contingent. But the curiosity of seeing a woman riding in front kept Lunt's gaze returning to her. She sat high in her saddle. Her chest was tightly wrapped in a bright red riding jacket with black trim, but its up and down rhythm revealed the fact that she was a woman. Beside her was a young man about Lunt's age in a naval officer's uniform. He had a thin frame and was concentrating on keeping his female companion in conversation. Many of the other riders were army officers, or members of the local militia. Most of the other military wore either red or green uniforms. The remainder of the riders wore red or black fox hunting jackets with high hats. They were likely local gentry. Some of the riders carried horns.

Lunt's gaze returned to the woman. She was very beautiful. Her auburn red hair was piled high upon her head in a saucer shaped bun. A second rounded bun sat atop the first and seemed to emanate from its center. Her cheekbones were prominent. There was a hint of light rouge on her face. For just an instant, she glanced at Lunt and O'Mally who were still sitting on the high side of the cart with their feet dangling over the side of the road. They were still trying to keep the potato cart balanced until the contingent of loping fox hunters passed.

The woman suddenly turned off to the opposite side of the road. As the party passed, Lunt focused on other members of the party. One well dressed army major was a striking, nearly bald man with just a wisp of white hair on the back of his head. He passed within an arm's length of Lunt without looking at him. Most of the party expended little time looking at the peasants along the road.

After the riders passed, from out of the evidently equally steep grade on the other side of the road, a horse's head now appeared. It was followed from Lunt's perspective by the woman's hair and then finally that face. She was looking directly at him. She touched her face with her hand. Perhaps she was giving him an indication of sympathy for the lashing he had just received. On the other hand, perhaps she was making fun of his prominent hawk nose. Lunt did not respond, but just looked straight into her eyes.

The woman's naval companion had circled around behind the group and now joined her. Oblivious to the three peasants he perceived in the cart, he questioned, "Are you alright, Alicia?"

"I thought Sugar had caught a stone," she responded. Her animal shifted its legs in the hereditary frustration that horses feel when they are held back from traveling with the herd. Her mare pawed at the ground in an effort to indicate that she wanted to catch up with the other horses.

Lunt noted the contrast between the two. Alicia was obviously considerably older than the Royal Navy Lieutenant, but, because of her overpowering beauty, he was very enamored with her and was not going to let her out of his sight.

"I guess she's fit," she said, and took one more glance at the partially toppled cart and then galloped off after the group.

"Quite a handsome piece of flesh there," said O'Mally. Then he added whimsically, "I meant the horse, of course."

Lunt and O'Mally concentrated on righting the cart and helping the old man collect his potatoes from the ravine at the bottom of the incline. As he did so, Lunt looked closely at the skin of one potato he had retrieved. On his next trip up to the cart, he carefully selected a large potato whose shape suited him exactly. He placed it into the large pocket of his vest. On his next trip down into the ravine, he took several long sharp bramble thorns and also put them in his pocket.

* * * * *

The wind blew briskly from the south creating white tips on the waves entering the southern passage from the Atlantic into the Irish Sea. The British squadron had just come abreast of Land's End during the first light of the new day. Her seven ships of war fanned out as they changed from fore and aft into running rigging.

Large square canvas sails were unleased from the flagship's various spars by over a hundred men who perched at regular intervals along each of the giant horizontal crosses, which hung out over the deck and ocean at great heights. As each canvas dropped from its supporting spar, it was barely a moment before the sails billowed out and took form in the stiff breeze. With each addition to the ship's power, the officers on the quarterdeck could feel Reliance press forward at greater and greater speed.

The Rear Admiral proudly surveyed his flotilla. Taking advantage of the fine southerly, he had decided to alter the search plan he had outlined to Lord North. Based upon the reports he had heard since his meeting with the Admiralty, he doubted that the Yankee pirates were still operating in the southern portions of the Irish Sea. It would be in the north where they would most likely be found. If this southerly persisted, they could streak up the Irish Sea well into the North Channel in just two days time. Why not cover the most area in the least amount of time, instead of initiating a time consuming search in the least likely region?

By signal flag, the Rear Admiral ordered his fleet to fan out and parallel each other's course by ten miles. It was a distance at which a good topman could still make out signal flags with a spyglass. In two days time, if the wind held, they could be at Belfast and into the narrow channel between Ireland and Scotland. With seven ships abreast, they would cut a search swath some eighty miles wide. In many places the Irish Sea was not that wide. He potentially could miss the pirates if they happened to be anchored in a remote, hidden cove somewhere but, overall, a swift run up the Irish Sea would offer the best hope of encountering the pirates and thus clearing the seas as quickly as possible.

The Prime Minister had told the Admiralty that he shouldn't have to do their thinking for them. Lord North may, in the weeks ahead, come to realize that a genuine sailing Admiral might be a suitable addition to his Admiralty Board.

As the Rear Admiral prepared to leave the quarterdeck, he left the details of calling for sail adjustments to Reliance's captain. If the wind held, they could be off Waterford by early evening. He needed to make plans to get a signal to H.M.S. Boston so she could join the flotilla as rapidly as possible. He must go below and decide upon how that was to be accomplished. He needed to look at the charts one more time, without a lot of junior officers jabbering in the wardroom.

Just before entering the doorway which led to his quarters and the great cabin, the Rear Admiral looked upward at the proud red flag with the Union Jack in its upper corner. It snapped straight outward in the breeze from a line attached to the mizzen gaff.

The Rear Admiral thought aloud, "I'm going to hang you right from that line before this week is over, Mr. Jones, or whomever you are. Let's see those little bee stingers of yours match up against Reliance's 54 twenty four pounders. And if you do survive that action, Mr. Jones, I'll personally yank the hangman's rope."

* * * * *

"We eat the evidence if we get caught," whispered a smiling O'Mally.

"If there's time," whispered Lunt back with a grin.

"Henry, we'd say in Ireland, 'that'll be a hot potato'," joked O'Mally as he moved up again from the potato bed to sit beside the old man to engage him in more trivial Gaelic conversation.

For the past quarter hour, the little cart had pulled past ships at anchor, in what was swiftly becoming one of the most prolific ship building sites of the British Empire. Lunt had carefully put tick marks into the skin of the potato to mark the relative position of each important looking vessel which lay at anchor in the lower end of Belfast Lough.

Now the potato cart pulled adjacent to the hulls of ships in various stages of completion. The bare wooden skeletons of the great vessels stretched upward from their keel bases like giant whales whose carcasses had lain in the beach for many months. Except these skeletons would be coming to life. Henry Lunt noted especially the second vessel from the end. It was going to be a giant. Easily over two hundred feet in length. The reinforced decks were being built to support something very heavy. Likely, large bore cannons. This skeleton might someday come to life to patrol American waters, fully armed and capable of creating immense havoc.

They must have a half year invested in it, with at least another half year to go. It would make an easy target, which would burn very well. Lunt made an extra heavy tick mark on the second of the row of four marks at the very tip of his potato.

As they passed the shipyard, out about a quarter mile lay at anchor a two masted vessel behind the construction site. Small vessels were carrying lumber supplies from the yards out to the ship. On her decks, Lunt could just detect the telltale glint of the morning sun off the metal of guns. Lunt looked at his potato and pushed one of the bramble thorns deep into the meat.

Street traffic was being stopped. Lunt lay the potato face down onto the pile beside him and glanced around. Coming from a street up toward the waterfront was a small detachment of British marines in bright red uniforms. They held muskets at the ready and stopped all traffic on the street. They were an advance party.

Rounding the corner now came a tall, rotund man in a blue captain's uniform. His large shoulders sported the braids of his rank. He was taller than most of his marines. Beside him was a younger officer with whom he was engaged in an animated conversation. The Captain had giant hands and with one he seemed to be intermittently poking at some breakfast morsel that was still lodged in his teeth. They were evidently going to their ship. A longboat with uniformed crew was waiting along the beach. Every member of its crew was at attention.

Lunt's eyes shifted to the vessel. For a moment, he had a chilling thought that the Drake might be setting sail. But by the vessel's position and the shoreline water marks, he knew that this was not likely. The tide was dead low and the coming flood would make it very difficult for a vessel to sail up against what must be a strong current, even with the assistance of the favorable southerly breeze that seemed to be building.

Lunt's craned his neck to view the vessel more carefully. There was something very familiar about it. Its hull shape was that of a common sloop of war, but there was something else. On the deck of the vessel Lunt could now see new wood stored between the fore and main masts. The crew seemed to be building a platform of some kind. More lumber was on its way out of the shipyard aboard the boat yard skiff.

Lunt looked up and down the lough for signs of another military vessel. He could see none. This must be the Drake. What were they doing to her? Why does she seem so familiar? Lunt's brain raced ahead to estimate the time of day when the tide might turn back the other way and then estimated a time for the next day. If Ranger could come in on the flood tide, even without sail up, disguised, they might be able to lay an effective broadside on the Drake, who would be turned bow first towards them. Jones could then board her, and ride out on the ebb.

If they could capture the Drake short handed, they might then be able to use both ships to do considerable damage to the remaining shipbuilding facilities here, including that number two ship, that new man of war. However, the Irish people had been very sympathetic to the American cause. A raid on Ireland, rather than England herself, might cause people like Edmund Burke to be less vocal in Parliament. But those were political decisions for Captain Jones to make. Lunt had been too removed from events in prison the past year to know what should be done. He would just provide his Captain with the information, and leave the decisions to him.

As the potato cart resumed its progress along the coastal road, O'Mally interrupted his thoughts, "We've seen the bulk of the shipping. Me sister's house is only a couple of streets over." O'Mally patted the old man on the shoulder and said something in Gaelic.

As Lunt got out of the carriage, the old man turned to look at him and smiled fondly. After first making a farewell gesture with his hand, he then applied a light slap of the reins to get his mule underway again towards the market.

5
Swim

"Jesus, Mary, and Joseph, get out of me house, you damn scoundrel. They'll be closing down me shop. You've caused enough trouble for six lifetimes, with all those damn United Irishmen notions. Be gone. Leave us in peace." The balding, irate Jim O'Toole moved with clenched fists towards another room behind the modest shop. As he departed, he kicked his foot against a wall in the frustration and rage he felt at seeing his hated brother-in-law return.

"You shouldn't have come back, Sean," his red haired sister said sadly. "But I love you." She ran into his arms and gave him an enveloping hug. For over a minute they clung together. When they finally broke apart, they were both teary eyed.

"How's mother, have you seen her?" asked O'Mally.

"She's grand, just the same, still at the little cottage on the outskirts of Galway. She speaks of her little carrot top every time, and prays to the Blessed Mary that you'll come home to her."

Embarrassed by the intimacy he was witnessing, Lunt turned away and stood in the doorway of the shop and looked out onto the street. In a casual way, he blocked anyone from coming into the shop suddenly and hearing a conversation that they should not. He looked up the narrow street which teemed with people going this way and that. Most of the extremely poor people he had seen along the Belfast road were not frequenting these busy streets.

O'Mally had said the poor people came into the city at night and wondered in droves along the streets looking for scraps of food, clothing, or other items they could use.

Some city residents left things at their doorways for the needy. But, generally, the inner city residents seemed to be far better off. Some of them, or members of their immediate family, must have found employment in this city, which appeared to be fairly prosperous. It reminded him of mercantile neighborhoods in Newburyport, or even Boston.

The street was cobblestoned, and narrow. Each cart that came up and down had to pass each other very carefully. At each intersection of the street, there was a lantern which must be lit every evening. In fact, Lunt could see a man on a ladder who was refilling a lamp for the next evening's use. Across from the victualler shop was a fruit and vegetable store, and, next to that, a merchant who sold books, candy, and some household goods.

Lunt hungered for one of the red apples he saw being placed on display across the street. But the woman who fussed about them and positioned them for the day's business, looked like she could be very inquisitive. He decided not to use one of his four remaining coins to purchase the apple because, while he waited for change, he would certainly have to speak to her. Lunt elected to remain in the doorway of the shop and guard its inhabitants.

Behind him, Lunt heard O'Mally tell his sister, "I've brought you a boodle, sis. But you must promise to give half over to mother in Galway." They were a bit loud, so Lunt turned back into the shop and put his fingers to his lips to advise quiet. At the sound of a cache of coins being shaken onto his counter top, O'Toole threw aside the curtain separating his shop from the family's living quarters. As he stood in the doorway, he looked first at the pile of money, and then directly at Lunt. He snarled, "And who are you?"

Lunt decided to close the door of the shop so that the conversation couldn't be heard. It was still very early in the day. It would appear that the shop had not yet opened.

"Ask yer brother-in-law," said Lunt trying to imitate an Irish accent. O'Toole raised an eyebrow when he heard

Lunt speak, but then glanced hungrily at the coins now piled on the table.

O'Toole said, "You didn't earn that money by an honest hand, I won't have it in me house. What's afoot, Sean? Why have ye come back?"

"To bring this money to me sister and me mother, and to see them for a spell."

Lunt observed O'Toole glancing at the money with obvious interest. He was visibly torn between greed and either hatred or perhaps fear. The man genuinely was unsure what he should do. He rung his hands nervously and asked, "Sean, how long do ye intend to stay?"

"Just tonight, Jim. We need to sleep here and be gone by midday tomorrow." O'Mally threw an arm around his sister, hugging her. "I'd like to talk to sis a spell. Share some stories. We'll be out of your hair tomorrow."

"Agreed," nodded O'Toole, again glancing at the counter. "But, you'll have to remain in the back of the shop. I've a large order to prepare this afternoon. If the constabulary knew of any connections between you and our shop, I'd be out of business in an instant. I've just gotten the Royal Navy for one of my customers. It's a big break for your sister and me."

"So's the money I've just brought to your home and there's no strings on it. Just that half must get over to mother." Sean paused until he saw O'Toole nod to agree to the arrangement.

O'Mally continued, "So you're preparing something for the navy?"

"Well, it's really for Entwhistle, the baker. He's been trying to set up a catering service to the gentry and he's got me supplying the meat. He's a couple of streets over and I've got a lot of preparation to do out back this afternoon. It's that sea captain's birthday. They're having a big shindig at Carnarvon House tomorrow evening. I've an order for an entire side of beef. If they think I've anything to do with the United Irishmen, I'll be blacklisted. It's no good, Sean, you have to go with the times to survive. Can 'ye imagine the money they must have to purchase an entire side of fresh beef for only about twenty people. That's where the real steady money is earned, from solid work over years of time."

While Jim O'Toole continued for many more minutes about the need for only a short visit from his rebellious brother-in-law, O'Mally and Lunt exchanges glances at the mention of a captain's birthday party tomorrow evening. Gradually, over the next half hour, O'Mally got O'Toole to talk more and more about his successful new customer, the British Navy, and how many of the Drake's officers and some non military guests would be at Carnarvon House the following evening. Jim O'Toole told all he knew, being completely unaware of just how very interested his listeners were in his successful new venture.

* * * * *

Lieutenant Dobbs' handsome lean face was extremely pensive while riding back from the fox hunt. It wasn't because of the three successive foxes that the hunting party had flushed from their warrens and then had seen torn to shreds by the hounds after an exhilarating chase through each fox's terrain. It was partly because he had finally gotten to be alone with Alicia, and he had kissed her.

As the other riders had gone gallivanting all over the countryside, up this hill and down the other, he had held her reins and they fell back to the end of the column. She had been exchanging furtive glances with him ever since he had been transferred over from Scotland a few weeks earlier.

In some ways he liked this kind of an assignment better than serving as a second officer on board a full Man of War like Reliance. He could survive a brief tour in this backward country, where the gentry largely didn't even wear wigs to evenings out. He could endure a spell now that it was announced that he was going to succeed Captain Burden with command of the Drake. It would be quite a triumph for the son of an impoverished minister.

If the new weapon system performed aboard ship in the same way that it had in the testing fields of the Scottish highlands, he would have his entre into an even greater assignment. One that could reshape the Royal Navy itself. In the meantime, it wouldn't be all bad to inherit the Captain's woman along with his ship. He would be willing to risk a little humiliation in order to hold and caress those beautiful breasts every night. The woman would be quite a prize, even if she were a bit older. He vowed under his breath that he would never let himself get into the disgustingly misshaped state of Captain Burden.

Under a tree, well out of view of the other riders, Alicia and he had made small talk for a few minutes, and then he had asked her, "Are you truly happy?"

She had looked down at his direct question. Then she looked up with a tear in her eye, "No, I want to stay here in my little Belfast apartment, I don't want to live in a pensioner's home in Britain. I have too much life to live."

Dobbs squeezed her hand and seized the opportunity of the moment. He moved his horse so that it was immediately beside hers, but facing in the opposite direction. He leaned forward and placed his hand across her thighs to grip the lip of her saddle. He stretched his face across the short distance between them. She was looking directly into his eyes, then she looked downward, but did not turn her face away. He lightly touched his lips to hers. She pressed her lips back at him.

"She wants me," he thought. He reached across to pull her closer to him. She, in turn, pulled him lightly to her. He could feel the softness of her breasts against his chest. As their lips opened he felt just the hint of her tongue brushing against the upper, most sensitive part of his inner lip. The hairs along the back of his neck tingled with excitement and he became immediately aroused.

As they kissed, his thoughts moved to the fantasy of perhaps making love to her here and now. She was side saddle and he could easily pull her across to his horse.

Then, in the background the shrill sound of a hunter's horn blew three times over the course of the long minute of their kiss. Dobbs was consumed with passion, but her hands started to push him off. Her lips free, she said, "You're very handsome, but they'll be coming back this direction. We can't be caught like this." She pulled on her reins to back her horse away. "We shouldn't ride together on the way back."

Sidesaddle, she reached across and struck her horse with her riding whip to gallop off in the direction of the reapproaching sounds of the hunt. She blended into the rear of the riders and gradually joined the hunt as if nothing had ever happened.

Dobbs, his disappointment rising, watched her depart across the meadow. She was beautiful. He would...

From behind, there was the faint sound of a horse's hooves crushing twigs on the forest floor, and then a soft walking tread across the underbrush. Dobbs turned suddenly around, embarrassment and even shame were already building in him. He knew he was caught. Who was it that had been behind them?

Major Pitkan moved his horse slowly out from behind the tree and trotted directly towards the Lieutenant, his eyes never leaving Dobbs' face. "Very, very ambitious, Lieutenant. So you'll get the Captain's lady, as well as his ship. Then he'll have nothing left, eh?"

Pitkan's stern face was accentuated by his sleek, bald head, with just a wisp of white hair at the rear. He trotted right up to Dobbs' horse, his eyes never leaving those of the Lieutenant. Then he simply turned and trotted off in the same general direction as the previous rider.

Dobbs was left alone with his thoughts. He sat under

the tree for a long time.

* * * * *

Lunt had been asleep most of the morning. Suddenly, there was a violent thud that shook the entire house. He sat bolt upright in bed. He first checked for his canvas bag. Then his hand felt his vest, the large lump of the potato was also still there. From outside he heard the frenzied bellow of a dying beast, followed by a gurgling sound as something kicked against the outer wall of his room, and then seemed to settle and slide down the wall to the ground.

Lunt stood up. He was very uneasy about staying in a house where O'Mally's brother-in-law did not want them. The temptation of reporting them to the authorities was obviously on Jim O'Toole's mind. But O'Mally had assured Lunt that his brother-in-law would take no action, as long as he wasn't told anything more. There would be nothing to be gained to report his brother-in-law for events that had occurred a long time ago. The names of O'Mally and O'Toole were not known, by the authorities in Belfast, to be linked. The knowledge that his wife was Sean O'Mally's sister would only discredit O'Toole and his current business plans. He might also have to turn the considerable money O'Mally had given his sister over to the authorities. That especially was something Jim would not want to see happen.

It was decided that, while Lunt rested, O'Mally would contact some old friends and see if he could somehow exploit the knowledge of the planned naval dinner so that they could find out more about the Drake. Having Lunt and his accent accompany O'Mally on the streets would be a definite liability.

Lunt tiptoed to the door of his tiny room and then out a corridor to the back yard of the house. O'Toole and his wife were kneeling over a dead cow. There was blood everywhere.

The slaughtering yard had become a gathering place

of flies. There seemed to be hundreds, who, enlivened by the warming heat of the mid April afternoon, buzzed, landed, and gouged themselves on the bits of flesh and blood that were strewn everywhere. The yard was thick with them and their continual scavenging. The O'Tooles were completely preoccupied with dressing the animal for the feast the following evening, and then using the remains for sale in their victualler shop. Lunt returned to the room and closed the door firmly to keep out the flies. He briefly pushed aside the curtain where O'Mally and he had agreed to leave messages for each other. There was nothing there. He massaged his feet briefly and returned to sleep, awaiting O'Mally's return.

* * * * *

Rhein van Zoot was a small, swarthy man. His extremely poor complexion had been exacerbated by his adolescent habit of squeezing his pussy pimples at every opportunity. As an adult, his embedded acne complexion and the deep hollowed pits, that seemed to perpetually ooze skin oil, did not make him attractive to most women. But physical appearance did not matter much to van Zoot. Most of his life he had been able to afford to buy the women he needed.

Van Zoot was in the business of collecting and reselling information, and opportunities. He found sellers and buyers, and made his wealth from identifying the needs which brought them together. Any commodity, whatsoever, represented a potential opportunity. In order to ply his trade, he had become a master of measuring each man's corruption and then exploiting it to his own advantage.

Over a fortnight ago he had taken a coach up from London and then a packet over from Liverpool, to visit the burgeoning Belfast shipyard to see if he could make contacts. Specifically, he wanted to identify procurement needs for the coming year. While visiting Lloyd's, he had become aware that much shipbuilding would be contracted to Belfast in the future. The American rebellion had resulted in the loss of about a third of Britain's total shipbuilding capacity. He had also heard that some vague, new ship enhancements were being tested for the Admiralty at Belfast. There was always a market for information about new developments. He had decided it was time to make a personal visitation, and to introduce himself to those responsible for letting contracts.

For days he had attempted to get an interview with the senior man in shipbuilding, a Mr. Robert Wright. But he had been put off handily. Mr. Wright seldom left the office or the gated confines of the shipyards, and he was a family man, whose obese wife dutifully picked him up in the family carriage every evening at the close of the day. It was difficult to arrange to see him in the off hours. The man did not seem to take his lunch in public places.

In the first week, this had proven an unprofitable excursion over to a country van Zoot never liked to visit. He would much rather stroll the cafe streets of Paris, than to be in this impoverished land. Too many beggars, from whom he could gain nothing.

Finally, determined to make the best of an otherwise disastrous commercial expedition, he arranged to inquire about the Royal Navy's senior personnel and their daily habits. From a tavern owner, van Zoot learned that there was also a possible contact opportunity in the person of a Captain George Burden, a rather rotund senior officer, who had command of the Drake, and also had responsibilities to oversee the Royal Navy's two contracts for new vessel construction in Belfast. Just by a slip of the tongue, the publican mentioned that the good Captain was soon to have a birthday. The publican had heard the Drake's junior officers discussing whether or not their Captain would take a holiday on his birthday.

This was the kind of lead van Zoot could exploit. If he could not get to Mr. Wright, perhaps he could initiate some beneficial contact through the Navy. It was worth the effort. Van Zoot identified Captain Burden's quarters and found that he lived with a whore when he was not aboard ship, that he ate far more than was good for his health, and that lately he had kept the Drake anchored deep within the lough in order to have some refinements made to her by the shipyard's carpenters. Each morning of late, Captain Burden had been in the habit of eating a very large breakfast of kippers and eggs at a local hotel before parting company with his live-in, and from there he would go over to the shipyard's planning office, or to his command aboard the Drake.

Van Zoot arranged to have breakfast at that same hotel the next morning. First, a Royal Marine corporal, sort of a combination orderly and guard, came to the door of the breakfast room and took a glance inside, and then discreetly stood aside for his charges to enter.

The Captain, in full uniform right down to his sword, came in escorting a very beautiful woman, a bit his junior. The stark contrast between the two made van Zoot look away, so as not to let a loose smile be seen to enter unto his lips. The Captain had a huge frame and was at least six stone overweight. His huge, moon like face sported enormous jowls, which hung on either side of his face so heavily that from the front the man seemed to have three chins. Beneath the jowls hung an enormous fleshy neck, that flopped as the man walked and talked.

The poor darling must have been really penniless to have taken up with such a slob, van Zoot observed. Some women will do anything to get half a pension. Van Zoot could see that she was playing on at least two parts of the Captain's vices, his vanity and his need for sex. Perhaps he could exploit a third, his love of food.

The very next morning, van Zoot had the waiter pass his calling card onto the Captain with a brief note. Van Zoot was invited over for a cup of tea. He explained that his company was in the business of supplying fine accoutrements for officers' quarters and other needs of the Royal Navy. He presented a letter from the Admiralty denoting his company as an authorized supplier.

During the tea, van Zoot told the Captain and his woman that it was regular practice for his company to honor distinguished naval officers on their birthday. He extended an invitation for the Captain and some guests of his choice to come for an evening dinner at Carnarvon House, a fine guest house located in the foothills behind Belfast. Van Zoot let the Captain know that the affair would be catered by a Mr. Entwhistle, who had spent years cooking in Mayfair hotels, and who could produce the most genuine roast beef and Yorkshire pudding.

Like most navy officers, the Captain was obviously a man who had taken a few donations here and there throughout his career. He was not particularly appalled by the suggestion of a dinner invitation, even from a relative stranger. And the dinner did sound inviting, what possible harm could it do? He had said he would send a message to van Zoot regarding the kind invitation. By late evening, an affirmative was received and that it would be Burden's pleasure to have twenty-two for his birthday dinner, including van Zoot, and that he would take the trouble to have Mr. Wright of the shipyards invited as one of his guests.

It was now the afternoon preceding the dinner and van Zoot hurried along the back streets of Belfast to the shop of Entwhistle, the baker and caterer. At the store, he made a final payment for tomorrow evening's affair and looked at the side of beef that had just arrived from a nearby victualler. A bit wormy for his tastes but, after a day's slow roasting and the sauces to cover it up, it would be sumptuous, at least by Belfast standards.

He gave Entwhistle the key to get into the vacant facility which was in the process of a property transfer. Van Zoot had bribed the caretaker to obtain part of the Inn's use for that evening. He was going to have elegant surroundings at a very little cost. After taking a final walk around Entwhistle's kitchen, he then departed to make other arrangements.

* * * * *

Lunt had never seen such a crude job of slaughtering an animal in his life. Lacking a sharp knife, Jim O'Toole had used a saw blade which had been supported by a circular bent pipe to break into the flesh and to sever apart the major bone elements. He had pulled and ripped at the flesh, and cursed it as he worked. Early on, it was obvious to Lunt that he had rarely before worked from a whole animal. O'Mally had made a few suggestions to him when he started, but had been told by his brother-in-law to mind his own business or to leave forthwith. Lunt had taken the cue and vanished back into his room to resume sleep.

When he awoke later, Lunt could find no trace of anyone in the house. He retained nagging concern that O'Toole could not be trusted. Lunt went to the front of the shop. Some of the ragged beef cuts were laid out on trays and were covered with paper. The prime side cuts were absent. Perhaps the O'Toole's had delivered those to the caterer. The shop door to the street was closed.

Lunt went down the hallway that led into the back of the house and the slaughtering site. Across the yard was a curing shed. He opened the door. Inside the shed hung pieces of the slaughtered animal, suspended on meat hooks which had been recently screwed into the wall. A few additional hooks were still sitting on a bench. Lunt closed the door to keep the population of flies within the curing shed to less than a hundred. He walked around to the far side of the shed where a large skin of the just slaughtered animal had been crudely stretched. Already, a large flap of the skin had folded back on the other and the two portions were drying stuck together. Lunt picked up a broken nail at the foot of the shed. He stretched the flap and then pushed the nail through the top edge, to improve the changes of a better piece of leather. Personally, he would have dried the skin on a flat surface, but this was not his concern.

Beneath the stretched skin lay Jim's tools. Lunt knelt down to examine them. They were still bloody. Flies buzzed away angrily as he reached down among them. There were three knives of various length, the crude saw, and a pair of tongs. He examined the saw closely. The moon shaped pipe holding the blade was worthless, but the blade itself seemed to be of very good quality, perhaps of steel. He took a nail and tried to scratch it. Yes, it was durable, capable of sawing not only through bone but perhaps iron as well.

Lunt stood up. Where was everyone? He cautiously started back across the yard to get his sail bag. Perhaps he had better wait in another place, in case his hosts had plans to turn them over to the constabulary. As Lunt started back across the yard, he heard the sound of a husband and wife's chatter coming closer. Then his hosts rounded the gate into the narrow yard towing a hand held cart laden with several buckets.

Lunt nodded to O'Mally's relatives. The sister, sensing his concern that they had gone off, said, "We find that sea water puts the flies off better."

Lunt went back into the bedroom where he had been sleeping and went into deep thought. For awhile, he heard outside the sounds of water being sloshed about in an effort to clean up what was possible. Then, he heard the couple pass his door on the way to their kitchen. Outside, the shadows in the yard lengthened. There was no sign that O'Mally would return anytime soon. He took the potato from his pocket and studied it carefully. He put one additional prominent mark on it and left it behind the curtain, as a message to O'Mally as to where he was going.

Lunt prepared to leave. He tied the knots of the canvas bag very tightly and carefully, so he would know instantly, upon his return, if the bag had either been moved or opened. He walked out to his hosts, who were sitting in their kitchen.

"I'll be going out for a walk," he said.

O'Mally's sister replied, "Better take something besides that vest, it's sure to be nippy this evening," and went in search of some additional clothing for her guest.

In the room alone with Jim O'Toole, Lunt bent over the kitchen table and placed his face directly in front of O'Toole. At point blank range the steel blue eyes over the hawk nose trained on the man intently. "There's a canvas bag in the bedroom. There's no money in it, only things that will bring you very great trouble. I'll be bringing it with me when we leave. Do not move it or open it. I'll know."

His directness obviously affected Jim, who trembled at Lunt's veiled threat, delivered with an accent he could not place. Jim remembered the kind of men that Sean used to travel with and so took the warning with an ominous feeling of dread. He was searching for something to say when his wife returned.

"You'll have some Irish stew before your walk," said O'Mally's sister invitingly, as she handed Lunt a black wool cloak.

"No, thank you," Lunt held up his hand, "perhaps when I return. Tell Sean that I'll be back in less than two hours." He smiled at her, gave one more stern look at her husband, who was taciturn, and then departed down the back corridor towards the small slaughter yard. In the yard, he stooped for a moment and picked up the saw and deftly removed its steel blade. Then he moved into the curing shed where heavy meat gorged flies buzzed at his annoying reentry. He took one of the unused meat hooks from the bench. He shoved both flat implements into his breeches and walked out the alley in the direction of the mouth of the river Lagan, which fed the base of Belfast Lough.

* * * * *

Captain George Burden moved his rotund frame about his comparatively small, but comfortable, great cabin. Two younger officers were sitting with him enjoying a glass of port. They would be on duty tonight. Because of the importance of his cargo, Burden had seen to it that a double complement of marines and a minimum of two officers were on duty aboard the Drake at all times.

During the afternoon, the tidal flow had shifted out of the harbour and the Drake had swung fully around, so that her stern cabin's windows faced up Belfast Lough. The occupants of the cabin were afforded a view of the city's street lanterns and candle lit windows, as the April sky darkened into nightfall. A partial moon revealed the forest of primarily small ships' masts that dotted the harbour. Here and there, bobbing whitewashed cork floats marked the position of crab pods resting on the muddy bottom.

On one crab float hung Henry Lunt, his eyes glued to the stern of the Drake. He shivered in the water but, through intense concentration of his brain, he maintained control over the effects of the numbing cold. He knew now to be true, what he had suspected when looking at the ship from the coastal road that morning. Her hull was nearly identical to his old ship, the Alfred. She might even be a sister ship, possibly constructed at the same docks. If he could get close enough without detection, Lunt knew a way to disable the Drake without her crew becoming aware.

As a mate aboard the Alfred, it had become his duty to replace the rudder chains periodically. It was the kind of difficult specialty job to which one tended to be reassigned, once you had performed it well the first time. The ship's flaw was that the architects had mistakenly designed the meeting point of the rudder and chain steering linkage to exit just above the water line.

Under average ballast loads, the steering linkage chain extended down from the helm, inside a tubing system, to exit through a point just a few inches above the water line. If, during sailing, the rudder needed to be held firmly to either extreme larboard or starboard, then the slack end was just long enough for a few links to dip for a time beneath the sea water. This accelerated the corrosion rate so that every four months or so the chains had to be replaced. If the Drake's crew had not performed this maintenance recently, there would very likely be a partly corroded link close to the rudder.

Lunt planned to swim to the rudder, find a weakened link, and then sever it with the crude butcher's saw blade. The Drake's steerage system would then be inoperative. Tomorrow, if the winds favored it, Ranger might be able to sail deep into the lough and capture or sink a disabled Drake. If Lunt's mischief went undetected, the only steerage of which Drake would be capable would be to wheel helplessly in circles because her rudder was locked to one side, without the benefit of counterbalancing pressure from the opposing linkage.

Lunt had left his vest, boots, and borrowed wool cloak beneath a bush on a sandy beach within sight of the shipbuilding yard. He had sat there until twilight, observing a family with children playing at the water's edge. As the light started to fade, people left the shore but Lunt remained. Then, in darkness he had removed his hated boots and entered the cool water. Initially, the gash on his cheek had stung, distracting his mind from the unpleasantly cold water. Silently, he swam out in the direction of a line of several crab pots which bobbed progressively closer to the Sloop of War.

Once out a few hundred yards into the water and clear of the high fence which had prevented a clear view into the shipyard from land, Lunt had been able to see that the equipment at the shipyard included a good many launches. There were also many soldiers near the water's edge, standing around a campfire. They seemed to all flow in and out of one building, presumably a barracks. This shipyard had a very strong military, almost wartime presence. If Ranger were to get this deep into the lough, and then become becalmed, grounded, or meet contrary winds, then these launches could be filled with heavily armed men, who could row into a position to easily outmaneuver a floundering sailing vessel. Captain Jones would need to know this disadvantage, if Lunt succeeded in disabling the Drake.

As he swam, Lunt continued to analyze the Drake. Despite her high freeboard, he was able to detect that there were an unusually large number of men active on her well lighted deck. Occasionally, some of them looked over the side. Reaching the first float, Lunt's hands groped in the murky water for the knot that must connect the floating cork to the crab pot resting on the bottom of the harbor. His hand found a slimly knot. He then kicked his feet more rapidly to give himself sufficient lift so that he could dedicate both hands to the task of untying the knot.

After several frustrating attempts to find a lose end from which to untie the knot, he decided to detach the floating cork another way. He reached into his breeches and withdrew the length of serrated steel and drew it across the line. Once, twice, and on the third swipe the buoyancy of the freed cork caused it to launch itself out of the water.

Lunt caught the bobbing cork and then held it firmly with one hand, while with the other he twisted the screw end of the meat hook into the cork's body. As his whole body twirled slowly in the water performing this task, his vision caught sight again of the shipyard and the campfire around which several soldiers stood. He judged himself to be about a quarter mile away. They would be unable to see him from shore. It was detection from the ship that he needed to avoid now. Holding the float end of the newly fabricated tool in front of his face, he slowly and deliberately began to paddle towards the Drake. The first fifty paces in the darkness were easy, but, as he came to the final fifty paces, he began to witness movement of the crew with great clarity. They could now potentially see him. Heart racing, he silently dog paddled nearer and nearer to the ship's broadside.

One uniformed marine suddenly stuck his head over the rail and spat a visible portion of flem directly into the water in the direction of Lunt and the bobbing cork which camouflaged his head. Lunt froze and then tread water slowly backwards, out of the rim of light from the ship's lanterns. His head and the cork remained aligned towards the guard. Lunt drew a deep breath, ready to submerge himself and swim underwater as swiftly as he could away from the warship.

"Ye could win the King's prize fer that lunger, mate." A small chuckle followed the crude joke as another marine joined the first.

Lunt's heart pounded and his breath became more rapid as he peeked around the painted crab buoy. He could see that the second marine had a musket in his hand. If he was observed, would they simply shoot at him or would he have a few extra seconds as they challenged him? Lunt wondered if swimmers would be willing to dive into the cold water to pursue him. Could he outswim them? He shivered, the delays had allowed the cold to penetrate his body.

Lunt slowly paddled back along the edge of the rim of light, towards the vessel's stern. The freeboard below the quarterdeck was higher than at the beam of the vessel, it would be darkest in the water there. Lunt again edged closer to the Drake's hull. There was no one peering over the rail at that point. There was only a small band of diffused light striking the surface from the ship's lanterns.

In the last fifteen feet before reaching the hull, Lunt submerged his head below the water so that only the floating cork would appear above the surface. For security, he clung to the floating cork. In the darkness, his head touched momentarily against the ship's hull. He pushed away slightly so that the bobbing hull would not descend on his head. Lunt noticed that there was a slight undertow tending to suck him beneath the vessel. He clung to the buoyant cork for support and, with his left hand shaped like a claw, he pulled his body along the hull towards the Drake's stern.

The area immediately behind the vessel's stern was brightly lit. Drifting out over the water and intermixed with the ambient noise of water slapping against the vessel's hull, Lunt could just make out voices from inside.

"Sir, just how did they actually measure its range?"

An older voice replied, "Over near Stromeferry in the north of Scotland, they set up great stretches of sail cloth in the meadow. There was no one around but the damn sheep. So every twenty or thirty paces or so... I don't know the exact interval they used but they could accurately tell not only the distance the projectile covered, but its accuracy as well as its momentum."

"I don't see, sir," said the younger voice.

"By the holes in the sailcloth. When you stop getting the penetration that you had up to the past twenty paces, then you know that you've established the ultimate range of the projectile."

Another young voice said, "Sir, Lieutenant Dobbs said this will revolutionize naval warfare. I don't see how."

Treading water immediately below the bay windows of the great cabin, Lunt struggled to hear the conversation. Bits and pieces of their talk were being interrupted by wind driven waves that lapped past the body of the Sloop of War. They were proving to be very distracting.

"....than you think, Lieutenant," said an older, pedantic sounding voice, "... a smaller, faster ship, the size of the Drake, will be able to carry the equal firepower of a much slower moving man of war. That's what we are going to test. Can you ..."

The voice seemed to be coming nearer the window. Lunt pushed himself off to one side out of the cabin light. He saw a shadow fall on the water very close to him. From within the cabin he could still hear bits of the conversation.

"But, sir, why do we need it just now? England is at peace, well, except for the thing over in the colonies. But surely, that can't last too much longer. Can it?"

"Gentlemen, when you have been in the King's service as long as I have, you'll come to know that England is always at war, in one way or another." The voice stopped. It seemed to be admiring the philosophical tone that it had initiated. After a moment the voice continued, "Oh, the American uprising will be over pretty soon, I suspect."

The mature voice continued, "Well, gentlemen, you'll forgive me. My appreciation for your kind, early birthday greetings, and the bottles of port. But as you know, I must to be off to my flat."

"Yes, sir." The phrase was echoed a second time and Lunt heard boots click upon the floor of the cabin inside, as two or three officers stood up at once. Lunt saw a shadow form and then increase in size across the reflected light shining on the waters behind the anchored Drake. Someone was again coming to the window. Lunt drew a deep breath and submerged, this time letting his crab float drift on top of the water. He swam downward into the murky water away from the light at the vessels's stern.

When Lunt surfaced, he was some thirty feet or more from the bobbing stern of the vessel. As he drew a breath, he could see a stout man in full dress uniform come to the cabin window and pull the shudders firmly closed, leaving the stern of the vessel in darkness. He could hear several cantilevers fall to seal the cabin windows from the ingress of wind and wave. Lunt knew that the occupant was locking the Captain's quarters, with a system of iron grates and perhaps a second wooden lid to protect the rear of the vessel from intrusion, or from taking in water during a high sea or rain. In the dark, it would be impossible to enter the Captain's quarters without a great many more tools than he had.

Lunt's eyes scanned the surface near the stern for a telltale bobbing. He did not want to lose sight of the crab buoy in the sudden darkness. He needed it more than ever.

There was something unusual going on aboard the Drake. After severing the anchor chain, he would need the hook screwed into the buoy for help in scaling the ship's freeboard to have a look topside.

* * * * *

Inside the cabin, just after the junior officers left his presence, Captain Burden took a set of keys from the drawer of his desk, went to his sea chest, knelt down, and opened it. After lifting the lid and pulling aside several items of clothing, his gaze settled upon his favorite winter cloak. He reached inside its pocket for a small box. His fingers caressed it.

In his hands he slowly opened the box to gaze upon a diamond clustered ring. He twirled it before his eyes in the candlelight of his cabin. It sparkled back in brilliant colors. It was a beauty. She would be proud of it. He would make her an honest woman. Captain George Burden was not only going to celebrate his birthday tomorrow evening, he was going to ask his beloved to marry him when he retired next month. Once the testing was firmly underway, he would simply turn the program over to Lieutenant Dobbs and be finished with it. Forty years at sea was enough, let the young people have it.

Burden stood up and looked at his profile in the cabin mirror behind the door. He sighed, tomorrow, yes, after tomorrow he was going to begin restricting his intake of food. He would make her proud of him. He checked his pocket watch. It was time to be off. The tender would be arriving for him. Visually he checked the security of his cabin again and then closed the cabin door behind him.

* * * * *

Lunt observed a tender being rowed out to the ship.

From the deck he heard the shrill undulating sound of a boatswain's whistle from upon the deck. A Jacob's ladder was being lowered, obviously to accommodate the Captain who was leaving for shore. He could hear men running on deck, most likely signaling a Royal Marine muster for the departure. As he tread water behind the vessel, Lunt started to shiver again, this time uncontrollably. He could no longer feel his feet, or move his toes. He had to get out of the cold water or perish. The night air was warmer than the water. It could give him relief.

Lunt swam silently and directly to the rudder, oblivious to whether or not he was being observed. On his way he encountered his floating cork buoy and carried it with him. Upon reaching the rudder, he tried momentarily to move it off center by holding onto its edge and then, by pushing hard against the stern with his feet. He applied considerable pressure in each direction to try and budge the steering mechanism. It was locked in place.

From the deck, the rudder must be fixed in place along the centerline of the vessel. Lunt could picture the steering wheel on the quarter deck braced in both directions by two or more stout cords. Each one applied equal resistance in opposite directions to prevent the wheel from rotating freely. The system may have been designed to hold the wheel in place but, more importantly to Lunt, it would also not allow anyone on deck to detect that the rudder chain had been severed.

If the Drake were left at anchor tomorrow, it would be unlikely that anyone would discover that she was without steerage. Ideally, Lunt should sever the chain tomorrow evening, but he could not risk waiting until then to return to the Drake and still be expected to make his way out to Carrickfergus to meet the Ranger that same evening. The sabotage would have to be accomplished now or never.

Lunt pulled his shivering body from the water and sat himself across the larboard rudder linkage. The rounded links pressed painfully into his bottom as the vessel bobbed in the relentless motion of a ship at anchor. He wedged himself into the rudder cavity, pulled his arms around his body, and tried to warm himself. After a few minutes of fitful shivering, he began to regain control of his body temperature.

Soon his fingers were feeling beneath him for a link which might be particularly corroded. He groped link by link along the chain, but did not detect any particular weakness, not even at the juncture of the large eye bolt attached to the keel itself. Lunt wondered if it was worth the effort to examine the starboard linkage. After all, when he had changed linkage chains aboard the Alfred he had always changed both sides simultaneously. Surely the English Captain would have also ordered it so.

Lunt pushed himself off the larboard linkage and quickly hauled himself up onto the great cabin's window sill. A fresh breeze was stirring and he was reminded of how cold his body was. Shivering again, his mind fought to stay in control. He examined the closed window fitting. It would take nothing less than an explosion to gain entrance into the well sealed great cabin. He lowered himself back onto the starboard linkage.

Just as he became settled on this new side, the vessel shifted in reaction to the breeze, and he found himself not more than thirty feet from the stern of the Captain's launch moving away from the Drake. There beside the coxswain, sat a large man. On his uniform were the epaulets signifying a captain's naval uniform. For an instant he felt the man was looking directly at him, right through him. Lunt froze in place. The Captain must have been deep in thought, for he voiced no alarm, no sudden shout. The vessel just moved off into the darkness towards the soldiers' campfire on shore.

Lunt shifted his weight on the starboard rudder chain. His fingers explored each link. The Captain of the Drake was presumably going off to dinner and, while he feasts, this

Yankee Lieutenant will render his vessel unsteerable, thought Lunt as his probing fingers found a very corroded third link. Within a minute, he was sawing vigorously. On his insteps, Lunt balanced the cork float as he worked, his back resting against the stern rudder cavity.

Within a quarter of an hour, the force of Lunt's bouncing weight caused sufficient tension on the sawed linkage that it severed. Unsupported, Lunt toppled into the water, nearly losing his grip on the butcher's saw blade. Lunt's head went under the water. Instinctively, he reached up to put his hand between his head and the bobbing hull which could crush his skull. He had succeeded. He tread water, mindful that he would have to make a decision of whether or not he should stop here, or to try and see what was being constructed topside.

All the time that he had been sawing on the anchor chain, the impact of the overheard conversation, between the Drake's Captain and some of his junior officers, kept spinning around in Lunt's mind. "How will it revolutionize naval warfare?" one of the Junior officers had asked. What was this unnamed thing? Why had the Drake, only a sloop of war and certainly not one of His Majesty's most important vessels, been chosen to test the device? What significance did the sail cloth spread out in a Scottish meadow every 20 or 30 paces have? Why had the Spymaster insisted that Captain Jones take the Drake at all costs?

Gripping the butcher hook in one hand and the saw in the other, Lunt proceeded to hack off bits and pieces of the sea hardened cork crab buoy from around the hook, reducing it to the size and shape of a handle. It would be a long swim back to the beach without the buoyancy of the entire cork float, if he made it at all.

After a few minutes work, Lunt tucked the saw blade back into his breeches. He dog paddled very silently up along the side of Drake. The deck of the vessel was lit up like the streets of Belfast in the distance.

As Lunt had hoped, the Jacob's ladder had not yet been retracted up the side. Perhaps they were expecting the tender to return directly after leaving the Captain ashore. If that was so, Lunt might only have the time needed to row the quarter mile in, drop the Captain off, and then return.

As Lunt floated on top of a small wave, he could just make out some figures standing around the bonfire at the shipyard. But was the crew of the longboat among those figures, or were they already rowing their way back across the water towards the Drake? He could not see the tender in the dark void between the beach and himself. If he now scaled the hull, would the crew of the returning tender see him dangling from the freeboard?

Lunt considered the possibility of returning to the stern, and attempting to the climb up over the captain's cabin windows, and up onto the quarterdeck. But there would most certainly be officers on the duty deck, increasing greatly the chance of detection. And from the quarterdeck, he might not be able to see whatever was being constructed amidships, between the two masts. The best opportunity would be to obtain an initial purchase midway along the vessel and use the Jacob's ladder netting to raise himself just high enough to get a vantage point through one of the gun ports. He would have only until the tender returned to do so. And he was starting to get very cold again.

Lunt swam up quietly to a particular point along the great hull. He waited as the waves raised and lowered his floating body relative to the freeboard of the Drake. Then, just his body started to rise upward, he thrust his right arm up out of the water in a great arc. In his hand he clutched the cork handle with its butcher's hook extending outward at the end. From beneath the water, he simultaneously kicked upwards with his feet to get as much lift as possible. As he crested the wave, his arm and hand slapped against the hull stretching as high as possible. The point of the butcher's hook sank deeply into the wooden hull with a dull thud.

As the next trough came between the waves, Lunt was left clinging to the hull of the Drake by his right hand, some six feet above the water line. His face was rudely pressed against the worm encrusted surface. The water only lapped at his feet, giving him fleeting buoyancy only as each wave passed below his dangling legs. As he rocked backwards and forwards on the hull of the Drake, he struggled to push his body around so that he could free his head to look above him. By the time of the third lift, he could feel the hook loosening. He needed to move fast or he was going to fall back into the water. It was very active on deck, he could hear several men talking. They might hear his splash, if he slipped.

As the next wave crested, it supported his feet momentarily. He quickly pulled upward with his right arm and simultaneously pushed himself away from the hull with his left. Then he arched his left hand outwards and upwards in the direction of the lowest end of the Jacob's ladder. He felt his palm strike the bottom rung at the base of his fingers. He closed his hand quickly. The pitching and rolling action of the hull caused his body to again smash against rough wood surface, but he maintained a firm hold of the bottom rung of the rope ladder.

Lunt let go of the meat hook, leaving it embedded in the hull. He shifted his right hand to gain the same grip as his left. His body again smashed against the side of the hull as the Drake pitched in reaction to the strength of the freshening southerly winds. His hawk nose hurt as it pressed against the rough hull. The gash on the side of his face felt as if it was going to open again and bleed. With his foot Lunt tried to loosen the meat hook from the wooden hull. But, from above, he only succeeded in embedding it deeper into the surface. He kicked at it several more times and then decided to retrieve it later on his way back down the ladder.

As Lunt cautiously pulled himself upward the seven or

eight rungs that would bring him level with the surface of the deck, a strong puff of wind succeeded in detaching a few lone strands of his thinning hair away from the damp briny mop that sat soaking on the top of his head. Water dripped from the loosened queue which drew the long blond hair to the back of his head.

Above, there was a sound of hammering. Lunt was oblivious to any physical discomfort as the adrenalin pulled his body upward towards the construction project he could hear proceeding on the deck above. As he looked up, he could see thin wisps of vapor drifting off the edge of the deck and then tumbling down the sides on top of him. The lantern lights above the deck gave the vapors an almost rainbow luminescence.

Slowly the top of his head cleared the level of the deck. As he raised his eyes to that level, the smell of fresh creosol pitch drifted into his eyes and lungs. He buried his face into the crook of his arm to avoid the discomfort. The acrid, stinging vapors filled his consciousness. His eyes stung. He struggled to stifle a cough. He had smelled creosol before, but he had never been subjected to having the full blunt of its acrid fumes fall over his face. He began to feel very sick. He shifted from the center of the net to the far right. As he did so, he turned his face away from the offending fumes and drew several deep breaths. Then he listened.

"Captain wants her coated three times, and then the excess sponged off so the wood will be dry by morning. They're going to mount it in the morning."

"Have you seen it?" said another.

"Tain't no one has seen it. Not with 'em marines sitting on it, eh, Jimbo?" offered another.

Lunt heard some kind of a reply whose thick cockney accent made it undiscernible. He drew another deep breath and glanced upward, squinting in anticipation of further eye discomfort. An open gun port was within a stretch of his neck at the right side of the ladder. It would be far safer to peer through that smaller crevice, than to openly poke his head up over the gangway. Lunt shifted his body to accommodate this new vantage point. The odor of creosol permeated everything. Lunt wondered at the possibilities of a fire starting because of the carelessness of having open fumes running along the deck while they worked by lantern light. In a moment he was going to see what kind of a situation had been so pressing, that the British had been willing to risk a fire to hasten the above work. Was Lunt's effort really worth all that he was risking?

Lunt cautiously raised his head to peek beneath the barrel of a four pounder and its caisson. Before him was a large flat wooden drum or cylinder, about four feet in height, and ten or twelve feet in diameter. It was made of bright new lumber. It had very likely just been constructed that day. Everything immediately in vicinity of the drum had been cleared away. It appeared to be kind of a platform, upon which a few deadeyes were attached. Lunt studied it, but could not ascertain its purpose. Forward of the drum there was a large rectangular packing crate on which three Royal Marines sat holding muskets supported between their hands.

Lunt's eyes returned to the great cylinder. The entire apparatus seemed to be supported on a kind of dowel that extended through the deck. Lunt observed that the drum was elevated just a few inches above the surface of the deck itself. From the positioning of the deadeyes, it appeared that the drum itself could be rotated and then fastened down at regular intervals. Something must be going to be placed upon it. Men were squatting around the drum brushing it with creosol to preserve the wood from the effects of foul weather.

The crate upon which the marines sat was difficult to see, with a portion of the drum blocking Lunt's view. It was aft a bit from where Lunt was perched. Lunt looked to his left. He would have to lower himself two rungs to traverse the Jacob's ladder unseen by anyone on deck. He lowered himself carefully, and moved hand over hand, and foot over foot across the netting.

Finally, Lunt was almost under a gun port, a good place from which to view the crate. He climbed slowly upwards. As his eyes reached the level of the deck, he saw the barrel of a freshly painted four pounder. He cocked his head slightly. The lanterns which lit the deck area gave off a flickering light that was difficult to read by. Lunt reached his hand through the gun port and grasped a hawser to pull himself up part way through the port. He was now just a dozen feet from the crate upon which the Royal Marines sat, their muskets held loosely in front of them. All of the marines were admiring the creosol coating which had just been completed. The crew and the marines were exchanging casual banter.

One marine shifted his leg, and Lunt could see writing stenciled on the side of the wooden crate,

The Carron Company
Stromeferry

Lunt stared at the box trying to make some determination about its dimensions and possible weight. Suddenly, from across the deck, one of the workers stood up.

"Who's that?" he screamed.

It seemed an eternity to Lunt, as he refocused from the wooden box to the man who had screamed the alarm. He found the source of the outcry, a man holding a paint brush pointing right at him. The three marines looked incredulously at the man, and then suddenly one of them looked around to where he was pointing. The marine saw Lunt. He was only a dozen feet away. He stood up and started to swing his musket around to aim at Lunt's face, beneath the ship's gun.

Lunt let go of the hawser and pushed himself back out of the open gun port. His feet pushed off from the top of the Jacob's ladder. He fell slowly backwards towards the sea. It seemed to him an endless length of time that his body hung in the air. During his descent, Lunt was conscious of the night wind blowing about him. Just as his body finally hit the security of the cold dark sea, he saw faces appear at the lighted gangway above him. In that fraction of a second that his body was on the surface of the water, he twisted frantically while he sucked in his last gulp of breath. Beneath the water was his only hope of survival. He clawed at the dark water, trying to burrow hurriedly beneath its surface. He felt a quantity of water close over his head and back. He thrust his face and arms further downward into the blackness.

As he groped frantically for deeper and deeper water, there was a blinding flash lighting the water about him. Beside him, he saw a stream of bubbles explode past his face to burrow into the black void ahead. He knew it was a musket ball. Then, he heard its echo through the water. He kept digging downward. There were more blinding flashes, punctuated by exploding sounds. About him, confused silvery fish also dashed about, trying to flee the sudden eruption of lightning and thunder from just above the surface of the water. Lunt turned his body to get below the safety of the hull. He must resurface somewhere, but to do it here was certain death.

Lunt swam vigorously under the dark hull of the Drake. He nearly collided with the keel, but another flash of light illuminated the water around him. One lone, disorientated fish almost swam right into his face before it swerved to dart off as darkness closed. Beneath the keel, Lunt executed a turn toward the stern to swim the remaining fifty feet or so beneath the hull towards the rudder. Through the water he could feel the hollow vibrations of many pounding feet running across the deck to look overboard in all directions to catch sight of him.

Lunt felt as if he was in a watery tomb. Twice he grazed his head against the bottom of the hull. He dived deeper to prevent the bobbing ship from crushing his skull as its great weight heaved atop the waves. His lungs ached from the creosol and he had not gotten a full breath of air. He hoped the rudder would be coming soon. He pushed on. He could see the lights of the deck which framed the water in a luminescent contour that encircled the hull. He would have to get through that luminescence without being shot.

The bottom of the hull suddenly gave way to open water above his head. Despite his desperate need for air, he controlled his rise to the surface so that he soundlessly entered again into the narrow cavity between the rudder and the chain links. Here he would be unseen for a moment. Above the surface he tried to control his breathing so that his gasping would not be overheard from the railing. To the side of the vessel, he believed he heard the longboat returning from shore. Men were shouting at it to circle the ship and search the surrounding water.

From the crew's shouts, Lunt knew that additional lanterns were being brought to all sides of the vessel to look overboard into the water. He had to leave now or risk close pursuit by a longboat with a lantern at its bow. Once he was sighted, it would be certain to detect him each time he surfaced until they finally captured him. Lunt took a deep swallow of air, as much as his lungs could contain, and then he pushed off by placing his feet against the rudder and dived deeply.

Just as he pushed off, the shudders of the great cabin were thrust open, throwing more light upon the water to the stern of Drake. It psychologically drove Lunt to pull deeper and deeper as he worked his way underwater away from the ship and the men who searched for him.

By swimming directly towards the deepest point of the harbour, on a different route than which he had initially come, Lunt thought he would have the best chance of eluding the search that would be widening. Now, in total darkness and several hundred feet from the stern of the Drake, he turned to look back for an instant. There were men running and lanterns being put over the side everywhere. The longboat circled the ship to look in the water for a possible body or swimmer. When they did not find him they would be broadening their search. It would take the longboat only five minutes to reach land, and probably another ten to mobilize a search effort. After that, every bit of coast would be patrolled to find the swimmer.

Lunt must make the beach before that amount of time and lose himself in the city. Then he would need to make it back to the O'Tooles for his bag. He must warn them. He breathed deeply and resumed swimming.

Each arm ached as Lunt pushed on, continuing to swim out towards the center of the lough. Lunt rapidly made headway, his efforts yielded great progress as the tide was still ebbing and the southerly wind was pushing surface water in his direction. After a few minutes more he changed his direction to head towards the land. Five hundred more yards to go before he reached the beach where he had left his vest and cloak under a bush. He hoped they were still there. Would he be able to find them? He would not only need them for warmth, but to disguise the fact that he had been swimming. Otherwise he would be walking barefoot through the streets of Belfast, dripping wet.

He stopped and tread water to look back at the Drake. Someone fired another musket into the water. Some fish must have darted in the wrong direction. As he turned again to continue his swim towards shore, his foot struck something. Surprised, he lowered his other foot and found his toes touched the bottom of the harbour. He put weight on his feet and found that he could stand. He was in shoulder deep water at low tide. He looked in the direction of the bridge that spanned the river at the mouth of the River Lagan. He was in line with the flow of the river. He must be standing on a sand bar formed by soot carried out into the lough from the river. This was certainly not a portion of the harbour into which Ranger should ever venture without very good local knowledge.

Lunt used his resting point to take a few deep breaths and then began to swim again. He was now very tired and cold but his brain told him that he must continue on. He must precede the search parties that would be soon scouring the beach. Arm over arm, he swam furiously, turning his head to each side with all the remaining strength he could muster. He was aware that his flailing strokes would cause attention if there were already observers on the beach attracted to the shooting coming from the Drake. They might be able to give the authorities a description of the man who emerged from the harbour water shortly thereafter. Lunt consciously struggled to make quieter stokes as he neared the shore. His arms must not slap and splash against the water. He closed his eyes and concentrated deeply. He thought of home and of wanting to get his part of the war over.

Finally, he felt he was close enough to shore to try and plant his foot on the bottom. He probed downwards with his toe. No contact. He must be off the sand bar. He swallowed a little water and managed to swim a few more strokes. How was he going to find his cloak, boots, and vest? They didn't really matter. All that mattered was that he somehow get back to Ranger. He must tell Jones that the Drake had something very important aboard.

Lunt swam a little more and then tried again. This time his toe finally made contact with the muddy bottom. Grateful, he breathed laboriously as he struggled through the chest and then waist deep water. When the water was just ankle deep, he collapsed onto the beach. He shivered uncontrollably but his hands pushed himself upright. He could not stay here. Up on the beach, he was conscious of movement. He struggled to stand up. He could see dark figures up on the beach. He must get away. He tried to run, but he was so cold. He moved heavy foot after foot. The waves splashed across his ankles as he ran. Then, there was a voice.

"Halt, right there."

6
Dinner

Captain Burden reached into his pocket. With the index finger of his right hand he fondled the facets of the diamond ring. Should he present it to her now, to avoid embarrassment if she hesitated in front of his officers at the dinner tomorrow evening? Lately she had been acting a little remote. The unusually long hours spent organizing the ordnance testing would soon be over. Lieutenant Dobbs would be in command within another month. Then they could hire a carriage for a trip down to Limerick to visit her family, perhaps a couple of weeks honeymooning around beautiful Kilarney, and then they might make their way over to Waterford or Wexford from which they could arrange passage back to England. He would make her happy.

There was a sudden knock at the door, no voice had preceded it. It was peculiar that his marine guard did not announce a visitor at this time of night. In this apartment house, with its Tudor architecture and small courtyard, there were only six flats. Two were owned by bankers, another by Mr. Wright, the shipwright of Belfast, and the other two owners never seemed to be in town. They lived in London, but had something to do with the shipping of commerce between England and Ireland.

As he was about to get up from his sofa, Alicia brushed by him to get the door as she always did. "I'll see to it, darling."

What a woman. She always takes such good care of me. For a few moments he heard her talking to a familiar voice in the foyer. Suddenly, the door was pushed open.

"I must see the Captain," the voice emphatically stated.

After receiving a formal salute, Captain Burden signaled for the young man to take a chair. It was one of the two lieutenants with whom he had shared a glass of port earlier in the evening, before departing the Drake. The man was out of breath.

"Sir, someone was around, or rather on the Drake," said Lieutenant Greene excitedly.

"On the Drake?" questioned Burden.

The Lieutenant looked at the Captain's Lady, unsure of how much he should say in her presence. Sensing his concern, the Captain said, "Alicia, bring us a spot of tea, will you dear."

For the next few minutes Captain Burden heard the brief story and the attempts the crew had made to find the intruder in the dark waters around the Drake. Then the Captain continued with his own line of questioning.

"Did anyone get a good look at this man?"

"No, sir. It all happened very fast. One of the crew thought he was fair haired."

"So he was only looking at the deck, he was not actually on it."

"Aye, eh, yes, sir."

"And the marines fired three rounds directly on top of the man?"

"Yes, sir, but we've found no body. Lieutenant Dobbs was awakened by the shots, sir. He's taken over the search in the water and making sure that there's no damage to the Drake. He sent me to alert you."

"It's not unusual you wouldn't find a body. Sometimes a man can continue a few hundred yards or so, enough to get out of range, and then die of loss of blood or exhaustion or whatever." Burden took out his pocket watch and then continued, "The tide would also be on the ebb and, with the wind, you'll probably not find the body until it gets light. It may be miles out into the lough by then. Was there anything missing on board?"

"Nothing, sir. Nothing at all. Lieutenant Dobbs has made a thorough inspection."

"And no member of the crew, excepting Lt. Dobbs and yourself and the longboat crew, have left the Drake since the crate arrived yesterday. And there are three marines constantly sitting on the crate, with a minimum of ten marines and two officers on deck watch at all times."

"All as you ordered, sir."

"Then I think what happened here is that some poor wretch climbed aboard to steal something. Dastardly poor country, you know. All the merchant vessels have a theft problem here. That's why they anchor out so deep and let the skiffs come out to load and unload. Because of the construction work, we have Drake in rather close. The intruder probably didn't know a sloop of war from a merchant schooner. When the poor chap stuck his head o'er the rail he immediately got more than he bargained for."

"Sir, I took the liberty of stopping by Major Pitkan's. He sends his compliments and is organizing a watch along the beaches. Is there anything else we should be doing, sir? asked Greene.

"Nothing till morning. I'll be out and have a look around then. That's all, Lieutenant," replied the Captain as he arose from his soft velvet sofa, smoothing down his uniform around its corpulent form.

Lieutenant Greene rose but paused, holding an object out in his hand. "There's one other thing, sir. The blackguard left this sticking out of our hull."

The Captain took the large iron hook with a crudely fashioned cork handle. The straight end of the metal was turned like a screw where it entered the cork. Burden unscrewed it from the cork a bit to look at the turning. Somewhere he had seen such a device before. He just couldn't place where.

Greene continued, "He apparently used this to reach up to grasp the bottom of the Jacob's ladder. We left it down after you departed so the longboat's crew could return after leaving you ashore. The man must have been in the water just as you departed."

"Peculiar," said Burden, turning the device in his hands. "Most peculiar. Deliver a note to Major Pitkan for me, will you?"

Captain Burden went to his writing table and dipped his quill pen into the ink well. He wrote a brief note to Pitkan, blotted it, then folded it, and sealed it with his personal wax stamp.

Burden handed it to his Lieutenant. "Of course keep me informed if anything else should happen during the evening. Otherwise I'll be out in the morning."

They exchanged salutes and the Lieutenant left directly. As soon as he was out the door, Captain Burden said, "You can come back in now, love." In his pocket he fingered the diamond ring. As he turned slowly, he saw her and his mood changed to one that might best be described as lust.

Alicia wore the white dress she had purchased for his birthday party. He had never seen her so provocatively dressed. She wore her hair in a double stacked bun, perfectly combed, without a flaw. A white beaded necklace hung about her neck and bare white shoulders. The white beads seemed like bits of white sugar all hung on a string, dangling over her decolletage.

The bodice of her dress was cut deeply to reveal nearly half her breasts. It revealed that everything which Alicia possessed was her own, not a seamstress' skillful preparation of some padding here and there.

Captain Burden stared at her and said, "My dear."

* * * * *

The embers of last evening's hot fire still heated the tiny stone cottage. Lunt stirred and then sat bolt upright on the ground. He was covered by five or six horsehair blankets. He pushed them aside. Vague remembrances of last night came to him, of his uncontrollable shivering, of several men tackling him on the beach as he tried to run away. Much later, there were blurry impressions of his being hauled somewhere in a cart, and then of men pinning him down and sitting on the edges of blankets to keep him warm. His head hurt now. He remembered the whiskey they had poured down his throat. It had warmed him from the inside.

"Good morning, Henry," said a familiar Gaelic voice.

Lunt turned his head. O'Mally smiled back at him. They were alone in a stone cottage. Outside through the shudders, Lunt could see that it was a new day.

"Like some boiled eggs and tea?" asked O'Mally.

Lunt nodded, leaning on his elbows. O'Mally got up and moved two pots to an iron rod that spanned the fireplace. He added a piece of peat to the fire. The room slowly grew warmer. Visibly sweating, O'Mally moved to sit beside him.

"'Twas a great risk you took last night. Did you find out what it was that Captain Jones had sent you for?"

"I'm afraid I made a muck of it," replied Lunt. "I managed to disable the Drake's steerage, but then I was discovered. They'll surely find it today. Now they'll know that we're after them, and it will be impossible to get the Drake out of Belfast. There are many sand bars in the lough. It'll be too dangerous to bring Ranger in as we'd likely run aground."

O'Mally nodded, "It takes a good pilot to work his way in or out of the lough, certainly it's not a thing to attempt in the dark, or while you're engaged in a sea battle. But don't you fret about tipping your hand. The Drake's Captain had been sent two previous messages, directly challenging him to come out and face the Ranger. He has chosen to ignore them. The fat man is a coward, that's what I make of it," said O'Mally as he got up to remove the pots from over the fire.

O'Mally continued to talk, while he placed four boiled

eggs into a wooden bowl and passed them to Lunt, "You see, one of the reasons that Captain Jones probably was reluctant to have me come with you was that I had a hand in delivering both of those earlier messages. He understandably wanted to try a different person the third time. But I know the man that delivered them. He was one of those that plucked you off the beach in the nick of time last night. Do you remember it?"

"Not well," said Lunt while he cracked open a hard boiled egg. He had only hazy memories of the past night but he wanted to correct O'Mally's misinterpretation. "Captain Jones does trust what you did. When I asked him about how he was certain that the challenges were actually delivered, he was very put out that I should question him. Where are your friends now?"

"They don't want to be seen by you, for fear that they could be identified later. But they'll be available to help. It depends on what we want to do next. I had a plan I was going to propose to you, but you went off on your swim," explained O'Mally.

"Why didn't we return to your brother-in-law's? Why are we in this place?" asked Lunt as he cracked open his third egg.

"Because you scared the piss out of Jimmy. You threatened him if he went into your bag. He remembers the old days and the murdering. Me brother-in-law was pacing back and forth when I got back. He had the look of a man who was about ready to bolt, or do something drastic. I didn't want to have to make my sis a widow. When I found the potato and figured out what you were up to, I moved us out of there. We'll not go back. I told him to hide the money well."

"My things?" asked Lunt.

"Over yonder, everything," O'Mally pointed to the corner of the small room where Lunt's vest, boots, and even the dark wool cloak were piled on top of his canvas bag. "I found yer clothes on the beach. It was still twilight so I must have just missed ye."

"What made your brother-in-law so afraid, can I ask about the murders?" asked Lunt.

"I'd rather not get into that, other than to say that some very innocent people were killed. Despite past and present injustices to dear old Ireland, what we did in return and the way we chose to do it was all wrong. I can see that clearly now. I've a new country now, America. It's still the same old enemy, but a fresh beginning is what I needed. It's better now not to awaken the old ghosts," said O'Mally solemnly. Lunt accepted his request.

After he had finished the fourth egg and sipped some tea, Lunt inquired, "What was your plan?"

"Before I tell you, can you tell me if you were seen by any of the Drake's officers. By seen, I mean your face."

"No," said Lunt, "and I don't believe I was seen by any of her crew either. Not clearly and, if so, only for an instant."

"Good," said O'Mally. "What I have in mind will take the greatest possible courage. It'll mean venturing right into the lion's lair but, in the short time we have left, 'tis the only thing that may bring us the Drake."

* * * * *

John Entwhistle heard the outer door of his shop open. It must be a late afternoon customer. He shouted out from the back room, "Sorry, we'll be closed for the day now. I've a catering this evening. If ye please, come back tomorrow."

His wife was talking up a storm as they worked busily. He was only half listening to her. He was roasting the side of beef in a portion of his baker's oven. In about an hour he would put the Yorkshire pudding onto the other side. He could not let the fire get too hot. He was thinking of slicing off a cut of the outer portion of beef for their supper. Their Lordships would never miss it.

He jumped very startled when he heard a Gaelic voice say to him very softly from a few inches behind his head, "You'll be pardoning me, Mr. Entwhistle, but we'll be taking over your operation for the evening."

Entwhistle turned quickly and was dumbfounded at the sight of five men in white hoods with large eye holes cut out. Each of the five men held a horse pistol. The hammers were all cocked back, suspended threateningly over their captive flint igniters. Beside him, Entwhistle's wife gave a shrill cry and then collapsed in a complete faint. He was alone.

"Well, that was easy. It's probably the first time the lady has kept her mouth shut for a long time." The leader's own chuckle followed the remark.

"As for you, Mr. Entwhistle, you'll be giving me lads a wee bit of instruction on the proper cooking of, what is it..." The hooded man strode over to the oven and opened the hot iron door using a nearby soup ladle to catch the handle. He peered inside and said, "Why, it's roast beef, and..." strolling around the little bakery further, "roast potatoes, vegies,..ah, and what have we here, could it be... ah, 'tis....Yorkshire pudding." Entwhistle swallowed hard.

The leader now moved to stand directly in front of the terrified baker whose raised freckled arms shook visibly. "You can put your arms down, Mr. Entwhistle. We'll be tying them behind yer back. If you attempt to escape, we'll use that carving knife over there...," Entwhistle's eyes followed in the direction that the leader pointed his pistol, "..to slit yer throat...from ear to ear."

The leader laughed heartily, a gesture that totally convinced Entwhistle that the man would relish doing it, if any resistance were encountered.

* * * * *

Rhein van Zoot was the first to arrive at Carnarvon House. It was just seven o'clock. He was exhausted by the morning and afternoon he had spent with Major Pitkan. The man had asked him question after question, and then proceeded to ask them all over again. His Sergeant Major with the square face had searched his room right in front of him, while the Major challenged his motives in hosting this dinner. Finally, without saying why he had detained him, Pitkan had simply said, "Very good, we'll see you this evening."

As he entered Carnarvon House, van Zoot was still shaking over the directness of the challenge. He opened the doors with his key and walked up the staircase to the three special rooms he had taken for the evening. To his surprise there was no one there, in either the drawing room or the formal dining room. The long dining table had been set for twenty-two, but only a few service candles had been lit. He frowned and went through the swinging doors into the narrow service room that ran parallel to the dining room.

There was no sign of the caterer or his crew, but they must have been here already or the places would not have been set. Entwhistle was going to cook the food at the bakery and wheel it through the streets in a covered container. This was to save van Zoot money on leasing the enormous kitchen and, as Entwhistle had explained, would provide his guests with the very best beef preparations directly from his own kitchen, rather than his having to use a unfamiliar stove.

Where were the caterers? Van Zoot had left explicit instructions as to when they were to be on duty not later than six o'clock. He pulled his gold pocket watch from his vest. It was now just after seven. There was time for him to go over the few blocks to Entwhistle's to see what was afoot. He descended the circular staircase in a hurry, midway down he heard the door open below.

"We'll inspect the rooms before we haul up the food."

"You're here to serve the food?" said van Zoot to the voices in the darkened hallway below.

"Aye, we're a bit late, but better late than never, me mother usta say," replied one of the men. "You be Mr. van

Zoot, the gentleman that's putting on this affair?"

"That's correct," replied van Zoot. "Where's Mr. Entwhistle and his wife?"

One of the men below ascended the stairs into the candle light that emanated from the recesses in the wall. For just a moment, van Zoot felt a little threatened by the approaching stranger. Then he could see the man's face clearly. The stranger was smiling from an impish looking face. He came up to van Zoot so that they were on the same stair, standing face to face. As he stepped into the full candle light, van Zoot could see that the man had bright red hair and freckles, which somehow made him look innocent.

"Call me Mike," said the man in a friendly sort of way. "Me fellow freckled cousin, John Entwhistle, 'tis a bit tied up, if ye know what I mean." Mike seemed to chuckle a bit, and continued, "He loves that cheese you know."

"Is the mistress at least going to be here?" said an annoyed van Zoot indignantly.

"Perhaps a wee bit later," replied Mike. "But don't be rueful, you'll have me for entertainment. I come to a lot of his banquets to sing. I'll keep yer guests entertained. That I will."

"I suppose Entwhistle wants more for the privilege," van Zoot snapped.

"Not a penny more," replied the man. Right in front of van Zoot the man opened his mouth and began to sing, "*The Rose of Tralee...........*"

Van Zoot held up his hand interrupting Mike after just a few lines. The entertainment might be a nice touch. He pointed to the other man in the darkness below. "And what's he do?"

At this inquiry, the man sprang up the stairs two at a time with considerable agility. He carried a large canvas bag, which he placed down on the stair below van Zoot, who peered down in the darkness towards the bag.

The man knelt down and reached inside. There was

a faint sound of metal clanking on metal as the man searched his belongings. Then he stood up holding something in the dark. Van Zoot squinted to see what the man was holding. The second man's eyes were looking right at him, studying him carefully as he brought a long carving knife into view. It was the distinctive one which he had seen at Entwhistle's yesterday. The sharpened edge gleamed in the candle light.

"This is Henry," stated Mike in a thick brogue for emphasis. "He'll be cutting the meat."

Van Zoot felt a shiver as he looked at the cold determined aspect of the young man just a step below him. He suspected that the man was capable of cutting more than just meat. The man's eyes were very intelligent, they looked straight at him over a patrician hawk nose. The man's skin was very white, as if he had been indoors a long time. He had a red welt on his cheek. Van Zoot turned back to Mike. He didn't want his well laid plans to be spoiled by amateurs.

"You have all the wine, beef, and yorkshire pudding with you?"

"All in the cart outside, wrapped tight as can be. Delicious it 'tis," replied Mike.

"Very well, but I'm disappointed that the caterer will not be here himself, very disappointed," said van Zoot for emphasis.

"Ah, don't you fret now," said Mike. "I can assure you me cousin would rather be here. We'll make this a very delicious dinner for your guests. 'Tis the navy isn't it?"

"Yes, most of them."

"Ah, Mr. van Zoot, we'll see to it that it's an evening the Royal Navy will not forget for a long time. That we will."

The man called Henry sheathed the cutting blade he had kept out while they had spoken on the stairway, and then moved aside to allow Mr. van Zoot to continue his descent. Mike and Henry ascended the stairs to look over the rooms from which they would serve the banquet. On the stairway Mike pointed upwards into the darkness, indicating that there was a vacant third story to Carnarvon House. It was not supposed to be used during the evening's festivities.

Van Zoot went outside to take a look at the cart of prepared food. The caretaker came out of his auxiliary house and, after van Zoot paid him, began to light the remaining candles in the stairway wall recesses. The polished wood stairway leading up to the dining room of the old mansion looked magnificent.

Henry and Mike made several trips up and down the stairway to unload food and wine from the service cart. Leaving Henry upstairs, Mike went outside to move the small wagon away from the front entrance. Just as 'Mike' O'Mally was about to reenter Carnarvon House, a noise he heard caused him to look up one of the streets approaching the house.

First, there was the progressively louder sound of boots pounding on cobblestones, then the bellowing voice of a sergeant called cadence above the din. There was an army of men approaching on the run, in unison. O'Mally shuddered.

O'Mally looked up to see a major round the corner astride a tan and white horse. The lantern at the corner revealed that, beneath the covering of his cap, he was almost totally bald. His uniform was blood red, garnished by gold epaulets. Also on horseback, closely behind him, came the Sergeant with the broad handle bar moustache, the one who had struck out at the occupants of the potato cart the previous morning. The Sergeant bellowed, "Bayonets at the ready, step lively now. Right turn, ho."

A column of troops, all dressed in bright royal red, with high miter hats and white cross straps, marched double time from round the corner and into the short square in front of Carnarvon House. Before each man was a musket whose newly shined bayonet gleamed in rows of four as each successive row rounded the corner beneath the street lamp.

O'Mally stood frozen at the doorway, and muttered under his breath, "Sweet Jesus, saints preserve us."

For an instant, O'Mally considered going back down the stairs, getting into his cart and driving off, leaving Henry Lunt to figure out what had happened. No, he'd live the rest of his life regretting it. He had to go back inside and see if they could escape together. There were two horses tied side by side at the rear of an ale house just two blocks away. They could make it there, if he could get Lunt to leave right away.

O'Mally took the stairs two by two until he reached the suite of rooms. He heard van Zoot directing his comrade, "There, that one up there."

O'Mally pushed the door open to observe Henry Lunt, dressed in his white breeches and shirt, perched atop a high ladder. He was lighting the candles of the chandelier above the dining table. This room would be well lit and very warm tonight. O'Mally had interrupted them, while from outside the sound from the arriving troops was beginning to be audible. They were already in the courtyard of Carnarvon House.

"Henry," said O'Mally, with a crack in his voice. Outside the thundering boots came to a halt as the deep penetrating voice of their Sergeant gave orders, one after another in rapid succession. Outside he could visualize a formation of troops developing. Had they somehow discovered the caterer's shop and found out what was afoot? Were they coming to get Henry Lunt and him? Perhaps this was what the bean chaointe had forewarned and now it was happening sooner than he had ever imagined. Had his damn brother-in-law turned them in after all?

Lunt turned his head in the direction of O'Mally. It was evident that he also heard the calamitous arrival of the troops. O'Mally jerked his head in a direction indicating they should go outside. Lunt took a step down the ladder, when van Zoot spoke up from a corner of the room, "Wait, there's just a few more candles, let's light them now, please."

For a long moment Lunt stood frozen on the ladder,

listening to the continuing sounds of troops forming in the courtyard. It was obvious to Lunt that bolting at this point was not the prudent action. Whatever was on, they must pretend it didn't affect them. He looked directly at O'Mally and then rearranged his body and raised himself up another rung to stretch his lighting stick to the wicks of the remaining candles of the chandelier. Had the British somehow identified that the intruder on the Drake was now planning to carve meat for their Captain and his guests?

Fine black tallow smoke rose from each candle in the chandelier and floated upwards to the ceiling where it gathered into a thickening layer above the dining room.

* * * * *

Van Zoot walked down the stairway, rubbing his small hands together. He was a much calmer man than he had been only a half hour ago. Entwhistle's helpers had efficiently transformed the empty service room into a storehouse of delectable food items, whose odors were now filtering out into the drawing room where the guests would congregate prior to moving through the sliding doors into the dining room.

If the Captain's guest list all came, van Zoot would have all the contacts of Belfast's burgeoning shipbuilding industry before him. What an evening it would be, he would find out what was planned in this remote location and have every opportunity to capitalize upon it. The prospects were grand for an exceptional evening.

He stepped outside the columned entrance to Carnarvon House. Major Pitkan was just dismounting, as Sergeant Major Hensley steered his horse around his men, barking orders and reforming them. The man perpetually carried a horsewhip.

The military still seemed to have a feeling that something was afoot. During the day he had heard rumors that someone tried to board the Drake the previous evening. Van Zoot had submitted to Major Pitkan's amateurish but persistent questioning earlier that day. Van Zoot believed that he had satisfied him that his motives were strictly commercial; perhaps the Major had not believed him after all. It would take him a long time to prove anything different. For an instant, van Zoot wondered if he should mention to Major Pitkan the fact that the catering personnel had been changed. No, it might cause him to call off the whole affair. He would never be able to reassemble contacts like these. Mike and Henry seemed to know their trade, and they had Entwhistle's knife. It was best ignored. He could waggle with Entwhistle tomorrow about reducing the price, because he had second class help.

The Major's manner of dress told van Zoot that the affair he was hosting was strictly provincial. Wigs would have been worn without question to any formal dinner either in London or on the Continent, but Captain Burden had specified that they be optional. Obviously, he was in doubt whether all of his Irish merchant guests possessed them.

Major Pitkan had apparently made it his style never to wear a wig. Van Zoot had seen the man about six or seven times since his arrival. The Major seemed to prefer to let his almost totally bald head serve as his hallmark. It was probably one of the reasons that he was still a major, thought van Zoot as he acknowledged the man during his dismount, "Good evening, Major."

Just as Pitkan was about to reply, Sergeant Hensley barked loudly at one of the soldiers who had dropped his musket, distracting them. The Sergeant stood up in the stirrups of his spotted brown mount. He held his horsewhip poised in the air threateningly. The Sergeant urged his horse to swerve amongst the soldiers who were trying to hold their formation despite their Sergeant's ranting. This was obviously a common incident. The Sergeant gave the man a loud rebuke and an order to report to the livery before dawn the next morning. The other soldiers were relieved that they would not be so honored.

Seeing that the incident was over for the moment, Major Pitkan turned back toward the stairs to face van Zoot. "I've taken the liberty of bringing some of His Majesty's finest over to say goodbye to Captain Burden. There's been a small incident around the Drake. You never know when a little military presence will deter a little rambunctiousness from the natives. After all, this is Ireland. Besides, having served with the Captain some years ago, I also thought a little cross service recognition would be in order."

"Ah, yes," said van Zoot, concentrating on just one thing the Major had said, about retirement.

"I say," said van Zoot, "I was given to understand that it is Captain Burden's birthday."

"Well, yes, but it is also his retirement. He'll be turning over the command of the Drake to a younger officer within the month."

Van Zoot was surprised, and did not answer the Major, who after a while turned back to watch the stern Master Sergeant continue assembling his red coated soldiers into two lines, one on either side of the entrance. There were about sixty troops all placed in a ready position, awaiting the arrival of the guests.

The Major turned again to van Zoot, and said, "'Twas a nice gesture of you to do this. I apologize for the questioning this afternoon, but it was necessary. The Captain's served King and country for over forty years. 'Tis nice to see the civilian side give a good man a little recognition."

Van Zoot was a little taken back by the retirement aspect of the Captain's plans. Had he stayed an additional week in Ireland, just to set up and pay for a retirement party? He'd certainly been misled. Here he was hosting a dinner party for a man who would be holding the command and the purse strings to naval contracting probably for only a couple of weeks longer. The cagey old devil had read his eagerness to make contacts in Belfast and had used him to foot the bill to invite his cronies to what would very likely be his final party in service. Although van Zoot would get to meet Mr. Wright, who had also been invited. Were the remainder of the guests of any consequence to him?

"I was unaware that Captain Burden was that close to retirement." stated van Zoot. "Who is going to be taking his place?"

The Major scowled a bit, "Very likely Lieutenant Dobbs. But that depends on the outcome of several things. The next commander of the Drake has not been named, that is, officially."

Alerted to the likely realignment of his priorities for the evening, van Zoot excused himself ostensibly to look after the arrangements, but in actuality to make some subtle realignments of the place cards before any of the guests ventured upstairs.

* * * * *

From a remote second floor window, the two seeming servants watched the military formation. They listened as the square faced Sergeant Major with the spotted horse moved about and called the troops to attention as each carriage arrived. They had heard the conversation between van Zoot and Major Pitkan.

"I originally thought they were coming for us," said Lunt.

"Unlikely. If they had a clue we were here, we would have been removed very quietly," said O'Mally, sighing. "It'll be the end of the plan to kidnap the Drake's officers and take them to Ranger tonight. The lads have probably moved the coach away by now. There's just too many soldiers. You can't blame them. This is why they never let you see their faces at Entwhistle's. They know that they can trust me but you are an unknown entity."

"I trust they left the horses for us behind the tavern so that we can get to Carrickfergus this evening?" asked Lunt.

O'Mally nodded, "I'm sure that they will still be there. What'll be the priorities now, Henry? What do you want to come of this evening?"

"Just listen. We'll serve them their fancy dinner, listen, and wait for an opportunity. If there's none, we'll just slip away after sweets are served."

Lunt concentrated to look out at the tops of the trees above the courtyard. The wind from the south was light but still persistent. It would make any attempt by Ranger to reach the Drake directly extremely difficult. Captain Jones would be spotted long before he could surprise anyone. If she were becalmed, Ranger would be overwhelmed by troops, sent at her in longboats. To try and take the Drake in this far corner of the horseshoe shaped lough would be a grievous mistake. He did not know whether or not the crew of the Drake had discovered the severed rudder chain. O'Mally's colleagues had watched the longboats circling the Sloop of War all day, presumably looking for Lunt's body, but they could not tell whether anyone had descended onto the rudder to repair the chain. The vessel was too far out in the water and, with tidal changes, the Drake's shifting orientation made reliable observation difficult.

Lunt stared outside and continued to think of all the possibilities of what could go wrong. O'Mally's brother-in-law would surely connect all the clamor about the harbour with Lunt's disappearance at precisely the same time the night before. But would he be willing to reveal their identify and risk having the money which O'Mally had given him confiscated, or also to risk being connected with O'Mally's past deeds, whatever they were? The man left to guard the bound and gagged Entwhistles would have been alerted that the military had surrounded Carnarvon House. He probably had quit his post already. If the Entwhistles managed to untie themselves before dinner was over, the jig would be up.

O'Mally interrupted his thoughts. "They're coming up

the stairs, we'd better have the wine ready."

Lunt looked at his companion, who now sported a regal white servant's wig. Lunt raised an eyebrow, to which O'Mally replied, "I've told you I'm a bit infamous in these parts. The wig will disguise the red hair, in case someone should recognize me. Although it's been some years. It's Mr. Entwhistle's, I don't have one for you."

"Good," Lunt said to O'Mally, who then vanished out of the service room to make some adjustments to the dining room table.

As the door to the service room swung on its hinges a few more times, Lunt was left alone with his thoughts. The southerly wind would also be shortening the time left to Ranger before the Admiralty's fleet arrived in search of them. It would be a disaster if they were caught inside the lough by even one of the fleet. No amount of good sailing could prevent the inevitable capture. The major question was whether this southerly was simply a land breeze, or one which prevailed over the entire Irish Sea.

And now there was a new complication; O'Mally felt he might be recognized. His discovery would surely involve Lunt and bring about an investigation of why the Entwhistles had not arrived themselves.

Dejected at the reduced prospects for a successful mission, Lunt quietly shook his head, drew a deep breath, and turned to assume his disguise as steward to the Royal Navy.

* * * * *

A group of fifty or so men, off watch, were huddled together on the second deck of the Ranger. Lieutenant Simpson had just come below and listened at the outskirts of the gathering. He had signaled the men to continue their conversation without his interference.

One said, "What will they do with us if we mutiny?

Will the Congress hang us?"

Another interjected to the hisses of his comrades, "The Continental Congress assumes that we'll follow British law, till the Marine Committee writes its own. For us that means hanging every offender at the very mention of mutiny."

"There are no formalized naval documents about conduct at sea," offered John Dougall, a highly respected member of the original Portsmouth crew. "That means we can do what we wish, especially when we're being led by a madman who brings a small corvette into the middle of the British Navy's home waters, and a Scot at that, who cannot even direct a decent raid in his home waters without waking up the entire town."

Another crew member spoke up in Jones' defense, "You weren't ashore last night, John. No one could anticipate that David Smith was going to bolt from the longboat and shout the alarm up and down the streets of Whitehaven. The man was a traitor all this time. Remember how he was always at our meetings, always offering something up against the Captain. And then how he'd be lick'in his boots the next day. It wasn't Capt'n Jones' fault about Whitehaven. He also couldn't have known that the son of a bitch had wetted down the grenade wicks, so we couldn't fire the shipping. But we did manage to spike the cannon at the fort. And Captain Jones did talk his way through the mob, to get us all back to the longboats safely. The mob stepped aside and let us go. He's a good talker."

"He's a good talker, aye, but the man does not have any clear plan. Lot of good that spiking a couple of dozen cannon in a remote English town will do for the revolution back home in America. Too damn far away, if you ask me. Now if those cannons were going to be used against General Washington, it'd be another story. I say we're without direction; going back to Belfast Harbour again is madness. The Drake's not coming out. Not on your life."

"What about O'Mally and the young Lieutenant?"

"I say we pick them up if they're there at Carrickfergus. If not, we skedaddle and go home to Portsmouth, without Captain Jones. Sooner or later we're going to run into a British man of war and then we're lost. I say we head for home tomorrow."

"Have we enough provisions to cross the Atlantic?" asked Elijah Hall.

"Well, we sure have the plates to eat from." The crew all laughed at the reference to family plates some of them had taken from the home of Lord Selkirk; the other failed mission in the intervening two days since Lunt and O'Mally had been put ashore. Jones had wanted to capture the Lord in an attempt to use the King's friend as hostage to force a naval prisoner exchange. Lord Selkirk had simply not been 'in residence' when the party had landed. So the crew had taken some of his family possessions, over the objections of Jones.

"Men," said Simpson putting up his arms to calm his fellows down. "There comes a time when action is required. As many of you have urged me, I will very soon take command of this vessel, as her owners originally intended. Captain Jones is on deck at the moment. When he goes to sleep, I'll make my move. I carry a boatswain's whistle, as I've told you before. Prudence is required in choosing the proper moment. The man will fight, you all know that, but when I see the opportunity present itself, when it will do the least harm to all members of the crew, I'll signal with four rapid blows that I am taking over command. The time and place will be of our choosing."

As the Ranger edged its way westward back across the dark Irish Sea towards Belfast, Simpson began to point at different men to give them assignments. "Crawford, you still have the spare key to the small arms stores..."

* * * * *

Lunt steered his tray among the various guests offering them wine, but avoiding conversation. As much as possible, he tried to position himself near the military men to catch tidbits of their conversation. As the drawing room immediately in front of the dining area started to fill with guests coming up the stairs, Lunt became impressed with the importance of the people at this function. Most had something to do with either the Royal Navy, commercial shipping, or the local government. Some of the gentlemen wore wigs. The few ladies present were formally dressed, and mostly of middle or advanced age.

One of the naval lieutenants was named Dobbs. Lunt had seen him before at the road clearing incident. He was lean, dressed in an immaculate blue and white naval uniform complete with dress sword. He sipped his wine very sparingly. His parents, a parson and his matronly wife, hung by his side constantly and appeared not to know anyone.

From the outset, Lieutenant Dobbs had positioned himself at the top of the stairs and made every effort to introduce his parents to as many guests as possible. Lunt stood behind Dobbs to offer the guests a glass of wine as they reached the top of the stairs. He listened to the introductions to learn the identity of the arrivals. Some guests he summarily dismissed as having no immediate bearing upon his mission. Two were bankers and their wives, a magistrate, an insurance representative connected with Lloyd's, and several local gentry.

Finally, one guest did warrant Lunt's scrutiny as he neared the top of the stairs.

Dobbs greeted him, "Ah, Mr. Wright, so good to see you this evening. I'd like you to meet my parents, the Reverend and Mrs. Dobbs."

"Anglican church is it?" After receiving an affirmative nod, the affable middle aged man in a light brown suit, wig, and brown eyes smiled back at the Lieutenant's parents. Taking each of their hands in turn he spoke, "I could tell from working with William here that he was that quality sort.

Now, of course, I know why." Wright looked directly at Mrs. Dobbs, who appropriately blushed at the compliment and looked downward.

Apparently very aware that the waiter called Henry was very close behind him, Dobbs waved a signal to hand a glass of wine to Mr. Wright, which Lunt did forthwith and then stepped backward out of the group, but close enough to continue listening to their conversation.

"Where is Mrs. Wright tonight?" asked Dobbs. "A bit under the weather after the foxes and hounds yesterday morning?"

"No," said Wright, stepping forward into the group. "Frankly, Martha wasn't invited. The invitation just had my name. I took that to mean that this was a kind of bachelor's party, but I see from the number of ladies present that I'm incorrect."

"I'm sure it was simply an oversight," said Dobbs. "The Captain is very fond of Martha, I'm sure you could go back and get her. Or I could ask one of Major Pitkan's militia to drop by your house, perhaps take my parents' carriage by. We can always find an additional chair and squeeze around a bit."

"Oh, heavens, no," replied Wright. "It would take my wife at least a few hours to dress. The dinner would be tucked away before we returned. No, I think I will enjoy being free for the evening."

Lt. Dobbs continued, "Mother, Mr. Wright is in charge of the shipyard construction here at Belfast. He has also been helping us get ready for our little ordnance experiment aboard the Drake."

"Afraid to tell you that it may take a few more days to get underway," said Wright.

"How's that?" said Dobbs raising an eyebrow.

"I've misplaced the screw parts. You know those four yard long calibrating pins that you wanted, for adjusting the platform angles. Damnedest thing, one of them has vanished. They're certainly not a strategic piece, just a nuisance that it is missing. I can't figure out where. I've sent for another set. Likely be here Tuesday next..."

Dobbs snapped, "We can't hold this up for something as simple as that...."

Then aware of the fact that he had begun to cause a scene, Dobbs asked with a forced smile, "Has everyone had enough wine?" When no more was requested, Lt. Dobbs pivoted to face the wine steward whose presence seemed annoyingly close, "That'll be all, Henry."

Their eyes met face to face on the same level and, after a brief moment, Lunt bowed his head deliberately and uncharacteristically backed off to maintain his cover. As he moved away, he observed Dobbs and Wright whispering very animatedly, their heads close together.

As Lunt looked about the drawing room for guests needing a refill of wine, he momentarily caught sight of van Zoot, who was actively moving about introducing himself to the guests. O'Mally brought out a plate of small scones, each adorned with a slice of ham. Many of the guests had moved out of the drawing room to the small foyer at the top of the stairs. From this vantage point they had a good look at each new arrival. Lunt decided to stand closer to van Zoot to hear his conversation with a man who had been introduced to others as a retired navy procurement officer working with Mr. Wright. Van Zoot started the conversation, "You know, I supply the Royal Navy at Greenwich, Plymouth and elsewhere. I've been interested in also helping to supply the Belfast marine construction projects."

The ruddy faced man in a rather ancient wig replied, "Awful nice of you to put on this dinner for the Captain." Van Zoot smiled and bowed slightly at the compliment, he started to excuse himself to try and meet another guest, but the man continued, "Actually there will soon be a chap here from the Admiralty office at Greenwich. Probably put in here towards the end of next week," said the ruddy faced man. "If they have the bloody thing up and running by then, we think it could be on every ship in the red fleet before the end of next year. That's where a firm like yours would be interested, I'd suppose. At any rate, Mr. Wright believes that the Admiralty really doesn't believe it will work as claimed. They think if it didn't come out of Greenwich then it could not be worth their while. Anyway, there has been sufficient interest to send someone up from London to have a look."

By the crane of van Zoot's neck, Lunt could tell that he was very interested in getting the pensioner to talk further. Looking around, van Zoot spotted Lunt immediately behind him and motioned to have the man's glass refilled.

After fulfilling the order, the conversation drifted off to talk of van Zoot's accommodations. Lunt waited nearby to hear more of what he sensed van Zoot would try and ask. Finally it came, "And how do you feel it will perform?"

The red faced man replied, "Sorry, Mr. van Zoot. Rhein is it?" Van Zoot nodded. "Can't tell you. Major Pitkan has in fact just reminded all of us at the shipyard to be on guard because of the attempted boarding of the Drake. Those of us in the know are all pledged to keep a tight lip. After we find out if it's worthwhile, then we'll let some firms like yours in on it. That's what usually happens. But for now, afraid I can't discuss the details further."

Van Zoot quickly apologized for asking the question and changed the subject. Lunt moved away and went to find O'Mally who was loading up another plate of befores in the service room.

Lunt leaned his head close to O'Mally's face. "Find out anything?" O'Mally was only able to report that he had heard that the Drake was going to remain at anchor several more days.

Suddenly, from outside, they faintly heard the Sergeant Major's bellowing voice announce the Captain's arrival. The drums held by the front line of soldiers in the court yard rolled in an announcement beat. Lunt opened another bottle of the before dinner wine, removed some fresh glasses from the cupboard, and went back out among the guests who were each straining to get a glimpse out of the bay windows.

Unable to see, some of the guests went downstairs and outside to greet the Captain and his Lady. Lunt was left peering out of a window behind three women who evidently thought they were alone.

"Scandalous isn't it. That old fat man living with that woman. They're not even married."

"If you ask me, she's just using him as a meal ticket and free transport to London. My God, will you look at that decolletage. She'll get a lot of glances tonight."

"That'll get your James aroused. He'll be very attentive when you get home later, dearie." The three ladies giggled.

Unable to bear the conversation any longer, Lunt cleared his throat and held out the wine tray as if he'd just arrived, "Wine, ladies?"

Outside, Major Pitkan, with full dress helmet, did his utmost to make the affair seem grander than it was. He sat on his horse as straight as his back could bear, while the Sergeant Major gave bellowing commands which changed the stance of the men at arms. They presented arms like crack troops. Some of their performance was driven by fear of their ferocious Sergeant Major, who all too often had relished punishing any miscreants into submission and conformity.

The drum roll continued as the corpulent Captain and his Lady moved toward their greeters. From a solitary window in the service room, Lunt counted the redcoats. Two on either side by thirty two long; sixty four men, all armed with muskets and bayonets, save the two drummers and the flag bearer. More than O'Mally or he could ever escape on foot, especially with their leaders being mounted.

As the Lady locked her arm in her Captain's she gave all of the troops a warming smile. Each man's eyes followed her. When the couple reached the end of the line, Major Pitkan drew his sabre and placed it before his face in salute. Beside him, his Sergeant also saluted.

Captain Burden returned the salutes and then said, "Why, my old friend how nice."

"Good evening to you, Sir, eh, Madame. I'd like to ask permission for the Sergeant Major to come inside for a brief glass of wine prior to dinner."

"Why, of course," said Burden nodding to the mustached Sergeant Major. The Captain took Alicia's hand and proceeded inside. From the bottom of the stairs, a voice called out, "Ladies and gentlemen, Captain Burden and Lady Alicia."

Everyone applauded as the guest of honor began to ascend the stairs. Halfway up the stairs the couple came into Lunt's vantage point.

The chandelier over the winding stairway threw down a brilliant golden white light upon the couple as they continued ascending the stairs. Into Lunt's eyes came an image of the most beautiful woman he had ever seen, an apparition which took his breath away. Her hair was reddish brown, and formed into two perfect saucer shaped buns one atop the other. Somehow they remained in perfect proportion to her face at whatever angle she moved her head. Her face was very high cheek boned and her complexion flawless. Her brown eyes were exquisite, as they dashed about taking in everyone above her with an engaging smile as she rose up the stairs. Round her neck and onto her bare white shoulders fell an awe inspiring necklace of white beads whose brilliance threw off small rainbows of light at their edges. Her white dress was cut low enough to show off her cleavage, especially to those standing at the rail above. Her right arm was locked in her Captain's, her left held her white gown to prevent it from trailing unnecessarily on the ground.

She was the Lady of the morning who had stopped her horse and looked hard at Lunt, and had seemed to signal regret at his wound. She was appealing then, but now magnificent.

Beside her was the Captain, a man close to his sixties, if not in them. The man's balding head and the full jowls which hung from his face revealed that he was very obese, but his hugh stomach was covered by a flattering white vest. The Royal Navy blue uniform, gold symbols of his rank, his gold buttons, and shining epaulets symbolized the power of Imperial England, masters of the sea. The many ribbons upon the man's left chest alluded to the decades of service and the many campaigns in which the Captain had doubtless served.

For just an instant Lunt could visualize in the Captain a thinner, more agile, younger officer, but that was a long time ago. Now, the man's immense jowls jiggled as he laughed and spoke to his guests, soon driving Lunt's brief imagery away.

Behind the honored couple, coming up the stairs were the handsomely dressed Major and his Sergeant Major with the great mustache. Their scarlet uniforms were bedecked with a multitude of ribbons, which sat proudly on their hard erect chests. Shining black belts adorned each man's waist. As they walked up the stairs, side by side, each carried his uniform cap in the crook of his hand, as had the naval captain preceding them.

As each attained the top of the stairs, O'Mally took their hats. Lieutenant Dobbs saluted his Captain as he reached the top of the stairs, and then spoke, "Captain Burden, I'd like to introduce you to my parents, the Reverend and Mrs. Dobbs. It was so thoughtful of you to have invited them." Courtesies were exchanged among the five and then Henry handed each of them a glass of wine. Lt. Dobbs nodded briefly to the two red coated soldiers behind the Captain and then ushered the party of five away from the head of the stairs.

After the exodus, Lunt was left facing the Major and

handed him a glass of wine. He prepared to do the same for the Sergeant Major who, from the expression on his face, was disappointed not to be introduced to the Lieutenant's parents.

Through Lunt's mind raced the possibility. Would the Sergeant Major recognize him as the victim of his brutality the previous morning? What if he did? Lunt refused to dwell on the things that could go wrong. He would try to hand the Sergeant Major the wine as innocuously as possible and hope for the best.

Lunt kept his body orientated to the right as he served the wine and the Sergeant barely noted him as he glanced around at the room full of people. It was obvious to Lunt that the Sergeant had rarely been accorded the privilege of socializing at formal dinners. The man looked a little stupefied about what to do next, until Major Pitkan led him by the arm to introduce him to some of the guests.

Henry turned to leave for the service room to help O'Mally strip the covering off the roast beef and pour the steaming gravy into porcelain cups with spouts.

The crowd walked and talked together for another ten minutes. After one uncomfortable round of wine, Sergeant Hensley descended the stairs to supervise the positioning of his soldiers outside Carnarvon House. Behind the closed sliding doors to the dining room, Lunt and O'Mally worked feverishly to lay out the dinner.

When all preparations were completed with the silverware, wine glasses, plates, all in place and the serving trays on the sideboards filled with rich food, it was O'Mally who first sought out van Zoot, and then, with his permission, slid open the doors with a flourish to reveal the dining room with its blazing candelabra, and a magnificent table set for twenty-two.

All of the guests turned at the sound of the sliding door and the bright light which bathed them from above the banquet setting. O'Mally, sporting his white wig, announced in his most perfect English, "Ladies and Gentlemen, dinner is served. May it be memorable."

7
Revelations

Lunt stood near the entrance to the dining room. His breeches and shirt were immaculately white. His straight brown hair was pulled back to form a tight four strand queue at the back of his head. His hawk nose stood out angularly over the meat trolley which he was to supervise during the dinner. He stood rigidly with Entwhistle's carving knife and a sharpener positioned directly in front of him.

The hugh slab of steaming meat would be sufficient for a party of twice this size. Lunt had tasted the meat in the service room. It was excellent as were the sides. The now bound and gagged proprietor and his wife did know their trade. All of the meat, potatoes, and vegetables had been transported in padded cloth warming containers and had remained piping hot. As O'Mally had opened the door to the dining room, the aroma of good food drifted out to the guests.

Although much of the food was ready, the majority of the guests were not coming to the table. They were taking their cue from the Captain who showed no signs of quitting an animated discussion he was having with Lieutenant Dobbs and Mr. Wright.

From across the room, Lunt made brief eye contact with the Captain's Lady, and then looked away. He was pondering the risks of bringing the group some fresh wine to see if he could overhear their conversation. When he looked up again he found that the beautiful lady was approaching him.

"Good evening," she said, "I'm given to understand that your name is Henry."

"Yes, Madame," Lunt replied very deliberately and tried to look away as if some other duties might require his attention.

She would have none of it and stepped closer. The smell of her perfume was compelling.

"You know, our Captain enjoys his food, so you will please see to it that he gets an extra thick cut this evening. And maybe some extra Yorkshire. He'll be on his little diet again tomorrow." She started to turn away and then turned back after glancing down a moment.

"I've been admiring your boots...seems since yesterday. Where did you purchase them? They were much the rage on the Continent last season. I thought I'd like to get a pair for my Captain. Did you find them here in Belfast or from a shop in Dublin...?"

"Alicia," mercifully it was an interruption from some group across the room. "I'll be back for my answer, Henry," she whispered back as she turned to cross the room. Many of the men pivoted to watch her pass by. She smiled to them.

Lunt looked down at the boots with the pointy toes that have been so uncomfortable. Now the damn things could be his undoing. Lunt set about to think of a brief answer that would satisfy the coming inquiry.

Small groups of people started to move towards the dinner table and to take the seats in front of their name cards. Lunt observed that van Zoot and Mr. Wright were now talking enthusiastically and something Wright had said had made van Zoot very happy. The greasy little man was smiling for the first time that evening. The two were about to approach the dining room, when Mr. Wright was hailed by Alicia.

"I'm sorry that there has been a misunderstanding and that your wife could not come. Robert, could I have the favor of your sitting by my side?"

"Eh, yes, Madame," the brown suited man bowed with a smile, conspicuously flattered by the request. At her direction, Mike moved the place cards so that Mr. Wright sat on the other side of the Captain's lady. Alicia smiled at Wright but he looked away, suddenly embarrassed by the special treatment he was receiving.

Van Zoot fumed as his intended plan to talk with Mr. Wright further at the dinner table was foiled. Instead he was surrounded by Lt. Dobbs, his parents, and several gentry, who were inquiring about the firm who were catering the meal. One of the ladies mentioned that she had brought a surprise birthday cake for the Captain, which she had given to the waiter, Michael. Van Zoot nodded his approval. Lt. Dobbs joined his parents, who moved over one chair so that he was seated beside van Zoot, his host. Van Zoot sighed, at least he would have the company of the likely new master of the Drake.

As Mike later passed near the Dobbs group, van Zoot put out his hand to whisper in his ear, "After dinner you'll be serving the birthday cake to the party, and would you sing a few songs as sort of a birthday surprise? I also understand that Lt. Dobbs has something to present to the Captain from the men of the Drake. Finish off with 'Hail Britannia' so that everyone leaves on a happy note."

Mike nodded agreement and then resumed filling the fresh wine glasses around the table.

When Captain Burden took his place at the very end of the table, closest to the drawing room, the remainder of the guests quickly took their places. The Lady Alicia sat to her Captain's left followed by Mr. Wright, to the Captain's right sat Major Pitkan. At the far opposite end of the table sat van Zoot, surrounded by the Dobbs. Henry's meat cart was stationed just inside the drawing room at Captain Burden's end of the table. Above them all hung the huge candelabra, with over a hundred lighted candles.

When Michael completed his tour of the table, which took five bottles of wine to accomplish, van Zoot rose from his place at the host's end of the table, clinking the crystal in front of him lightly with a spoon to get everyone's attention.

He held his wine glass out over the table in the direction of his honoree and stated clearly and dramatically, "To Captain Burden, who has served King and Country faithfully for over forty years."

The guests at the dinner table all rose and raised their wine glasses in salute to the Captain. The glassware sparkled in the hands of the well dressed assemblage. Silver wigs, starched shirts, spotlessly pressed silk waistcoats, and evening gowns adorned their bodies.

"A few words about your career, Captain Burden," asked one well wisher. Burden pulled his large frame up from the chair. His jowls shook and he nodded to his friends about the table. There was just the glimpse of a tear in one eye. He wiped it away and then began to speak.

"Ah, yes, my career. Forty years ago I was a cabin boy, and then a sailmaker, and then boatswain's mate. I came up through the ranks, you see. Finally, it was in India that I was commissioned. Served there eight years as a midshipman. Damn beastly hot place it was. Men died of this or that disease like flies, and pirates. Ah, most people think about the Caribbean when they speak about pirates, but in the southern ocean the word pirate brought new meanings of terror to honest people. We hung many a pirate in those years, particularly in and around the Andaman Islands, below the subcontinent and as far over as the shores of Madagascar. That's an island, larger than England, off the coast of East Africa."

All in the room were silent and respectful to hear their Captain speak of far off places and adventures they could only dream of. He continued for some time.

"Then, there was the French and Indian War. I was in support of General Wolfe in the defeat of Montcalm on the Heights of Abraham in the province of Quebec. In fact that's where I met Major Pitkan here. We were both a bit younger then, eh, Major. I was a bit trimmer and you had bit more hair."

The guests chuckled at the reference. Lunt compared the ribbons on each man's chest. His own father, Michael, had the same blue, yellow, and silver ribbon which each of the two British officers displayed. They were both about the same age as well. His father had fought with the Massachusetts Bay Militia at the same battle, on their side.

Captain Burden took his seat and invited Major Pitkan to speak. The Major put down his glass, looked down the table and began to recall the battle, "To get to the Heights of Abraham, we had to move troops at night across the Lawrence, a large and treacherous river. We were under cannon fire, the current was against us and the weather was horrific. Most of my men couldn't swim. It was in '59. You know who the naval lieutenant was who steered that barge across the river from upper New York to Canada? It was none other that Captain Burden here. A good man to have around in a tight situation. I propose we toast again to the man who helped deliver Canada from the French."

"Here, here," everyone stood, and glasses were raised again.

The Major continued, "So you see, ladies and gentlemen, I was especially pleased to find Captain Burden at this post, when I was assigned here just a few months ago. It was an old comradeship renewed."

"Yes it was," confirmed Burden. "What Major Pitkan has not told you is that he was captured during the last war. You spent how many years as a prisoner of war with the French?"

"Three," revealed Pitkan, "unhappy years."

Lunt began to get very pensive about his mission, when van Zoot interrupted his thoughts by announcing, "We'll likely have much more to tell about. But can I suggest that we let the waiters serve us the food while it's still hot."

Above the warming candle of the service trolley, Lunt began to cut a good sized portion of meat for each guest which O'Mally, with great cordiality, first served on a plate to each lady around the table. Captain Burden's plate was the next to be served. Lunt cut deeply and firmly into the meat so that an extremely large cut resulted, one which nearly filled the entire plate an inch thick. It was blood red in the center and oozed with a rich supply of its own gravy. Upon it Lunt placed the largest Yorkshire pudding in his basket. O'Mally raised an eyebrow when he took it and placed the enormous portion in front of the Captain.

The Captain looked down. His small chin quivered in anticipation, and he remarked, over his shoulder at Lunt, "Why, very generous of you, young chap."

Lunt smiled quietly and continued cutting. After all had been served, he stood at attention and listened to the conversation. O'Mally retired to the service room and continued to refill serving plates of vegetables, potatoes, and the other garnishings which were being consumed.

While they were eating, one of the bankers asked Captain Burden another question, "Sir, before you end your illustrious career, is there one wish that you would make for something you'd still like to accomplish?"

Burden looked down at the dinner plate that he had managed to empty before him. He made one last cut of a remaining piece of meat from a larger piece of gristle. He took the morsel, chewed it thoughtfully, and then spoke, "You know, if I had one last mission to accomplish, I'd like to rid the Irish Sea of this damn pirate chap, Jones or whatever his name is. It's fashionable these days to call this sewer swill, Privateers. The past couple of weeks he has been spotted here and there off the coast of England. He's taken all sorts of plunder from innocent commercial shipping. Tell me he's not in it for the monetary gain. The war with the colonies is just his excuse. If I could get him in my gun sights, I'd blow him out of the water. That'll be my last wish for service to my country, to blow that Yankee pirate to kingdom come."

There was general applause around the table. Robert

Wright spoke up spontaneously, on the strength of several glasses of wine he had consumed, "Wouldn't it be nice to run into him next week, we'd give him a little more firepower than he'd be reckoning from a sloop of war. It'd be a fine test, eh, Lieutenant Dobbs."

Dobbs smiled in reference to Wright's enthusiastic remark, but put his finger to his lips. Wright whispered something to Alicia. She nodded in agreement. Major Pitkan scowled.

Captain Burden discretely changed the flow of conversation, "About a fortnight ago, we had the Drake anchored off of Carrickfergus which, of course, is our normal station from which to protect the lough. We don't like to anchor all the way into the lough, as we are now. It can be difficult to work your way out again in a hurry, if the weather or tide conditions are not just so. You all know that. Well, in the middle of the night, we were closely passed by a small three masted vessel. Since then there has been a rumor that it was the pirate Jones, disguised as a innocent merchantman with his gun ports closed. Anyway they got all caught up in our anchor line. Told the watch they were sorry and drifted by before I was wakened. If they wanted a fight why didn't they simply say so, instead of coming by like thieves in the night."

Major Pitkan added, "I've just come from duty in Boston where I served since '73 and then from Halifax after the evacuation of the Royalists. That's the way they fight on land as well. They squat behind trees and stones, instead of facing us like men in the field of honor. It was the same way on the Heights of Abraham, those colonial regiments would not stand up and fight with the regulars. Did they, Captain?"

Burden moved his head in a signal of agreement.

"That reminds me," spoke up Burden. "Has anyone ever seen this sort of an implement before?" The Captain pulled a large hook with a cork attached to it from beneath his dress coat. "It was found stuck into the hull of the Drake. Perhaps some of you hadn't heard, just after twilight yesterday, we had an intruder aboard the Drake. I brought this over for all of you to see, because it has to be a common implement of some trade. I just can't place it, I've seen it before though. I thought that, as many of you are from different professions, you might have a look and see if you can identify it for me."

The eyes of everyone at the table were fixed on the implement as Burden began a lengthy account of the discovery of the intruder and the subsequent search. Slowly, Lunt took off his apron, left it by the meat service trolley and began to slip as inconspicuously as possible around the dining room table towards the door to the service room.

News of an intruder brought a hush to the table. Mr. Wright motioned for the implement to be handed across the table to him. Alicia looked at it a moment, and then glanced over her shoulder towards the empty trolley and then back at the Captain who was still describing the previous night's events. Major Pitkan was passed the implement and speculated, "Because it's made of cast iron, it must be from a mold. And since it was not individually tooled, there must have been a lot of them made. If we can identify the trade it's from, we might be able to trace the source of the intruder."

While still listening carefully to the discussion around the dinner table, Lunt slowly opened the door to the service room and departed the dining room.

Wright asked of Burden, "Did the intruder see anything of what we were doing? The, eh ...device, is still in its carton?"

"Yes, assuredly," said Captain Burden. "My marines think that they may have killed or wounded the man. But we have searched all day without finding a body. I'm inclined to think it was just a common theft attempt," added Burden.

From the far end of the table, Lieutenant Dobbs spoke up, "We checked the Drake over thoroughly today, nothing seems to have been disturbed."

"Well, whatever clues any of you can offer, we'd appreciate your input," directed Captain Burden to his guests at large. "Please pass that implement about and see if anyone recognizes it."

The conversation continued along the same lines for several minutes, while in the service room Lunt whispered to O'Mally, their heads side by side.

"They have not discovered that the Drake's anchor chain has been severed but it looks like the cat will be out of the bag in an moment. I want you to take the remnants of our canvas bag with you. Walk down the stairway and get into your cart as if you're starting to pack up to leave. Tell them you're going for a larger cart. Take a few of the larger dishes with you to make it look like everything is finishing up. Walk slowly away until you round the corner. Get one of the horses at the alehouse, and ride like the world is going to end to get to Carrickfergus.

"What's afoot, Henry, I thought we were going to serve them dinner and quietly leave after they depart?"

"They're passing the meat hook around now to see if anyone knows what it is. I believe the Captain's Lady may have figured it out. It won't be long before they connect the meat cutter with the meat hook."

O'Mally eyes enlarged.

"You warned your brother-in-law, like I told you, to take the rest of those hooks out of his meat locker, and to hide the money you gave him, and to say he didn't know who you were if asked?"

"Aye, twice, and he's the nervous type, probably has buried the money and hooks a mile or so into the woods."

"Good," said Lunt. "Now leave, I'll keep them busy for as long as I can. Tell Captain Jones to either come in and take her tonight and take advantage of the severed rudder chain, or to expect the Drake at Carrickfergus in the morning. That lying Captain Burden will never be able to say he didn't receive this, his third invitation to fight. Not after his last career wish a few minutes ago."

Lunt reached in his canvas bag and drew out a wad of heavy canvas material, which he unfolded to reveal his lieutenant's waistcoat and a slightly crushed tricornered hat, complete with red, white, and blue cockade.

"Oh, good Jesus, you brought your uniform here," quivered O'Mally looking back nervously over his shoulder. "Think man,...think of sweet little Sarah, having to raise your child alone. Let's wait it out. We may not be discovered. If we are, we'll fight it out together." O'Mally was wringing his hands in anguish, he was visibly crying.

Lunt hurriedly put on his uniform while he talked, "The point is to get the Drake, above all to get the Drake, and there is no other way now but to publicly embarrass the Captain into taking her out to face Ranger, especially after that bravado in front of all of Belfast's gentry. He'll have to do it........"

Behind them the door squeaked a little and van Zoot peered in, but could not clearly see the partly uniformed Lunt, who was squatting on the other side of O'Mally. "You about ready to sing some songs and then serve the birthday cake?"

"Rr.. ready in a few minutes," snapped O'Mally. The swinging door closed again.

"Ya see, Henry, they're ready for the entertainment. You have not been discovered. Think man, think of your wonderful family."

Lunt stooped to take one of three heavy round objects out of a special pocket in the side of the canvas bag. When he pulled it completely out of the bag, O'Mally shook his head.

Lunt asked calmly, holding the round cast iron ball in his hand, "Are naval grenades still calibrated at five seconds, as much as these things can be timed?" O'Mally nodded, his eyes filled with tears. "Then, I'll make this one about...one and a half."

Lunt held the naval grenade in his left hand and cut

two thirds of the fuse off with the sharp knife he had used to cut the meat earlier. He looked up at O'Mally who said, "They'll hang you."

"They probably will. It's time to go, my friend. If they take action before I do, we'll both be lost, and so will the opportunity to take the Drake."

Lunt withdrew two pistols from his canvas bag and stuck them neatly into his breeches, so that the cover of his naval waistcoat just covered their handles. He then reached in and brought out the short sword and scabbard which Captain Jones had given him before his departure from the Ranger. He used its leather belt to fasten it about his waist. He took one of the pistols, checked its prime, and tightened the lock of its flint with his thumbnail. Then he looked up. "Why are you still here?"

O'Mally fell on him, tears streaming from his eyes, and hugged him tightly for a long moment. Lunt pushed him off. "There are two pistols and two grenades left. Try and take the canvas bag with you. The potato's in it, wrapped in a patch of flannel so that there'll be no misleading marks. Captain Jones can finish off those ships as well, if he comes in for the Drake tonight. Make sure you tell the Captain about their weapon. It is made by the Carron Company from a place called Stromeferry, wherever that is. You must get this information to Jones. I will endeavor by my challenge to make the Drake come out tomorrow morning. Tell Captain Jones to be ready."

O'Mally started to object again but Lunt continued, "Sean, if they ask to search you downstairs, blow that Sergeant to hell. A lot of Irishmen will be proud of you."

Lunt lifted the canvas bag up for his friend to take.

O'Mally nodded teary eyed and walked out the far door to the service room which opened out to the top of the stairs. He kept his body as close to the stairway wall as possible, so that Captain Burden's end of the table would not notice his departure. Lunt heard him descend the first few stairs.

After that, the noise from the dinner party drowned out any possibility of hearing further footsteps. He probably would not be able to hear O'Mally pass through the guards outside, or drive away. But if there was a pistol shot, Lunt was ready to take the necessary action. On the other side of the wall the diners were laughing. Lunt's mind raced. This was going to be it. The most important few minutes of his life. He might be dead within moments, or face a hanging in the morning. Would Sarah ever find out what had happened to him? Did he have another child, from their brief weeks together last summer? Had his father put the new veranda onto their Newburyport home, or was he at war as well? How bad were things in Newburyport? Likely he would never know the answers to those questions, but what he was about to do needed to be done. It was certainly better than rotting in a stinking prison, smelling your own defecation day after day because the guards were too afraid and too ignorant to let the men out. Lunt straightened his tricornered hat so that it was as perfectly aligned as he could make it.

From behind him, the door was pushed ajar again, "Is the entertainment ready?" van Zoot inquired in a irritated tone.

"Make your introduction," said Lunt. He made no attempt to disguise his Yankee accent. There was a slight hesitation, but the swinging door closed again. Through the wall he heard van Zoot tap his spoon against something that gave off a shrill noise. The voices about the dining table stopped for a moment, as their host said something about entertainment.

Lunt took a deep breath and then, feeling that it was not enough to calm him, he took another slowly. He had to get beside Captain Burden quickly or it wouldn't work. He hadn't heard any unusual noise from the courtyard below so O'Mally must have gotten through the guards. He held one of his pistols cocked in his right hand, the short officer's sword dangled by the hand guard from the little finger of the left hand which otherwise clutched firmly the dark, round, black ball of a naval grenade, its fuse cut short to the quip. His last thought before pushing through the door was, "This is your moment, Henry Lunt, make it your best."

Lunt pushed open the door through which O'Mally had departed just a few minutes earlier. He walked tall and erect across the foyer at the top of the staircase and then into the drawing room. He stopped in a position behind and to the left of Captain Burden, where Major Pitkan would be less likely to make a dive for his weapon. Most of the table was already looking in his direction, waiting for the Irish tenor to appear. They stared at Lunt, not knowing what to perceive. While continuing to chew some food, the Captain pushed his chair back and around a few inches and stared at the strangely uniformed man.

Lunt stood before the table, his pistol leveled across the table in general. His eye watchful to the right. He spoke in a clear, strong New England accent, with its characteristically crisp nasal twang, "Ladies and gentlemen, my name is Lieutenant Henry Lunt of the American Continental Ship of War, Ranger. I serve under the authority of Captain John Paul Jones and you are all my prisoners."

There was a long moment of silence. Some eyes staring at him expressed instant fear and hatred, but most were totally expressionless. Like a herd of sheep, they appeared puzzled and looked to one another for direction as to what to believe. Was this the beginning of the entertainment?

Someone shouted, "It's your birthday wish, Captain Burden."

The laughter started somewhere from one of the middle seats. It was a nervous laugh, one which attempts to overcome peril by pretending it away. It became infectious as each contributor tried to chase away the brief moment of terror that they all felt by also taking up the laughter. This was to be thrilling entertainment, that was all. But the dark side of each dinner guest's brain told them that this somehow seemed all too real.

The laughter reached the very ends of the table, overtaking Captain Burden himself. His head tilted back. His great jowls bounced in rhythm with his great whale like belly rolling in merriment beneath the white breeches and vest, whose immaculate white expanse was only interrupted by the column of gold buttons which prevented his great protuberance from showing itself to the world.

Determined to be taken seriously, Lunt pointed the barrel of his gun directly into Captain Burden's face. The motion caught the man midway through one laugh, but the surrounding laughter urged him to exhale a few more bellows before quieting.

Lunt looked him straight in the eye and said, "This, sir, is no jest." With his left foot he pulled the meat trolley within reach. He placed the grenade on its corner and with his sword now firmly in his grip he impaled the largest remaining piece of roast beef, and held it up high for the dinner guests to see. A few continued to laugh, as drops of gravy dripped from the fresh impalement. Lunt swung the blade and its burden across the table and placed the dripping chunk of blood red meat directly on the Captain's immaculate white stomach. He kept the sword in position through the meat, with the Captain pinned below it.

"Oh, my gawd," shrieked one lady. Several chairs were pushed back from the table.

Lunt spoke up commandingly, "If any man or woman cries out or moves from their chair or makes any effort to interrupt me, I shall be forced to blow your esteemed Captain's brains across this room. Believe me, it is not my desire to have to do so."

Lunt's eyes looked past the now slouching Burden towards Major Pitkan, who resembled a cat getting ready to pounce. The last sentence calmed the dinner table from reaction out of sheer terror. They were dealing with someone with a purpose, not just a blind madman who wanted to kill them all.

Lunt continued to choose his words, deliberately and cautiously, "For the third time in a fortnight, Captain Burden, our vessel does challenge yours to meet us on the high seas. We propose you meet our Ranger at Carrickfergus tomorrow morning, or we intend to lay havoc to your harbour and all its ships, should you again ignore our challenge. The choice, sir, is yours."

Lunt held the oozing slab of meat still pressed onto the Captain's chest with the point of his sword. In his right hand, his pistol pointed directly at the Captain's head at less than two feet away. But the man did not tremble, he looked resolute despite his awkward position. Two determined black eyes set amidst a large moon face studied Lunt.

"Sir, I have never received a challenge from the Ranger or your Captain, for had it been so, I would have been there."

"But, sir," pressed Lunt. "My information is that you have been challenged twice before and both times you have chosen to ignore it."

"When and where?" demanded Burden. "And could you kindly remove this slab of hot meat from my chest, it is damn uncomfortable. You have made your point."

Lunt pushed in on his sword which caused one squeamish dinner observer to gasp as she saw fresh red fluid suddenly pour from the Captain's midsection. With the sword held in his left hand, Lunt retrieved the side of meat and placed it on the Captain's plate. His great white uniformed chest and stomach looked as if they had served as the primary destination for a cannon ball. An oval pool of blood red, natural gravy adorned his front. Here and there a colored drip line left a trail where a streamlet of blood had trickled off onto the floor.

Realizing he was vulnerable with just a pistol, Lunt used his sword to tip the meat tray off the trolley which clattered to the floor. The base warming candle was now left exposed to the air. Quickly, Lunt put his sword down on the trolley rim and picked up the round iron ball that he had placed there, just a moment before.

"Ladies and gentleman, for those of you not familiar with the tools of warfare at sea, this is a naval grenade and you can see that the fuse is extremely short. I have cut it that way myself. You see, when this fuse is brought in contact with ...," Lunt waved the iron ball perilously close to the candle, "...this warming candle, it will be only the blink of an eye before there is an explosion. It will very likely kill us all."

Several of the dinner guests moaned, but kept their wide eyes on Lunt's left hand which he held less than a foot from the candle flame.

"I repeat," emphasized Lunt, "that I have no purpose here but to establish this military challenge and then to return to my ship. I wish to harm neither any civilian nor any of the King's officers while they are my prisoners. Remain calm, quiet, and in your seats, and no harm will befall anyone in this room."

"Lieutenant Lunt," it was Major Pitkan who spoke up. "When and where did you present these challenges to the Drake?"

"I did not deliver these challenges myself but it is my understanding that one was delivered over a week ago, and the other four days ago."

"To what place were they delivered?"

"As I understand it, both were delivered to the Captain's flat. It was too dangerous for our agent to try and deliver such a written challenge directly to the Drake. I know that the second was delivered in a small package and was signed for."

"Truly, I have never seen such challenges," offered Burden. Then looking past the barrel of Lunt's pistol, he said, "Alicia, did you receive them?"

The woman to Lunt's left looked down and placed a handkerchief to her face. She did not answer, but seemed to sob into her handkerchief.

From the far end of the room there was a persistent chime of silverware on china. Lunt glanced up. Lieutenant Dobbs was spinning a spoon on a desert plate. He was looking at Lunt with vengeful eyes, his high cheekbones revealed a gaunt aspect under the lights of the overhead candelabra.

Dobbs spoke up as he continued to twirl his spoon gratingly on the empty plate, "You know you are going to hang, Lieutenant Lunt. You were here in our presence without a uniform most of the evening. Tush, tush. Just how do you figure that you are going to get away? A platoon of sixty four crack soldiers led by the fiercest sergeant in the regiment sits just a loud holler away. From one lieutenant to another, this was a very foolish operation. It does not speak well of your Captain."

Just then, the service door at Dobbs' end of the dining room pushed open, and from the other room came an eerie glow. Lunt tensed and looked to his military prisoners, who had also turned their heads at the distraction. A cart rolled forward with a birthday cake complete with lighted candles. Finally, a bright red head of hair appeared pushing the cart.

Lunt grinned in relief that he was not alone. The man the dinner guests had known as Michael smiled and spoke, "Ladies and gentlemen, I could not bear the thought of this beautiful cake going to waste."

O'Mally held a pistol in each hand and pointed them over the top of the lighted birthday cake. Beside the cake stood a stack of dessert dishes behind which were two more naval grenades, each visible to the occupants of the room. The wicks had also been shortened.

"We're all going to stay clam, aren't we?" O'Mally spoke soothingly with a soft Irish brogue, his deceivingly happy eyes danced about. He looked down at van Zoot who was perspiring heavily, "I promised you a memorable dinner, Mr.

van Zoot, let's finish it, shall we."

O'Mally pointed to the grenades and said with a broad smile directed at the entire table, "Oh, and do remember, me darlings, that we Irish are well known for having a very short fuse." There was another series of shrieks and moans from among the civilian guests.

O'Mally put down one of his pistols and took up a cake cutter. He began to cut pieces of cake, some with burning candles fell over on their plates as O'Mally sliced each piece. His hand visibly shook as he transferred them one at a time to van Zoot. "Pass the cakes along, Mr. van Zoot, if you please. We're all going to enjoy the Captain's birthday party and then, two by two, you'll all come with me for a trip up the stairs to some guest rooms I know on the third floor above. Let's be eating our cake now. Everyone's hands above the table, if you please."

Major Pitkan spoke up calmly, "Lieutenant Lunt, I'd like to continue with our little discussion." He looked across the table and spoke sharply, "What happened to the challenges, Alicia?"

Alicia looked up from the handkerchief that covered her face. She looked directly at Captain Burden, who was studying her with closely discerning eyes, "I didn't tell you, darling, because I didn't want you to be hurt. You're going to be retiring soon. I thought they'd just, go away!" She started crying into her handkerchief.

Pitkan commented dryly, not convinced, "Very selfless and touching, my dear. If your love for Captain Burden is so complete why did you need to exchange rather passionate kisses with Lieutenant Dobbs yesterday morning in a little side escapade at the fox hunt?"

A shocked reaction went up and down the table. Alicia looked down. At the far end of the table, Lt. Dobbs' mother uttered, "William, you never."

Dobbs snapped, "Shut up, mother," and resumed the twirling of his spoon upon its plate. The grating sound was unnerving every one of the guests. O'Mally reached across the birthday cake and thumped the Lieutenant's arm with the barrel of his pistol. "If you speak to your mother like that again, or if you continue twirling that spoon, I'm going to personally break your fingers, one by one."

Lt. Dobbs glared at him in hatred, but ceased the movement. The hearts of the remainder of the dinner guests pounded in numb terror while a few of their number continued the bizarre conversation. At the far end of the table, Major Pitkan smiled to himself.

"What do you say to this, Alicia?" demanded Burden, obviously in distress.

Alicia looked up at her Captain. "It was just a small flirtation, just a quick moment, that's all. I pulled away from him and rode off. I haven't said a word to him since."

Major Pitkan spoke again, "There's more, I'm sorry to say, old friend." He looked with sad eyes at Captain Burden and then continued, "I've been having your Alicia watched. Last Wednesday, when you were starting construction of the ...eh, special platform on board Drake, and had to be present to move positions of some of the Drake's rigging to accomplish it, why did Mr. Wright visit your apartments in midday for a span of four and a half hours?"

Wright looked down and folded his fingers on his chest. He said nothing in defense.

The Major continued, "Either we have one of the most sexually adventuresome women in the world in our presence or there is another purpose." Alicia suddenly sat straight up in her chair, her attempt at crying her way out of the situation now cast aside. She glared angrily at Major Pitkan who continued to unravel the mysteries surrounding this dinner.

"Why, Mr. van Zoot, was Mr. Wright's wife left off the invitation list?"

Van Zoot was quick to turn around the possible allegation. "It was the Captain's Lady who prepared the guest list for me. As I told you this afternoon, I was just seeking commercial contacts. I was not even told the Captain was retiring, otherwise I would likely never have paid for a dinner in his honor." About him, people looked shocked at the statement. "I'm sorry, but it's true," said van Zoot after a few seconds pause.

"And likewise, Alicia would have seen to it that Lieutenant Dobbs' parents received their last minute invitation to this dinner. It would keep the likely future commander of the Drake busy until she was ready to use him," added Pitkan, who directed his next question back across the table.

"Mr. Wright, what do you have to say?" Wright shook his head slowly and continued to look downward. His silence seemingly an admission of some guilt.

Lunt stood with the gun still leveled at Captain Burden's head. His intensely intelligent eyes occasionally flashed about to the other occupants of the dinner table. He wanted to hear this out. It might lead to an answer that would reveal why the Drake was of such intense interest. He let Major Pitkan continue his line of questioning.

"Isn't it an interesting coincidence that our Alicia has had a liaison with the two, nay, three most important men in the little experiment going on aboard the Drake."

Major Pitkan turned towards Lunt and nodded his bald head towards the meat hook now lying in the center of the table. "Lieutenant Lunt, is that your hook? Were you our intruder aboard the Drake yesterday evening?"

Lunt nodded.

"What kind of an implement is it, we're all curious."

Lunt made brief eye contact with O'Mally who had just finished passing the last piece of cake to van Zoot. Lunt decided to leave a white lie to protect O'Mally's relations.

Lunt explained, pointing with his pistol, "It's a meat hook. It was lodged in the side of beef sitting at Entwhistle's, the caterers. I took it from there to help get aboard Drake, but I didn't get far."

"Good," said Major Pitkan. "Now we are back to the

motives of the Captain's Lady. It's very good of your Captain Jones to send you here this evening, Lieutenant Lunt, seems that we did not get all the foxes yesterday morning. May I be permitted, Lieutenant Lunt, to put my hand just inside my uniform's lapel to withdraw a letter?"

Lunt nodded and shifted the barrel of his pistol to point just past the head of Captain Burden, directly at the Major. With his left hand he continued to hold the short fused grenade threateningly. Slowly and deliberately, Major Pitkan folded back the lapel of his uniform. From an inside pocket, the corner of an envelope protruded. Slowly, the Major withdrew the missive and then looked at Captain Burden.

"You see, old friend, you're not the man you once were. None of us really are, myself included." Burden turned his head over his right shoulder to look directly into his friend's eyes. The Major continued, "A month ago, when I first arrived here from duty in Halifax, I wondered why such an enormously beautiful, younger woman would have taken such an interest in you. I knew you did not receive your commission through family ties as so many others have in our service. You had no great fortune coming to you after retirement. At first, frankly I was rather jealous of your good luck. But then I began to notice things. How much she seemed to be in control of your life. That you tended to stay with her in that apartment, rather than on your ship. That she seemed so well informed about your activities. Ordinarily, for a routine defensive mission in a relatively unimportant port like Belfast, who would care?"

"But, after awhile it became apparent to me that the Drake was being signaled out for special testing. Lieutenant Dobbs had been reassigned from Reliance, a top front line man of war, in order to take command of a relatively small sloop of war. So one day, over a month ago, I took the liberty of asking the Captain's Lady of her origins. She was very evasive, but I got some details out of her. She said she was from Limerick, in the south of Ireland. She did not know that I had an acquaintance there, a colonel in the local militia. This is his letter. I received it only three days ago by morning post. That was the same day I started watching the Lady's flat. The very day Mr. Wright here, of our shipbuilding operation, spent a rather long tea time at her flat rather than his own. Goodness knows how many times he has been there before."

Major Pitkan slowly and deliberately opened the letter. The sweat on top of his bald head glistened in the light of the candelabra as he looked directly across the table at the woman with the white shoulders, bewitching eyes, and deep cleavage, above which hung a cluster of white porcelain beads.

"*My dear Major Pitkan,*" he started to read. "*It was a pleasure to hear from you after so many years. I hope the years have been as good to you as they have to me.*"

Each time that he completed a sentence from the letter and glanced up to measure its effect, Alicia's green eyes glared directly back into his.

"*Regarding the Lady Alicia Warren, I regret to inform you she passed away on November the 16th of last year. I believe that she died of pneumonia, this being a very damp place in the winter. I'm given to understand that she was a very short, heavy set woman with dark black hair and a large black mold on her right cheek.*"

The Major folded his letter and returned it into its envelope. He looked up directly into the beautiful but deceitful face across the table. His friend, Captain Burden, had placed both of his hands in front of his own face in anguish. "Did you get that name from an obituary column? It was just about five months ago that you came to Belfast, wasn't it? Just who are you, Alicia?"

O'Mally spoke up, "Reverend and Mrs. Dobbs, and the next couple, Roberts is it?" The banker and his wife nodded. "I'm going to ask you to come up the stairs. Absolutely no harm 'twill come to you, if ye behave yerselves." O'Mally motioned for them to rise.

"You won't hurt my boy will you?" said the minister hesitating, apparently afraid for his son.

"No, Reverend, not unless he does something foolish," replied O'Mally in a calming voice.

The party of four arose and walked out around the dining room table, ahead of O'Mally who carried two pistols leveled and had wedged one grenade under each arm, pressed close to his body. As he passed close to Lt. Lunt he placed one of the grenades on the meat table, a foot from the burning candle.

"Can ye hold 'em?" he whispered.

"I did before you came," said Lunt. "Now there will be less of them to watch."

After O'Mally and his party of four disappeared up the stairway to the floor above, there was a sharp series of movements to his left. The brown suited Mr. Wright was struggling with the Captain's Lady. Lunt could do nothing but keep his gun leveled at Captain Burden's head. He held the grenade high for the other people at the dinner table to remain aware of the threat. Finally, in the midst of the struggle, he saw the woman called Alicia form her right hand into a fist and punch Wright directly in his adam's apple. The man gurgled and fell over onto the floor, a small pocket pistol fell to the floor at Lunt's feet. Lunt placed his boot on it.

Wright sat up and coughed violently, while clutching his throat. He was spitting up blood.

Alicia snarled at him, "When you sleep with a lady, she learns all your secrets." Alicia turned and looked up into Lunt's eyes. Amidst a background of coughing, she stated, "Lieutenant, I need to escape with you, please. I can help you with your prisoners."

Lunt's mind raced. It might be acceptable for the two servants to leave before the rest of the diners. After they secured everyone into an upper room, they could haul down a group of dishes for show and wheel the cart away. If they weren't searched coming out and could just get out of musket range of the military guards, they had a small chance to make it to O'Mally's horses. But there were only two horses. Taking a third person, of whose motives he was uncertain, was an impossibility. Lunt looked at her and shook his head.

"I don't know who you are, or what you are up to, madame. I can't be expected to take you on an escape plan designed for only two." He saw Major Pitkan smile.

When O'Mally returned alone, Lunt stooped and picked up the small pistol and placed it in the pocket of his uniform jacket. He looked down at his principal prisoner.

"The question now, Captain Burden, is will you meet the Ranger tomorrow morning at Carrickfergus? I do apologize for questioning your courage and integrity. It seems there were more complex plots going on in your world. I'm sorry for them and for the destruction to your uniform."

Burden nodded, made a disdainful glance at his former mistress, and then replied, "The Drake shall be there, sir. But I feel that unless you surrender to me now, that you will not live to find out the outcome."

"Really, Captain, in the light of what has happened, an inquiry would be in order," said one of the magistrates. "The Governor General will have to be consulted, before you engage in such a reckless endeavor."

Burden spoke up firmly, "This evening I'm still the senior naval officer present in Belfast. I know for a fact that the Governor General is far away from Dublin, otherwise he might have been at this dinner. Thank God for small blessings that he wasn't. I have not been relieved, and I am fully capable and determined to meet the challenges placed to my country."

Burden put his hand to his eye and pushed away a tear. He continued to speak, "There is an old saying, that there is no fool like an old fool. I have attained a new level of understanding of that adage. I suspect that many of us at this table, who have had their lives and careers disrupted this evening, will for one reason or another desire to reclaim at least a portion of their honor aboard the Drake. Am I right, Lieutenant Dobbs, Mr. Wright?"

Burden focused on his captor, whose pistol was resolutely aimed at his face. "Now, Lieutenant Lunt, will you surrender to me? I promise you humane treatment."

"Sir, I am still the one holding the pistols and the grenades, so I shall not surrender, but I expect you to keep your promise and to meet my ship tomorrow, whatever befalls me," stated Lunt.

"The Drake will be there, may God have mercy on your soul," said Burden.

Before one of the English officers could contemplate doing anything, Lunt spoke to O'Mally, "I think it's best if we move the entire party upstairs at once. I'll take the lead with a candle and two of the short fused grenades. You take up the rear with pistols at the ready."

Lunt asked of his companion, "Can you first cut a couple of long lengths of rope from the curtain sashes, and take a half dozen forks up with you, and two of the candles off of the candelabra?"

O'Mally looked at Lunt curiously but collected the items without question. The entire assemblage watched in wonder, while O'Mally performed the tasks.

Lunt put the second pistol into his breeches and then motioned for everyone to rise. He started to walk up the dark stairway backwards, holding the candle in one hand and one of the short fused grenades in the other. A second grenade was wedged into the crook of his arm. His prisoners were told to follow him up the stairs, O'Mally took up the rear.

The woman called Alicia continued to try and persuade Lunt to listen to her, but he advised, "We'll speak upstairs, when the rest of the prisoners are under lock and key."

Captain Burden, Major Pitkan, and Lt. Dobbs formed the first row ascending the stairs following Lunt. At one point, Lunt momentarily slipped and the trio started to rushed forward. But he quickly recovered and brought the short fuse to within a few inches of the candle. Rather than face a deadly explosion, they all backed off.

At the top of the stairs, Lunt said, "Which way?"

"Down the corridor, first door on your left," said O'Mally.

Lunt followed O'Mally's directions and found a single raw candle burning on a table of the large guest room with two beds. There were two doors, very likely closets of some kind. One of the doors was shut, apparently where O'Mally had put the first four prisoners. From the other side of the door, Lunt could hear the voices of the Dobbses and Roberts, whispering. Lunt let all of the remaining prisoners precede him into the large bedroom. He directed them into a corner.

Lunt gave the candle and the two short fused grenades to O'Mally. He then took the items he had requested O'Mally to gather below. He tied one end of the drapery cord in a bowline knot to the door knob of the closet and its other end to one of the unlit candles. He stood the unlit candle upright to the side of the door. He dug the prongs of two forks deeply into the floor to channel the direction of the falling candle. Lastly, he placed the grenade on its side in the path which the candle might be pulled if the closet door were to be opened.

Lunt spoke to his prisoners, "This is what I wanted you all to see. I'll also be setting up this sort of arrangement in the companion closet for the rest of you. If you push open the door before the candle burns down, the cord will pull the candle forwards. It'll fall between the two forks where it will certainly make contact with the fuse of the grenade you see lying on its side. Once it does, you'll all be blown to kingdom come.

"So I'd advise strongly that you look under the crack beneath the door, and wait until you see the candle light burn out before you smash the door down. Otherwise there'll be a lot of dead people at this range. And you know, with one grenade going off, the other beside it will likely be set off as well. You never know about these things. I wouldn't try to burst out until both candles burn themselves out. I will see to it that both candles are well sealed down to the floor with wet candle wax. I'd judge there'll be about an hour or so more left in each candle. It's windowless here and from the third floor of the back of this mansion house, I doubt if shouting will draw the attention of Sergeant Major Hensley below."

The assemblage looked at Lunt somberly as he used the key to turn the latch of the door in which the first four prisoners were confined. The unlit candle was pulled between the two forks and fell right beside the grenade as Lunt had predicted. He picked up his implements and ushered most of the military into the closet with the two older couples. Pitkan, van Zoot, and the others were ushered into the second closet. O'Mally stood guard at the bedroom door with pistols poised.

Lunt set up the trap at the first closet door which contained the military. He then turned to the Lady Alicia who waited at the door to the second closet. Her eyes pleaded with Lunt to take her.

Lunt whispered, "There's only a moment or two to talk and I want you to tell me everything, or I'll leave you here."

Inside the first closet, Major Pitkan whispered for his fellow prisoners to be quiet. He pressed his ear to the crack in the door and strained to listen.

"I'm the agent of a continental power. Your Spymaster knows who I am."

"Really," Lunt said in disgust, and pointed with his pistol for her to enter the other closet.

"Please, outside," she put her fingers to her lips and pointed towards the first closet. She did not want to be overheard. Not wanting another mention of the word Spymaster in front of the British, Lunt acceded and ushered her out of the guest room towards the stairs. Pausing at the top of the stairs, he said, "The truth then, or we'll leave you to the fate you have made for yourself."

She whispered to him, "My name is Marie Chatelain, I am an agent of Louis the XVI. At first, I thought because of your French boots that you were a careless agent sent to help me. Your Spymaster, the one who uses the little telescope and the severed snake stamp, knows me."

"No one knows who the Spymaster is."

"We have our suspicions."

"I don't have time to discuss suspicions. What secret does the Drake possess? The answer or I leave you here."

The lady in the white gown sighed, "They have the Carronade."

"The what?" said Lunt.

Alicia's true French accent began to emerge as she continued to whisper to him, "It is half the length and weight of a traditional eight pounder, yet it can throw a ball of eighteen or twenty pounds over a thousand paces."

"Impossible," said Lunt.

She looked at Lunt. "They've done something, I have not found out what, to the design of the barrel to make the shell go further than ever before. An alteration of the dimensions of a lighter round fired from the same carronade can increase the range of that lighter round dramatically. A eight pound ball can do better than three thousand paces, while a traditional naval cannon can only fire two thirds that distance."

She continued with an intensity that Lunt had never before seen in a woman, "Think of it, Lieutenant Lunt, if we can capture this secret, your light weight American corvette could out sail and have greater firepower than a frigate. You have to take me with you."

"Why, if you don't know the design secrets to this miracle weapon?" said Lunt.

"Because I am the only prize that will bring the Drake out of Belfast Harbour to meet the Ranger."

"The Captain promised."

"Promises are for children, not great military powers, Lieutenant Lunt. With what Captain Burden, Lt. Dobbs, and the others have done, within an hour they will be relieved of their command by the local magistrates. Certainly, Captain Burden would like to take the Drake out against you to defend his honor, so would Dobbs and Wright, but they won't be allowed to. You heard some of the civilian disapproval beginning already downstairs. Don't you see."

Alicia continued her line of reasoning, "The only way that you can be sure that the Drake will meet the Ranger at Carrickfergus is if I'm aboard. They do not know how much I know, and they must get me back, before they lose the secret of the carronade. That is the only thing that will, with certainty, cause the Drake to meet the Ranger tomorrow. Nothing else.

"And, there is another reason you should take me!"

"What's that?" snapped Lunt, realizing very uncomfortably that O'Mally and he had just joined company with a very persuasive individual.

"Your Ambassador Franklin has been urging France to declare war on England, in order to come to the assistance of the American Revolution. But Admiral D'Orvilles of the French fleet will advise Louis not to do so, if he feels that England has such a superior weapon aboard her ships and he does not."

As Lunt, O'Mally, and the former Lady Alicia descended the stairs, Major Pitkan gloomily watched the flickering light of a candle from beneath the door of his temporary closet prison. One word he had heard Alicia say reverberated back and forth in his head with the force of an exploding cannonball, "Spymaster, Spymaster, Spy......"

8
Escape

Sergeant Major Hensley was questioning one of his troops about dirt on his cross strap when the Lady Alicia came out of the front door of Carnarvon House. She was accompanied by the two Irish servants, Michael and Henry. All evening Sergeant Hensley had kept thinking of them as being particularly familiar. Somewhere recently he had seen that distinctive hawk nose and the red mop of hair on the smaller man. Where was it? Well, he passed many people in the streets of Belfast every day. The rest of the party must be getting ready to leave earlier than expected. He called his troops to attention.

The Lady Alicia was walking down the stairs alone. She held a handkerchief to her face and seemed to be crying. Damn females, what was wrong? Where were the officers, and her Captain, or even Major Pitkan, or that Lieutenant Dobbs, can't imagine he'd let her leave alone?

Sergeant Major Hensley, tough leader of men, veteran of action after action in the service of the crown, placed his foot into the stirrup and easily swung himself into the saddle of his giant spotted mare. He met the threesome just before they reached the hansen.

"Pardon me, Madame, is the dinner party over?"

"No, it'll go on a bit but I have a cold coming on. The affair will likely continue for hours. The Captain and the Major are telling old war stories about the capture of Montreal, and I didn't have the heart to make them leave. They're having such a good time." She sneezed once, and then again. "Besides, as you know I don't enjoy stories of intrigue and violence. They thought it best that the two servants take me home, and then return with the hansen for Captain Burden."

"No, Madame, I can't allow that," said Hensley.

"But,.."

"Madame, the reason we're here tonight is to protect you. I can't let you go home with them. Corporal Higgins will help you." The Sergeant Major turned and called for the man, "Take the Lady Alicia to her home and check her flat, and then come back with the Captain's hansen."

The Corporal saluted and then helped the Lady Alicia into the carriage. She smelled so good. He'd be the envy of the boys for this duty. He'd try and delay returning as long as possible to give them a tease as to what he had been doing alone with the Captain's Lady.

The hansen drove away. The two servants started to put their dishes into their wagon.

The Sergeant looked down at them, "Are you sure you're not wanted?"

"No, sir, they're talking military stuff up there. They really didn't want us to remain. In fact, they kinda requested us ta leave," explained the red headed man. He held a canvas bag in his right hand.

Hensley decided he'd have a look inside before he let them leave, so many servants were stealing things these days. He didn't have to be courteous with them, he'd just order them to open the bag when he came back out.

"Remain here, 'til I verify this."

The Sergeant turned his horse, rode back to the stairs, and dismounted. He strode up the stairs and, before entering the mansion, he took off his ornate helmet and put it in the crook of his arm. He quickly brushed his hair into place, and then proceeded to open the door and take the stairs one at a time, listening. He could not hear any sound. They must be praying or whispering. He hesitated, years of formal training had conditioned him not to break in on officers, even when there were civilians around. Major Pitkan was a good officer, strong and tough, he wouldn't have let the Lady go if it weren't all right.

Hensley paused a few more moments. Damn funny that I can't hear 'em at all, he thought. Damn funny too that they would have the servants all leave. Maybe they were talking about the little cannon and didn't want anyone to overhear the conversation. Maybe that's why they wanted the Lady Alicia to go. The Major had said that he didn't trust her. Slowly, Hensley strode up the stairs. Still no sound. Wait, he heard something distant coming from upstairs, in the darkness.

He came to the top of the first flight of stairs and peered around the corner. The dinner table was still set. The dishes were dirty, the waiters would have never been permitted to leave a table in that mess. The overhead candles were still lighted. There was uneaten birthday cake in front of most of the places. The birthday candles had all gone out, but they had burned down to the frosting. Something was terribly wrong. He heard sounds, where was everyone? The staircase to the next floor was dark and that was where the sounds were coming from.

Hensley walked slowly up the staircase. His right hand closed on the hilt of his sabre. There was the faintest of flickering light coming from above.

It was dark and Hensley hated the dark. His entire career he had always fought in the daytime, where he could see the enemy face to face. He paused. No, don't pause, push forward. It's going to be all right. He reached the top stair. The banging sound was louder. He heard Major Pitkan's voice yelling through the darkness, muffled. He saw flickering light coming from under a door jam, down a dark corridor which must have run the entire length of the third floor. He drew his sabre, tiptoed to the door, and opened it slowly.

It was a large, elegant empty bedroom. Where were the noises coming from? His eyes were drawn immediately to a far corner, on the ground. There were two candles standing sealed in their own wax to the floor, burning, and two forks were stuck upright adjacent to each candle. There was a cord tied to each candle and, damn, that round shape. A grenade, he tiptoed over to try and understand what this was. Some kind of a trap. Dare he touch it? The cord from each candle led to each door handle through the upright forks.

"Who's out there?" said a voice from behind a door.

"It's Sergeant Hensley, what is this contraption?"

"For God's sake, Sergeant, don't let the candle fall on the grenade. Put the candles out," shouted Major Pitkan from the other side of the door.

"I...I won't be able to see," said Hensley, confused.

"Then pick up the grenades, man, both of them and pull them out of harm's way first, then break us out," commanded Pitkan.

Sergeant Hensley was relieved to follow orders. But to be safe, he decided to snuff out one of the candles before picking up the grenade. A moment of fear passed through him as he picked it up. Would it explode as he lifted it? No, he had it. As soon as he announced that he had the second grenade moved out of the way, he heard the closet door smash; bodies were pushing against it to get out. Finally, the occupants of the closet came tumbling out as the door gave way. The force of the movement tumbled the last lighted candle over, the cord pulled the lit candle between the two upright forks. On its side the candle flickered momentarily and then went out. They were in total darkness. Bodies collided with each other as they sought to locate the door.

"Major Pitkan," shouted Hensley.

"He's in the other closet. You must stop them," said one of the magistrate's voices. "We'll release the Major and the others." From somewhere he heard Pitkan's voice confirm the order, "Sergeant, go after them. Kill them if need be. They must be stopped. The two servants are Yankee pirates. The woman, Alicia, is a spy and has the secret of the naval gun. She above all must be stopped."

Sergeant Hensley took the stairs down two at a time. The two waiters should be still outside. His men wouldn't have let them leave. He reached the second level, still brightly lit by candles, he turned the corner and began to shout as he descended, "Stop them! Stop them!"

He reached the ground floor still shouting, as he burst out of the building. There, in the darkness, his troops stood at attention under the lantern light. Only a couple had broken ranks, and stood staring at him, "Sir?"

"Where are the two servants?" demanded Hensley.

"They've gone down the street there, towards the city." The soldier pointed to a street where two men were just barely visible in the dark. They pulled their service cart along after them.

"Didn't ye hear me tell them to stay?"

"Aye, sir, but you left us all at attention. Beg your pardon, Sergeant Major, you have always told us to follow the last order you've given us. Since they were just walking away, we figured we could catch up with them. They are right there, Sergeant," he pointed again to the street where the two waiters were towing the cart.

Sergeant Major Hensley ran to his horse, took mount, and turned to gallop in the direction of the two men wheeling the cart, now two blocks off. But, from another direction, he heard the sound of a low, muted gun shot; a small gun, but its ominous sound echoed up the cobblestone streets sending an announcement that something was very wrong. The sound had come from the direction the Lady Alicia had gone with Corporal Higgins. He was alone with her and Major Pitkan said she had the secret of the naval gun. She was the one he had to catch.

"Men," he shouted to his assembled platoon, still mostly standing at attention, "Those servants are Yankee spies, go after them, stop them. Shoot them if they won't stop. Charge!"

Sixty-four men broke ranks and began to run in the

direction of Michael and Henry, who were still with their cart. The soldiers' muskets were in their hands, their bayonets flashed like darning needles in the lantern lit demesne. As each man ran, he was conscious that another followed him with the blade close at his back. A stampede mentality started to develop, just as in an infantry assault. The men in the front felt great pressure building from behind, and moved faster. The formation erupted into a dead run, as it reached the end of the long courtyard of Carnarvon House and tried to rearrange itself to proceed down the narrow neck of buildings that led to the beginning of the cobblestone street. The men at the rear, frustrated that they could not go faster, began to emit a blood curdling infantry cry as they ran. The sound carried ahead of them to the terror of those that heard it. The hounds had scent of the foxes again and would tear them apart when they caught them.

Satisfied that his troops would catch up with the two pirates or whoever they were, Hensley turned his attention to the pursuit of the gunshot. The hansen had traveled down the street southward in the direction of the Captain's flat. He entered the long cobblestone street. At each cross street ahead there was one lighted street lamp. Hensley could see ahead for four or five streets, but he could not see within the intervals between the lights. There might be a hansen there. Scattered about were a few people pushed back against the buildings, the homeless, who eternally wandered Belfast's streets in the darkness looking for scraps of food or cast away clothing. Obviously frightened by the sound of a gunshot and the troops yelling in the courtyard, these dark figures hid in the doorways and alleys, or crushed against buildings while he passed. All the women seemed to wear black shawls in this country. He didn't see some of them until he almost rode over them. Despicable place. He hated it.

The Sergeant Major rode cautiously along, to gallop would be to miss something. At each block there was that nagging, hollow feeling that he should go down one of the cross streets. At each intersection, he stopped and looked left and right, his eyes strained into the darkness. This was beginning to remind him of a maze. But there was no reason to deter from going straight ahead, so he continued onward.

As he reached the third cross street, lit by an especially pale street lamp whose glass must have been filthy dirty, Hensley observed a booted leg at the edge of the light. As he turned and rode closer, above the top of the boot he could see white breeches. He dismounted and knelt beside the body. His instincts knew who it was. He turned the body over and pulled the face into the dim light. It was Corporal Higgins.

His eyes were open, just a slit and there was a sticky wetness coming from his side. "She shot me, Sergeant," the weak voice said.

"Hold onto your side, man. I'll get you help. But I have to find her, now." He yelled into the darkened street, at the dark figures that hugged the walls along the block he had just passed, "This man is hurt. Help him, for God's sake."

He mounted his horse and continued up the street slowly and deliberately. Behind him, in the far distance he heard a great volley of gunfire, followed by a few isolated musket shots. His men must have caught up with the waiters. They'd come his direction now and find the Corporal.

Sensing that his quarry was near, he withdrew his horse whip from its place on the saddle. He jabbed his heels into the sides of his great horse whose iron hooves began to pound with great intensity on the cobblestones as they moved forward at a greater pace.

* * * * *

Lunt and O'Mally pushed the cart along with them, and looked back to see the assembled troops break rank and begin to run towards their street at a quickening pace. The redcoats, with their white cross straps, tall miter hats, and flashing bayonets, were clearly visible as they reached the first street intersection off the courtyard. Then, from the throats of their pursuers, they heard the savage cry of a full bayonet charge. The soldiers were only a couple of hundred paces behind.

Lunt put his hand into the cart and grabbed the canvas bag, which was now much lighter because it no longer bore the heavy grenades, only the scored potato, his sword, four pistols, and the uniform he had hidden again in order to exit Carnarvon House.

O'Mally shouted, "Help me push the cart over, it'll slow them down. The horses are only another street over." They executed the maneuver in a moment, leaving one uprighted wheel spinning as they departed.

"Run for it!" screamed O'Mally. They could hear the pounding tread of heavy military boots in pursuit, and the increasing howl of the full bayonet charge building behind them. They ran as fast as they were able. Lunt considered tossing the canvas bag aside as it was slowing him down, compared to O'Mally who was building distance between them. No, he'd keep it, damn it. He would not lose his sword. He pushed his body harder and lengthened his stride. Behind him the roar of sixty screaming redcoats became deafening.

O'Mally rounded the corner ahead of him. Five more strides and he'd make it, four, he dug in, three, he heard the word, "Fire!" shouted from behind him. Oh God, he wasn't going to make it. Lunt had to reduce their target fast, there'd be fifty or sixty bullets flying up the street at him. He dropped to the ground and covered his head. As a second reflex, he closed his legs. His last thought was of his brother, Ezra, who had said it was the bullet that you don't hear that will kill you.

There was a blinding series of lightening flashes that swept up the narrow ravine of the cobblestone street. They engulfed everything in their path. Whistling sounds and impact noises immediately followed. Sparks flew as musket balls struck and ricocheted off the stone buildings that formed the tunnel of a street. Chips of masonry bounced off Lunt's forehead and the hands that protected his face. From his squinting left eye, as he lay flat, he had seen three rounds and their ricochets raise sparks as they careened off the stone edifices and street. Now everything was strangely quiet.

Lunt was not hurt. He couldn't believe it. Behind him he heard the soldiers pushing the cart aside. He had to go now. Most of them would take a full minute to reload, especially in the dark. He looked back. Smoke belched forwards, and only here and there beneath the street lamp could he see bits of red uniforms. He got up and sprang around the corner in three strides. A single bullet followed him harmlessly by.

O'Mally was on his horse and held the reins of a second, "God, man, I can't believe you survived that, St. Christopher is with ye. Here, get on yer horse and let's get to Carrickfergus before they reload and catch up with us."

"No," said Lunt, "the woman, she's the prize."

"You're daft, man, no."

"Yes, she has the secret that the British are afraid of losing. We need her to make sure the Drake comes out to meet Ranger." Lunt turned his horse's head and then shouted, "This way," as he kicked his horse's flanks to propel it across the intersection twenty or so yards ahead of the advancing column of lobsterbacks. A few lone shots rang out, far too late. Reluctantly, O'Mally followed, kicking his horse, crouching low, and propelling his beast across the narrow street opening. One lone shot rang out, again far too late as the target had already vanished from sight. The soldiers began to run to the corner, most of their weapons still empty.

Lunt and O'Mally galloped together down the cobblestone streets. Sparks flew as iron hooves met rock at blinding speed. Three blocks along, Lunt pulled up. "Where will she have gone?" Behind them they could hear the voices of angry soldiers, with empty muskets, yelling, "Halt! Halt!"

"Find the hansen," said O'Mally. "That'll be the last place she'd be. You take one street down from here in the same direction, I'll go one up. Watch fer the homeless ladies, with the black shawls, she could be one of them. Lunt said, "Wait," and opened the canvas bag, hastily strapped behind his saddle. He reached inside and handed O'Mally two pistols.

"If, we're separated, make your way to Carrickfergus," shouted Lunt as he turned to the left.

"Ha, that one again," O'Mally laughed and rode off to the right.

Lunt cantered down to the next intersection and looked right and left. Left led back to Carnarvon House, right was the direction to take. He turned and proceeded one more block. On the ground he saw the Corporal, a few dark shapes around him. She'd got rid of him quickly. He had known instinctively that she must be carrying a gun. She went alone with the Corporal too willingly. Lunt rode past the group squatting around the wounded man. He continued ahead two more intersections and there was the hansen parked on the corner. For a moment he thought he could see another rider pass through the intersection two streets over to the right. That must be O'Mally. He would run into her if she went in that direction. He would concentrate on streets to the left.

He galloped to another intersection, there was nothing except the occasional dark shapes of people who seemed to live in the streets. They jumped aside. He went another street further and looked again to his left; this street curved away to the right. He had a feeling that he could see movement of a shadow against the lantern lit walls. Movement of a hand going up.

He went down the street at a gallop, reaching back in his canvas bag for his sword. He had the hilt in his hand but couldn't get it released. He tugged, damn, it was stuck. His horse careened down the curving street, forcing him to hold onto the reins with both hands. He quit his attempt to retrieve the sword. As he rounded the curve in the street, he heard the crack of a whip and, as it made contact with flesh, he heard a muted female whine.

"Murdering bitch," he heard Sergeant Major Hensley scream as he was trying to drive his horse over a black shawled form that was on foot, striking out at him with an iron rod. Hensley was on one side of a lamp post, Marie was on foot on the other. The rod must be the missing cantilever, thought Lunt, the adjustment device Wright had been missing. She must have had it all along.

The Sergeant was moving in but, whichever way he moved, she countered to keep the street lamp between them. He used his whip again to get at her around the light pole. Beneath her black shawl, Lunt saw a flash of her white shoulders and part of a naked breast as the whip struck her again and withdrew, pulling her shawl to the ground.

Slowing his horse to a walk some twenty feet from the Sergeant, Lunt didn't have time to check the prime of his pistols. The flints might have slipped away, or the ball and powder shaken free with wadding loosened in the jostling ride. Lunt reached back into his canvas bag and extracted his sword, sheath and all, from its bag. As he withdrew the sword from its sheath, metal grated upon metal. Hensley heard the distinctive noise and turned around. He had been about to use his whip again but half way in the motion he stopped, and then lowered his hand, the heavy breath of his mount exhaled a layer of fog into the chill night air beneath the street lamp.

"So, the Yankee pirate has come for his whore," taunted the Sergeant.

He saw Lunt raise his sword and continue on towards him, moving his horse a step at a time. Hensley threw aside his horse whip and reached for his sabre. The sound of grating metal upon metal reverberated again along the narrow cobblestone street. The Sergeant kicked his horse violently in its flanks to propel his spotted mount forward. The animal snorted and then lunged forward. Lunt raised his sword in front of his face and screamed in rage as he kicked his own mount into action.

The two blades met in mid air, each side propelled into the impact by the combined momentum of over a ton of raw human and horse flesh. Sparks flew and the sound of the clash rang out along the street for blocks away. The Sergeant Major's sabre had a razor sharp edge intended for slashing. Lunt's naval sword lacked a sharp edge, its intended use was to thrust forward to impale human flesh. As Hensley's sword grated down Lunt's blade, he tried to rotate it so that its edge would cut into Lunt's face. Lunt shifted in the saddle to avoid the action.

Momentum lost, Hensley withdrew his sabre and poised for a backhand slash as the two horses passed by each other. Lunt again countered by placing his blade into the sweeping path of his enemy's sword. Upon collision, the swords bounced apart and the sharp edge of Hensley's sabre bit into the flesh of Lunt's horse. The animal whinnied in protest and lifted its body upwards onto its hind legs in panic. Lunt held on tightly, feeling his saddle hitch begin to slide, he clutched the beast's mane.

Sergeant Hensley turned and watched his adversary struggling with the horse and then planned his next stoke. This horse was not trained for action like his own, he would use that against his opponent. He poised his sword forwards and charged into the floundering beast with a dragoon's battle scream, "Eeeeyyyyaaaa!"

Lunt had just settled the horse down when the Sergeant Major was on him again. Hensley was not going for another series of great swinging stokes downward on top of him with his longer sabre. Instead, he was keeping just out of range of Lunt's sword and jabbing forward. This was going to be different. The Sergeant Major was not aiming at him, but at his horse, damn, he was trying to kill his horse to put him on the ground where he could ride over him. Lunt jerked his horse's mane to the left, his own body still sliding on the loose saddle.

Suddenly, Hensley found an opportunity. He jabbed the tip of his sabre fiercely into the horse's eye. Lunt heard his animal give a blood curdling whinny of pain. Incensed by the sound, the Sergeant pushed forward more. He was going for the animal's brain. As his opponent held his longer sword forward, Lunt could feel his animal try to back up and then start to shudder. His horse was about to topple. He had one chance; pulling on the dying animal's mane he reached over its head and grabbed tenaciously onto the back edge of the Sergeant's sword. Lunt used his adversary's sword blade to momentarily hold his weight as he lunged his entire body forward, the sword in his right hand leading the assault.

Seeing the unexpected action, Hensley tried to jerk the tip of his sword free from the eye socket of his adversary's horse. But Lunt's weight on the sabre hilt made it difficult to retract. The point of Lunt's blade was coming at him. Hensley tried to fall backwards to avoid it but his horse moved contrary to his wishes. He felt the tip of the naval sword drive into his throat, break his larynx, and sever his juggler vein. He felt enormous pain as he fell backward, his life's blood spurting out uncontrollably. He was mildly aware when his body hit the Belfast street. He kicked a few times trying to shout but was unable to form words. Finally, he lay still, his last conscious memory was of a man stepping on his face and withdrawing the sword as he struggled helplessly to scream through his own blood.

The woman, who had been called Alicia, was quick to mount the Sergeant's horse. She was about to kick the animal into action when she glanced back down at Lieutenant Lunt, who was staring at the dying Sergeant. Lunt turned to look at her. Two on a horse would be slow. She was not going to turn the Carronade over to the Yankees but this man did help her.

"There's only one horse, Madame. Are we both going to ride it, or are you going to make me walk?" asked Lunt still shaking from the deadly sword duel. As he spoke he removed the canvas bag from his dead horse. He glanced momentarily up and down the street for his sword's scabbard, but it was gone.

"Promise you'll let me go, when we're past the redcoats." said Marie Chatelain.

"Yes," said Lunt. "Do you want to take the turning screw?" He pointed with his sword to the yard long rod she had been using to defend herself.

"It's not of any strategic value," said Marie, "I just took it to delay the testing until my own liaison arrived."

The horse whinnied with the feel of an unfamiliar rider, as she started to turn the animal to go up the hill towards the cross street. Just in case she was not going to stop, Lunt caught the horse's bridle and executed the turn with her. For a long moment the two looked into each other's eyes.

By the light of the street lamp Lunt perceived an extraordinarily beautiful, but very deadly lady. Looking down at him, she perceived a rather perfect innocent but handsome man, in a sort of rustic way. She could control him. She pulled the reins in tight and moved forward on the saddle. Lunt placed his foot in the stirrup and pulled the saddle toward him as he swung his leg up over the mount, taking his canvas bag with him. From the high position on the saddle, he glanced once more at the Sergeant Major who had ceased any kind of movement. The dark pool of liquid had ceased to bubble at his throat.

Lunt then turned the horse back towards the direction in which he expected to see O'Mally. By the time he had moved only three paces, a figure on horseback moved into the lamp light at the next intersection. Lunt recognized the red hair immediately, even in the peculiar light. A hand signal indicated that they should turn at this street and move left.

The two horses began to gallop. Lunt was very conscious of the woman's softness as he rode with his arms obligingly wrapped around her to control the reins. Her perfume was still apparent over the smell of the sweating horse. He concentrated hard on following O'Mally who maneuvered through the darkened streets. Suddenly, his fellow rider shouted, "Wait!"

"Why?" said Lunt, not slowing up.

"We're just a street over from the paddocks. They have the finest horses in Belfast. We'll not be able to outrun mounted dragoons with these two horses, one doubly mounted," said Marie.

"We'll waste too much time putting new saddles on the horses," said Lunt.

Marie began to protest, but Lunt kicked their horse onward in pursuit of O'Mally, who had just turned the horse to the right. They were almost to the slope of the hills which stood behind the town.

"There's no road up there," said Marie.

"O'Mally knows the terrain," said Lunt coolly.

They rode onward and upward in the darkness. The density of buildings began to thin. The moonlight gleamed, and occasionally a spark was ignited by the hooves of O'Mally's horse striking a stone in the roadbed. Finally, up ahead, his horse stopped on the slope of a steep hill. O'Mally turned to look back at the city. He could hear commotion in the streets below. Reaching O'Mally, Lunt briefly turned his horse to look behind them. His horse panted from obvious over exertion.

"They'll be buzzing all night," said O'Mally. "We need to make our way across this hillside and ahead of them before they get to the Carrickfergus road."

"Which way are you going?" asked Marie.

"Why, out to the Ranger," said Lunt.

"I mean, how are you going to get there?"

O'Mally answered for them, "Don't know, ma'am, we'll

swim I presume, but I guess that Cap'n Jones will have a longboat just a couple of hundred paces off the beach, waiting for us."

Marie reasoned, "Don't you think that the first place that they'll send cavalry, after your challenge, is to Carrickfergus? You'll never get through that road, no matter how far you go around to get there."

"We haven't done badly getting away so far," replied Lunt.

Marie persisted, "There's a small cove up about five miles along the road towards Carrickfergus. The Royal Navy keeps a small tender there. If we can cross the road undetected, we can surprise the guards. There's usually only two or three of them."

"And just how do ye know about that?" questioned O'Mally.

"I was the Captain's mistress for four months. There's not too much I don't know about the way he had fortified this harbour. The boat is at the point where the lookouts can see up the lough and flash a signal about incoming ships to the Drake. Because the cove is a little far from the Carrickfergus road, a lot of people forget it's there."

Once again, Lunt detected that Marie's manner of speaking was changing in their presence. He could now detect a very definite French accent. She continued, "I'll lead you there, adjacent to the cove along the highway, and then leave you to take the boat on foot. You'll have to overpower the guards. They'll be marines but, on a night like this, they'll not be the best men."

"Why on a night like this?" asked Lunt.

"Because tomorrow the Drake was originally to set sail. Captain Burden has filled the boat with all his best men for the ordnance testing. Anyone arriving aboard since the carronade was moved to the Drake has not been allowed to depart, excepting the officers. A few younger marines have been left ashore to perform shore duties."

"There'll be a boat there, you're certain?" quizzed Lunt.

"Yes, Captain Burden took over an old coal tender in January and was planning to use it for training. Unofficially, he named it H.M.S. Innocence, because of the new personnel it was to help train. He even had the name lettered onto the stern in a sort of mock ceremony. I was there. It won't be fast but you can sail it out to Ranger, out of the way of the dragoons," said Marie.

Lunt looked up at the tops of surrounding trees, there was still wind. "It might work," he said looking to O'Mally, who also nodded approval.

* * * * *

Captain George Burden wrung his hands together fitfully as he paced back and forth, still on the second floor of Carnarvon house. "I've been such a fool."

Lieutenant Dobbs was standing with his parents, consoling them. He offered an additional glass of wine to his captain, "Sir."

Burden glanced up. He shook his head and looked at Major Pitkan, who gave him a consoling glance. "Dragoons have been alerted?" Burden asked.

Pitkan reported, "At least two squads are already mounted and on the road to Carrickfergus. I've sent a message to get every force possible out, including the local militia. My men are combing every street. They had contact and then lost them. The three of them were on horseback. At last sighting they were heading up into the hills."

Burden rubbed his chin and then gave orders, "Lieutenant Dobbs, get every longboat out on the harbor with a full complement of marines. Send someone to the signal boat, up at the second cove along the Carrickfergus road. That damn Alicia knows about that one too." Burden pounded the dinner table again, causing an unfortunate plate of half eaten food to fall to the floor.

Lt. Dobbs hugged his parents and had started down the winding staircase, when he heard Captain Burden call his name. He looked up towards the railing. The Captain seemed to have a lot more power in his voice than he ever remembered. "Lt. Dobbs, have all hands ready on the Drake. We'll be setting sail for Carrickfergus at dawn."

"With the carronade, sir?" asked Dobbs.

The voice of Mr. Wright interdicted, "The Governor General will want an inquiry, surely you wouldn't risk the weapon by taking it out to face Jones?"

Burden wheeled his huge frame around to face the speaker. His stare hushed the brown suited man. "You're not so innocent yourself, Mr. Wright. Nooners, eh?" Burden walked right up to the man and stared down into his sweating face. "Maybe you should consider coming aboard H.M.S. Drake yourself tomorrow morning, before your wife hears the story from these blabbermouths." Burden motioned in the direction of several matronly women who had been along during the evening's ordeal. They gasped aloud at his frank reference.

Burden shouted to Dobbs, who had just begun to descend the stairway again, "Hold up a moment, Lieutenant."

Burden moved his hugh frame swiftly across the drawing room to stand in front of van Zoot. He leaned down to bring his face nose to nose with the little man. "And what role did you play in this, Mr. van Zoot?"

The greasy little man looked up. His upper lip perspiring in the candlelight. The large Captain seized him and was shaking him. Van Zoot was afraid. He appalled physical danger. That was for his customers, not himself.

"I had nothing to do with this," van Zoot screamed as his body was being shaken violently.

"We'll see," said Burden. "I've put up with you stinking profiteers all my career. I'm not letting you out of my sight. For the first time I suspect in your life, you're going to see what happens when your crappy molding doesn't hold under stress, or a cannon bursts on deck from metal fatigue."

Van Zoot stared up at the large faced Captain with astonished eyes. "Surely.. you're not taking me to sea, to a battle?"

"You're damn right I am," snapped Burden.

"I'm a Dutch citizen, I'm neutral," protested van Zoot.

"That's all the better reason to keep you in sight. Lieutenant Dobbs, go immediately to the Drake and take this scum with you. Put him in the brig for the night. As I said earlier, launch every longboat you can towards Carrickfergus, with armed marines aboard."

Lt. Dobbs stood bolt upright, relieved that he was being ordered to do something and would not have to submit to more embarrassment about the Alicia incident in front of his parents. He asked again loudly, "Sir, do you want me to prepare the carronade?"

"Yes," replied Captain Burden. "But make no attempt to move the Drake from her anchorage until dawn's light. I know you checked her, but I feel we need to look over the vessel again from bow to stern. I've a notion that Lunt fellow did something to her."

Lieutenant Dobbs saluted, nodded goodbye to his parents, and then hurried down the stairs out of Carnarvon House.

"Major Pitkan," the Captain turned to address his long time friend, "can you see to it that we have a good armed force aboard the Drake, in case we grapple with Ranger? The marine force is low. I could use an extra forty of your men."

"You have it," replied the Major. "I will take the rest of my command towards Carrickfergus with a mounted force and some light field pieces. Perhaps we can lend a hand, if the privateer ventures close to the north shore of the lough."

"Very good, Major."

Robert Wright, the master shipbuilder, stepped up to the Captain. He had tears in his eyes. "George, I was a fool as well, I should have known better at my age. I would be proud to accompany you. I'll do anything on board you need done. I can assemble a group of my carpenters and we can repair anything damaged under fire. We can finish the carronade mounting while you're sailing out to meet Ranger. I can make it work without the leveling rods."

Captain Burden looked at him for a long moment. He had never thought of Wright as a fighting man. But seeing that the man was sincere and determined, Burden nodded approval. Wright smiled, and then started to run down the stairs.

Burden shouted after him, "I'll have the last longboat at the usual landing a half hour before dawn. I'll expect you and your carpenters there, Mr. Wright."

Burden turned to the remainder of his astonished guests, "I have been a certain fool but almighty God has given me an opportunity to rectify a grievous error. For my King, I shall be victorious. I am truly sorry that all of this has happened. Good night to you all."

The Captain picked up his hat, fitted it upon his head, and quickly descended the winding stairway out of Carnarvon House.

* * * * *

High in the foothills surrounding Belfast, the two horses of the pursued worked their way eastward through trails that were at best incomplete, or did not exist at all. O'Mally rode first, Lunt followed. Several times during the transit, Marie volunteered to be let off. Each time Lunt deterred her.

"When we arrive at the cove, if the collier is there, we'll have no further need of these horses. But if there's no ship, we'll need them. On foot, you'd be caught when the sun comes up, as sure as can be."

Marie did not reply but continued to make suggestions to help their forward progress. Overhead, the moon was clearly visible and the cloud cover began to thin out. The town of Belfast began to fall behind them as they worked their way back down again into a neighborhood of hedge rows and tiny divided farms. Whenever they were challenged, crossing or passing by some farmer's field, O'Mally was quick to reply, "We're on the King's business, all is well."

Lunt guessed that they had made five or six miles progress before O'Mally came to the top of a road that went back in the direction of the harbour. From their vantage point they had a panoramic view of the lough. "Is that the cove?" O'Mally pointed and moved his horse close to question Marie.

She pointed, "You can't quite see the stone signal house but there's the fire. It's lit there continuously every night, so that it can be seen from the Drake. If it goes out, that's a signal that there's trouble, or that the marines have fallen asleep. I think that this road comes out on the Carrickfergus road just a little to the south of the cove. The cove is a bit of a distance on the other side of the road. The horses will be no further use to you once you reach the road. It's marshy on the other side.

"Then let's move as fast as we can back towards the lough," said O'Mally. Lunt replied with a simple, "Yes," and the two horses proceeded to gallop. As Marie was flung backwards onto Lunt, she clung to the pommel with deliberation, while Lunt managed the reins. Their animal was overburdened. He was unable to keep up with O'Mally, who gradually pulled ahead of them.

When the two riders inhaled, their mouths filled with the grit of dust kicked up by O'Mally's steed. In the space of five minutes they covered a long mile. The road was fairly straight and Lunt was conscious of people in small cottages or sleeping in lean-tos coming out to view the night riders. Lunt concentrated on riding the powerful spotted horse that had once belonged to the Sergeant Major. The moonlit bay grew nearer and nearer.

Ahead of them, Lunt saw O'Mally pull off to the side

of the road. He was very near the intersection of the Carrickfergus road. He had stopped beside a stone wall. As Lunt pulled up, he saw O'Mally dismount and talk to a man who smoked a long pipe. Lunt and Marie could smell the tobacco smoke as they approached.

Lunt pulled the horse to a stop. O'Mally put up his hand for him to be silent. Lunt waited, conscious that the man to whom O'Mally was speaking was very alarmed at seeing the woman with him. He started to look about nervously. O'Mally was speaking to him in the high pitched sound of Gaelic. Once, Lunt overheard the word, "Yankee," and the old man immediately replied using something like, "Ah, Yankee."

Lunt could tell that O'Mally had used a bit of humor to calm the man, because the respondent gave a slight chuckle and then the pace of the conversation quickened. The man was pointing in an animated fashion towards the cove.

O'Mally turned and walked his horse back to where Lunt and Alicia waited. He spoke softly. "About fifty dragoons passed here ten minutes ago. There were looking for us, especially the Captain's Lady." O'Mally nodded to Marie.

"They woke this man up. He thinks that a few of the dragoons turned up towards the cove and the rest of them went along to Carrickfergus." O'Mally pointed to a field across the road. "We can go across the road there, and then take a path that leads close to the signal house the Royal Navy uses. My friend here says there's usually a small sloop there and two or three marines. We should be able to get fairly close before we're detected. He is going to give us three black capes to camouflage us in the darkness. They'll also keep us warm on the water."

As Lunt listened to O'Mally speak he was vaguely conscious of Marie shifting her weight slightly in the saddle in front of him. Suddenly her face turned and, looking right at him from inches away, she said, "I've gotten you as far as you need by horse. I need to get away too. Can you get off, Lieutenant Lunt? We made a bargain."

For a long moment Lunt looked at her. O'Mally was still speaking about how they would be able to surprise the guards across the road, but Lunt was not conscious of his words. "I think it would be best if you come with us."

Marie looked at him intensely, "Are you going to break your promise?" Her eyebrow was raised.

"You did say to me that promises between great nations were not to be trusted," replied Lunt.

"You don't represent a great nation, Lieutenant Lunt."

"It will be," said Lunt.

"I'm not so sure that your Captain Jones can defeat the Royal Navy. I'd rather take my chances on land," stated Marie.

As she was speaking, Lunt was conscious of Marie's arm whirling around behind her. He saw the flash of a metal object in the moonlight. Lunt grabbed the back of her dress and yanked her after him as he leaned away from whatever she was bringing about. Carrying her with him, they both tumbled off the horse to the ground. Lunt hit the ground on his back, his leather vest absorbing some of the bite of small stones that would have pierced his flesh.

Marie had fallen on top of him, still with her left hand free. Just as she was beginning to bring whatever weapon she had to bear on him, he threw her off to one side. The impact disorientated her. Lunt scrambled in the dirt. He grabbed her foot and pulled on her dress to keep her off balance, as she sought to turn around. She held a small pistol.

Suddenly into Lunt's view came the broadside view of a cocked flintlock's barrel. The muzzle was placed at the side of Marie's face. She stopped all activity and looked up frozen in surprise.

Squatting before them was O'Mally, holding the pistol. "Now, now, that'll be enough. Drop your little stinger, me lady."

Marie looked over her shoulder at Lunt whose knees pinned her white dress to the ground and whose hands held each of her wrists. She ceased struggling and let the pistol fall to the ground. O'Mally picked up the pistol. "You'd best search her, Lieutenant."

Henry looked down at his prisoner. Her magnificent dress was dirty and torn. Her bare neck and shoulders were caked with dirt. He indicated she should roll over. He avoided eye contact.

His voice quaked slightly, "I'm ..I'm sorry, I have to..."

"Why, you're embarrassed," Marie taunted him, laughing.

O'Mally grabbed one of her wrists, permitting Lunt to conduct a search. Lunt glanced down at the bodice of her dress and then back up into Marie's eyes. "Do you have any more weapons concealed on your person?" asked Lunt nervously.

Alicia stared into his eyes with a mocking smile, and did not reply. Lunt waited for a response, there was none, so he swallowed hard and proceeded to place his hand along the outline of first her right leg and up into her crotch. All of this time he patted rather than felt. He did not look into the eyes of his captive. On his search behind her buttocks, his hand felt something thin and hard. "I've found something," he announced timidly.

Marie snarled, "It's a knife. I have two of them. I'll save you further embarrassment, if you let me stand up, Lieutenant Lunt."

Lunt looked briefly into her eyes. "Thank you," he said and stood up to let Marie rise. With O'Mally's pistol trained on her body, she turned briefly and positioned her dress until she could get access to a small pocket. From one and then the other side she extracted two shiny, narrow bladed daggers which she presented, handle forward, to Lunt who watched her intensely.

As Lunt took the two daggers, she commented, "If you're

too embarrassed to search a spy who has just tried to kill you, how can you really expect me to believe that you're capable of getting us out of this difficulty?"

* * * * *

At the campfire, the two dragoons were sharing a warm tea with the three permanent Royal Marine guards. The dragoons' short barreled carbine muskets were still slung over their shoulders. The marines' weapons were stacked along the side of the stone signal house. Their muskets were fully primed, ready to fire, but none of the them really expected to be part of any action that evening.

On such a clear night it was a pleasure to stand around outside, and keep watch over the bay and the small collier which lay beached behind them. By signal they were in direct contact with the watch aboard the Drake, some five miles distance over the water. They huddled about their combination signal and campfire.

"You mean the Captain's tart was a Frog spy?" said Marine Corporal Hastings, his Yorkshire accent cutting harshly into the night air.

"They don't know where she was from, but a spy she be," said one of the dragoons.

"'Twill be the Frenchies no doubt, who else would dare? Boy, how'd you like to capture her. Give her a little private search. She's a corker that one."

Most of the soldiers roared approval for the dream assignment. One man licked his fingers in an obscene gesture, and they all laughed.

Frederick Leigh, one of the Royal Navy's youngest marines stood, looking over the fire, when his glance happened to fall towards the south, to the very rim of the fire light which was cast out across the marshy land. Between bits of his companion's laughter, he noticed that the marsh had grown curiously silent. Was their laughter upsetting the toads and insects which continually buzzed, chirped, and clicked in the darkness? He moved to one side so that the direct firelight was not in his eyes.

Something was wrong. He'd had this assignment every evening for a fortnight, and the toads and marsh creatures were never silent, no matter how loudly his fellow outpost guards talked and kidded each other through the night. Something was different out there. He squinted to look outwards, several hundred feet in the distance. His fifteen year old eyes focused into the limits of sight. For an instant he thought he could see something, and then there was nothing.

"What's the bother, Freddie?" asked his Corporal.

"Not certain, no animal sounds, something's wrong."

Everyone at the campfire stood up. There was something out there. The dragoons removed their musket carbines from their shoulders. A figure in white came out on the marsh towards them. It was difficult to see with the lights of Belfast behind the figure. Squinting, they saw it was a woman in a white dress, or what seemed to be a white dress, hurrying in their direction. Suddenly, around them one of the dragoon's horses bayed. The mood became eerie.

The five soldiers and marines continued to focus towards the south. It was a woman all right, walking across the marsh in a white dress which was ripped at the top. She was still over a hundred feet away. They could not see her face clearly in the firelight.

Suddenly one of the dragoons shouted, "It's her, the Captain's whore."

"Best grab the muskets," said the Corporal.

From their left, a strong, firm voice interrupted, "Don't even take a step! You're under arms. I'll kill the first man to move."

The five men whirled at the sudden voice. The two dragoons already had their muskets at the ready. The man on their left stood on the edge of the firelight. He wore a dark cape. While they were watching the woman in the white dress he had snuck up on them. He was only thirty feet away. With the wave of his arms, the man flipped the cape back over his shoulders to reveal white breeches with a leather vest over a white shirt. He was tall and sandy haired. In each hand he held a cocked flintlock pistol at the ready.

As one of the dragoons turned, he moved the barrel of his carbine in the direction of the intruder. The short musket exploded with a flash of light as its cock and flint hit steel on the descent. The other dragoon made a motion to fire and brought his carbine to the ready.

The twin pistols of the intruder roared almost simultaneously. Gunfire spit from each, followed by a billow of smoke which roared out in their direction. The second dragoon seemed to be lifted into the air and was flung backwards by an unseen force. The first, who had just fired, fell to the ground clutching his thigh, falling in anguish on top of his discharged carbine.

Leigh and the other marines broke for the wall where their muskets were stacked. Early in the evening, Corporal Hastings had ordered them all to fix bayonets.

"It'll be the end of your lives if you use those muskets, lads." The second voice carried a thick Irish accent. They paid no attention as they grabbed their muskets and whirled. Leigh dropped his amid the confusion and scrambled on the ground to retrieve it. The Corporal and the other marine turned in the direction of their new adversary and aimed their guns to fire. There was a man standing near the lady who was now only fifty feet away. The marines fired at the man who had spoken. He fired back, discharging both pistols. Roaring sound and light was again followed by billows of smoke that filled the space between the opposing men.

As he continued to grope on the ground in search of his musket, Leigh sensed a body smash against the wall near him, the face angled towards him, as his own hand closed on the barrel of his musket. His fingers checked the cock.

There was no flint. It had snapped off when the musket had fallen. He looked in the direction of the second assailant, the man was not in sight. Against the wall, his Corporal's face was turned up at him in a weird angle. The neck broken in the fall, the eyes blank in the firelight.

Leigh regained his footing. The other marine was screaming and charging at their first assailant to the left. Now only twenty feet away, the man had a sword drawn and stood his ground while the Royal Marine careened towards him screaming a battle cry, his bayonet thrust before him balanced on the long barrel of an empty musket.

Leigh started forward just as he heard the sword and bayonet collide. Sparks flashed amid the reverberating sounds. The vested man stepped quickly to the side letting the first marine whirl past, missing him. He turned around to glance at Leigh's advancing position. As Leigh continued forward, he was conscious that he was out of breath and that his heart was pounding. Through his mind raced the thought that this was going to be the end of his life. Right here and now. He felt no fear. He would do his duty.

The other Royal Marine was coming back, and the assailant's back was briefly to him. If he could get a bayonet there, it would be over. He rushed forward. The man was quick and deflected the other marine's bayonet rush by grabbing the barrel of the musket. Leigh heard the other marine wail as the intruder jabbed him in the stomach with the sword. Leigh rushed onward, it was only a few feet to the man. He was conscious of the intruder turning towards him, away from his friend who was kneeling screaming on the ground in mortal pain, his hands clutching his stomach.

"My guts, he's stabbed me in the gut."

Leigh faced the tall, lean man who held the sword pointed directly at him. Leigh stopped his forward movement. The two circled in a death dance amid the agonizing cacophony of the wounded marine in mortal pain. The firelight cast strange shadows about him. He studied his adversary and then lunged forward. Just before he made contact with the man's chest, a sword bashed downward on the barrel of his musket. The heavy force from above deflected his onrushing bayonet down into the ground. He started to slip. He mustn't die like this. He'd get around but then he felt a fist strike against the side of his head.

Suddenly, Leigh was on the ground. Eyes shut, he grit his teeth waiting for the pain. He felt the point of a sword pressed against his temple. He was down on his stomach. His face was ground into the dirt. His musket lay uncomfortably beneath him, its flintless hammer stuck upward into his chest. A foot stepped on his right shoulder pinning him to the ground, the point of the blade moved across his cheek to his throat. Leigh hoped the pain would be brief and over quickly. He didn't want a slow death.

"I'll not take your life, if you promise to cause me no further resistance," a firm even voice with a slight nasal accent spoke out of the darkness.

Leigh opened his right eye, the left side of his face still pressed roughly into the dirt. He could see up the infinitely long sword poised at his throat. Above the hilt of the sword, he saw a hawk nose and clear blue eyes in the firelight.

"You've done your duty, lad, no grown man could have done more." The statement made Leigh feel strangely proud. "I'll spare your life, if ye promise no more hindrance to our taking the sloop. Blink your eye twice if you agree."

For a long moment Leigh swallowed and then blinked his eye in the required signal. The pressure on his shoulder was released instantly. He sat up to look at the man who pointed his sword towards his fellow marine, who still hollowed in agony.

"Help that man keep his guts in his stomach and try to stop the bleeding. You may be able to save his life if you can keep him still."

As Leigh held his comrade, who was now shaking violently with chills, he was conscious of the woman and the two men examining the collier. He heard the woman say, "Collect the muskets, we may need them." The red haired man went to each dead soldier's body and paused for a few moments to kneel over the marine with the leg wound before he collected their weapons. The man who had spared his life returned to his side, where he knelt with his wounded comrade.

"How is he?"

"He's passed out," answered Leigh.

"Probably for the best. If the surgeon can stitch him up properly, he may survive. Keep your hand here," the sandy haired man placed Leigh's hand on a place above the man's wound. The bleeding seemed to slow.

"Your powder and shot are in the cottage?"

Leigh nodded and as the man was about to leave, he asked, "Sir, why did you let me live?"

The man turned, "Because you remind me of a young cousin of mine, Micajah, he's out here in the war somewhere, about your age. Our objective was to take your collier, we didn't want to kill anyone. You just spotted us a bit too soon. Our fight is with your King, not with you." The man turned and ran into the cottage. Moments later, he ran out carrying a small keg of powder and a canvas bag of shot. He rushed to the sloop, placed the contents inside, and then he and the other man pushed the small ship from the beach out onto the water. Moments later, the single sail was hoisted and very slowly the vessel departed out of sight.

Within five minutes, Leigh heard the galloping of hooves, coming down the road toward the stone signal house. The horsemen turned into the small access road and stopped at the campfire. The officer in charge looked about and then spoke to Leigh, "Where are they?"

"They got the collier, sir. They're out there." Leigh moved his hand from his friend's stomach momentarily and pointed a bloody finger out into the dark of the harbour.

"Damn," said Major Pitkan.

9

Pursuit

Lieutenant Greene and his marines heard the sounds of musket fire coming from the signal house on the north side of the lough. He immediately ordered his men to alter course in that direction. As they turned, there were more flashes of light, followed by reports of musket and pistol fire that carried out over the water.

"Put your backs into it, men," he shouted. Something was very wrong ahead.

The twelve seamen dug their oars stoutly into the water. The longboat's coxswain began to call off a cadence. Greene could feel the speed of their boat improve now that they had a destination. He squinted ahead into the darkness. A lantern mounted on their bow gave them light for close-in observation, its influence shown out only twenty or so paces directly ahead of them. It was shaded from behind to minimize the destruction of their night vision as they gazed into the far distance.

They had just left the Drake to search along the north shore of the lough for the Captain's Lady and the two Yankee pirates. Greene had been briefed about the events at Carnarvon House. The three spies were ostensibly attempting to meet up with the American pirate Jones, off Carrickfergus before morning. Dobbs was busily preparing the Drake to engage the pirate ship. Captain Burden would be on board soon.

Dobbs had assigned both Greene and one of the midshipmen to each take command of a longboat and search the lough for the trio of spies. According to Dobbs they were to shoot the spies on sight. In fact, he had emphasized several times for Lieutenant Greene not to bring them back alive, should he catch up with them. Greene listened as the order was given, but inwardly he felt that he would have difficulty following that order, especially concerning the Lady Alicia.

As they rowed along, Greene recalled how the Lady Alicia had met him in the vestibule of the Captain's quarters and had wanted him to give her the message about the intruder on the Drake. Thank God that he had pushed past her into see the Captain. Captain Burden had not really been indisposed as she had whispered to him. In fact, when Greene had entered into their quarters, the latter was still dressed in his uniform. Could she really have been a spy? Perhaps she had just rejected Lieutenant Dobbs at one time or another and he was trying to get even by giving an order to shoot her. Greene had seen his immediate superior looking at her rather lustfully over the past few weeks. Did Captain Burden really want her shot on sight or was this just Dobbs' interpretation? If he found the threesome, Greene would have to make a decision about what he was going to do with them. He was not about to ruin his career to become a scapegoat for Dobbs, or Burden, or anyone else. No, sir, his father had paid too much to buy his commission. He would do his duty, but carefully.

According to the hasty plan Dobbs had issued, Lieutenant Greene's longboat was to patrol within a mile of the north coast of the lough and stop or detain anything that looked suspicious. The other longboat was to proceed up the middle of the harbour. If there was a signal of two cannon shots, both longboats were to return immediately to the Drake. If the wind was light in the morning, the longboats might be needed to help tow Drake out of the harbour, otherwise if the morning wind was favorable the Drake would catch up with them. Finally, Dobbs had been emphatic that they were not to try and engage the American privateer. If they made a sighting, they were to row back and report the position of the American ship.

It had been a quarter hour now since the sound and flashes of musket fire had been seen at the lookout station. Greene extended his telescope and planting his boots firmly on either side of his thwart to steady himself. He managed a wavering glance in the direction of the signal fire but did not notice anything. They would be there within a quarter hour if the men could maintain this pace.

"Keep it up, men," he encouraged them. To his right, Greene could faintly see the bow light of the second longboat approximately two miles distant. It had maintained its original course, while Greene had turned towards the western shore and the signal house. It was difficult to believe, but perhaps they had not heard the disturbance that far out. Momentarily, he turned to face back towards the Drake. The southerly wind had subsided, there was no trace of wind on the water. With no wind to drive sailing craft, his oarsmen would now make their longboat the fastest vessel on the lough this evening. There would be time for them to catch anyone fleeing from the signal house by water. First, he must find out what had happened there. They might have already caught the spies and, of course, he needed to see if others had received the same orders which Lieutenant Dobbs had given him.

* * * * *

"There's not a wisp of wind, Henry," said O'Mally, sitting amidship and looking up at the mast.

Marie sat sullenly, leaning against the mast that was close to the bow of the squat twenty foot vessel. She looked at Lunt questioningly. The sail flopped this way and that, more in response to the rocking movement of the waves than to any wind pressure. Finally, she asked, "Are we moving at all?"

Lunt looked out across the harbour where the moon's reflection could be seen on the water. "Tide's on the ebb, we're being carried out but not swiftly. I think we should consider rowing or we're not going to make Carrickfergus by dawn. If the wind had held, we'd have made it in another two hours, perhaps less."

Still holding onto the tiller, Lunt proceeded to search through a pile of oars that were stored beneath the bottom boards of the longboat and chose the longest. He looked up at the solitary gaff rigged mainsail and shook his head. Back to the south he could still see the campfire of the signal house. They had made a few miles before the wind died but they had a long way to go. In response to a vague puff of wind from the opposite direction, the boom suddenly swung across the deck, slamming into the stays supporting the mast.

"O'Mally, set the boom back on larboard and rig a preventer line. That boom will smash one of us on the head if we don't." After the task was completed, he signaled for O'Mally to take the tiller.

Lunt moved forward and squatted beside Marie. "You can help instead of just sitting there."

She looked at him with a pouting face. "You should have let me go. I'm not going to tell you, or Captain Jones, or your Spymaster anything about the gun. No matter what you do to me."

Lunt looked at her steadily and winced inwardly at her outright mention of the name that Captain Jones had said never to mention aloud. He decided not to react. By having mentioned it twice now, she was obviously trying to prove something. It would only give her an edge if she knew it bothered him.

Marie offered, "Why don't you let me load the muskets? We may need them."

Lunt shook his head, "If we do, we'll have time."

"You don't trust me," she said teasingly.

Lunt started to stand up, but Marie put out her hand to grab hold of his breeches at the knee and tugged downward in a signal that they should continue talking. He squatted again.

"That was a grand gesture, letting that boy live," she said.

"He was just a boy," Lunt paused, "there was no point to... would you have killed him?"

"Yes," she said looking directly into his eyes searching for a reaction.

Lunt remained stoic. "And Captain Burden and his dinner guests. You would have killed all of them?"

"Certainly, yes." Marie's voice became stronger. "This is not a glorious endeavor, Lieutenant Lunt. This is war. It's been an hour and now you have no wind. The boy will have told the dragoons or the navy that you're in this collier. There are probably a dozen vessels rowing around in the water right now looking for us. If you had left everyone dead, and we had scattered the dragoon's horses, no one would know where we are. Better still, we should have rode the horses out of there, instead of taking this slow boat." She shifted around, obviously annoyed at their predicament.

Lunt continued to squat, his eyes studied her as she talked. "If we had eliminated the dinner party or at least the officers, there would have been no one to sail the Drake who knew anything. It would have been especially easy pickings for your Captain Jones to sail in and blow the Drake out of the water at dawn. Now they will be coming after your Ranger. Captain Burden may be fat and a bit old, but he's a very good sailor. Lieutenant Dobbs can also command. They're both very good."

"You should know," said Lunt crisply.

The inference made Marie suddenly lash out in an attempt to slap his face. As the hand ripped out towards him, Lunt seized her wrist roughly and wretched it backwards against the gunnels until she shrieked.

"All right, Henry?" inquired O'Mally, looking forward concerned.

"Yes. Hold the rudder on course," replied Lunt.

Lunt continued to apply pressure to her arm. "What you are going to do, Lady," his voice became deep and authoritative, "..is to sit up on the boom close to the mast. It will keep the sail shape full, while I trim her. We'll catch as much wind as we can. Mr. O'Mally and I will row. If each of us does our part, we'll stand a chance of reaching the Ranger before the British patrols can catch us."

He let her arm free and shifted back towards the tiller. He looked back towards shore where he could still see the fuzzy image of the campfire from the signal house. They must be moving very slowly. His eyes scanned the water. He squinted. More towards the Belfast city lights he thought he could see a solitary light way out on the water. It was a considerable distance. If there were patrol boats out after them, they were not close.

Lunt returned to the mast, let out the main sheet, and then observed the sail react to the wind. It flopped more than it should and then patiently, over the course of the next five minutes, he tried three other sail adjustments. Between adjustments, he leaned on the boom to hold it in place. When the boom was adjusted to its best position, he tightened the preventer line from leeward to the boom to remove the possibility of an uncontrolled jibe which could sweep the boom across the deck with devastating swiftness.

Lunt then squatted to talk to Marie, "I'm going to put you up on the boom now."

"I'll fall off. I can't swim." She looked up at the freely shifting boom. "It's unsteady, it won't hold my weight."

Lunt corrected her, "It will hold far more than your weight. Over the course of the next hour or two, your being there might improve our position another mile of two closer to the Ranger. Your sitting on the boom, while we row, will also help the sail take the shape of a spoon so it will catch more of the soft air. If you were not up there, our forward motion from rowing would cause the sail to work against us." He consoled her further, "It will make a difference. I'm not putting you up there needlessly."

Lunt held out his hand to help her get up. Together they walked to the base of the mast. About six feet high, the boom was jointed to the mast by a series of iron rings. He put his hands on her hips and lifted her up onto the boom. She shook unsteadily. The sail flopped unnervingly against her back.

Suddenly she was pitched forward on top of Lunt. Her soft female bodice made him aware of her again as it had just a few hours ago during the galloping ride through the dark streets of Belfast. He turned his head to avoid eye contact with her and then strained his arms upward again until she was reseated on the flopping boom. For the first time since Lunt had met her, Marie Chatelain genuinely looked frightened.

Lunt coached her, "Lean back, as if you are in a giant chair. Relax! If you're stiff, it'll pitch you out again."

"I can't swim," she repeated, her voice quaking.

Marie leaned back trying to become adjusted to her unsteady perch. From her vantage point she studied her two captors who set the tiller bar with guide lines and then both proceeded to row. Beneath them were all the muskets, none within her grasp. She was becoming used to her perch. She sighed and leaned backwards to stare out into the night.

* * * * *

Lieutenants Simpson and Hall were huddled together, speaking softly to each other on the quarterdeck. Jones suddenly strode out of the door to the officers' quarters and came up behind them. He cleared his throat to announce his presence. Simpson gave an unusual start as he turned around. He had a boatswain's whistle strung by a cordage about his neck, he had been fingering it.

Simpson noticed immediately that Jones wore his sword and that the butts of two pistols were detectable beneath the open flaps of his uniform jacket.

"Isn't this Lieutenant Hall's watch?" Jones inquired of Simpson, who rarely spent time on deck at night when it was not his watch.

Simpson offered, "I couldn't sleep, sir."

"Neither could I," admitted Jones. "What's our position, Lieutenant Hall?"

"We're a couple of miles inside the mouth of the lough, sir, but wind's nil now, has been for about an hour, and the tide's on the ebb. We'll have a difficult time getting to Carrickfergus this evening."

"We must get there," stated Jones with a exaggerated Scottish burr. He turned to look up at Simpson, "If you suddenly had command of this ship, would you do everything possible to get her to Carrickfergus to meet our men?" As he spoke, Jones moved closer to Simpson, his eyes never leaving those of his Lieutenant.

"Yes, I would," said Simpson firmly.

For a long moment Jones continued to look at him. "Yes, I believe you would." He started to turn and then his eye caught the boatswain whistle's reflection in the moon light as it rested at the tips of Simpson's fingers.

"Ah, the missing whistle," said Jones smiling. "I'll take that, Lieutenant Simpson, pleased that you found it. We've has been looking for it everywhere." Jones held out his hand. Simpson looked above him. Three marines were leaning over the fighting top of the mizzen, looking down at their officers. Simpson reluctantly removed the whistle and handed it over to his Captain.

"We'd better get some sleep, Lieutenant, I expect we'll both have an arduous day tomorrow. Let's not make it any worse, shall we," said Jones, who turned and departed the poop deck to return to his quarters, his hands clasped behind his back, the whistle clutched in one of them.

* * * * *

Lunt's arms were beginning to tire; O'Mally and he had rowed now for over a half hour. The wind had been almost non-existent. The boom would have been flopping back and forth all night in the vacillating breeze, if it had not been for the preventer Lunt had rigged. Looking out over the stern, he was surprised to still see the light from the signal house fire. It seemed as large as ever.

"I'm going to reconnoiter," Lunt told O'Mally. He pulled his oar inboard and passed the handle to his companion, then moved forward to the mast. Marie seemed to be motionless, still perched on the boom. Lunt moved close to her. He asked softly, "All's well?"

Somewhat startled, Marie jerked her head up from its resting place against the canvas mainsail. "It's hard to believe but for awhile I was asleep." She rubbed her eyes and looked at him.

"I'm going to shinny up the mast."

"What?" she quizzed at his statement, not understanding his meaning.

Lunt pointed up. "I'm going to climb up the mast and see if I can better determine our situation. We should be at least a little closer to Carrickfergus, yet I can still see the light from the signal station. It appears to be about the same size. I have to get a more accurate indication of how we are doing."

Lunt grabbed around the first of a series of metal and rope bands which held the mainsail's flopping luff close to the mast. He wedged the toe of a pointy French boot into the separation between the boom's iron support collar and the mast and pushed upward. His knee creaked and his feet ached again in a now familiar constricting pain as he pushed the whole weight of his body upward. He encircled the mast with his arms and joined his hands through a gap between the luff and mast. He leaned his body weight backwards as he heaved upward to place both knees on either side of the mast. His outward and downward pressure and the friction of his breeches were sufficient to hold his body aloft. He quickly moved his encircling arms upwards together, and then again lifted the entire weight of his body to meet them. His knees again found a new resting place. As he moved higher, the mast started to wobble.

"Everyone stay in place, as you are," Lunt called down in a tone just above a whisper. He then moved considerably higher in a series of lunges. As he shifted, the natural swaying movement of the collier in the waves caused his body to be swept out into a greater and greater arc with the mast. He wondered if his body weight at this height was sufficient to upset the small vessel's balance and at some point send it capsizing over into the water. Surely the builders must have designed a sufficient depth of keel and ballast to allow a person to climb the mast at sea. Yet, the vessel was supposed to be sailed with cargo and now it was virtually empty. His position felt precarious. He hung on as the sail flopped and banged in response to the next rolling of the harbour's surface. The shaking luff of the sail ground into the backs of his hands and arms. Marie's body weight resting on the boom was losing its effect on sail shape at this height.

Lunt looked back toward the signal fire. He needed to continue upward. He waited until the next large wave passed and then he shinnied to the top of the mast. The gaff at the top of the solitary mainsail was not secured and, in reaction to extreme waves, flopped about wildly. He hooked his leg over the wooden strut to steady it.

After a moment, he assimilated into the environment of the lough. He became more conscious of the sound of waves and the dampness of a light fog, than of the creaking noises of the deck below and the sound of O'Mally still rowing ineffectively. Out over the water, towards the direction they were heading, Lunt could see a few lights ahead on the shore, but no vessels in the water. The waves ahead lapped as the lough's tide was beginning to turn. Very soon it would be on the flood and the current would be against them. They had been making little progress in the almost flat current, the incoming tide would only push them back, deeper into the harbour.

Lunt shifted his body around the mast. He looked back at the fuzzy light he had been viewing immediately off their stern. He was high enough now that he could discern two lights instead of one. The nearest was much better formed, the one above it was fuzzy, perhaps the dull light of the now distant signal fire. Lunt concentrated on the lower light, it appeared relatively close and had the steadiness of a lantern. He rested his foot on the deadeye that controlled the gaff and attempted to stretch higher. Lunt guessed the distance to the nearer light to be only a mile. After some moments of observation, it appeared to be closing fast. He looked across the water in all other directions and identified nothing else. He descended to the deck.

Marie looked at him with curiosity. "See anything?" she asked as Lunt reached the deck, standing for an instant beside her position on the boom.

Lunt did not answer and moved to sit in front of O'Mally who still rowed. "I think we'd best lower our aspect," Lunt announced.

O'Mally looked up at him and stopped, breathing heavily from the arduous but futile rowing. Lunt continued, "I'm going to take the sail down, lower the boom and gaff onto the deck, and change course towards shore. I think we've got a longboat in pursuit. It's dark and a bit foggy, perhaps they won't spot us. It's our only hope."

O'Mally shook his head in obvious concern. "Do ya suppose they've seen us yet?"

"Don't know," said Lunt, "but get the bow pointed inshore at an angle oblique to them. As they come parallel with us, we'll make the angle towards shore more direct. They'll see only our stern in view, not the larger beam."

"What?" said O'Mally not entirely sure of Lunt's intention.

"The surface of the transom will be smaller and consequently less likely to be seen than the beam, we'll keep the stern of the vessel directly towards them at all times." Lunt pointed out a course with a hand signal. Understanding, O'Mally nodded and then shifted his oars to change course. Lunt moved forward to the mast and stopped in front of Marie.

"There's a pursuit vessel, probably a longboat. They're coming up on us fast, must have a full crew of oarsmen. We need to take down the sail to lower our visibility. Down off there now." Lunt extended his arms as she pushed off the boom towards him. Contact with her again stirred him for an instant.

She said, "After all this, we're not going to make it, are we?"

"It doesn't look good, but let's give it our best," said Lunt.

Marie nodded and asked, "Can I help?"

Lunt nodded and pointed to a series of ties which held the luff of the sail to the mast. "Take these off as I lower the sail onto the deck. Then help fold the entire sail beneath the boom and gaff so that the white canvas can't be seen as they pass us."

Lunt felt the direction of the vessel change slightly while he unfastened the halliard from its cleat. The main was lowered gradually onto the deck. Several times he paused to gather in the canvas. Marie stood beside him loosening the ties. By the time he had lowered the sail fully, the sail was also free from the mast. He shifted the rigging onto the floor of the vessel and then began to hastily stuff the sail material into the hull cavity. Ideally, there should be no white of sail to flash their presence in the darkness and no large dark silhouette that would be detectable as it blocked out lights from shore.

To keep down the noise, O'Mally had ceased rowing. With a lack of headway, he struggled with changing the direction of the vessel. They were drifting now under the influence of the waves of a flood tide. O'Mally took the helm and, after each wave, tried to utilize the vessel's momentum to carry it towards shore. Lunt judged that there was still over an hour before daylight. If they could get some wind, they could outsail the rowers, but it seemed not to be.

Lunt finished securing the gaff and boom amidship and then shifted back to O'Mally, who was continuing to have trouble getting the vessel headed properly. They were losing precious time.

"I'll take over the tiller," said Lunt. "You check the muskets and get them loaded with powder and shot. Over charge them a bit for long range."

O'Mally got up and turned the steering over to Lunt. "Aye, 'tis best. I don't have the knack, but guns are something I know."

While O'Mally proceeded to uncover the muskets and powder they had taken from shore, Lunt concentrated on the movement of waves into the lough. His first objective was to keep the stern of his vessel facing his pursuers. If he could get out of the range of their vision before they reached a point parallel to his position, they might have a chance of going undetected. He turned and looked back, the light was much larger now. He could heard voices across the water and just see the outline of the bow of their longboat and the flashes of the oars as they dipped in the water and then splashed in the lantern light. They were going to pass very close-by, but it appeared that they had not caught sight of them yet. Their distance was under four hundred paces. They were singing something, a rowing chant.

Lunt again concentrated and, as a moderate wave lifted them, he gently changed the course of the collier to coast downwards off its crest. At the bottom of the trough he turned slightly with the prevailing current to pick up momentum. Suddenly, he thought of something and stretched his head to look over the transom. The stern of the vessel was painted royal blue, but on the transom the large, block white lettering of Captain Burden's humorous name, H.M.S. Innocence, stood out in sharp contrast to its dark environment.

Lunt shook his head and looked around for something with which to cover the transom. The only thing he had close at hand was his dark wool Irish cloak. He would be cold but it was all he had. He fit one button hole over a cleat and draped the garment over the stern of the vessel. It was only large enough to cover half the transom. He looked around for something else with which to cover the other half. Nearest was the dark wool garment which Marie wore. He motioned quickly to her.

"I'll need your cloak," whispered Lunt, "..to cover the transom. The lettering is white."

In reaction, Marie immediately began to unfasten her cloak, the same one which O'Mally's friends had given them all before they reached the signal house. Marie handed it to him, the faint light revealed her white dress, now muddied from head to toe, her white shoulders were bare. Lunt flung the garment out over the remainder of the exposed transom.

Lunt whispered to his crew, "Each of us will crouch low and be still until we are discovered, then you are to shoot for their water line. If we can get a ball or two into their hull, it'll splinter enough to cause some injury. At best, we can slow them down. If we can get some water in their boat, we could get away."

O'Mally handed Lunt a musket. He did not hand one to Marie.

"I'm sorry," said Lunt to Marie. Then he turned to O'Mally who was dressed in dark clothes. "Forward, sit on top of the folded sail, it's still visible. Keep it covered with your body. Take most of the rifles, leave me two and a pistol."

O'Mally moved forward towards the bow carrying some

of the carbines. Marie stayed beside Lunt, lying low with her face pressed against the bottom boards, shivering from the cold. Behind them, the chorus of their pursuers' song was becoming clearer and clearer, despite the cockney accents forming the words...

"*Yankee Doodle, on the run.*

Yankee Doodle, on the run."

...was being repeated again and again. The sound of the rowers' chanting was now obliterating any sound of oars hitting the water. Lunt peered up over the transom. The longboat was now only two hundred paces away. He again shifted his tiller to point the vessel down the crest of a wave and then in a direction perpendicular to his pursuers. He put his head down and listened. Marie moved up from the deck to lay with her back on the opposite side of the tiller. Her arms encircled her shoulders. She was visibly cold.

"How close will they come to us?" she whispered.

Lunt's face was just a foot from hers, under the tiller bar. He whispered, "Probably less than a hundred paces. They're distracted by their own song. We could be lucky." The soldiers were laughing about something. He asked her, "Can you really shoot?"

"Of course," she replied.

Lunt looked at her and then spoke, "You heard what I said about the water line. If I'm hit, fire the muskets at it and then go overboard. The seat there," he gestured, "is pretty loose and should float, you might try and take it with you into the water. If you have to go over." He paused, "You can't swim at all?"

She looked at him and shook her head.

In the background behind him, there was a lull in the chanting song. The sound of rowers' oars striking the cold dark water intensified. Lunt glanced upwards at the tall mast to see how visible it was. Overhead, a cloud cover had returned. It was dark and ominous. Almost automatically he moved the tiller down to make the small collier fall down another wave to continue to inch away from the likely path of their pursuers. In the trough of the wave, he again hardened up slightly to carry the vessel away from the pursuers. Cutting through the darkness he could hear the voices resume their rowing chant,

"*Yankee Doodle on the run,*
Yankee Doodle on the run."

Moonlight began to seep through a break in the cloud cover. It might reveal them. Lunt looked at Marie, in her eyes he could see the reflection of the longboat's bow lantern. The British were almost parallel with them. Lunt turned the tiller as he reached the bottom of a trough. He tried to keep the black cape covered transom facing right at them. The sound of several rowing oars descending into and rising out of the splashing water was now very intense amid the chanting.

Lunt heard someone on board say something in a cockney accent and then the entire crew laughed. From the direction of the laughter, the longboat seemed to have moved past them.

"*Yankee Doodle on the run,*" started one strong voice, presumably the coxswain. A chorus of oarsmen's voices repeated the refrain, as their oars dipped into the water again with an audible splash.

"*Got a tart on his lap,*
Ain't no feather in his cap.
Yankee Doodle on the run."

A chorus of male voices laughed in approval of the new contribution to their rowing lyric. Gradually, their voices became a little more distant across the water.

Lunt looked at Marie. Her eyes were shut. She had her hands and arms were clasped across her bodice in a vain attempt to control her shivering. A few crow's-feet showed at the corner of her eyes. Who was she really, thought Lunt? So beautiful, yet so capable to have maneuvered herself into a position to spy on the Royal Navy, seemingly all by herself.

Was she really French or perhaps Russian, there was a slavic quality to her features.

Suddenly, the sound of rowers' raucous laughter was punctuated by the shrill call of a boatswain's whistle. Lunt's every instinct jerked his body into action. Facing Marie, he saw her eyes flash open. He looked down towards the bow, O'Mally was holding a musket and was drawing back the cock. In the distance they heard a midlands accent.

"Up oars and silence, mates, the Lieutenant wants us to listen a bit. No sneezing or breathing, if you please."

Lunt peered up carefully. He judged that the longboat was some two hundred paces past them. He could see the outline of the lantern and a man standing above the others looking towards shore with a spyglass. As another wave carried them up onto its crest, Lunt turned the tiller ever so slightly to keep the dark transom facing their pursuers. For a long moment there was silence. Crouching low, Lunt reached for a musket and handed it under the tiller to Marie. He then took one himself, pulled back the cock and checked the positioning of the flint.

In the distance, he heard the coxswain resume the rowing chant. He sat up a little and lifted his head to look at the departing vessel. He could see the reflection of water drops spinning off the tips of oars in the light of the bow lantern. He let out a sigh and then felt a hand close on his as it grasped the tiller. The touch was light. He turned his head.

"You're a very brave man, Henry Lunt." She shivered, "Oh, I'm freezing."

Lunt stood up and unfastened the cape from around the tiller and lifted it off the transom. The edge of the cape was wet from contact with the sea. Lunt squeezed it to get as much water out as possible. He then threw it over her head and helped fasten it at her neck. She gazed up at him all the while.

"Why do they call you Yankees? And why do they

always say Yankee Do..oodle?" she asked with a French accent.

Lunt smiled at the way that she pronounced the words. He explained, "My father told me that the word Yankee came from the Dutch. A long time ago, when New York was called New Amsterdam, they used to refer to the British colonists across the Hudson over in Connecticut, as John Bulls, still a popular name for the English.

"How do you say John in Dutch?" Lunt queried.

"I speak many languages very well, Henry. But I know only a little Dutch. I suppose your Yankee sound could have come from the word Jan, or John in old Dutch, if it were mispronounced. It's an interesting theory," said Marie.

"My father thinks the colonists of the time just accepted the term good naturedly and after time it lost its original meaning. It eventually came to mean everyone in the British colonies east of the Hudson," Lunt continued as he slowly shifted the tiller. During his explanation, Marie had placed her hand on top of his. He became conscious of it again, as he continued talking.

"During the Indian Wars, against the French," he looked over at her for a reaction, but there was none, "...the British regulars did not have much respect for the colonials, they felt we were too inefficient and they began to call us Yankee Doodle, meaning wasting time."

"Did your father fight against the French and Indians?" asked Marie.

"Yes," said Lunt, again looking at her for a reaction, "and in the same campaign that Captain Burden and Major Pitkan were discussing at dinner."

"What are we going to do now?" Marie changed the subject.

"Sit and pray for wind, when it gets light they'll be able to see us both from shore and water," said Lunt. "It will take more rowing power than we've got to overcome the incoming tide."

Lunt turned and looked at Marie. "Why did you let

yourself get into this sort a thing? You're very beautiful, you could just sit at home and be married to a handsome lord, or whatever your country calls its nobility."

"Boredom is my reason, Henry. For many years I sat at home and let my husband take the front role. It was my duty to give him children. But it was never to be." Marie bit her lip. "When I was a child, I had a fever. You see, Lieutenant Lunt, I am barren."

Lunt looked at her a bit shocked by her forthrightness. She continued, pulling her cape about herself tightly for warmth, "You are right, Henry. I was from a noble family, not high nobility but medium level nobility, if you can understand. But with any position of nobility comes the expectation of children. A responsibility, so to speak. My husband's family were very disappointed and created a lot of pressure on him to have our marriage annulled by the church. For many years he resisted and then, when there were financial difficulties a few years ago, he found it expedient to let his beautiful wife out for hire."

"For hire?" said Lunt.

"There is a special phrase at court...*La belle sterilite*. What is meant is that the husband can let his wife sleep with other men, without complications. You see, since there could be no issue from the liaison, it is a very attractive attribute to men in very high places. And then there was an arrangement for a change in title to obtain some additional land and then ultimately," Marie looked Lunt straight in the eye, "I slept with the King."

Lunt looked down, obviously embarrassed by her frankness. "Do you want me to go on?" she said. Lunt shook his head and said, "It's not necessary."

Lunt stood up suddenly and raised his hand up into the air. "I think there is a whisper of wind." He looked at O'Mally, who nodded. There was no longer any sight or sound of the British patrol.

"We'll wait another quarter of an hour and then see

if we can sail, Mr. O'Mally." The Irishman sat upright on the bed of canvas and raised his hand to acknowledge the order. Lunt looked around and then sat down again.

"Do you have a wife?" asked Marie.

"Yes," replied Lunt.

"Has she given you children?"

"Yes, a son. I have not seen them for over a year."

"Where have you been?"

"In prison. First, Mill prison in Plymouth, later Wales until two days ago."

"You've just escaped and then were put on this absurd mission?" asked Marie, somewhat startled.

Lunt shook his head, "I have to tell you that the absurd part of this is that it all just happened. It just became more and more complex. I couldn't stop things. Captain Jones only intended for us to locate the Drake, and find out if and when she was coming out.

"The original idea was that we should just walk around the perimeter of the lough and observe the vessels anchored. Between O'Mally and I, we just got carried away. One idea led to another. The dinner service was too great an opportunity to pass up." Lunt looked at her from across the tiller bar. "Do you understand?"

"I understand more than you know, Henry. Then, you did not know about the naval gun before you came to Belfast?"

Lunt retraced the conversation, "You never answered my first question, why do you spy? Aren't you afraid of being hanged?"

Marie looked at him and went along with the change of subject, "You see, as a liaison without complication, I suddenly learned that I could accomplish something meaningful in my life. I mentioned my King earlier."

Lunt nodded, and Marie continued, "When my husband first let me sleep with the King, it was to forgive certain taxes he owed, but the King liked me. He wanted me to serve him in affairs of state. The annulment, which my husband's family sought for so long, was immediately theirs and I was then far beyond their power. My husband soon had his new wife."

"Did she bear him children?" Lunt inquired.

"Yes," replied Marie who began to laugh hysterically, oblivious to the danger of their being heard by the British patrol. Lunt moved to put his hand over her mouth. She held up her hand to let Lunt know that she was still under control.

Annoyed at the breech of security but curious beyond himself, Lunt asked, "Why did you laugh?"

"Because my loving husband's four children were all girls. In France that means that he has no direct heirs to his titled estates."

For the first time, Lunt believed he saw Marie's eyes fill with tears. He placed his hand on her arm and said, "I'm sorry."

Marie took a frilly part of her dress and began to dab at her eyes, yet she continued, "You see, Henry, my King kept me at his court for two years. I became bored by the petty circumstances about a King's court. All nature of people are continually trying to get this or that privilege or advancement. After a while you can see through the false ambition and pride. I decided that I wanted to do something more important, to participate in deeds which would influence history. Most women don't get such opportunities, you know, they just latch onto a man and use his power and title."

"And so you became a spy," concluded Lunt.

"Yes, and you, Lieutenant Henry Lunt of the American Continental Navy, why did you become a spy?"

Lunt shook his head, "I don't know. As I said I'm not really a regular spy, it was a situation. Captain Jones rescued me and some other men, and nearly lost his ship to do it. I felt I couldn't let him down."

"How old are you?"

"Twenty-five," he replied. "And you?"

"My, Henry, what a personal question! Do you not know it is impolite to ask a woman her age?" Marie batted her eyelashes in a coquettish way and then leaned forward. "I'm over forty, Lieutenant Lunt, and I intend to live life to the fullest until the day I die. Being a spy for my King allows me to do a great deal more of what I want."

Suddenly she felt a portion of her hair lifted in a stiff breeze. The same thought passed between them instantaneously. Lunt turned around and whispered to O'Mally, "Yank up the main, we've wind, thank God, we have wind."

"'Tis the breath of life from the little people," commented O'Mally, sheer delight evident in his voice.

* * * * *

Royal Navy Lieutenant Greene was a mile directly off shore and almost two miles short of the ancient stone pillar at Carrickfergus. His men had rowed relentlessly all night. He himself was exhausted after his second consecutive night out on the lough. They had encountered nothing and it was almost dawn. He drew out his spyglass and checked everything about him once more. The wind had begun to blow stiffly from the southwest. It might favor the escaping spies.

He should try to search for the collier again. They had neither seen nor heard anything in the darkness. He asked his coxswain to order the men to stop singing and be silent. He turned slowly in a deliberate revolution starting with the fading lights of Belfast along the south shore of the lough. As he swung towards the southeast, he picked up the other patrol boat easily, it was way off course, nearly to the south shore of the lough. He continued turning. There were three, ..no, four merchant vessels anchored in the usual place off Carrickfergus. Still no sign of the collier. It was still dark along the north shore as he swept his glass slowly back towards Belfast to complete the circle without success.

Greene decided to concentrate on the north shore again, perhaps he could see Major Pitkan's patrols and exchange a signal with them.

Suddenly he saw a light on the north shore where there had not been one an instant before and then another light was blotted out. Something was moving close to shore on the water, blotting out one successive light after another. It had to be the collier. He shouted to the pilot, "Three points to larboard, Mr. MacKensie."

"Aye, aye, sir."

"Bear into it men, we have contact," shouted Greene. One of the marines beat a small drum from the stern as the men increased the tempo of their stokes. Twelve oars, six on each side, rotated rhythmically from the sea to the air and back to the sea again. With each assent into the night air, the oar blades feathered together in the tradition of the Royal Navy. Among the rowers, six Royal Marines began to prime their weapons at a furious pace as their Corporal shouted a series of commands.

They moved closer to shore in a effort to cut off the vessel which was obviously trying to beat along the coast towards Carrickfergus. They should intersect within a quarter hour. Greene looked towards the east, towards the mouth of the harbour. The sky was beginning to lighten.

"We can likely get a volley on the target in another ten minutes. Shall we use one of our rockets now, sir?" asked Corporal Johnson.

"To establish a trajectory it would be fitting, Corporal, as you wish." Lieutenant Greene shouted encouragement to his men, "Backs into it, men, there'll be a night's leave and a flagon or two on me if we catch the damn Yankee spies before they get to Carrickfergus."

Greene turned to look at the four merchant ships laying at anchor. He could not see what the spies might be trying to reach. There was no warship. The longboat pressed across the bay to intercept the collier.

* * * * *

The hijacked H.M.S. Innocence continued to beat forward. O'Mally steered the course which Lunt had set, while Lunt adjusted the sheets almost continuously. He let the lines lose until the main luffed from too open a sail. He then pulled the lines taunt and cleated them down. As the collier proceeded on an ever more westerly direction, he tightened the sail to make a sharper angle with the new wind. At times he positioned Marie in different windward positions to give the tub shaped vessel better balance. The loaded muskets lay stacked in the center of the craft.

Anxiously, Lunt looked towards shore, they were five hundred paces away. They might be seen but there was little that small arms fire could do to affect them at that distance. He looked out into the still black void of the lough. Approaching them was a single point of light, about a half mile distant. He squinted and stood up, with his hand on the boom for leverage. There was something closing in on them.

As he stared for several moments, he saw a flash of light and then a long arching flame streaked into the sky and then hurled downwards towards him. He ducked instinctively as the incendiary whirled by them and fell fifty paces beyond them into the water.

"Rocket," shouted Lunt, just as the swooshing noise of the round reached them. "There'll be a musket volley shortly. Everyone down on the deck. Heads below the gunnels."

Lunt noted the position of the patrol boat's light relative to a cleat on the gunnel. He would know in a minute whether they were going to evade the British on this heading. He ducked his head, as did O'Mally and Marie. The former coal carrier had a high freeboard. Lunt kept his hand in control of the main sheet, while O'Mally stayed on the tiller also keeping his profile low. Their vessel moved as fast as possible.

"Fall off from them a half point," shouted Lunt.

Marie spoke up, "I said I can shoot. Will you let me take a try? I will be able to hit the mark."

There had been no volley as yet. Lunt peered out over the gunnel. The patrol boat had moved back along the stern. He could not tell whether it was due to O'Mally's slight change of course or if they were going to beat their pursuers to Carrickfergus. The morning light was getting brighter, it was going to be close.

"We'll both make the attempt," Lunt finally responded to Marie's offer to help. He cleated the main sheet to a belaying pin and took up two standard British issue army muskets. He had never fired this model before. How he wished that he had an American rife, one of his father's hunting pieces with a long barrel. He doubted if these weapons would have the range he needed.

He watched Marie take up the musket and rest the barrel half way out over the gunwale. The butt rested against her shoulder as she squatted in the middle of the boat. He smiled and thought, she may be brave but that recoil will pitch her backwards on her fanny. He was about to move to help her when suddenly he looked around to see the flash of a volley of musket fire.

"Incoming," he shouted and threw himself low on the deck. Above he heard the whistle of musket balls pass through the early morning sky. Most of them erupted into the water about them as small water spouts. Two rather spent rounds hit the sail; one ripped a small circular hole some inches above the boom and the second musket ball lacked sufficient force to even penetrate the canvas and simply fell from the sail to the deck, bouncing loudly to announce its arrival. The pursuers had their range.

Suddenly, Marie fired her musket as the vessel hit the crest of a wave. The deed surprised Lunt who was still estimating whether or not they could get an effective shot off from this distance. He had chosen to save his shot until the pursuers were closer. Fire shot forth from her muzzle and black smoke at first gushed forward out over the water, and then drifted back as it was carried with the wind. Before making the shot, she had braced the weapon against a support upon which the tiller ordinarily rested. It had absorbed the shock rather than her shoulder.

Lunt stared in the direction of the developing dawn. The colors of the sky were dark and ominous but among the objects that he could now make out were a series of ships sitting peacefully at anchor, each pointing towards the crisp southwesterly. The first was only a mile off. If he could pass the first one, he could put it between them to block the patrol boat's fire as he continued to make his way up the coast in search of Ranger.

There were at least three vessels at anchor, finding Ranger might be difficult unless they gave a signal. Lunt glanced in the direction of the pursuers who were still closing but seemed to be slowed up. The bow lantern had gone out suddenly, in reaction to Marie's shot. She must have hit it, or been so close they had snuffed out the lantern themselves.

For a long moment, he could no longer see his pursuers, until the lights of a second volley lit the sky for a brief moment. He threw himself onto the deck.

* * * * *

The mutineers proceeded through the sleeping quarters awakening men they knew would be sympathetic to the cause of giving the Ranger a new commander. They let any sleep who might support Jones, including any of the men he had rescued two nights previously as they would naturally have loyalty to their liberator.

The mutineers currently had four pistols among them.

Colwell Haggart had just been elected to lead the mutiny. Lieutenant Simpson had said that Captain Jones was on to them and had come below earlier to advise the crew council to attempt nothing tonight, as it was not prudent. Then, he had simply said goodnight and retired to his quarters leaving Lieutenant Hall on watch alone. It was not the first time Simpson had delayed their plans. Captain Jones had been seen to retire shortly before Simpson.

After Simpson's departure, the Portsmouth council had been left below sitting around. They talked all night past eight bells and into the beginning of the morning watch. Then, they decided in the wee hours of the night to take immediate action. The morning watch was to be under Midshipman Benjamin Hill. He was not especially loyal to Jones and would be slow to act against his fellows from Portsmouth. The marine guards would be due to change at four bells into their new watch. The old guards would be tired and the new marine watch would be getting dressed and opening the armory.

At three bells the mob had begun to move. They started up the narrow stairway to the gun deck, Haggart was fourth from the lead. Things would go properly this time. They were right on time. They'd get the marines coming out of their powder room stores and seize them and their muskets. It would be over quickly once the mutineers dressed as marines and ascended up the ratlines to the fighting tops.

Haggart whispered encouragement to his men, "'Twill be smooth as silk men, they'll not be expecting it. No one'll be hurt 'cept the Captain maybe. We don't need to be doing this kind of duty. We signed aboard this ship to take prizes, not warships."

On the second deck level the mutineers waited until they heard the marines moving across the deck towards the quarterdeck armory. It was still dark and would be for another quarter hour. Darkness would be on their side. Haggart went with his men up the stairs towards the gun deck with a finger to his lips and a gun in his hand. Midway up the last flight of stairs, he peered past his men's shoulders towards the quarterdeck.

The high deck appeared to be devoid of officers and there was no one at the wheel. Haggart looked around. Where were the marines who were supposed to be perpetually assigned to sit aboard the capstan when Ranger was at anchor? Gone, damn, if only he had known. The men in front of him now stopped on the stairs and were looking back over their shoulder at the forecastle behind them. Haggart followed their gaze.

There, big as life, was Captain Jones. He raised a lantern over their heads to peer down at them. He was dressed in white breeches and a plain shirt, his uniform jacket discarded. Very visible in a wide leather belt were two pistols. His hanger swung from a scabbard at his side.

"Top of the morning to ye gentlemen," said Jones in as thick a Scottish brogue as he could command. "'Twas such a fine morning for a fight that I've asked Lieutenant Wallingsford and his marines and some other good men to post triple duty aloft this very morning. I'm very pleased that the men of Portsmouth and others have shown fit to get up over an hour early to volunteer for watch as well. Such enthusiasm for duty 'tis an inspiring thing to see."

The mutineers were caught red handed. Haggart looked up to see marines piled onto each of the masts' fighting tops. Many of the marines visibly had two or three muskets beside them in addition to the ones they pointed downward at the mutineers. Haggart noticed that Jonathan Harken and some of the other men that Jones had recently rescued stood with the marines on the ratlines above the deck. Jones motioned for the men on the stairs to continue out onto the deck. As they did, he walked amidst them holding up the lantern so that he could look each man in the eye. He was a head shorter than most of the men he surveyed.

He started to speak, "For shame, 'tis such an awful thing

to be asked to fight for liberty early this morning, instead of succumbing to greed..." Before Jones could utter another word, from the starboard side there erupted the swoosh of a rocket out over the water. The bright tail of the comet like flame lit the sky and diverted all their attention.

"Perhaps, gentlemen, the search for liberty has started without you. Let's postpone our discussion and go to the rails to see what's afoot," suggested Jones.

Eagerly accepting the excuse to avoid a head-on confrontation with their fully prepared Captain, most of the men left the assemblage and rushed to the starboard rail, hoping to avoid further association with the mutinous group. As they peered out over the rail, a musket volley lighted the air followed in a moment by its sound. Lt. Wallingsford stood beside his Captain and estimated aloud, "Five count between flash and report, be little over a mile off, sir."

Jones whispered over his shoulder, "Collect the pistols from the three or four that have them, Lieutenant. We'll get to the bottom of this mutiny another time."

Wallingsford and two marines walked behind the seamen and requested that Haggart and the others turn over their pistols. All complied without a struggle and were allowed to turn their attention back to the starboard rail to witness the fire fight that was fast approaching them. In their midst their Captain asked for rail space, the men parted and gave him room.

"Who they shooting at, sir?" asked one seaman.

Jones was silent. A moment later a single musket flashed much closer to shore. "There's your answer, lad," said Jones.

"Spyglass, Mr. Perkins," shouted Jones, his hand waited behind his head for the familiar cylinder to be delivered. Within a few seconds he was extending the telescope, training it towards shore.

On the first boat the bow lantern went out suddenly. A volley seemed to explode from the vessel simultaneously from the middle of the harbour.

Jones reported to his crew, "There's a small sailboat close to shore. I presume that'll be Lieutenant Lunt and Mister O'Mally. Do you think that the men of Portsmouth would be willing to fight the enemy and leave their Captain 'till later?"

Every man within earshot sounded, "Aye, aye, sir."

"Well, let's be about it then. Mr. Hutchins, double red signal lights aloft from the mizzen so Lieutenant Lunt will know which of the vessels at anchor is his. Otherwise he can't tell us apart from these merchantmen about us. But we did mean it to be that way, lads, didn't we?"

"Aye, aye, sir."

"Starboard gun crews out of the hammock. I want slow matches lit. All starboard guns primed but keep the gun port lids covered until I announce it to be different"

"Aye, aye, sir."

"Fifteen men and no less to stand by the capstan, if we have to weigh anchor in a hurry. Mr. Cullan, lift the main staysail partly so we can get some directional steerage at anchor."

Ranger bolted to life as men scurried about their vessel. Captain Jones continued to bark commands. Ranger was ready.

10
Daybreak

After the last volley passed, Lunt pushed himself up from the deck. A sense of pain came from his left arm and he looked down to see it was bleeding. A large splinter of wood was lodged in the flesh of his upper arm, the sleeve of his shirt was turning dark. He pulled out the splinter and saw that the wound was not serious. He ripped off part of his shirt sleeve and tied it around the wound to stop the bleeding, while shouting to his fellow crew members, "Everyone all right?"

Marie and O'Mally shouted that they were uninjured and then each fired muskets towards the pursuing longboat. The wind was increasing in tempo. As he fixed a makeshift bandage, Lunt looked across the lough which was just beginning to reveal an early morning sky of glorious dawn colors. He could see his pursuers clearly but they were not moving any faster than his collier under sail. He looked again at the anchored merchant ships. They were going to arrive in their midst a few minutes ahead of the longboat but it was going to be close. He turned the tiller to fall off further towards shore for a couple of minutes so he could view the sterns of the vessels. The early morning light was behind them, they were all just dark silhouettes against the coming dawn. He examined them. One had only two masts, it could not be Ranger. All the others had three.

Suddenly, Lunt saw two red lanterns appear, one atop the other. They had been hung from the stern of the vessel nearest him. Good fortune. He glanced at his pursuers and saw another flash. The pain in his arm made him lower his body below the gunwale. A few of the rounds descended onto the deck but they hit no one and lacked the momentum to create major damage. One ball did tear a second hole in the canvas but not at a stress point.

Lunt called out from the tiller, "Mr. O'Mally, leave the gunnery to Ranger. We need sail trim more than a single musket shot." His sentence was interrupted by the sound of Marie firing another round. He ignored the interruption and continued to give orders, "Let off the sheet a few inches and tighten down the boom, if you please, Mr. O'Mally, before there's another volley."

O'Mally laid down the musket and attended his duties, during which another volley was fired by the pursuers. All of the rounds fell behind them in the water. They were widening the distance from the longboat.

Lunt pulled the rudder hard right after passing behind Ranger's transom, the little collier's mast barely reached above Ranger's freeboard. The longboat was five minutes behind them. Lunt looked up to the rails for a reassuring face on the larboard side. Suddenly, he saw many. There was a cheer from above, Lunt knew he was home.

"Release the halliard, Mr. O'Mally."

"Aye, aye, sir."

The flapping sail was pointed directly towards the wind, stopping the vessel within a few paces. Momentum drove the vessel forward and then the buckling force of the wind striking the collier's bow started to make them lose headway. Suddenly, two lines were cast down upon them.

Lunt and O'Mally each seized one and secured the small sloop to the ocean side of Ranger. Lunt looked up to see the familiar face of John Paul Jones smiling down upon them. A Jacob's ladder was lowered. The Captain saluted him before he was able to secure the ladder to the collier. Lunt returned the salute and started to help Marie, but she pushed by him and proceeded quickly up the rope ladder ahead of both O'Mally and him.

When Lunt and O'Mally reached the deck they were immediately surrounded by well wishers. As the crew surrounded him and kept patting him on the back, Lunt looked up at the poop deck to see Marie with her arms around the Captain. She was kissing him as if she had been waiting to see him for a hundred years. Jones suddenly became very conscious of the display he was making before the crew and removed himself from her embrace. The next time Lunt looked he could see Marie and Jones talking excitedly. Finally, he saw Jones take the lady he had known both as Alicia and Marie and lead her by the hand to the quarterdeck rail. They stood together in silence a moment before the eyes of his crew.

"Men of the Ranger, I would like to introduce you to Madame Marie Chatelain, a friend of Ambassador Franklin and mine, and an emissary of His Majesty, Louis the XVI. It seems that Lieutenant Lunt has made both a successful reconnoiter and has also managed the rescue of a very beautiful lady." Laughter followed. Jones started to speak again but Lieutenant Wallingsford interrupted, "Sir, the longboat is approaching."

Jones looked to the starboard rail and pointed. "All hands drop down from sight immediately. We'll give the lobsterbacks a surprise they'll never forget. Swivels to the starboard deck, Mr. Simpson, but keep them out of sight to the approaching vessel. This officer will do the talking."

Still coatless from the encounter with his crew only a few minutes before, Jones strode to the starboard rail and looked below. Conscious that the two pistols still in his belt would give him away, he laid them beside a belaying pin for support, climbed atop the rail, and held onto the mizzen shrouds to make himself visible to the approaching craft. Jones glanced above him, Ranger flew both the commercial flag of Lloyd's and the Union Jack. He leaned outward, the gold stripe which disguised the outline of his closed gun ports would not reveal the Ranger's true purpose.

* * * * *

Standing off some two hundred paces, Lieutenant Greene cupped his hands around his mouth and began to shout up at the first anchored vessel he encountered. A man standing on the deck rail with a white shirt motioned for them to come closer. The man pointed to his ear as if he could not hear.

"Row up to them, Mr. Grant."

When the patrol boat arrived alongside the three masted vessel, Lieutenant Greene shouted up to the man, "Can you hear me now?"

"Aye, it'll be just fine, speak yer intention," said the man with an Scottish accent.

"Sir, I'm Lieutenant Greene of His Majesty's Sloop of War, Drake. Have you seen a small sailboat pass by here, just before dawn?"

"Pass by, you say?"

"Yes, sir, there was gun fire. Surely you heard?"

"Is that how that man got injured?" The man on the rail pointed at one of the oarsmen who had been wounded in the face and chest when their signal light exploded during the fire fight.

"Aye, yes, sir. He was shot by spies," replied Greene.

"Goodness gracious, spies you say."

The man seemed to be mocking him. Greene began to say something, but then the man spoke up again.

"Sir, the boat you are missing. What was her name?"

"Sir, it was H.M.S. Innocence."

"So, Lieutenant, you've lost your *Innocence* and are out here on the water trying to find it again."

Behind the man, Lieutenant Greene could heard the raucous sound of laughter. It came filtering down over the freeboard. Greene squinted up at the ship's rail. There was no one else there. Just one man.

He looked down at some of his crew, they were also laughing. The young officer became enraged. He shouted,

"Sir, if you could speak decent English, you'd understand that I haven't lost my innocence, but ..."

The young Lieutenant's utterances were lost in a great roar of laughter from the three masted ship, but there was still no one else apparent except the Scotsman. His own men about him were still trying to suppress their laughter but they also felt a nagging fear that this conversation was not going to have a pleasant ending.

"Ah, Lieutenant," said the man in a thick Scottish accent, "What is it ye really want?"

Greene shouted out, "To stop the spies from getting to the pirate Captain Jones. Sir, can you help me?"

"You want to find this Captain Jones then?"

"Yes, sir."

The man above him on the quarterdeck rail squatted briefly and then stood up again into full view. In each hand he sported a pistol, fully cocked. Greene and his crew of sailors and Royal Marines stared upwards into the barrels. They sat frozen. The man was right above them. During the brief conversation, their vessel had been drifting closer to the hull of the strange craft.

The man on the rail said, "I'm sorry to make such sport of a young enterprising officer but I can tell you that you've accomplished your mission. You have found Captain John Paul Jones. I am he."

"Surely you jest, sir."

"No, Lieutenant Greene, I do not jest." The man motioned with one of his gun barrels and a hundred heads seemed to appear over the starboard rail. They smiled down at him mockingly. The man continued talking, "You have before you a group of Yankee Doodles who are on the run no more. I advise you and your men to lay down your arms, or be blown to kingdom come. You are too small in number to offer any kind of meaningful resistance. It would prevent the lost of precious life, if you agree to lay down your arms now." The man shouted, "Now, instantly,

Lieutenant!"

Lieutenant Greene looked up on the gun rail to see five swivels now pointed down directly at him. Over a hundred men watched his every action. His six marines stood frozen. From his tormentor, Greene heard the command, "Gun ports open. Roll 'em out for the Lieutenant to see."

Nine gold colored gun ports were thrown open. Gun barrels rolled from the hollows in the golden stripe, which had disguised their deadly presence as part of the upper freeboard.

"I surrender, sir," sighed Greene, still in shock at the sudden calamity.

"Good," said Jones. "You will receive humane treatment, better than your country gives ours. You will be exchanged, when your arrogant King deems it to his advantage to exchange prisoners with the Continental forces."

Jones climbed over the rail, looking at the crew of the longboat. "Which of you seamen are Irish? Born here?" Three men raised their hands.

Jones pointed his pistol to indicate that he was talking to each of them. "I want you men to take your wounded man back to the Drake and let Captain George Burden know that Captain John Paul Jones and the American Continental Navy awaits his pleasure. You are to inform the Captain that this is my third invitation for him and his ship to meet me in an honorable struggle.

"Tell your Captain that I have no more patience and that if I do not see the Drake round the mouth of the lough this day, I will destroy every ship in the harbour, beginning first with the three vessels behind me, then working my way up and down from Carrickfergus to Whitehall, and even into Belfast itself. Since Captain Burden is charged with the protection of this harbour, it would be a sheer dereliction of his duty for him to fail to meet this challenge."

* * * * *

Lieutenant Greene and the rest of his prisoners were escorted below to a holding area on the second deck. As the undermanned longboat rowed off back towards Belfast, the green hills of the town rose majestically into the morning sky.

Jones turned to his crew and spoke loudly, "It'll be some time before we see the Drake. A lot of you have been up all night for one reason or another. I want every man, not on this morning watch, to get some sleep. I need a fresh crew when we meet the enemy. Get some rest, lads. Any man who gives his full measure of devotion to the successful capture of the Drake shall not need to have later concern that past events will come back upon him. The slate is clean from this time forward."

The crew cheered spontaneously.

* * * * *

Lunt tossed and turned in the small sleeping cradle. His quarters was separated from the most aft gun position by only a curtain. Behind the curtain, he could hear some of the gun crews checking their equipment and bantering about the surprise of the young Royal Navy Lieutenant that he had indeed found John Paul Jones.

Lunt's quarters were boarded on the other side by the firm wall of the great cabin. From within he could hear his Captain's low muffled voice and some occasional female laughter. They seemed to be speaking in French. Lunt tried to concentrate on getting his body to sleep but invariably his ear was tuned for a hint of additional sounds which might be forthcoming from the captain's cabin. Despite the physical ordeal which his body had experienced over the past two days, his brain raced with the thoughts of seemingly unimportant questions. How well had Jones known Marie? It must have been a very long time from the intensity of her greeting. Had Jones actually wanted Lunt to foil her spy mission? Had they been lovers before and were they still? Is that why Marie had not even glanced his way once she had set foot on Ranger? She had not even thanked him or chosen to recognize him, despite the closeness he had felt during the adventure.

Lunt continued to toss and turn. He was just another of the countless men she had tried to use throughout her life. Thank God he had not allowed her to do that with him as well. He had given her nothing. He had brought her to Ranger against her will, although she did help during the final pursuit. She had made a remarkable shot with the musket, shooting out the bow light of the longboat. Apparently that had slowed them down, just enough.

Suddenly a voice interrupted his thoughts. "Lieutenant Lunt, beg your pardon, sir. We have to turn your quarters into a ordnance storage area for the rear starboard gun. You'll have to move, sir." It was Thomas Palmer, the gunner's mate.

Lunt arose from his struggling attempt to sleep. He threw his feet out of the hammock. As they hit the deck he winced and then stared down at the damn French boots. He had tried to take them off but they seemed stuck on. He bent over looking at the little pointy toes he despised. The French must have funny feet with itty bitty toes for these things to be comfortable. Grudgingly, he stood up and walked over to the few clothes he had. He wrapped them in the bed roll which had been loaned him for the cradle and picked up the canvas bag that still contained his uniform and sword. He pulled aside his own curtain and found himself facing Jonathan Harken.

"Sir, Mr. Palmer thought I could help you find another place."

Lunt patted the shoulder of his old cell companion, "Thanks for suggesting O'Mally over Smith. I guess I'd have been on a hangman's noose by now if you hadn't."

"He seemed a very odd sort, sir. I saw him always

sneaking around, looking about before he did anything. Knowing you as I do, I didn't think he'd be the kind of man you'd want to land in Ireland with. But I had no idea he was a spy. None of the crew did, that's pretty much the truth. The Portsmouth men feel it was he who let the capstan slip, the last time they were trying to board the Drake."

Again Lunt thanked him and then changed the subject. "You say you know where a very tired person can get some sleep?"

"If you wouldn't mind where it was, sir, I know where there's a quiet place with a soft cushion."

"Get me to it," agreed Lunt.

"Well, sir, it's below the forecastle, near the crew's quarters. Some of the crew are already sleeping there. But it's quiet there. If you don't mind the company."

"Lead me to it, Jonathan," smiled Lunt, relieved that he was going to get away from the sounds in the great cabin that were disturbing his sleep.

Lunt followed Harken to a lower deck until he stood looking at an emergency stairway whose access route had been blocked off for some time.

"Here, sir," pointed Harken.

Harken pointed to a place on the deck among some soft canvas rolls. Lunt threw his bedroll on them and knelt to smooth it out.

"Beg your pardon, sir."

Lunt turned around and looked up at the man, "Yes?"

"I just wanted to say, the crew's real proud of you, sir. How you faced the Royal Navy at their dinner table with just two pistols and how you sailed that fat little tub out from the range of that longboat, with them shooting at you and all."

"How did you know about all that?" asked Lunt, who had not yet given a full report to anyone, even his Captain. Jones had been too busy entertaining Marie in his cabin, after they had taken Lieutenant Greene prisoner. Lunt had not even had the full opportunity to provide Jones with the information he knew about the new gun or the position of merchant ships in the harbour. He would have to do that long before Jones engaged the Drake. Just now he knew Jones was not interested in speaking with him.

"Mr. O'Mally, sir, he's a bit in his cups, sir. The Captain allowed us all a drop of rum to celebrate your return. None of us had the heart to deny Mr. O'Mally all he wanted. Besides, he keeps talking about this being the last day of his life."

"What's that?" said Lunt looking up suddenly from his sitting position. He had his knee bent so that he could get at the right boot which he had clenched in both hands and was again trying to wrench off his severely swollen foot.

"Says you crossed the path of some woman crying by the water when you came into Belfast. Says she's a Banshee who was warning of his death to come. Kind of spooky, sir."

"Damn, foolish notion. He's still up top?" quizzed Lunt.

"Yes, sir, drunk as a skunk, if ye don't mind me saying so. Is there anything else I can do for you, sir?"

"Well, go up top and tell Mr. O'Mally that he has a gun crew to take care of later this day. And that Lieutenant Lunt orders that he get to sleep. Now!"

"Is there anything else, sir?" asked Harken.

"No." Then Lunt hesitated, "Yes, there is. Are you a man who can keep a secret, and carry it out without telling anyone? On your honor."

"You know I'm that man," said Harken.

"Well my last request, if this day bodes ill for me and not for you, is that you get these damn French boots off my body, even if you have to cut them off. I'll have to fight with them later today because I have no other, but I'll not enter the next world with them, if it can be helped."

"Do you want me to help you get them off now?"

"It doesn't seem possible, I've tried and even if I could now, I'd never get them back on again 'till the battle was over. I can't fight the Drake in bare feet."

"No, sir," said Harken, looking down at his friend's boots and then saluting as he left.

Lunt removed his old leather vest and folded it to support his head. After a full ten minutes of struggle he did finally succeed in pulling off both his boots. Then he laid down and his mind dreamily thought of the walk along the coast road into Belfast. Of the poor people in their dark shawls who lived by the side of the road, of the wail of the woman by the stream, and of O'Mally's reluctance to let him go back and try to help her. He thought of O'Mally's sudden lack of talkativeness during much of the rest of the adventure. Was that superstition why O'Mally had come back up the stairs to help him secure the prisoners? Did he believe that he was going to die anyway? Was that why he did it?

Lunt remembered one evening long ago, when O'Mally and he had gone ashore from the Alfred into Nantes. Several of them had drank the entire evening. While in his cups, O'Mally had spent much of the night talking about all the mythical creatures of Ireland. As they were stumbling along the quays he had begun to tell everyone of the Banshee. How every native born ancient family in Ireland had its own. And that when a male member of that family was about to die, that the Banshee would appear a few days ahead to warn of the coming event. Once the Banshee appeared, the death was irreversible.

As his mind drifted off into sleep, Lunt recalled how he and some of the other crew of the Alfred had sat on the pier that evening wailing in imitation of O'Mally's Banshee. It seemed a thousand years ago but now just like the other day.

Lunt's thoughts of the Banshee and her wail seemed to bring him back again to the coast road. But this time, Lunt overcame O'Mally's objections and returned to the stream where the woman had wailed. He walked up the middle of the stream through the cold water in search of her. He shivered in the cold. His eyes did not look up until at the edge of the narrow stream he saw a pair of duck feet. The sound of wailing was unbearable. Lunt waded closer to the edge of the stream to better view the feet. Then, just as he looked up, a woman turned away from him. He tried to reach out to her but the more he tried, the more she seemed to move off. She seemed to float on a mist above the fog. Lunt followed her.

Then the figure stopped and the cloak fell from the back of her head. In the moonlight, the back of her hair was bright rusty red and beautifully arranged in two buns, one atop the other. As Lunt began to reach out for the figure, the head slowly turned as the intensity of the wailing increased to deafening proportions. The turning figure revealed no beautiful white face with high cheekbones. There was only a skull.

In startled reaction, Lunt's body seemed to fall backwards as if he was tumbling off a cliff. His arms flailed but he could not find anything to hold onto.

* * * * *

Captain George Burden strode the quarterdeck glancing upwards at the fill of his sails. He had not eaten since the eventful dinner of the previous evening, yet he did not feel hungry in any sense of the word. Ordinarily, his breakfast would consist of three or four eggs, plenty of biscuits, cheese, possibly some kippers, and tea. Was it just yesterday morning that he had enjoyed such a breakfast at the hotel, getting his fill before going over to the ship to inspect what the interloper might or might not have done aboard the Drake? Alicia had been with him and they had discussed the trip that they would make through Ireland immediately after his retirement. A trip, he knew now, she certainly never intended to make. His finger poked into his pocket, the ring was still there. What a colossal fool he'd been.

Burden tried to keep his mind on the conflict which was certain to lie ahead of him this day. He felt somehow trimmer and filled with renewed purpose. For twenty years he had served in the backwaters of the British empire and had let himself slide and fall victim to too much food and drink. His mind drifted again.

He thought of that young colonial officer, Lunt, who had dared to come masquerading into his birthday party. In some sense the man had been right to place the slab of dripping red meat on his chest. This morning, his housekeeper had wanted to clean his dress uniform but he had ordered her never to wash it again. He would leave it in his closet until the day he died to remind himself of what he had become. A grotesque fat man.

Major Pitkan and he had returned hastily to his flat to search Alicia's things for a clue to her origins. There was nothing, everything was carefully arranged to support the fact that she was a lady from Limerick. What a magnificent Jezebel she had been. He had never suspected. He pulled his mind away from the whirling torment of humiliation.

"Half point to larboard, Mister Whiting," he said.

Why had he not made the connection between the meat hook and the beef carver earlier. The Colonial had coolly cut meat for his table, while he had passed the meat hook around to see if anyone could identify what it was. And the man never spoke the entire time. Whoever heard of an Irish servant who could keep quiet for over two hours. It was so obvious, yet he had not seen it. But the young Colonial officer did have a certain pluck and style about him. Imagine the audacity to walk up to his dinner table, at his birthday party, with no way of escape. He was a brave, foolish young man. It was a pity he would have to hang. Yes, hang them all he would, even Alicia.

Months ago, all Royal Navy captains had received standing orders from the Admiralty to hang all Yankee privateers. It would be a pleasure. Those directives would be his guide for action this day.

Marshall and the other magistrates had tried to suggest he should not go anywhere with the Drake until the Governor General was briefed. Ha, that hypocrite was off gallivanting west of Dublin, likely screwing one of the local ladies. This Captain was not looking back to land for a signal and if one was seen, he would ignore it. This was going to be Captain Burden's day. He felt good, he had not had liquor with which to start the day, as had been his custom of many years. He felt very fit and more purposeful than he had in years. The Admiralty would no doubt investigate him and his actions for months. He would certainly be court martialed and might lose his pension for dereliction of duty. But if he were the man to hang the Yankee pirate Jones and his accomplices from the yardarms of an English warship, much could be forgiven. The press would make him a hero.

"Mister Whiting, send Lieutenant Dobbs up here."

He must forget all thoughts of yesterday. He must concentrate only on the present, on today. He must sail his ship with all the skill he could muster. These were the parting words of dear Major Pitkan, his loyal friend. Because the wind was coming from the south, Major Pitkan himself had taken a force of a hundred horsemen and some light cannon along the road to the north end of the lough. That was the shore towards which a disabled vessel might be blown and if the pirate could be driven aground, or close to shore, the Major's dragoons would render assistance. He had also sent a lesser force to the south end. God bless him.

Burden's mind continued to whirl as he looked aloft. To think that shipbuilder Wright had been sleeping with Alicia at midday while he had gone aboard Drake to prepare for the ordnance test. 'Course who could blame him with that fat little wife of his, getting the chance to bed with a woman like Alicia. What was her purpose, did she think she could get something out of Wright that she couldn't obtain from him? Burden glanced down on the holystoned gun deck,

Wright was looking up at him with sad eyes. At least the man had the gumption to volunteer to come aboard. 'Course he wants to kill her too, before anyone from the Governor General's staff can question her and ruin his business. We all want to kill her.

Burden glanced out at large group of red coated soldiers and a few civilians which peopled his deck. He had taken on as many additional soldiers as possible. In his preparation for this fight, Burden had left his way open for several alternatives. His primary strategy would be to catch the Ranger and board her. If he could get a little help from the new gun he'd take it, especially if it could cripple the enemy from afar, before the Colonial's guns were within range of the Drake. If they could use the carronade to launch a large eighteen pound ball against Ranger at close range, the effect would be devastating. At any rate, it would give Lieutenant Dobbs a change to try his new toy. If it worked in action, England would have a way to catch these damn privateers and to help smash the American uprising before it spread here to Ireland and who knows where else in the Empire.

Burden glanced up. The slight change in direction had improved the sail set. It was a good ship, the Drake. Her twenty cannon should be the equal to whatever the Ranger carried. He had not seen his opponent but, with the extra force of fifty of Major Pitkan's finest and some dozen or more volunteers, the Drake should be carrying nearly twice the manpower of the Ranger. If they could close and grapple her, it would be over quickly.

"Sir," spoke Lieutenant Dobbs.

The man had visibly lost a bit of his shine since his own 'kissing' incident with Alicia had been revealed in front of his Church of England parents. But he was a good competent officer. The events of the past twenty four hours had ruined his career and he damn well knew it. Privately, after they had been released from the closet prison, Dobbs had apologized to Burden. He had said that he had never been "intimate" with Alicia but that he had been thinking of it. Alicia, or whatever her name was, had encouraged his advances. He did not deny Major Pitkan's observations during the fox hunt. He had simply apologized.

"Lieutenant Dobbs, you say that in addition to firing an eighteen pound ball, that the carronade can be made to fire a lighter sabot shot, a very great distance?" asked Burden.

Dobbs stood at attention before him. "Yes, sir. I had made up four of the wooden shoes earlier for the testing which was to have occurred this day. I believe we will be able to get a range of 3,000 paces from such a lighter, six pound shot. Twice the range of our four pounders, and certainly a greater range than anything a lighter vessel like the Ranger would ordinarily carry."

"But we have never fired this carronade from a pitching deck at sea, have we, Lieutenant Dobbs? You have previously only tested the carronade by shooting at canvas spread out across trees in an empty Scottish field. And canvas doesn't shoot back."

"But, sir."

"My point is, Lieutenant, that you must be doubly and triply sure that your little toy does not damage the integrity of this ship, or all will be lost."

"Yes, sir," replied Dobbs. "I have checked the platform, it was well constructed by Mr. Wright's group. We have also double braced the cannon with lanyards. There will be sufficient absorption of the shock. You can trust me, sir."

Burden reminded him, "I trusted you yesterday to check this ship over for possible damage from the intruder. Yet, this morning I was the one who found the rudder steerage chain had been cut."

At that remark Captain Burden turned to look directly into Lieutenant Dobbs' eyes. He raised his right eyebrow, and then calmly and forcefully set priorities for his Lieutenant.

As he spoke the great flaps of flesh which hung from his neck swayed back and forth, and from his great belly he pushed wind upward into his larynx with a forceful roar.

"Your first responsibility this day is to man that gun with all the alacrity you can muster. And to keep it operational. If we can get close enough, we'll employ the eighteen pound ball to blow that damn pirate apart. If the carronade fails for any reason, we are to abandon it and concentrate your efforts on our other weapons."

"Yes, sir." Lieutenant Dobbs started to move away.

"I'm not finished, Lieutenant."

"Sir," Dobbs turned as his Captain continued speaking.

"If there is a sign that this vessel could or just might fall into enemy hands, you are under my direct order to make it your first priority to toss that pop gun overboard. If it should perform in the manner you have described, can you imagine the damage it would do to England to have those little American privateers all capable of being able to toss something as heavy as an eighteen or twenty pound ball?"

"Yes, sir," said Dobbs, now listening intently to the older officer who expanded upon the gravity of the situation.

"Be it understood, that at all costs this weapon cannot fall into enemy hands, or within the year all those little nasty pirates will be able to directly challenge England's Men of War in open battle. Instead of running away from us, because they are out gunned, they will instead be able to turn and fight us at sea. We could lose the uprising in the colonies and God knows what else."

Burden motioned for the other officers and masters on his quarter deck to gather round him. First, he looked directly at the Sailing Master, "What kind of speed are we getting now, Mister Whiting?"

"Sir, the first log estimates over seven knots on a quarter hour glass."

"We need more speed. I want to hit the Ranger with full force when we round the bend into full view of

Carrickfergus. Attend to getting the topgallants launched after I have spoken to all of you."

Burden looked about at his officers and masters. He spoke with an authority and strength that they had never heard from him before. "Our strategy will be to roar into view and head directly windward of the place where the longboat survivors indicated Ranger was anchored. When we're within 3,000 paces we'll dip to leeward to give Lieutenant Dobbs a brief change of course with which to try the carronade. No matter what the effect, we will then resume the former course immediately and try to get windward of the pirate. If we can, we will either be able to drive her towards shore where Major Pitkan's batteries can be brought to bear, or we will be in a position to close and board. Our superior numbers should make that an effective strategy. God save the King."

His officers and men saluted him and answered back, "God save the King."

Burden picked up his speaking trumpet and went to the rail of the quarterdeck which overlooked from shoulder height the remainder of the crew who were dispersed accomplishing their assigned tasks. As he paused to clear his throat, he observed van Zoot clinging onto a line attached to a belaying pin at the foot of the main mast. His eyes were filled with terror as they glared back at him. Burden thought to himself, after all the men you have ill equipped for profit, it's time you and your kind experienced a real fight.

Then, after a drum roll, Burden spoke to the entire ship. "I have invited volunteers, the civilian militia, and the standing army regiment to also serve upon the Drake this day because I expect to board the pirate vessel and may need your numbers. However, in order to accomplish this victory, my seamen need, first and foremost, to be able to sail this vessel to within range of our target. It is imperative that all of you, without a sailing mission, stay within the boundaries already laid out by the gun captains for you. You are also under no circumstances to load or discharge your muskets or to fix bayonets until specifically ordered to do so by my naval officers. If you follow these instructions, we will prevail this day. God save the King."

The nearly one hundred and seventy seamen, soldiers, and volunteers, a good many of whom had never sailed in sea action before and ignorant of the carnage of war at sea, stood to their feet and raised their arms in anticipation of the coming triumph and repeated the cry, "God save the King."

Captain Burden looked back at them with his hugh moon face. His great body filled their gaze. Above him the topgallants were unfurled to a hungry wind, they snapped as their lines were tightened down from the fore and main masts. Visibly, the ship increased its speed as the added power first pushed Drake down into the sea until her buoyancy overpowered the driving sails and the great hull was again hurled forward, up over the water. Captain Burden brought the telescope to his eye to study his adversary.

* * * * *

Major Pitkan galloped at the head of a column of red coated dragoons. As they moved northward towards Carrickfergus, they had picked up strength from the local Irish volunteer regiments. In their midst they towed two light cannon, secured from the armory at Belfast. Ahead a few miles distant, lay four ships at anchor, one of which must be the Ranger. Pitkan glanced over his shoulder and smiled, the Drake was coming out under full sail at last. Burden must have corrected whatever was wrong with her steerage. His old friend was going to have his day of victory. He was determined.

Behind the body of troops followed a considerable number of the gentry, merchants, and the curious, all in their horse drawn carts and wagons. As word had spread through Belfast, they had rushed from home and work, slamming doors and closing windows. Also attracted by the movement along the coastal roads were great mobs of other city dwellers, all running along the coastal roads to follow the army to the place where the great lough met the Irish Sea. With the call for local volunteer militia, all secrecy about the coming sea battle had been discarded. Everyone in Belfast now knew that there was going to be a fight. The Drake was going to take on the Yankee pirates and John Paul Jones. It would be a fight of the century for all of Belfast to witness.

As the great body of horses and carriages pushed along the coastal roads, there arose a great column of dust which could be seen for miles in the high noon sky. It moved up the green hillsides surrounding the lough to whirl in eddies among the homeless, and the tenant farmers who populated the green farms and hills on either side of the lough and who, by their majority, made Ireland the most populated and impoverished country in late eighteenth century Europe. The people whose ancestors had lost all rights because their religion did not agree with those of their English conquerors. The clatter of horsemen, cannons, and carriages alerted them that something they largely did not understand was about to happen. A message went through their numbers like wildfire as they too joined the rush towards the mouth of the lough that opened to the Irish Sea.

"The Yankees are going to fight the Drake!"

* * * * *

Lunt was aroused by a seaman. "The Drake's coming into view, sir. Captain Jones wants you on the quarterdeck."

Lunt got to his feet and searched around for his canvas bag. He changed into his uniform and attached a new scabbard about his waist. Then, he struggled for several minutes to put back on the boots which he had succeeded in removing from his feet just a few hours before. His feet protested angrily. He hurried up the stairs to the gun deck, where men were busily rushing this way and that, pulling lines. He heard the Sailing Master and then the Boatswain shouting their series of commands.

"Anchor's aweigh," "All jibs and staysails up."

Lunt avoided the men who were inserting bars into the windlass and starting to turn her to draw up the anchor. The Ranger had already shifted from her anchorage with just the few sails which were already up. The wind was brisk south by southeast. Lunt took the few stairs up onto the quarterdeck. One green and white uniformed marine moved to block his path.

"Lieutenant Lunt," he announced.

"Sorry, sir. I didn't recognize you for a moment," said the marine, stepping aside.

Lunt approached the circle of blue uniforms that surrounded the Captain. Jones was speaking "....by the look of her, she'll be attempting to come windward of us. We are not going to be pushed within range of those dragoons, we will sail a tight reach to windward and pretend we are attempting to close with her. When the moment is right, we'll fall off rapidly and give her a broadside in passing at fifteen hundred paces or thereabouts.

"I'll speak to the men now." The officers about him opened up and Jones was left facing Henry Lunt. "I've made no regularly assigned duty aboard Ranger for you, so you will stay within earshot and be ready to fill in as I direct during the engagement."

Looking at Lunt's uniform, Jones suddenly whirled about to face the other officers. It reminded him to say something. "When we are in the thick of it, I will let each officer decide as he wishes, but I suggest it might be more prudent than not for each of you to consider discarding your uniform jackets so that sharpshooters from the Drake are not as likely to concentrate on our officers. On our part, I have given Lieutenant Wallingsford specific orders to concentrate his marines' fire on the Drake's officers. I leave it to be your individual choice, gentlemen. But you have my permission to discard your uniform jackets."

Lunt glanced around at the other officers' expression. He could already tell from Lt. Wallingsford and Lt. Simpson's faces that this was not going to be to their liking. Lt. Hall, Midshipman Hill, and Lunt exchanged glances and decided to take a 'wait and see' attitude.

Jones took his speaking trumpet and strode to the foredeck. The ship's boatswain piped a whistle for attention.

"Men, Liberty is the prize we seek this day, not personal gain. Some of us have had our differences on this voyage. As far as I am concerned, the slate is clean, only the future is what counts. Let me tell you what Ambassador Franklin told me when he was last aboard this vessel. He said that if we could just succeed during this voyage to capture a British warship of equal or greater size to our own, that it would go a long way towards securing European help for the American cause. You see, men, the French and the rest of Europe do not in their hearts believe that we can defeat John Bull."

Jones paused and looked at the men of his ship from the marines and sailors stationed in the high rigging, to gunnery crew below on the deck. All were silent, listening.

"Can we do it?" asked Jones.

"Aye, aye!" shouted the crew.

"Then, lads," shouted Jones drawing his sword and pointing it with dramatic effect towards the starboard rail, "Let's take the Drake!"

The gaze of the crew fell out over the ocean towards an approaching ship whose every sail was set fully in a dead run up the harbour towards the ocean entrance to the lough. The mid afternoon sun was now just above the vessel. Rays of sunshine made translucent the full endowment sails which propelled the Drake out towards them at breakneck speed. Canvas billowed in full shapes from the spritsails, which drove the leading bowsprit, to the topgallants which adorned each of the Drake's upper masts. The sea beneath her churned from their power.

Seeing that the anchor was up and secured, Jones shouted, "We'll fall off to larboard two points, Mr. Cullan. We need to build speed." The Helmsman set the course so that the Ranger pointed out towards the mouth of the lough.

Lunt shaded his eyes and looked aloft to the mizzen above them. The sheets had already been let out to accommodate the fuller wind angle that they would meet on the new course. He looked at the uniformed green and white marines which now filled the upper reaches of the rigging. Each of them had two muskets, some of which had exceptionally long barrels. Above the fighting top of the main mast, at the doubling, he could see Lt. Wallingsford fifty feet above the deck directing his men to occupy specific positions. The giant swede, Miers, now an American marine sergeant, took a similar position at the doubling of the foremast.

Ranger's fore and aft sails began to fill with the new position. From bowsprit to mizzen, the taut fore and aft sails bit into the driving wind. Ranger began to lean to the leeward as her sailors applied trimming adjustments to her sails. The vessel began to increase in speed. At first, her hull pushed deeply against the sea but then its buoyancy lifted her above the green water. Sunlight gave emerald tints to the ocean as the vessel churned forwards, her bowsprit pointing its course out of the harbour. Drake's position, as viewed from the deck of the Ranger, no longer moved forward. If each held course, the two vessels now appeared as if they might collide at some far point in the future.

Lunt could see the Drake changing her sail position. Her yards were tilting further forward on the windward side, and falling behind to leeward. Drake was using all the running power she could muster to intercept the Ranger.

"What do you reckon the distance, Lt. Lunt?" asked

Jones.

"About a mile, sir," responded Lunt, who was handed the Captain's spyglass. Lunt walked up the inclined deck towards the starboard rail. They were beginning to come into contact with the rolling waves of the Irish sea which would be churning against the ebbing waters of the lough. In this wind, sea conditions at the entrance to the lough would be dicey.

At the rail, Lunt took the glass to his eye to observe the Drake. She had all sails out but her new position was causing the vessel to heel excessively. Lunt strained his eyes towards the vessel. At moments he could see her deck as it tilted towards him from the force of wind. He saw for an instant the raised circular platform he had briefed Captain Jones about but behind it the deck appeared red, a moving pulsating red.

Lunt moved the glass from his eye and rubbed the lens with the sleeve of his jacket. As he looked again, the Drake was infinitesimally nearer. There was red on the deck, between the masts. It seemed to be moving, or was it just an illusion of light contrived by an odd refraction of his spyglass above the pitching sea? If only the glass would be steady for a moment's time. Lunt wrapped his arm around a mizzen shroud at the first ratline. He balanced the spyglass through the crook in his arm. He strained his eyes a third time. Yes, the deck was red. It was not a solid red but little dots of red that, because of their intense hue, tended to overcome their background of oak planks. The little dots were clinging to each other on the pitching deck. Now he could see that the red dots were men, or the red coats of men, and there must be half a hundred of them sitting between the fore and main mast. They all wore crisscrossing white bands. Captain Burden had taken a company of lobsterbacks with him with which to board the Ranger.

Lunt turned from his position on the windward rail to look down at his Captain who had been calling for an adjustment to one of the sails that stretched between the fore and main. The Sailing Master flew down the stairs off the quarterdeck to personally direct his men to adjust rigging. The two vessels were on a race to see who would first cross the other's path and deliver the initial volley. Lunt looked back over the rail. The Drake's position had stayed the same relative to his first sighting from the deck. If neither vessel changed its course, the two would collide or cross very near to each other.

Lunt turned to find Jones looking in his direction. He shouted down the deck, "Sir, the Drake appears to be carrying a full complement of lobsterbacks."

Jones nodded and then called to down to the gun deck with his speaking trumpet, "Mr. Simpson, have grape shot on the ready for all starboard guns. We may have need to clear off her decks." From the gun decks, Simpson signaled acknowledgement of the command.

Lunt moved down the deck to join his Captain. "Sir, it appears that he is trying to cross our path before us. We are on a collision course."

Jones shook his head, "He'd never do that, unless he's a fool."

"Sir?" questioned Lunt.

"He's got to take a different heading of some kind. On this course he may pass just in front of us but his facing guns are leeward. If he fires at us from this tack and heel, it'll be directly into the water. Only we have the proper elevation. He must think that I'm a bloody fool. Thinks he can bluff me into licking my chops, waiting until we cross before he makes his move."

Jones continued to think aloud, "I'll wager he will be doing something else. He's left his yards fully loaded and cannot point to windward any higher because of it, unless he transfers the bearing weight to his fore and aft sails. What's his distance now, Mr. Lunt?"

"I estimate just over a half mile," replied Lunt staring

at Ranger's adversary, whose deck was still pitched at a treacherous angle.

Jones replied, "Then what he plans is to continue on course another quarter mile or more until he is within range, and then fall off and shoot at us from his windward rail. He might even be hoping to get in two broadsides on this pass."

Jones raised his speaking trumpet to his lips, "Sailing Master, be advised to ready your crew for a possible coming about."

Just as he finished speaking, Lunt pointed to seaward. The Drake had already begun to fall off, long before her time. She was again on a broad reach that would bring her back on a crossing path this time to the stern of Ranger. Jones' eyes froze on Drake as she drifted back from the race towards the two small islands at the south entrance to the lough.

"She's moving away from us. What the hell is that Captain Burden....," Jones voice trailed off as a single violent tongue of flame spit out from the mid deck of the Drake. There was then an eerie fraction of a moment of silence which was followed by a whistle that pierced the surrounding sky. As they stared, the Drake's deck became flooded with a heavy puff of smoke. Their attention was suddenly diverted as the massive mizzen boom directly above their heads lifted unnaturally as the sail above it shook violently upwards and then gradually resumed its position. At the leech of Ranger's mizzen, they could see a massive hole about the size of a man's body. The strain of the violently shaking boom on its supporting sail was causing the canvas to split further before their eyes. Jones shouted, "Ease the mizzen sheets, before she splits in two. What was that, Mr. Lunt?" asked Jones still looking upwards at his rent sail.

"It was the carronade, sir," said Lunt gloomily. "I fear Lt. Dobbs' little toy works."

11
Battle

Lieutenant Dobbs triumphantly waved his sword over his head in elation, while behind him, Mr. Wright and the rest of the specially selected gun crew cheered enthusiastically and patted each other on the back. At nearly twenty-five hundred paces they could see that the special six pound ball, encased at one end with a larger diameter wooden shoe, had worked. The carronade was going to be useful in both extending the range of a small calibre ball, as well as in its planned role of delivering the killing stroke of a very heavy ball at close range from a short, light weight piece that could be carried on a sloop of war. No matter what might have happened to his naval career because of the incident involving Alicia, the expertise he had gained during his meticulous testing and then cataloguing of the various shapes of the sabots would be needed by the Royal Navy if it were to duplicate the performance and accuracy of this successful long distance shot from the stubby carronade.

The idea had not been Dobbs' own. It was the inventors at the Carron Company who had first suggested trying it. But the first few shapes they had tried had been wrong and they had left their young Lieutenant in charge of carrying on the experimentation with other new shapes. As a result, he had spent much of the past autumn and winter shooting sabot shapes out over the Carron Locke. As he reveled, he recalled how each round would echo back from the mountains on the other side. It had been a peaceful half year in Scotland.

Now only Mr. Wright and he knew which shapes had been prepared for the Drake. Since Dobbs' arrival in Belfast,

Wright had spent many days with him, helping to tool the shapes that had brought him the greatest success in Scotland. Now, in battle, the carronade had wounded the rebel ship with one round at a distance never before possible with a cannonball and gun of that size. Wright came over to him and they shook hands heartedly, knowing that together they had a bargaining tool that would transcend beyond the events of the past day. The Admiralty would not discard them. There would have to be forgiveness.

Dobbs turned and glanced back at the quarterdeck. The Captain still had his eye trained through the spyglass, He was visibly issuing orders to Mr. Whiting, the Sailing Master. Then the Captain turned back to look down the gun deck, tipping his hat to the gun crew in acknowledgement of their prowess. Across the distance, Burden's and Dobbs' eyes met and they exchanged a smile. There was hope to escape retribution from the Admiralty. All they needed was a stunning victory.

The Drake again hardened up to pursue the pirates. Across the deck, seamen responded to commands by tightening lines which moved through deadeyes and pulleys to change the sailing angles of over a dozen sails. In the center of the main gun deck, fifty redcoats remained where they had been ordered but, as the sight of the wounded adversary was pointed out to them, they too responded with enthusiastic cheering and waving of their hats.

Sailing Master Whiting continued to stare through his spyglass and reported to Captain Burden what he observed, "Sir, it appears her mizzen has sustained damage. I can see men on the mizzen boom, trying to repair canvas. There is a hole in the sail. They are taking it down."

Burden directed himself to the Helmsman, "Mr. Snead, stay hardened up and follow right after their stern. That damn pirate will not be able to get too far ahead of us with a missing sail. Perhaps we'll be able to get Lieutenant Dobbs in range for another shot. He has only a few of those hand carved wooden shoes on hand.

"Eventually, we need to get close enough to the pirates to use an eighteen pound ball from that gun. That'll be the crippling stroke. Craft that size will break apart with a ball of that weight flung against her hull."

Suddenly Midshipmen Warren reported, "Sir, we're seeing a shift in the wind, the pennants are veering."

"Just follow the pirate," ordered Burden, glancing out at the mouth of the lough where a grey blanket of fast moving clouds indicated dicey weather to come. "She'll be ours this day, if we can catch her before sunset. Trim every sail as flat as you can, Mr. Whiting."

* * * * *

As the water sluiced by Ranger's hull, all officers stood about Jones. As they conversed, on the deck before them were the sailmakers working feverishly amid a pile of canvas and the mizzen's boom and gaff, which had been lowered to the deck. With less sail area aloft, soon the Drake would be gaining on them. One sailmaker hurriedly rammed his fid through three layers of canvas, while others held the hastily cut square canvas patches in place on either side. As each stitch of the needle holder was pulled through, the repair began to cover the rent.

On the now crowded quarterdeck, Jones discussed the coming strategy with his junior officers, "We'll continue to beat to windward for the next quarter hour. We'll let the Drake believe that we have sustained far greater damage than we have. Mr. Cullan, do not sail as efficiently as we can. I want them to feel every encouragement that they can catch us if they chase us."

"Sir," interrupted Simpson, "isn't she just going to fall off every few minutes and shoot at us with that thing until we're crippled and they are still out of range to us?"

"That is probably what she is planning, Mr. Simpson.

But I'll not allow Ranger to serve as her target. Lieutenant Hall, you have the helm from this point on. For the next quarter hour you are to be ready to fall off a full four points each time that the Drake falls off to discharge her weapon. Then, without command from me, you're to harden up again within a half minute's time. You will repeat the sequence after another half minute. There will be no sail adjustments, Mr. Cullan, only a zigzagging movement generated solely from the helm. We'll not present a steady target that is constantly going away on the same course. With rapid alterations in our course, it will reduce their likelihood of hitting us. Lieutenant Lunt, take one of the spyglasses and from the taffrail give notice to the helm the instant that Drake begins to alter her heading."

Within a few minutes, Lunt shouted back from the stern rail, "Sir, they have again closed the distance to 2,500 paces. Their sail preparation appears that they are planning to fall off again."

"Be ready to do as I have said, Mr. Hall. Mr. Cullan, run that mizzen back up. The repair is sufficient and we are out of time. We must lead the Drake out of this lough, then we'll engage her where she can't get help."

Lunt shouted, "They're just falling off, sir, reaching to us on a perpendicular course."

Jones turned his attention to the helm, "Lieutenant Hall, prepare to fall off, upon my command." Jones raised his hand directly in front of Hall's vision. As the Captain held his hand suspended, the Sailing Master alerted the men aloft to be on guard for sudden shifts in heading. Jones' lips visibly counted out a routine, estimating the time needed to sight a gun properly along a straight line and execute a fire order.

"Now, four points off the wind," commanded Jones, as he lowered his hand rapidly. Ranger's crew felt their hundred and ten foot world whirl from a reach to a beam as they suddenly headed violently to the east. As Ranger met the wind at its new heading, the over tightened sails caused her to heel over at a severe angle towards the churning sea to her lee. Masts and rigging creaked in protest to the strain but then bent away from the wind. Excitedly, Jones admired their flex, pointing up, "Ah, 'tis the Kauri trees. They'll take it. Finest masts in the world."

Behind Ranger, there was a flash of light from amidships the Drake. Most of the officers and masters had rushed to the stern railing to join Lunt in a direct observation of the enemy. But as many anticipated impact, they crouched in self defense. Lunt swallowed hard. Death would be quick if Drake's ball were to hit any of them. A worse fate would be to have the ball hit wood and be struck in the eye or body by a flying splinter. Lunt preferred sudden death, than to be dragged below to the whimsies of the surgeon. He swallowed hard, his eyes straining to see if something were coming at him, moving at terrific speed. Sometimes he could just see cannon balls when they were fired away from a deck on which he stood. Would he be able to see one coming at them? A whistling sound reached his ears just as he saw a puff of white smoke form on the Drake's deck and then dissipate back through the rigging. Suddenly, Ranger began to turn back again to windward.

Lunt looked to his left as an object collided with the crest of a wave where they would have been just fifteen seconds before. The green water gushed upwards forming a momentary spout just windward of Ranger.

"Stay on course to weather, without further zigzag, Mr. Hall," shouted Jones. "They have lost some distance and they'll chase us now a bit, before they try again. Remain on the stern watch, Mr. Lunt. A little better sail trim, Mr. Cullan."

Suddenly, Jones turned around and looked upwards. "Gentlemen, in our haste we have never shown our true colors. Prepare the ensign. All officers and masters to the quarter."

As a hundred men strained to adjust her rigging, Ranger

shifted in anticipation of the higher waves that would greet them as they hurtled out of the shelter of the lough and into the open Irish Sea. Under direction of the Sailing Master, a refined tack was established, the wind crooned as it wove its way through the full complement of fore and aft canvas. Miles of running rigging strained against their attachments to support the sails aloft. Beneath Ranger's deck a small mountain of ballast rock counterbalanced the forces which would otherwise topple her over into the foaming water. Ranger moved forward as she assumed a rhythm with the heavy seas about her.

Once again, officers and masters gathered around him, as Jones spoke with a commanding voice. From the stern rail, Lunt could just hear him. "Gentlemen, we've been luring Drake eastward of Mew Island. When they attempt their next long shot, we'll not harden up but will fall off downwind and put out the running rigging. It'll be the Serpentine. Mr. Cullan, we'll keep lower course sails brailed and thus free of fire, but have the topmen remain alert in case we need the speed. Remember, the Serpentine is best executed slowly. Understood, Mr. Hall, Mr. Cullan?"

"Aye, aye, sir."

"Lieutenant Simpson, you will continue to direct the gun deck with Mr. Palmer. It'll be the Serpentine, in a slow steady pivot. I want balls, grape, and chain, all at the ready. We'll likely use them all. Where possible, fire all guns in threes, with adjustment orders given to the succeeding gun masters. No coins needed for the first round, put the wedges under the wheels for elevation, the first salvo will be a long shot with the sixes at two and half charge."

"Sir, we have never fired more than two bags. There could be a rupture," cautioned Simpson.

"You will this time, Mr. Simpson. We've never needed long range as desperately as we do now!" ordered Jones.

"Lt. Wallingsford, I want all marines well up into the fighting tops and some all the way to the uppermost crosstrees.

Mind that those aloft keep within the iron rings or to tie themselves onto anything they can as it'll be a wild ride up there as we twist the serpent. Tell your men to aim well and, when possible, to shoot at the Drake's officers. The more they are disorganized the sooner this will be over and done. Mr. Lunt reports they have a good sized party of lobsterbacks on deck. We cannot afford to let them board, nor allow that damn gun to strike out at us. It will be peppery."

"Mr. Lunt," Jones called over his shoulder, "I want you to move four of the swivels to the stern. Take three men and man them. As we sweep by the enemy, be prepared to use them at your discretion."

"Lastly," said Jones as he began to unbutton his own uniform. "I'll not look down on any officer who sheds his uniform waistcoat in the fray. 'Tis foolish to increase your chances of being shot by a Royal Marine." Jones looked at Simpson in particular and jested, "I'll wager, Lt. Simpson would not want to see his Captain shot, and to get command of the Ranger in that way. You can be sure that Captain Burden has just given similar orders as I've just given Lieutenant Wallingsford."

"Will they shed their uniforms?" asked Wallingsford.

"'Tis unlikely that a British officer would ever shed his uniform, Mr. Wallingsford," Jones replied. "But I'm given to understand it was their undoing at Saratoga. The lobsterbacks were so thin on officers that they had no direction. Our sharpshooters had picked them all off, one by one."

Suddenly Jones turned and looked above his head, shading his eyes with his hand. He pointed upward with his finger. Nearly every man on board followed his gaze.

The flag had just been hoisted to the top of the mizzen gaff, and had immediately filled in the stiff breeze. For the first time in his life Henry Lunt saw the blue field in the upper left corner, with the circle of thirteen white stars. The remainder of the flag was as he remembered from earlier voyages. A pattern of red, white, and blue stripes. The flag snapped defiantly in the face of the vessel which pursued it.

* * * * *

"Lieutenant Dobbs," shouted Captain George Burden through his speaking trumpet. He turned to his long time Helmsman, "Hard to windward, Mr. Snead."

Burden set his feet astride the sloping deck as he waited for his First Lieutenant. He looked up at each mast in turn and shouted a few incidental commands to the Sailing Master, "We'll be to windward with speed, Mr. Whiting."

Burden thought better of his earlier order and commented to the Helmsman, "Belay that, Mr. Whiting, I think we'll sacrifice a bit of direction to weather to catch up with them in the drive west. Fall off a third of a point."

"Lieutenant Dobbs reporting, sir."

Burden turned to face his second in command. "You see our adversary is no fool. Pity that they avoided the second round, but the trajectory was good and true. I will be attempting to catch up with him before dark and close the distance between us. I have set a course to give him a little windward direction in favor of our paralleling his position. The next time I give you an opportunity, he will be closer. We are getting veered, so Jones will eventually have to move into our course. Get the four pounders run out and overpowered for longest range. Leave the firing of the next carronade shot to Mr. Wright. Do not neglect the use of the other twenty guns under your command. Remember what we discussed earlier."

Dobbs saluted his Captain and returned to command the gun deck.

The two vessels moved out past the heads of Belfast Lough and into the Irish Sea as the late afternoon sun began to cast long shadows across the water. The wind roared, and the tightly drawn white sails of both vessels made a brilliant display for the thousands of spectators: from hillside peasants, to prosperous merchants in carriages, to several small Belfast craft which had sailed out behind Drake to observe the sea battle first hand. Major Pitkan and his red coated dragoons gathered at both extremities of the land hoping for a chance to join the engagement.

In time they saw the trailing ship close the distance and again fall off to shoot its powerful single shot ahead at the rebel vessel. The observers again saw the great puff of white smoke form on the Drake and then dissipate rapidly as the crisp wind carried it back towards Belfast.

* * * * *

Lunt ducked low to the rail as he saw the flash from the Drake. He again tried to focus on the cannonball, but failed to detect anything until he heard a whistle for a brief moment before an object he could barely see hit the sea to the stern of Ranger, and then bounced off two succeeding wave crests before vanishing forever. As the Ranger continued to fall off, he was left facing the two small, sea gull encrusted islands which were situated at the southern entrance to the lough.

According to prearranged signals, over half of the Ranger's crew swarmed from the ratlines out onto each mast's series of two or three wooden crosstrees. All but the lowest set of square running sails were being let out. Fore and aft sails were collapsed rapidly as Ranger turned full about on a dead run back at the Drake. The British vessel had already turned back up to windward to continue to chase the enemy vessel, an enemy her Captain had felt would continue to try and evade her. The two fighting ships now drove at each other head to head.

Jones' voice was heard everywhere as he initiated all

major orders, "Run right for her bowsprit, Mr. Hall!... Two and a half powder bags on starboard sixes, Lieutenant Simpson... Distance, Mr. Lunt?"

"Twenty-five hundred paces, sir, and closing fast," Lunt reported as he hung out over the mizzen ratlines to observe the closing vessel.

Jones initiated a new set of commands, which were translated into a further detail first by the Sailing Master, and then by each crew chief as they were implemented across the vessel.

"We'll swerve to larboard at 1,800 paces. Call out each 100 yards, Mr. Lunt," requested Jones, who then turned to Cullan again.

"Not much tension on the running rigging as we make each bend of the serpent, slow is the key. Give Mr. Simpson time to discharge his batteries in groups of three, Mr. Cullan. Immediately initiate the jibe after the third discharge, Mr. Hall."

Cullan shouted up from the gun deck, "Understood, sir. Loose, we'll not put our rounds into the sea, sir."

"Twenty-two hundred paces," shouted Lunt. His voice carried back across the quarterdeck.

Jones shouted from the poop deck, "It'll be larboard battery following, Mr. Simpson. Two full charges with ball. On the wedges, if you please. Take out their rigging."

"Aye, aye, sir," shouted Simpson.

An erect Lieutenant Simpson walked up the mid deck screaming orders, he drew his hanger from its scabbard, "Six pound balls, to be loaded both sides. Two and a half bags on starboard, two on larboard. All crews fill. Watch those slow matches. Downwind always. Mind the opened bags. Give 'em to the powder monkey to stow away."

* * * * *

O'Mally's gun crew was fourth along the starboard rail.

His would be the lead gun in any adjustment volley. O'Mally unleased the storage lashings and the gun was backed up to the extent its braces would permit with training tackle. The powder monkey first tossed a limp flannel bag into the barrel as far as his slim hand could reach, and then two full flannel bags of powder were each pricked and loaded. A more experienced gunner, named Elijah, pulled the ramrod from its perch, placed a wad of old sail cloth at the mouth of the barrel, and then thrust it down the barrel on top of the gunpowder. He rammed hard several times to further split open the flannel powder bags within. A six pound ball was extracted from the shot rack and more wadding would come next.

O'Mally looked briefly out to sea and then poked his wire down the touch hole to clear the way for fine powder which was poured out until the cavity was filled. O'Mally checked over his shoulder to see that his slow match was still smoking at its position by the main mast. It had formed a crust of ash and would need a good blow to give a quick ignition of the fine powder. About him, he was aware of the sounds of other gun carriages being pulled back and their gun captains shouting similar orders, and of the sounds of grunting and cursing as men strove to fulfill duties in as minimum a time as possible. From the center of the gun deck, he heard Mr. Palmer repeating distance estimates initiated from the quarterdeck.

"Two thousand paces, Drake is falling off again. They'll be delivering another round. Brace yerselves...," warned Palmer.

From the poop deck they could hear Captain Jones initiate orders, "Steady as she goes, not till eighteen hundred."

O'Mally concentrated on the work of his gun crew. The wedge had been thrust in place against the rail. The ball had been rolled down and the ramrod was now packing the final wad of slightly damp cloth about the ball to prevent its rolling out until the gun was fired.

Behind him Simpson bellowed, "All gun captains signal when ready. All crews stand well clear for discharge. These sixes are loaded to maximum, ensure your guns are well braced."

Each of O'Mally's men pushed the heavy gun to the rail. The muzzles now protruded out two and a half feet beyond the freeboard. Men lashed the side tackle to the freeboard and deck. O'Mally raised his smoking slow match over his head. His was the third gun ready. Soon all starboard crews were prepared.

"First starboard battery fire on my command," shouted Simpson with a high voice. His wrinkled, middle aged face was already perspiring from tension. His officer's sword was poised above his head.

In the fighting tops and on ratlines and spars far above them, marines and seamen assigned to trim the spars clung precariously to the rigging. From the fore top, Sergeant Miers' voice shouted a warning to all, "Incoming!"

Ranger had just started to turn when the larboard side of a spar in the fore mast shook violently and a hole appeared in the fore topsail. The shock and sound of splintering wood penetrated to all levels of the ship. Debris and a human form dropped from above onto the deck. A gun captain from the larboard side squatted to look at the green and white uniformed body briefly and then covered the head and the surrounding pool of blood with his vest. Above them, a seaman was calling for help as he clung by one arm to a line that had saved him from joining his fellow marine on the deck. Two comrades were attempting to pull him to safety as Jones gave the signal to round up into position for his first broadside. The man swung in a violent arc, but clung on teetering as he screamed for help.

"All guns ready. First battery, on the uproll, fire!" shouted Simpson.

Within an instant the three lead guns exploded with belching fury. As each gun captain stood aside, he put his slow match to the powder filled touch hole at the base of the barrel. Each gun roared back with fury as its recoil attempted to free the gun and caisson from the hawser securing it in place. The guns literally lifted from the deck and then crashed back again, unable to shake off their restrainers. A great billow of acrid black smoke swirled among the men who manned each position until it was caught by the wind and carried out over the water. Eyes stung and men coughed from their brief encounter with the scorching fumes and debris of exploded gunpowder.

"We're left of the mark," reported Simpson. "Remaining batteries adjust one peg forward, on the uproll, be quick, fire!"

O'Mally stood aside and touched his slow match to the edge of the touch hole. His gun roared and as did the two adjacent. Beside him the adjacent gun lifted with its brothers, but then spun crazily in the air as one of its training tackles snapped, allowing one end of the ton of gun metal to spin uncontrolled for an instant through the air.

O'Mally stepped quickly backwards but the young powder monkey, Matthew Weatherby, who had knelt near his feet screamed in agony as a portion of the cartwheeling caisson slammed into his leg and pinned him to the deck.

Ignoring it, Simpson shouted, "Third battery, no further correction. On the uproll, fire!"

Smoke from the mouth of the disheveled cannon flowed out over the deck to form an eerie low cloud. Men coughed and stepped aside to avoid the recoil of the third group of cannons bellowing a final salvo. Immediately afterwards, Ranger began to careen through a full half circle onto a completely new tack. Amidst the confusion, O'Mally was first to his injured boy's side, he shoved his thick wire pin into the boy's mouth crosswise lest he bit off his tongue due to the pain he was expressing. Glancing down, O'Mally saw that the boy's lower leg had been crushed almost in two by the fifteen hundred pound caisson. He could see bone splinters protruding from the profusely bleeding leg. About him, men sought to upright the cannon off the boy with their arms and backs.

"Get him to the surgeon," screamed Simpson.

Starboard gun crews stared as others carried away the lad whose leg swung freely from the knee joint. Mercifully, the boy had now fainted and was still. He was delivered up through the doors into the officers' quarters. The great cabin had been designated as the temporary hospital of the surgeon, Ezra Green.

The Ranger continued to turn and then adopted a new heading. Her fresh broadside was delivered five hundred paces closer to her adversary.

From the larboard side the first three groups of six pounders roared. From above a topman called down, "We've hit their foremast, dead on."

The starboard side was still dazed from the sight of their favorite young boy from Portsmouth, who had been wounded in their midst.

Simpson turned to them shouting orders, without hint of pity, "Reload all starboard guns. Grape. It'll be close work."

From the topmasts someone shouted, "Incoming!"

Fifty yards in front of the whirling Ranger, a broadside from Drake's ten starboard guns fell short in the water, but created a brief mountain ridge of spray that obscured each opponent's view of the other for a long moment. One of the cannon balls from Drake proceeded toward Ranger, ricochetting like a flat rock across a series of wave crests until it thudded against her hull harmlessly.

O'Mally pushed his gun crew to their task. The coiled worming iron was pushed down the muzzle to extract any large wads of unexploded powder and packing wads. Elijah then used the sponge end of the ramrod to dampen any remaining spares within the barrel, lest they ignite a new load of powder prematurely as it was being thrust down the barrel.

"Good and thorough soaking, Elijah," shouted O'Mally. "I've seen men have their arms blown off because the sparks were still alive. That's it, soak it again." Similar efforts at each gun station brought forth a clatter of wood striking metal across the deck. Ranger started to jibe again, she was now only eight hundred paces from Drake.

High above as they spun, a marine on the very top of foremast glanced briefly to the south. The horizon was becoming obscure in the fading light but, for an instant, the man could just discern several tiny but distinctive stacked trapezoidal shapes dotting the far southern horizon.

* * * * *

Portions of the rebel's second broadside had smashed directly into the upper half of the Drake's foremast, showering the deck with a great clutter of upper mast, sail, rigging, and men. Extensive canvas was left hanging in mid air, being blown in various directions by the roaring wind and hampering the vessel's forward progress. In reaction, Burden had swerved the Drake for a broadside prematurely and it had fallen short in the water.

Burden shouted into his speaking trumpet, "Men in the foremast, cut the debris away. Mr. Whiting, take charge directly. The damage is slowing us down. For God's sake, clear it.

"Lieutenant Dobbs, you will issue the next broadside upon my command," shouted Burden. "Aim up into their rigging, we must first cripple them for boarding. Then use the eighteen pounder at their hull. They'll be close." Burden watched as the rebel corvette whirled to a broadside tack in the opposite direction. They were less than five hundred paces away.

From the gun deck, the boatswain shouted a secondary command to a group of seamen huddled near the main mast, "Grappling teams ready at the bowsprit. Captain will be attempting to close."

In obedience, a team of seamen carried four light, foot long treble hooks to which had been attached light, strong hemp lines. They were experts at twirling the sturdy hooks well over their heads and casting them over a hundred feet to catch another ship along side and pull it close to them for boarding. The men proceeded with their equipment to take positions among the Royal Marines who were already perched upon the bowsprit, hanging out over the water to the front of Drake. Amidships, the red coated regulars were beginning to load their muskets and fix bayonets according to their officers' direction.

Burden spoke to the men beside him on the quarterdeck, "We've lost our upper foremast and its sails. Now, they'll be faster than us. We must close to utilize our superior forces on deck. Mr. Snead, as soon as they are within a few hundred feet, aim at their bow no matter what else happens. If we can attach we can..."

In a murderous whistle, the roar of Ranger's third broadside of nine guns all simultaneously poured their beehive of grapeshot into and over the Drake's deck. The Drake shuddered in a thousand places simultaneously. It seemed for a moment that the vessel was going to be shaken into oblivion. The huge masts and their supporting rigging wavered as wood, canvas, hemp, and flesh were impacted in a thousand places at once. Pieces of wood were chipped off rails, masts, and planking by the razor sharp pieces of grape. These created secondary missiles which carved without pity into human targets. For just a fraction of a moment, it seemed to Burden that there was silence and that most of the broadside had mercifully not hit anyone. But then the sounds of injured crewmen began to build from the deck into a miasma of horror.

"Aagh, my eye, my eye!" cried a dragoon sitting on the floor of the gun deck, who had taken a huge splinter through his eyelid into his eye, and was flailing across the deck in berserk frenzy. Dobbs shouted to other wounded men about the dragoon to suppress his movement so that he would not interfere with the gun crews. A seaman from one of the spars had been shaken loose from his hold and had tumbled head first onto one of the larboard guns. His brains spattered across that gun's crew, many of whom, already wounded from grape, vomited convulsively. Burden estimated that thirty or forty men had been wounded from the salvo. They had to hit back now.

"Ready to fire?" Burden called questionably of Dobbs through his speaking trumpet. The enemy was starting to turn again. In a fraction of a second their bow should be facing his broadside. A good volley could tear through all three sets of masts. Dobbs waved his hand back at Burden. He saw the opportunity. He had his sword raised and waited for the uproll of the next wave which would carry Drake into an elevated position from which to rake Ranger's sails.
"Fire!" Dobbs screamed.

Tongues of flame lashed out from long barrels over the tumbling ocean as all ten of Drake's larboard four pounders roared into the air, some carrying balls, others chain shot with which to rip the rebel's rigging to shreds. At five hundred paces the British gunnery could not miss. For a fraction of a second, the shock of the roaring cannon and the bright flash of light into the twilight caused even the mortally wounded aboard Drake to be silent. The facing wind driven by the dying, blood red sun drove the acrid smoke back over the deck. Eyes and throats burned, and men vomited in nausea from the sights, sounds, and smells of the carnage.

As the Drake's deck cleared of smoke, Burden could see that his men had aimed well. The pirate's main mast was split in two at the upper doubling. Men and their weapons were falling from the upper rigging. But still the rebel ship was able to complete its turn. Drake's headway was still being slowed by the great tangle of canvas hanging from its toppled foremast. Mr. Whiting had climbed into the rigging himself and was chopping wildly at lines, trying to rid Drake of her obstruction.

"Fire the eighteen, now, damn it!" shouted Burden through his speaking trumpet over the resumed cries of the wounded. "Now!" he screamed, but something was wrong. Rigging had fallen in the way of the carronade. Damn, he had told Dobbs that the platform was a novel idea but impractical. Since they had not expected it to be used in battle, Burden had decided to let them experiment with it. He should have had the carronade remounted on the rail this morning.

Just then, in response to Whiting's axe, the entire top half of the foremast was released and fell backwards, crashing to the deck. It landed atop the carronade, and Mr. Wright and the crew which manned it. He saw Dobbs immediately shouting orders to clear away the debris. A runner came to Burden's side to tell him what he already knew, that Dobbs would not be able to fire the carronade for several more minutes. He was reloading the portions of the larboard battery unaffected by the fallen debris.

* * * * *

A moment before, the boy from Vermont had been positioned just below Lt. Wallingsford. The young officer had prepared his men to be ready and then the world about them had suddenly been blown away. The Vermonter was left untouched but Lt. Wallingsford had vanished so quickly that the boy's brain had not registered the event. All the rigging that had been above him had fallen below. Some of it was hanging, flapping in the breeze. The wind whistled through the sharp V shaped splinter that had once been a stalwart portion of a larger mast. The starboard portion of the small platform, on which he had been standing, had also been blown away and was dangling. All the men in the upper third of the main were gone, except him.

"Help me!"

The boy looked down. Dangling by some top rigging was a fellow marine. The man was clinging on the base of the small platform with both hands, preventing himself from falling some fifty feet below onto the deck. To clear himself of encumbrances, the Vermonter pulled his own spare musket over his head and hooked it across the splinter V that had once been a mast. The world about him turned as the Ranger continued to change course. He squatted and reached downwards. He had to hold on with one hand. Like this he would only be able to use one hand to grasp his comrade. It would not be enough. He squatted and tied a severed halliard line around his own shoulders. He tried it, it was taunt. He stretched himself on the remaining platform and grasped his comrade's arms below the elbows with both hands. Below him, the deck shook with a terrible roar of a new salvo being fired. Beyond the other marine's face, all he could see was a cloud of billowing smoke instead of the deck below. He pulled hard until he felt the man lift free, just a foot more to get his chest onto the platform. The man was going to make it.

* * * * *

Burden cursed as he saw a group still attempting to clear the debris from around the carronade. His larboard crew was still reloading their fours. Many members of the gun crews had been wounded by the grape. The rebels were still completing their turn. Drake was going to have to endure another broadside before they could return fire. There was only two hundred paces between the two vessels. They were moving on a parallel course, the wind was at their beams. The rebels were the windward vessel which would cause them to gradually slip towards Drake. He could see the enemy gunners preparing to fire. Burden braced himself and shouted through his trumpet, "Commence firing all muskets. They are in range. We will close, boarding parties prepare, we will attempt to close ..."

Suddenly, there was a thousand whistles piercing the air. Burden looked down at his protruding white vested stomach. It was red. He had been cut by a fragment of shrapnel. Many of the gun crews and soldiers on the deck below screamed in agony. Blood was visible on nearly every man.

"Grapeshot," shouted the Boatswain. "Everyone to the deck, down." Another battery of three guns flashed at them, this time striking more forward on the deck. Burden turned to face his Helmsman, "Now, turn up into them, we'll board those murderous bastards."

As the Drake suddenly changed course to stab directly at Ranger's broadside, the third battery of grape shot sent a torrent of whistling shrapnell obliquely down the long deck. It struck some in the boarding party forming at the bow. Red coated men in white cross straps screamed and held their hands clinging to their faces, necks, and hands. Burden could not see Dobbs anywhere.

The gun crews was crouching low in chaos. Burden screamed into his trumpet, "Any gun ready, fire at will!" Two larboard guns quaked and answered his orders immediately, and a moment later a third gun roared. Because of the altered angle for boarding, only one of the three rounds hit the rebel's stern taffrail while the others passed the vessel's stern, landing without effect in the water.

Burden's mind concentrated on tactics. They would be able to reach Ranger's stern before she passed. The rebels had come too close, Ranger was trapped by the wind on one side and the Drake on the other. She would have to pass them before she could either jibe or harden up further. Otherwise, she would stall right into them. They would be able to grabble. They would make it.

The two vessels were very close now. The Royal Marines were firing from the rigging. Soldiers on the deck had gone to the larboard rails. There was a constant crackle of musket fire as tiny puffs of white smoke formed everywhere at the muzzles of a hundred muskets. Ranger's three masts also were filled with tiny puffs of smoke. Aboard both ships men began to fall from the hail of bullets.

"We're close enough, pull into her sharply!" screamed Burden. Snead began to spin the wheel directly at the broadside of the enemy. Once on his new course, he corrected his wheel so that it was straight and waited for impact. Then, the Helmsman turned to look toward his Captain but instead found himself staring at the deck in front of him with horror.

* * * * *

The boy from Vermont was alone again on the stump of the upper main mast. His fellow marine had been safe on the top of the mast with him for an instant, but then was hit from musket fire and was now trying to lower himself to the deck below, while he was still able.

The enemy ship was starting to turn into them. The boy grabbed his musket from its position on the stump and cradled it in the crotch of a masthead. To his right and left, the green and white uniformed marines were firing intensely from the fore and mizzen masts. They were shooting into the human sea of red jackets that were, in turn, shooting back up at them from the enemy deck. For a moment, the boy could not see a clear target, then his glance looked backwards. There at the stern was a large man in an officer's uniform. It must be their Captain, Jones had said to shoot at their officers. The boy shifted slightly, the closing spars of the two vessels were beginning to obstruct his view.

He had just an instant more in which to fire. He squeezed the trigger and felt his musket boom. Its recoil pounded against his shoulder. He clung to his perch. Unable to see the results of his shot, he reached around for his powder and ball to reload the single musket he had remaining.

* * * * *

Ranger's batteries exploded with a fifth broadside that largely swept ahead of the enemy vessel which had suddenly altered its heading to hurl directly towards them. Drake's bowsprit pointed like an avenging sword right towards the midships of Ranger. There was scarcely a hundred feet between the vessels.

Jones seized the helm of the Ranger from Lieutenant Hall shouting, "Over, man, they'll ram us!" Jones jumped with the weight of his entire body onto the handholds of the wheel. One, two, three spokes were jerked around as Ranger was steered to windward, her sails not properly set for this new heading, she was not going to make good speed. Two of Drake's guns, and then a third, returned fire and part of the stern rail of Ranger exploded sending splinters flying across the quarterdeck. Jones shouted orders for Cullan to release the yards to windward and to tighten further to leeward, back as far as they would go. Ranger needed fore and aft rigging for a close haul, but there was no time to rig it. In trying to avoid her opponent's thrust, Ranger was in danger of going into irons.

* * * * *

Inspired by his Captain's last order, Bartholomew Snead turned the wheel over further. He tried to keep his eyes away from the deck immediately in front of him where his Captain lay, half of his head blown apart by whatever had hit him. It seemed a lifetime that he watched his ship plow ahead towards the stern of the privateer. The rebel ship was trying to turn away; heading higher into the wind but her running sails were wrong to come about efficiently. As Snead waited for the impact, his ears heard a tapping sound. He forced himself to look down at his Captain.

Despite the man's massive head wound, Burden's hand

was moving. His fingers were tapping on the deck, then his hand was moving into his pocket, searching for something. The Helmsman wanted to go to his side and help him. The poor man, all this and he was missing something when he was dying. Finally the hand ceased moving.

Snead jerked himself back to the real world of carnage and brushed aside a small piece of human gore that had fallen on his uniform when his Captain was hit. Coming to a decision, he screamed down into the smoke filled gun deck peopled largely by wailing men, "Captain Burden's dead, tell Lieutenant Dobbs he is in command. We are going to ram the bastards. Tell Lt. Dobbs he is in command! Send him to the bridge."

Snead kept shouting as he directed the momentum of his ship forward into the enemy. The bowsprit would certainly make contact. He kept waiting. Amid the smoke, he could not see ahead clearly. But he felt contact was imminent. Finally the entire vessel shook with impact. Men aboard both vessels were tossed to the deck. He had fulfilled his Captain's last order, he had rammed the enemy. He threw over the wheel sharply to pin the Drake further into the enemy vessel and then left the helm momentarily to kneel at his Captain's side.

* * * * *

Lunt crouched at the stern rail and focused on bringing his swivels to bear on the boarding party. Midshipman Powers and one other seaman had been hit as one of the last of the Drake's broadsides had impacted against the taffrail. Powers' arm had been badly mauled and they had both been carried below to the surgeon in the great cabin.

The enemy's bowsprit had wedged itself among the mizzen's stays and ratlines. Already two grappling hooks had been flung successfully across to the deck of Ranger. The British were trying to lash themselves deck to deck.

If they succeeded, the entire space would be open for their greater number of men to come over the rails at once. In the meantime, a small group of men were trying to cross to the Ranger's deck across the bowsprit. Lunt fired his first swivel and saw three men drop from their perch into the water.

Out of the smoke of the last exchange, a single man sprung forward and leapt across the deck at them. Marines from both sides poured musket fire into each other. Behind him, from the center of the quarterdeck, Lunt could hear Jones shouting commands, "Mr. Cullan, come about, more fore and aft rigging, we must come about, now." Somewhere on the Ranger's deck and in her rigging, seamen struggled amid a torrent of small arms fire to fulfill his command.

Lunt crouched and focused on the bowsprit. He saw a green and white uniformed man jump from the ratlines to intercept a single boarder on the rail. The British seaman's broadsword descended onto the musket barrel, but the American marine used his musket's leverage to force the man back onto the bowsprit. The two struggled a moment and then dropped together into the dark water below. The sun was descending and the western sky had taken on a bright red cast.

Ranger began to swing around to fall through the wind, burdened by the Drake, whom she carried. The Drake's forecastle was filled with soldiers. They were forming. Lunt aimed across the short space of water and fired his second swivel into the mass of red coated soldiers. Men screamed and then returned fire concentrated on his position. He looked up to see British marines on the stump of a foremast firing down on him. Beside him a man screamed and then slumped over. Lunt was alone to defend the stern rail. He moved back to the next swivel and crouched, waiting for the bowsprit to again fill with crossing boarders in scarlet red uniforms and white cross straps.

Suddenly, Ranger began to break apart from Drake

and the redcoats, who were beginning to attempt to cross the bowsprit, fell backward. Lunt heard the single sound of a musket fire from just below him and one solitary boarder fell off into the water. He peered over what was left of the taffrail. The stern windows of the great cabin were open, a slim female hand was retracting a musket, Marie.

Lunt looked up to see the bowsprit, still attached to Ranger by a web of lines, running to high on the mizzen mast itself. The lowered parts of the stays had been chopped away from their deadeyes by an axman. The Drake still clung to the Ranger by slim tendrils. British fire was being concentrated on anyone in the mizzen who might sever the tenuous link. Lunt fired a swivel as a group of desperate men again tried to cross the bowsprit. They retreated back to their forecastle.

Above Lunt, a red haired man ascended the far side of the mizzen stays carrying only an axe. British marines continued to concentrate their fire on the poop and mizzen positions. American marines fell from the mizzen to the quarterdeck, including one who had been trying to cut the final stubborn attachments with a bayonet. Across the deck, Lunt could see another group of redcoats forming for a run across the bowsprit to gain the deck of Ranger before it was too late. He crouched and waited until several were in line and then laid his slow match to his last loaded swivel. Some of the boarders fell, but others continued across, their bayonets gleaming through the musket smoke. One of them leaped from the tip of the bowsprit to land in front of Lunt, who had been starting to reload a swivel.

Lunt picked up his sword, but suddenly there was a pistol shot from behind him. The redcoat fell backward. Lunt turned to see Captain Jones standing behind him with one of his two pistols smoking.

Jones turned and shouted down the deck, "Every available man to the quarterdeck to repel boarders." Jones drew his sword and started to the rail. Lunt followed. Men on the bowsprit retreated back to their ship.

Below him Lunt heard another single musket roar as Marie claimed another redcoat in crossing. Overhead came the sound of a thump, thump, thump of a battle ax being wielded with fervor. Lunt glanced up to see O'Mally, amidst withering fire, chopping away at the stays. Several were cut but O'Mally was hit, yet he still kept chopping, and then, ever so slowly, Drake began to fall behind. Both crews continued to shoot at each other, until the distance again widened so much as to make small arms fire impractical. Lunt looked up but could no longer see O'Mally. Below him, Marie tried one more long distance shot before closing the Captain's shutters. Lunt turned to Jones, and said, "Thank you, sir."

Jones nodded to acknowledge the comment but his real attention was still focused on the ship. With his sword still in his hand, he moved rapidly forward to the quarterdeck rail to shout orders. "This is not over yet. Mr. Cullan, cut the upper main mast rigging free and pitch it overboard. Prepare to come about."

Jones turned to Lieutenant Hall, who was still acting as helmsman, and said, "Stand off a thousand paces and circle them, then bring me close in behind their stern."

Within a few minutes Ranger came within a couple of hundred paces of the enemy stern. Jones spoke through his trumpet, "Do ye wish to strike?"

From across the water, Lunt heard the voice he recognized as Lt. Dobbs' answer back, clearly and distinctly, "Sir, I'll see you in hell first."

Then Drake with her two remaining sails began to fall off to the west, away from Ranger. She was obviously trying to make it back into the lough and had stayed in irons deliberately until Ranger had completed her pass from east to west of her.

"Larboard batteries load bars and chain, Mr. Simpson," shouted Jones. "Let's immobilize her, shoot for the rigging."

Jones directed the movement of the Ranger so as to bring the larboard guns into position on the stern of the Drake, which was moving slowly to the west under limited sail. Great holes appeared in her canvas, through which the crimson sunset was visible.

"Fire in threes," commanded Jones from the quarterdeck rail, as Ranger began to pour a broadside into Drake's defenseless stern.

The impact of each of the first two batteries was visible from Ranger as they ripped through the remaining rigging and shreds of sail. The set of main sails all toppled to the deck. Drake's main mast was now just a bare severed trunk. More men were buried alive on the deck amidst tons of rigging and canvas.

Jones yelled, "Cease fire," before the third set of threes were fired. "Fall off and pass to the lee of her stern rail."

* * * * *

Dobbs was wounded in several places and a splinter from the fallen mast had lodged deep under his ribs. He teetered at the helm, amidst a torrent of men who screamed advice at him, "Strike, sir, strike. It is hopeless. We can't make it back to Belfast with them shooting at us."

"Not while the carronade is still aboard," Dobbs shouted.

"Sir, it's buried in debris."

"Well, let's unbury it." Dobbs stumbled forward with his sword drawn and descended the stairs from the quarter-deck. He breathed heavily, faint from loss of blood. The carronade had been his weapon. He should not have mounted it amidships on the platform, the old fat Captain had been right. He had not been able to use it during most of the battle because there was always something in its way. The advantage of putting it in the middle so that it could be fired to either side had been minimal during the action. Why had he been so stubborn?

Dobbs stumbled over bodies whose blood had soaked the fallen canvas that covered the deck everywhere. Moans of wounded men filled the air. Dobbs shouted, "Every man that is able, man the starboard guns. Let's send them to hell. Fire at will."

Dobbs continued making his way over bodies buried beneath the canvas. On one footfall he heard a man moan. There was another sharp pain across his side. He felt nauseous again and put his hand to the wound. It was sticky. He looked at it momentarily and then pressed it back to suppress the bleeding. He stumbled forwards again, gathering men to come with him. Most of them were wounded. In the center of the deck was the remnants of the main sheet spread over a hump which had been the carronade. Dobbs thrust his sword into the covering canvas and began to cut a circle around the gun. Someone disturbed him.

"Sir, the Yankees want to know if you'll strike."

"Tell them to go to hell, Mr. Warren."

Dobbs and his men continued to cut a circle in the midst of the canvas which smothered the carronade. Side by side, seamen and red coated soldiers pitched in to uncover the weapon. Drake was without steerage, her position now at the mercy of the waves which pounded against her. Her two remaining sails had been toppled by the last Yankee salvo.

Over his shoulder, Dobbs heard his Midshipman reply to the Yankee pirates through his speaking trumpet, "Yankee Doodle, go to hell."

Dobbs hurried to pull the rest of the canvas off the carronade, before the next inevitable broadside from Ranger. "Pull, men, .. crop it there,.. all right."

As layers of canvas were pulled aside, Dobbs found a body in a brown civilian suit. Turning it over, he saw Mr. Wright, his friend who had struggled on his wood lathe in the evenings to build the sabot shells and the platform for their experiment. He was dead, another good man who had fallen prey to that whore. He had not been afraid to do his duty and had manned the carronade to the last. Clutched in his hands was the last sabot. Dobbs picked it up and gave it to a seaman to pitch over the side.

Behind him he heard one and then a second of the Drake's four pounders fire. Everyone knew that the inevitable broadside was coming. The crew thought Dobbs was going to try and use the weapon against the pirate. "Sir, shall we try to turn her about?"

"No, they're coming up on the wrong side. We'll never be able to do it. She is already loaded with an eighteen. We are going to fire her into the deck," answered Dobbs.

"Sir, would you sink the Drake?"

"Only this gun. Help me, men," moaned Dobbs who struggled to point the barrel down from its mount towards the rail.

As they pushed together to aim the carronade, their world exploded around them. Men, still alive on top of the canvas and manning the last few guns on Drake's starboard, suffered from a full volley of whirling grape shot that whistled before it careened into human flesh and wood. Aimless splinters flew again and men left standing became human pin cushions.

Dobbs had fallen over from the blast. He struggled to upright himself. He could feel enormous pain in his hand.

A seaman looked at him gasping, "Sir, your arm has been shot away."

Dobbs ignored the pain. "Aim the gun at the deck and fire at will. We must sink the gun."

Dobbs and two other men climbed on top of the cleared gun. Dobbs lunged his body against the weapon in an effort to turn its barrel down. "Another coin, below the barrel. Touch the slow match. Now, damn it!" shouted Dobbs.

The carronade exploded and at point blank range, the eighteen pound ball blew out the far side of Drake so that, after smoke and splinters cleared, there was only a gaping hole which extended to the crews deck below. Twelve feet of the Drake's side had been blown away. In front of Dobbs lay a canvas coated runway into the sea.

About them another volley of grape whistled. Its razor teeth largely flew over dead men.

"Cut her free!" shouted Dobbs while using his left hand to mitigate the loss of blood from his right arm. He fell backward onto the hemp rope and canvas, and watched as two men started to lead the carronade down into the sea. Dobbs held up his head to observe the two seamen push her down across the canvas. For a moment the gun stalled and then, with a tugging on the training lines, it began to gain momentum. The gun reached the edge of the hole it had helped create in the Drake's side and then fell barrel first out into the sea. One lone line, still attached, held the gun like a thread. A seaman cut the line with his broadsword.

"It's in the ocean, sir. Shall we strike?"

"I'll not strike!" shouted Dobbs.

The shocked men about him winced at his statement. Dobbs continued in obvious pain, "Is Midshipman Warren still alive?"

"Yes, sir."

"Then tell him that he is in command of the Drake and the choice is his. I'll not do it." Dobbs' head fell back against the canvas. Amidst the pain he recalled the dreams of glory he had expected for himself as a boy. Just one day in his life had shattered them all. Death would surely come now. Would his parents be proud of him? He had done his best. He waited for death.

12
Victory

"Signal from the Drake, sir."

"Hold fire, Mr. Simpson," Jones shouted through his speaking trumpet. He turned to the stern rail and asked, "Lieutenant Lunt, what do you make of it?"

Looking through his spyglass, Lunt saw two men at the stern of the vessel, one held aloft a lantern while the other waved furiously with a strip of white canvas. The man waving the canvas wore an officer's uniform. There was no mast left from which to support an ensign. Lunt conveyed his thoughts to Jones.

Jones continued to shout orders, "Mr. Cullan, we'll circle and come astern. Mr. Simpson, load grape again. If it's a deception, they'll pay the price."

In the semi-darkness, Ranger cautiously circled the Drake at a distance of 2,000 paces. The maneuver would take some minutes. Jones bent over and snatched up his uniform jacket and pulled it over his shoulders. He then descended to the gun deck and began to talk with his men, several of whom had been wounded but had been able to remain on duty. At one location, he paused and ordered nearby crew members to clean up the blood surrounding a dead marine who had fallen from the fore top spar when it had been blown away.

From the gun deck, Jones squinted upwards at the condition of the main mast. He saw a young marine who stood beside the splinters at the top of the stump, some fifty feet above the deck. Jones called up at him, "Any sign of Lt. Wallingsford?"

"No, sir," the boy from Vermont responded, "I believe that Lt. Wallingsford was blown into the sea when the cannon ball struck the uppers, sir."

Jones nodded silently and continued along the larboard side speaking encouragingly with individual seamen and patting some of them on the back. Finally, he crossed to starboard and on his return he noticed that a group of men were standing about the most aft six pounder. Jones approached but, because of his height, was unable to see over his men's shoulders. Squatting between the bodies he saw a hand supporting a head of bright red hair.

"Let me through, men," said Jones.

Lunt was bent over O'Mally's body, his ear at the man's lips. He turned when he saw the Captain and shook his head, his intelligent eyes sad as he whispered, "Sir, he was shot from the mizzen while chopping the shrouds free. He was hit twice but we've got the bleeding stopped. I think he'd survive the musket wounds but apparently his back was broken in the fall. He can't feel anything in his legs."

Jones stepped forward, but Lunt caught his arm and whispered into his ear, "Sir, he fell on the gun while it was red hot. His skin is fused to the barrel. None of us have the heart to move him."

Jones started to speak but was momentarily halted as his nostrils and eyes were repulsed by the sight of O'Mally, his face contorted in visible pain. His back was arched hideously over the iron barrel. The lingering stench of scorched flesh intermingled with the smell of gun smoke. O'Mally's leg was pinned to the six pounder by a remnant of the mizzen spar. Beneath it, O'Mally's leg was shattered.

Jones called up to the quarterdeck, "Mr. Ryan, where is the double ration of rum I ordered for every man?"

"Coming, sir,"

"By God, man, pass it out quickly but bring the first tankard here," commanded Jones.

Jones knelt over and started to say something when O'Mally interrupted him, "Have we won, sir?"

"It appears so," said Jones glancing up across the water

at the Drake, from whose stern a signal lantern illuminated a bit of white canvas still being waved vigorously. "We'll know in a couple of minutes."

"Be very careful, sir," advised O'Mally with a grimace. "They could be tricky. They'll not want to surrender a Royal Navy vessel to you, sir."

Jones looked again at the Drake. "I have eighteen gun barrels of grape at the ready, Mr. O'Mally. But I don't think it will be needed."

Jones touched a tankard of rum to O'Mally's lips. The man sipped and then smiled. "Not as good as poteen, but it'll do, sir."

After a moment he added, "Sir, are they surrendering? If they are, I want to see it. Will you hold me up, sir?" requested O'Mally, his eyes pleading.

Jones looked up again and saw that they were approaching the Drake. To those immediately about him he ordered, "Get the spar off this man." To another he said, "Get the Surgeon down here! I don't care what Mr. Green is doing, get him down here now!"

Captain Jones held O'Mally's head in position as Lunt and a few seamen moved the spar inward across the deck to a securable position. The distance between the two vessels closed again to less than 200 paces. Ranger was in an excellent position to administer several ruthless salvos without the Drake returning fire because of her lack of maneuverability. Ranger's crew observed for the first time a large gaping hole in the vessel's larboard freeboard that extended into the lower deck. A few pathetic men were roaming the deck, seemingly delirious, one or two carried lanterns.

Jones looked down and asked, "Ready?"

O'Mally nodded faintly and drew a breath. Jones stooped over to grip O'Mally's body and lift him from the gun barrel. Bits of O'Mally's flesh stuck to the gun as the Captain gently began to rock the collapsed body from its position. As he performed the extraction, Jones reminded him, "You can't stay here, man. If we have to fire another volley, we'll need this gun."

O'Mally cried out as he was moved. Jones tilted him upward and carried him to the rail. Despite the man's larger frame, Jones held the crumpled body upright and then shifted his position so that O'Mally could see the Drake waving its surrender signal. The lantern signal was still being given.

Now, scarcely one hundred paces from Drake, Jones yelled over his shoulder, "Where is that surgeon? I want Ezra Green here now with a stretcher."

As Jones supported O'Mally, he pointed towards the smoking hulk of the once great vessel, its two masts now mere stubble. Jones looked briefly into O'Mally's face to see if he was still conscious and then back across the water at Drake. Lunt heard the words whispered by his Captain, "These people for too long have gone unchecked. Their officers and their King believe that they can behave in any way they wish. Today, we have shown them that they cannot. We have beaten them in a like vessel. This day at least, Britannia no longer rules the waves."

Lunt could see that O'Mally gave a weak nod in response to the Captain's spoken thoughts. Captain Jones bent over him further and spoke directly into his ear, "And you, Irishman, are more responsible than anyone for this victory. If you had not snapped those stays with your axe, we would have been engulfed by an army of soldiers. If you had not gone into Belfast with Lieutenant Lunt and issued the challenge, this victory could not have been won. I shall always remember what you did."

The Surgeon arrived and O'Mally passed out as he was laid upon the stretcher to be taken to the great cabin. All eyes on the deck were upon their Captain.

Jones took his speaking trumpet and stood at the rail facing the Drake, "Where is Captain Burden?"

"Dead, sir," came the reply.

"And Lieutenant Dobbs?"

"Dy...Dying, sir. I am the only officer left," shouted Midshipman Warren. "I formally surrender, sir, and pray that you give assistance to our men."

"You will retract all cannons and close the gun ports. You will then shine a lantern on each gun position to indicate that the lids are closed. After that we will board to windward."

Jones turned to the Helmsman and indicated that he should sail off some distance from the Drake so that the orders could be seen to be obeyed.

Then dramatically, Jones ascended the stairs to the quarterdeck rail, drew his short naval sword from its scabbard and, pointing out over the water towards the Drake, shouted, "Victory is ours!" to which the crew gave a rapturous cry, danced on the deck, hugged, and congratulated each other. After a moment, Jones announced, "A moment of silence for Lieutenant Wallingsford and the others who gave their lives or their health for this proclamation of Liberty. Be they never forgotten."

For a moment, each man reflected on the events of the past hour and five minutes, then Jones spoke again, "One of the missions of the Ranger in this voyage was to encourage the King's ministers to exchange our prisoners of war for theirs. Today they still hold our beleaguered comrades under the unjust threat that they will eventually be hung as traitors when this conflict is over. We failed two nights ago to seize Lord Selkirk, in order to later offer him as part of a first exchange for American seamen. I was disappointed in the outcome of that enterprise, but I think this night we have..," Jones raised his voice to a roar, "..a greater prize! This is the first time to my knowledge that an American warship has fought and captured one of a like size of our enemy. This, men, is something we must endeavor to show the world. It will bring America much help from Europe."

Lunt's gaze extended beyond his Captain to the cabin door. His eyes briefly met those of Marie who was dressed in her dark cloak, her hair hanging down over her shoulders.

Lunt turned his attention back to his Captain.

"We will be judged as much by the quality of this victory, as by our behavior after victory. Remember, men, that half of the seamen on the Drake did not want to be there. They were taken by press gangs from their villages in Scotland, Ireland, Wales, and even England, too. Unlike you, they were forced to serve in German George's navy. I know this to be true because at twelve I was so taken from my native Scotland.

"These people are afraid of us and of our ideas. Let them not find out that we are really the wild barbarians which I know you all are." The Ranger's crew laughed and held up their double ration to cheer him. Jones put his hands up.

"Therefore, it is my order that there be no cruelty or open hostility toward any member of Drake's crew. We very much need their help to repair that vessel and make her seaworthy for a long voyage out of British waters. I have just been informed that a large flotilla of vessels has been spotted to the south during the engagement. It is imperative that we leave this location within the hour. But it is also most essential that we attempt to take the Drake with us to show the rest of Europe what a well equipped American Navy might be able to do. This victory may win us much support..," Jones turned his gaze over his shoulder towards the cabin door, "...in France."

Jones ended his speech by raising his flagon high and shouting, "To the men of the Ranger. I salute you." The crew cheered for a few minutes and then returned to their stations.

Jones stepped back from the quarterdeck rail and turned to his Helmsman, "Approach the windward side and grapple her. We will tow the Drake into the lee of Mew Island and anchor for a short time to make repairs, bury the dead, and let some of the wounded ashore. Lieutenant Simpson, take charge of the details."

Jones proceeded to the great cabin to check the Surgeon's progress with the wounded.

* * * * *

Lunt pulled his uniform jacket onto his back and sipped the rum which had been provided. It felt warm and soothing. The Drake's Midshipman was standing by the larboard rail. He and another crew member caught the first line thrown from Ranger. As they drew close to Drake, Lunt became glad for the dullness which the spirits provided him. At first he was able to hear the undercurrent of moaning as if the Drake herself were wounded, and then he began to be able to distinguish the individual voices as they cried in torment.

From the bowels of the Drake, they heard a hideous scream, "Not my leg, sir, please, aah...ah..ah!"

Beside Lunt, one of the crew men raised his lantern to view the deck of the enemy ship. He shrieked aloud, "God in mercy!"

Before them was the carnage of sea battle. Everywhere in the heaps of canvas and rigging that covered the deck was blood and pieces of human beings. Those that were not moaning, were either unconscious or dead. Each would have to be examined and cared for.

Lt. Simpson stepped to Lunt's side with a voice trumpet and spoke clearly and slowly towards the other deck, "I am Lt. Simpson of the American Continental Navy. You are all prisoners. My Captain has ordered us not to harm any member of this crew further. But in order to earn this leniency, I order each man aboard to bring any firearms on or about his person to this spot, immediately." Simpson pointed in the lantern light to a place a few feet away from him on the Drake's deck.

Simpson continued, "Any man not accomplishing this order within five minutes will be shot." Lunt turned his gaze towards Simpson. That had not been Jones' order, but it might be effective.

Simpson put down his trumpet and leaned across the rail to speak to the Drake's Midshipman, "How many have you lost?"

"Over half the seamen are dead, sir," said the Midshipman, "most of the rest are wounded in some way."

"What about the soldiers who were aboard?" asked Simpson.

"A lot of them are buried, sir, under the rigging and canvas. They were pinned down when you shot away the main. You can hear 'em," replied the British Midshipman.

One man who had been listening to the conversation, sounded off to indicate his presence below the wreckage.

"What about the rest, the Royal Marines?" demanded Simpson.

"Well, sir, about a dozen won't have anything to do with surrender. They are below, sir," said the midshipman.

"Well, you tell them that they have five minutes to get up here or we will sink the Drake with everyone aboard." The midshipman saluted and started to hurry off, and then turned again to withdraw his sword and toss it onto the growing pile of small arms.

A few minutes later the Midshipman emerged from below, followed by a snarling Royal Marine sergeant in a bright red uniform. His men followed with their muskets held over their heads in a surrender mode. Simpson nodded and then looked back at the Ranger's crew and issued orders for the men waiting at the rail to board the Drake.

"Collect all wounded men and transport them to the Ranger. Throw all debris over the side, except large pieces of canvas or rigging, and any single length of wood twenty feet or longer. Lt. Lunt, you will take charge of checking the security of the hull. Mr. Gale and our other carpenters will assist you, as well as any British seamen so capable. Mr. Hall, you are to supervise sweeping all gore over the side as soon as possible."

"Midshipman," Simpson pointed to the surviving British officer, "you are to take some of your men and assemble the dead at the bow for burial later."

Lunt was one of the first to cross to the Drake's deck. He needed to inspect the gaping hole in the freeboard which looked into the second deck. As he walked, his boots stuck to the deck in what he knew was human blood. Everywhere were the sounds of men suffering. By his lantern's light he had glimpses of human horror that made him avoid focusing on too many details, except the security of his deck. As he passed behind Simpson, who was looking about, the First Lieutenant remarked over his shoulder, "Better repair her well, Lunt, she'll probably be yours."

Under the light of an assistant's lantern, Lunt approached the mound of entangled canvas and rigging piled between the two masts. He looked up and saw the canvas had been cut away in a crude circle. He held his lantern higher. He saw the heavy track of two sets of wheels which had descended from the pile burdened with an enormous weight.

"You didn't get it, Lieutenant Lunt."

Lunt turned to the voice and shifted his lantern to see who spoke. Laying backwards on the mound of debris was Lieutenant Dobbs. There was an obvious wound in his abdomen. Someone had put a crude canvas bandage over it. His right arm had been blown off below the elbow and a leather throng tourniquet had been placed on his upper arm. A large wooden splinter had been twisted tightly in the leather. About the stump of Dobbs' arm was an unsatisfactory bandage that dripped. Dobbs' eyes stared out as in a trance. They seemed to have no particular focus.

"Bring him a double ration, no, make it a triple," ordered Lunt to one of the carpenters, who hurried off.

Lunt went to Dobbs' side and knelt beside him as the man spoke, "Suppose you'll be able to tell your grandchildren how you took the Drake. You see, I'm not going to have any, not now. I don't even have a wife to cry for me and to carry my portrait around in her locket for the next forty years. Won't now."

Lunt placed a large flagon of hot rum to Dobbs' lips to soothe him. "I've had so much pain already that it seems like an old friend now," said Dobbs as he accepted another sip before continuing, "But who'd want a one armed has been, who let the colonials capture his ship. I used to have my pick of women, too many choices. Until I fell in love with a spy." Dobbs' vision seemed to clear, and he tried to sit up. Unable, he then screamed, "Jezebel!"

Lunt turned to follow Dobbs' hate ridden gaze. Marie Chatelain stood behind him on the deck of Drake, looking down at Dobbs. She was wearing the same black hooded cloak, her hair piled up on her head again in her usual fashion. The wind blew at it and in the lantern light her face seemed unusually white. Lunt turned back to Dobbs to calm him. A moment later he glanced over his shoulder again and she was gone. He stood up and was unable to see her dark figure on the Drake's deck. Where had she gone so suddenly?

* * * * *

Marie walked quickly along the edge of the rubble. As long as she stayed away from the lantern light, her dark cloak would blend into the shadows. Only Lunt had recognized her amidst the confusion. She shouldn't have stopped to look down at Dobbs. She started to ascend the stairs up onto the quarterdeck and then paused midway. There was Snead. The British Helmsman was still at the wheel. He seemed frozen in place, his eyes glued on some imaginary position in the far distance, as if he were in a trance. The Yankees had not even noticed that he was still at the helm.

Cautiously, Marie ascended the remaining two stairs. Snead was very faithful to Captain Burden. They had sailed together for over twenty years. She must be wary of him.

She passed behind him. He seemed not to notice anyone was close to him. If she called out his presence to the Americans, she would never be able to complete her mission. The Yankees had never captured an enemy ship before. They did not know the first priority of action. They were busy treating the wounded and making sure the Drake did not sink. They were so naive.

Marie cautiously evaded Snead, who seemed not to move. The Captain lay still by the rail and she went to his side. For a brief moment she took his hand. It was cold. She put her head on his chest, facing away from his head, not wanting to look at the bloody pulp. Poor George, you were such a good man. I did love you. I did mean to trick you and steal from you, but I did love you. I have loved all the men I have slept with, each in his own way. No time for sentiment. I must find it. As her head lay on his chest, her hand searched through his jacket. She withdrew items she found and placed them on his chest. His pocket watch, his pipe, the gold toothpick, and then in his vest pocket was a round object.

Marie sat up. Stray beams of the lantern light drifted up to the quarterdeck. Before she looked at the item, she glanced quickly to her left. Had the Helmsman moved? No, she assured herself, he was still there in his trance. Marie held the ring up to the flickering light. The diamond sparkled in great colors. George had really planned to marry her, not just to keep her as his whore. He had really loved her. She placed the ring into a pocket of her petticoat and continued to search in the vest pocket. There was something else there, hard and thin. She drew it out, the key. It was usually tied to a string in the bottom of the Captain's vest pocket. But the key was loose in his pocket. She took it and looked down on the deck from beneath her dark hood. In the lantern light, Lunt was still kneeling beside Dobbs, giving him rum. Lieutenant Simpson was busy below deck. Many wounded men were being helped over to Ranger.

Marie looked at Snead. He just continued to stare forward, his face rigid in the lantern light. She crept behind him, careful not to expose her white skin to light. She bent and opened the outer door to the officers' quarters. Men lay heaped in each of the officers' rooms. She looked at them briefly, some of them moaned. These must have been the early wounded, they were still there. She opened the door to the Captain's quarters. There was no one inside. She closed it behind her and turned the bolt to lock herself in. There was a single lantern already lit. Which panel was it that Burden kept his papers behind? Marie searched hurriedly.

If she could find it, she would have the carronade. The Americans were bemoaning the fact that they had not captured the gun but the plans were much more important than having the gun itself. She climbed to stand on top of Burden's writing desk, it was up there. He'd had a false wall void put in above his locker. She had convinced him to have her stay one night aboard the Drake, with the fib that she was lonely and that she had never spent a night at sea. He had accommodated her. She moved the stiff chart hung over the panel. There was the key hole. She slid the key in and opened it. The false door swung open to reveal the cabinet behind. There were deep circular holes drilled in the wood, suitable for the storage of rolled charts or plans. She reached inside.

* * * * *

It bothered Lunt that he had seen Marie on the Drake and a moment later could not locate her on the deck. He was still with Dobbs. The man's glaze fell to the soothing rum and Lunt helped bring the cup to his lips. Dobbs swallowed and continued talking in a stream of memories, "You did a brave thing back there, the dinner challenge and the escape. You killed Sergeant Hensley, didn't you? He was a bastard, he really was. Captain Burden, bless his soul, said he was the cruelest man he'd ever met. Liked to inflict pain."

Dobbs' pattern of thoughts changed again after a pause. "You know why I wouldn't surrender Lunt? It was you, I admired you. You never faltered all last night. It was you that inspired me never to give up. You didn't get the gun, did you?" Dobbs looked up for reassurance.

"No, we didn't get it," said Lunt looking around to escape the intensity of the conversation. But Dobbs continued talking, "That closet bomb. It would have blown us to bits, wouldn't it, or was it just a trick?"

"It was no trick," Lunt said lifting the cup to Dobbs' lips. His hand momentarily grazed the remnant of Dobbs' arm. Lunt felt the man's pain.

"I liked you. We could have been friends. If...," Dobbs pattern of speech changed. He began gasping for air. "Tell my parents I love them. Write them for me, Lunt," Dobbs' head fell to one side. Lunt checked his pulse at the throat. He was still alive. He had just passed out. Lunt stood up and called, "Get this officer to the Surgeon."

Was Marie still on board the Drake? She must have been aboard the Drake in the past. Was she somewhere on board now looking for something she knew was there? The captain's cabin. Lunt turned, and called to the carpenters, "Mr. Gale, get this mess overboard. Mind the men underneath. Throw off a little at a time, but nothing large from which we can construct a sail. I'll return shortly."

As he started to turn to leave, a marine called to him, "Sir, what will we do with this man? He had locked himself in the provisions locker."

Lunt turned to see the small pocked face of van Zoot. He was trembling with fear as the marine held his collar.

"How did you get aboard the Drake?" asked Lunt.

"Capt...Captain Burden made me come. I didn't want to. I'm a neutral, you know that. I'm a Dutch citizen."

Lunt turned to the marine, "We'll never get to the bottom

of why he was here before we have to leave this anchorage. Put him in the brig aboard the Ranger. Captain Jones will speak to him tomorrow."

Lunt turned a deaf ear on van Zoot's protests and looked anxiously up at the quarterdeck. The lights were tricky, but he believed that he could see the door open to what must have been the officers' quarters. Was it Marie? There must be plans on board for the carronade. Was she trying to get to them first and hide them away somewhere? He rapidly ascended the stairs and opened the door. There were three men standing in the corridor. Two were American marines. The third man turned to look at him briefly. It was Captain Jones. He put a finger to his lips. Before Lunt could say anything more, Jones turned again to peer into the key hole. Then, he stood up and motioned for the marines to break open the door.

Musket butts were lifted and smashed against the door violently. The lock broke immediately and the door swung open. Lunt saw that Jones carried a pistol in his right hand.

"Find anything that your friends should know about?" Jones asked.

Marie looked up. From her expression, she was immediately resigned to the fact that she had been caught. She held her head up straight as she spoke, "Captain Burden had a false locker there in which he kept all his most important charts and papers. The carronade plans could have been there, but all the chart pigeon holes are empty." She pointed at the ground. "You see, there are bits of paper on the floor and the port windows were open. Someone was here before me. If the plans were here, they are not now."

"Had you found them, would you have shared them with us?" asked Jones. Marie only stared back at him, expressionless.

After an uncomfortable silence, Jones spoke, "Madame, you are to return to my cabin on the Ranger and you are to go nowhere else. If you disobey my order, I shall leave you on Mew island with the wounded, for the British to do with you as they wish." Jones turned to his marines, "Escort Madame Chatelain to my quarters and remain there with her. She is not even to relieve herself out of your presence."

Jones and Lunt were left alone in the Captain's quarters. Jones searched about the cabin hastily, opening drawers and cabinets. "We must get underway quickly again. I estimate the flotilla is only a few hours behind us and they have good wind. Every minute that we don't get underway, they are closing the distance. We will have to tow the Drake, at least until some masts can be reconstructed. That'll take a couple of days. If we are closely pursued by a British fleet, I may have to abandon the Drake. I did not have the time to find the plans without Marie. I deliberately let her steal away to the Drake. We would never have found the false cabinet in this short a time." Jones reached down on the floor, "Here!" he exclaimed.

Lunt turned, Jones was holding a hard linen tube. A type in which charts and items were frequently stored. He turned it over in his hands and handed it to Lunt. Lunt looked inside, "It's empty, sir," and then he examined what was printed on the outside:

The Carron Company
Stromeferry, Scotland

"Is that the name you saw on the boxes, when you climbed aboard the Drake?" asked Jones.

"Yes, sir, it's the name," said Lunt enthusiastically.

"We may not have the plans or the gun, but I believe we do have the location where it is being developed," commented Jones.

"Do you know this town, sir?" asked Lunt.

"Aye," said Jones looking at the name on the tube. "You have never mentioned this name to her?"

"No, sir."

"That may be a piece of knowledge that we possess and that she does not. Continue to keep it to yourself, we'll let the Spymaster know of it in due course."

"Sir, she knows that name," said Lunt.

"I'm sure she does, Lieutenant Lunt, but I'm sure she doesn't know who it is and that's the key."

Jones left the great cabin carrying the tube. Lunt followed him. Jones stopped directly beside the Helmsman "Are you the man who steered this vessel into the Ranger?"

Jacob Snead slowly turned his head towards Captain Jones and smiled, "Yes, sir."

Jones stared back at him, "Since the two vessels have closed, have you seen anyone enter the cabin before the lady or myself?"

"No, I've not seen anyone else," said the man.

"Except yourself?" pressed Jones.

The Helmsman smiled and looked into Jones's eyes, "I had my duty to do, sir. I followed the Captain's orders. Even though he was dying, sir, shot in the head, sir, he managed to pull the key from his pocket for me to see. I obeyed his last command, sir. That's all."

Jones called down to a seaman passing below, "You, take this man forward to help Lt. Simpson! Come with me, Lunt, there is much to do and very little time."

* * * * *

A brief burial ceremony was conducted en route to Mew Island. Under lantern light, Jones read briefly from a bible over the bodies of the dead. Over fifty bodies were slid into the sea from beneath their respective flags. Able British and American seamen and marines stood on opposite sides of Drake's bow. After the last body departed the deck, Jones spoke to the assembled prisoners, "All British wounded, as designated by our surgeon as being unlikely to survive a voyage at sea, will be transported to Mew Island by longboat along with a sufficient quantity of hard tack, dried potatoes, and water for several days. Is Mr. Snead present?"

"Yes, sir."

"Mr. Snead, you are to be in charge of all wounded on Mew Island, until your countrymen can effect a rescue. It should not be long. I regret to inform you that within the past hour Lieutenant Dobbs died. I was with your brave officer at his death. I have been moved to prepare a missive for his father, the Reverend Dobbs. I regret that time did not allow us to transport the dead to this island.

"We will be underway within the hour. All British sailors and marines are to assist my lieutenants as required in the repair of the Drake. The Drake will initially move out under tow."

* * * * *

Lieutenant Simpson was asked to report to Jones' wardroom. He knocked and entered. At the officers' table sat Captain Jones with his clerk, James Gooch, Lieutenant Lunt, and the Sailing Master, David Cullan.

"Yes, sir," said Simpson saluting.

"How are the repairs going?" asked Jones.

"Satisfactory in the time we've had, sir. Lt. Lunt will have to do a lot of work but she should be seaworthy." As Simpson spoke, Lieutenants Hall and Midshipman Hill also each knocked and entered the cabin. At Jones' invitation they took their seats. Simpson nodded to them and then continued to give his report.

"The hull damage actually looks far worse than it really is. Dobbs' gun broke open freeboard no closer than ten feet above the water line. The prisoners are removing some rock ballast. She should float higher. The hull damage should be able to be repaired by tomorrow. I would leave the two ship's carpenters aboard with Lieutenant Lunt," Simpson nodded graciously to Lunt and then resumed speaking.

"We have transported the remaining two lengths of Kauri masts over to the Drake. In daylight tomorrow, Lieutenant

Lunt should be able to extract the old stubs and raise two short masts to get nearly forty feet of elevation above the deck. That should be high enough to mount a spar on the top of each. The old main doubling was intact. It should be able to be reamed out. In another day's time they should be able to get up another twenty or more feet above the new main for a second spar and sail to be mounted. That will have to be done at anchor, of course. The Drake should be able to sail by herself after two days at sea. She will be slow, sir, but the hull integrity is still sound."

"You feel Lt. Lunt should be able to manage with a good prize crew then, Lt. Simpson?"

"Yes, sir," replied Simpson.

"Good," said Jones. "Have a look at this," Jones handed him a piece of paper. Simpson looked at it and then looked up at his Captain.

"Sir, this is a list of men. My name is at the top. You promised, sir, on your honor, that there would be no reprisals for the past trouble." Simpson was visibly shaken.

Jones spoke calmly, "Since the Ranger left Portsmouth last summer, I have endured petty disputes over the prize agreement. These disputes have forced Ambassador Franklin to remove one very competent marine captain from this ship, because in your eyes his rank would have eaten into your share of the booty. The man would have been very useful to have in our various landings. Instead, I have had to go ashore myself. I have had someone mysteriously drop an anchor a fortnight ago so that we became entangled in the Drake's anchor lines and had to withdraw." Jones' voice became louder and intensified with rage, "This very morning I have broken up an attempted mutiny. I have been twice almost left behind at Whitehaven and again in Wales when we rescued Lt. Lunt and the other prisoners. I have had to endure the humiliation of having my crew steal dinner plates and silver from Lady Selkirk's house like common thieves!"

Jones hammered his fist down on his desk and then continued, "No, this list you see, Lt. Simpson, contains those of your closest friends from Portsmouth. Those who principally came to this war for profit, rather than cause. This is a list of men who quite naturally would prefer that you be their Captain."

Simpson shouted back, his usually slouched frame stood erect, "Sir, you promised that there would be no reprisals, if all helped in the engagement with the Drake."

"I did, Lt. Simpson, and I am a man of my word. All of our officers and men fought today with courage and determination. You personally manned the gun decks with skill and bravery. I'll never say anything differently. This is not a reprisal list. It is simply a list of *your* crew."

"Crew, sir?" asked Simpson, his voice a little calmer.

"Aye," said Jones, "you, not Lt. Lunt, are going to command the Drake and sail her back to Brest."

"Sir, we are in the middle of the British Isles. There is very likely a flotilla only a few hours away. The Drake will not be fast enough to evade."

Jones slammed his fist on the table, "You would have been willing to send Lt. Lunt aboard, why not yourself? I will tow you this evening and..," Jones emphasized his next word, "*I*...will not abandon *you*."

Jones unrolled a chart and spread it out on the table. The officers stood up and gathered around. "If the wind persists, we can make it by the channel between Fairhead and the Mull of Kintyre by dawn. 'Tis forty miles to the north and it is the narrowest point out of the Irish Sea. If there are any British men of war stationed to block egress from the Irish sea to the north, they will be in that point. But, knowing the habits of ships as I do, if they have had to be there for several days, I've a notion they would prefer to anchor at night very close to the Scottish side. There are some good ale houses there." Jones looked up and found a few smiles.

He continued, "Both of our ships will run without any deck lights whatsoever. We will proceed straight up the Irish coast, very near to land. It is largely deserted along the Irish side. In the daylight we can go to either side of Rathlin Island. If we are under pursuit on the morrow, I will transfer all Americans to the Ranger and we will run for the Hebrides. If we make them, a thousand ships will not find me there."

Jones continued with emphasis, "But the symbol of our success, gentlemen, will be to haul the Drake back to France for the world to see. Otherwise, it is the word of the English against us. They will deny we ever took the Drake or simply say that they recaptured it right afterwards. We cannot let them do that. Ambassador Franklin needs this vessel in a French port so that he can bring the French, the Dutch, the Spanish, and perhaps even the Russians aboard. Without her, we have only a story that can be discredited. With her, we have a prize to show the world."

"Do you understand now, Lieutenant Simpson, the importance of this assignment?" asked Jones.

"Yes, sir," replied Simpson.

"During the engagement, I had Mr. Cullan haul up Ranger's lower course sails. They should be largely undamaged and capable to bear the brunt of hauling both vessels away on a run this evening," said Jones. Cullan nodded his agreement.

Jones held three pieces of paper in his hand. He looked right at Simpson. "If you follow the orders I have had written out for you, Lieutenant Simpson, we should make it together around the west of Ireland and back to France. I shall not abandon you. Mr. Gooch, read the orders aloud. After you hear them, Lieutenant Simpson, you are to sign two of the copies in acknowledgement that you have received them. What you do with the third copy is your own concern. Mr. Gooch, read Lt. Simpson his orders."

Gooch began to read from one of the papers:

By John Paul Jones, Esquire
Captain in the American Navy

Lieutenant Thomas Simpson,
Sir,

You are hereby appointed Commander of our prize, the English Ship of War Drake. You are to keep Company with me and to pay punctual Attention to the Signals delivered herewith for your Government. You are to Superintend the Navigation and defence of the Ship under your Command and to support me as much as possible should we fall in with and engage any of the Enemies Ships.

The Honor of our Flagg is much concerned in the preservation of this Prize, therefore keep close by me and she shall not be given tamely up.

You will take your Station on the Ranger's Starboard Quarter at or about the Distance of a Cable's length. Should bad weather or any Accident Separate you from the Ranger you are to make the best of your way to France, and I recommend the port of Brest to your preference---you will secure all the Books, Charts, Instruments and Effects belonging to the deceased Captain & Officers etc.---For which this shall be your Order---

Given on board the American Continental Ship of War Ranger the 26th day of April, One Thousand Seven Hundred and Seventy eight.

Gooch handed Simpson a pen and the man signed each copy. Others witnessed the signature with their own marks. Simpson stormed out of the Captain's cabin.

* * * * *

Jones visited the hospital area which had been set up near the crew deck. At Jones' direction, each of the officers had given up his cradle to the most severely wounded. It was the middle of the night and the wind was still brisk. Progress to the north was excellent. Jones stopped and spoke with each of the dozen most severely wounded men if they were awake. The young powder monkey, Matthew Weatherby, who had been wounded when the cannon overturned, was berthed beside O'Mally. Mercifully, he was asleep. O'Mally held his hand across the short distance between their two cradles.

Jones remembered that during the battle, the Surgeon had tried for over an hour to brace the boy's bones together and then probe with his tenaculum to find the split artery to halt the boy's bleeding. As Green had explained to Jones, immediately after the surrender the only way to ensure that the boy did not die from loss of blood was to use the screw tourniquet to close off all the arteries, just below the knee, and then to amputate. The Surgeon had left the operating area for several minutes after the amputation. Jones had seen him outside crying.

O'Mally looked at Jones, who noticed the boy's hand clasped in his.

"It's helped me keep my own mind off the pain."

Jones nodded. "Like some rum?"

"I've never refused a good drink, sir." After he accepted the Captain's offering, he spoke softly into his ear, "Sir, bean chaoint, a Banshee, has wailed for me. When I die, in the next few days, will you promise to wait to drop me over the side until we come past Galway Bay, so that I'll come home again. Please, sir."

Aware that everyone about him was listening, Captain Jones replied, "I'll promise you more than that O'Mally, you will go back to Galway alive one day." O'Mally looked at him tearfully and Jones patted him on the shoulder and moved on.

Seeing the Surgeon as he was leaving, Jones inquired about O'Mally's condition. Green indicated that O'Mally had not only lost one leg but that his back was hopelessly broken. He would never be able to even maneuver himself out of bed for the rest of his life, should he live. Captain Jones murmured something to the effect that it was a shame that he could not do more to help a man who had done so much for his adopted country.

* * * * *

For four days and nights Ranger and Drake maneuvered their way around the Irish coast. To avoid detection on the horizon view of any pursuer, they hugged along points of land or between islands, when they were available for camouflage. Although they never again saw any ships pursuing them, Captain Jones was ever mindful of his treasured prize and its importance to the American cause. Increasingly, he also had difficulty with the Drake's keeping up with him and her responding to the signals he had ordered. Twice, he returned to Drake's side and spoke to Simpson through the speaking trumpet about the importance of their staying together.

As the Ranger rounded the northern tip of Ireland, Jones became more tolerant of both van Zoot and Marie Chatelain. He allowed each of them to walk the quarterdeck at alternate hours during daylight. During the morning watch, Jones began to have long conversations with Marie, primarily about the French court and which personalities should be first made aware of the capture of the Drake. She advised him as to which members of the court would be the most favorably disposed to renew hostilities against the English. Several of the personalities she discussed were people about whom Dr. Franklin may not have been aware. Most of the time Jones and she spoke in French.

During those days, as they hugged the northern and

then western shores of Ireland, Lunt primarily slept during the day and took the night watch with Midshipman Hill. He did not have much occasion to see Marie, except in passing. On the fifth morning, he was still on duty at daybreak when she came out on deck.

"What do you think of me, Henry, this spy?" asked Marie.

"I know that your King is fortunate, you have given your utmost in his cause," replied Lunt.

"No, Henry, I'm really asking about your feelings," she said.

Lunt turned to face her, bristling, "You know I have a wife. She is not as beautiful as you, or as polished. But I love her," and he walked away.

She followed him across the deck. Lunt looked around, hoping Captain Jones would appear to relieve him of his watch. "Did you like spying, Henry? Wait, don't answer, you were terribly good at it. You were so honest. Like just now, most men would think of saying the things I wanted to hear so they might have an opportunity to visit my boudoir after we arrived safely in France. Your faithfulness is astounding, with your wife so far away," Marie taunted him.

Lunt whirled and spoke abruptly, "I have asked the Captain to hereafter keep me on duty as a naval officer. I did not like lying even to Captain Burden, Major Pitkan, Lt. Dobbs, and the others. I think that's why I really made the challenge. No longer could I stand the deception that you seem to relish. I would rather perform my duty to my country, honestly, from the deck of a fighting ship. I have communicated these feelings to Captain Jones."

"No, no," said Marie, "I think you...."

"Huhmm, huhmm," coughed Jones, who thus announced his presence.

"Good morning, sir," said Lunt. "We have lost sight of Drake again during the night. Since the wind was light I decided not to wake you. It was only an hour ago. They are likely just behind that head, probably only a few hours back." He pointed to the north.

"Damn it, Simpson, won't you do anything as I ask?" Jones shook his head.

"Sir, are you going to go back for them?" asked Lunt.

"Excuse me, gentlemen," said Marie and she returned through the door to the officers' quarters where she had been given a berth.

"Aye, I suppose 'twill be necessary, before he goes off somewhere to sell our prize," answered Jones.

Lunt interrupted, "Sir, I have completed my watch but there is something I wish to discuss with you."

"Speak up," said Jones.

"O'Mally, sir. You know he has a broken back." Lunt pointed to a nearby land feature, "Around that point is the entrance to Galway Bay. Sir, I could use one of the small skiffs and sail O'Mally into one of the coastal villages and leave him. He'd be close to home, where his mother lives. It's probably just a day's ride. He has half a share coming. A little money in the right place and I could get someone to bring him to his mother, or to have his mother come for him. If you are concerned about getting Ranger too close to shore, you could meet me on an island. On the charts, sir, are the Aran islands at the entrance to the Bay. The note indicates there's a small fishing village there. I could light a signal fire tonight and tomorrow night so you can find me on your way south again."

Jones turned, his demeanor angry. "So that's why you did not wake me when you first lost sight of the Drake." Jones shook his head, "Lieutenant Lunt, I can't afford to lose you. The Ranger cannot afford to lose you. For a man who...may not live."

"You said he was going to live," retorted Lunt.

"I'm not God," snapped Jones.

"Don't you see, a few nights ago you gave him hope. That is why he is still alive, sir. You helped him will it. You made him forget all about that Banshee nonsense. You promised that he'd go back to Galway alive one day. You could make that promise come true now."

Jones moved away from Lunt and continued to shake his head. Lunt followed him along the rail.

"Sir, what is going to become of Mr. O'Mally in France? Because of his condition, and without a good knowledge of the language, it will be worse that any prison. You know that we will be off again, somewhere. After that O'Mally will be alone, an impossibly crippled man. He deserves better."

"Did you know that Marie wants to teach you French, humh, in her chateau. She is in love with you, Lieutenant." Jones raised an eyebrow.

"Sir, I am a married man. You have met my Sarah. You can take the French lessons."

"I have already learned French, Lieutenant," said Jones smiling.

For awhile, the two walked along the deck together in silence, changing direction several times.

Jones resumed the discussion, "Ah, yes, Sarah, a fine lady but you are three thousand miles and at least one or two years away from home. You have been in prison for over a year. Live a little, damn it. You have never been to Paris, have you, Henry? The greatest city in the world. A city of bright colors and remarkably beautiful women. I have much for you to do in Paris and you are going to become a hero there when Dr. Franklin introduces you to the French court."

"Sir, I have requested only sea duty from this point on. I am a sailor, not a spy, and certainly not a diplomat."

Jones pointed his finger directly at Lunt's face, "But you were so good at it. Marie said so. She is, as I have told you, quite genuinely the courtesan of Louis XVI himself. She can wield great influence for the American position and she was there. She saw us take the Drake. You understand that this little ship we have just taken is just a drop in the bucket compared to the overall might of the Royal Navy. The damage we have wrought is in the ruin of their prestige. A contribution to the buildup of doubt among their Parliament and among their people. A contribution to having England's enemies find the courage to help us. Dr. Franklin will be able to say it better than I can. You must meet him."

Jones continued to talk, "Henry, if our cause is going to be triumphant, I need men about me who will be willing to work with the French, and the Spanish, and maybe the Dutch. Men who will make us friends for the cause of Liberty. Men who do not steal plates and silver for profit, but are willing to attempt extraordinary things because they are right."

Lunt interrupted in the same theme, "Men who look out for the safety of their comrades. Men who see that those who saved their lives, and their ships, can find peace when they are in trouble."

Jones intertwined his fingers and flexed his hands inside out several times. He extended his clasped hands out over the rail and pointed with two index fingers at the Irish coast. "Ireland is a wild country on this western side. Men have vanished without a trace. Besides, who will help us get the Carronade? I plan for you to meet the Spymaster. And this summer the Marine Committee from the Continental Congress is expected to arrive in France. Mr. John Adams will be among them. The men I have mentioned are excellent contacts for a good young officer."

"Are we to go to Scotland together to steal the Carronade?" asked Lunt excitedly, "You're Scottish."

Jones avoided an answer and instead returned to ponder openly Lunt's request, "On this side of Ireland the sentiment will be against the English, unless you happen upon the land owners, the gentry. But if you stay among the peasants, or if you can locate a priest, you could make arrangements to get O'Mally home. Priests are outlawed in all of Ireland but they are everywhere among the people."

"I know, sir, O'Mally told me about them. It was a priest, after all, who helped us get into Belfast. He was an old man with white hair, who when the British stopped us, was far more concerned about his relics beneath the cart than the potatoes within it. A man who took money from me for the potatoes and let me toss them out to the poor.

"And later, I understand, he went and gave the money I had given him to the poor. He told O'Mally in Gaelic that I was a double bonus, like winning twice on a horse race. O'Mally said he prayed over me all the night I was delirious from the cold water of the swim out to the Drake. He had sent all his parishioners out to look for me along the coast. They found me only minutes before the British would have. He let me sleep in his cottage the night we were afraid that O'Mally's brother-in-law would turn us in. I'm not afraid of the priests," concluded Lunt.

"Let's make a bargain then," said Jones. "If I let you bring O'Mally to Ireland, you will be back on the Isle of Inishmore no later than tomorrow night, and you will subsequently serve me and the cause of our young republic as your seniors require."

"Yes, sir," answered Lunt.

"And one more thing, Lieutenant Lunt, you will attempt to slay no dragons in Ireland. Only to provide for the comfort of our shipmate," said Jones.

"Dragons, sir?" asked Lunt puzzled.

"In Belfast, I sent you there only to scout out the Drake. Not to climb aboard her, or to challenge the Royal Navy to a duel by yourself, or to almost steal the enemy's secret weapon. *Dragons*, Mr. Lunt. Promise me there will be no more dragons attempted on this mission. I do not want to miss you two days hence, and later find that you have begun a rebellion of your own in the west of Ireland."

Lunt laughed and then saluted, "No more dragons, sir. I will wait 'til Ranger gets to France before we begin another adventure."

Author's Historical Notes

Henry Lunt and the Ranger is fiction, based partly upon little known historical events. My first priority in writing this novel was to prepare an entertaining adventure and espionage story, not a biography. As a young man, many stories about the Lunt family's involvement in the American Revolution and the early history of the United States were passed on to me by my stepfather, George P. Lunt, a renowned scientist in his own right. Among my most prized possessions is Henry Lunt's naval sword.

Henry Lunt did accompany John Paul Jones on at least five of his ships: the Alfred, Providence, Bonhomme Richard, Alliance, and Ariel. On at least the last three ships he served under Jones with the rank of Lieutenant. However, there is conflicting information as to whether he was on the Ranger. Several accounts, all seemingly stemming from one source, not written until over a hundred years after the actual events, indicate that Henry Lunt was a prisoner of war from December, 1776 to March, 1779 overlapping the period of this book. However, within Plymouth, England's Mill Prison, records were inaccurate and escapes and recaptures were frequent. As readers of subsequent sequels will find out, Henry's young cousin, Micajah, became a veteran of such escapes by the time he was sixteen. French records of American prisoner exchanges were largely obliterated during their revolution, only eleven years later.

Within the Lunt family, a legend has persisted that it was Henry Lunt who brought the challenge into the Drake's captain at a dinner party, so embarrassing Captain George Burden publicly that he was obliged to sail out and meet the Ranger. Collaborating this, some Irish newspapers of the time seem to refer to a party or gathering, at which many of the Belfast gentry found out in advance that there would be a battle the next day and thus had time to organize themselves to ride out to the tips of Belfast Lough, or to hire small craft from which to witness the action. These newspaper accounts, largely very sympathetic to the British, tended to give a biased version of the battle. A list of only about one third of Ranger's crew exists and this largely came from those involved in possible court martial action against Lieutenant Simpson, who in Jones' opinion did not follow the actual orders he signed in the last chapter of this book. We simply will never know conclusively whether or not Henry Lunt was ever aboard the Ranger. However, I have favored the family legend in this fiction.

The carronade was very much a real secret weapon being developed during 1778. In the early experiments it was tested as both a long and short range weapon, capable of either hurling a light ball a great distance, or a very heavy ball a relatively short distance. The technology behind the weapon was deliberately not described in this book. It is something our Spymaster must find out in the sequel. By 1781, the carronade was being used aboard a number of the Royal Navy's ships of war operating in the American theatre. By the time of the Napoleonic wars it had become a major naval weapon used primarily to hurl very large balls a short distance. Since H.M.S. Drake was very likely the closest permanently stationed Royal Navy warship to the site of the ordnance testing at Stromeferry, that ship could conceivably have been involved in testing an early version of the weapon. This may have been why Captain Burden was reluctant to take the Drake out to face Jones. At any rate, I couldn't resist the premise that an early version of the Carronade was aboard the Drake, especially since Jones, despite many other possible targets, did keep coming back to get the Drake as described in my novel.

Jones' crew on the Ranger, especially those from Portsmouth, N.H., were very hostile towards their Captain and tried to mutiny or leave him ashore several times as described. Jones, despite the fearless man he was, had no choice but to keep forgiving them in order to get his mission accomplished. In addition, early in the voyage, several of the crew suffered from a smallpox outbreak, which I elected to leave out of my novel out of concern that my story would have too many subplots. The British spy, under the alias of David Smith, may have been responsible for the first boggled attempt on the Drake and was certainly responsible for alerting the citizens of Whitehaven, England to the raid.

Very little of the actual tactics of the sea battle are known. In one historic letter, Captain Jones mentions only that the action was "warm, close, and obstinate" and then goes on to describe the ultimate destruction to the Drake's rigging. Several Irish newspaper accounts seem to agree that the Drake's foremast was hit fairly early in the battle by American gunnery, otherwise I have utilized my imagination to depict the engagement.

Captain Burden, Lt. Dobbs, and over forty others died heroically in the defense of their flag, much as has been depicted in this novel. Many others aboard the Drake were wounded. Jones was very impressed by the determination of Lt. Dobbs, against all odds, not to surrender his ship. Irish newspapers indicate that Jones sent a sympathetic letter home to Lt. Dobbs' father with the Drake's wounded, hinting further that some of Jones' crew must have been ashore to scout out the Drake and subsequently might have had some knowledge that Dobbs' father was a member of the clergy. Among the casualties aboard the Ranger was U.S. Marine Lt. Samuel Wallingsford, but little is known of the exact circumstances of his death, except that he would have been commanding sharpshooters in the tops.

Many other circumstances described in my book are either wholly fiction, or a blend of fact and fiction. So as not to ruin the suspense of the sequel, I can say no more.

Tom McNamara

In Appreciation

Although this work is fiction, not a biography, a considerable amount of background research was accomplished with the help of the following organizations. The author wishes to express his appreciation to:

The National Maritime Museum
Greenwich, England
The National Library of Ireland
Dublin, Ireland
The United States Naval Academy
Annapolis, Maryland
The Navy Historical Center
Washington, D.C.
The Old South Church
Newburyport, Massachusetts
The Portsmouth Historical Society
and The John Paul Jones House
Portsmouth, New Hampshire
The H.M.S. Rose Foundation
and especially the crew of the H.M.S. Rose
Bridgeport, Connecticut

About the Author

Born in 1944, Tom McNamara was raised in the Boston area where as a boy he received first hand exposure to the historic surroundings from which the American Revolution evolved. He attended the oldest public high school in the United States, Boston English, and by 1966 had received a degree in chemistry from Boston University. After military service, he received an M.B.A. from Northeastern University.

Upon graduation from college, Tom joined the United States Army and after completing Officer Candidate School, served in Vietnam as an ordnance officer. After Vietnam, the army assigned him as a project officer with the Army Missile Command, where he worked on assignments at both Redstone Arsenal and Cape Kennedy.

For most of his professional career, Tom has been involved in corporate market research and new product planning. He has conducted business research for many of the world's largest corporations, often traveling internationally to conduct many of these assignments. Over the course of his business career Tom has also been a frequent speaker at conventions and conferences, and has contributed articles to various industrial and trade magazines.

In 1974, Tom received considerable nationwide publicity as the recipient of both a Presidential and Chicago Police Department commendation for capturing a mugger in downtown Chicago.

In 1977, Tom married his wife, Ellen, and in 1983 they moved with their company to San Diego. They have one child. In 1990, Tom co-authored his first book, *America's Changing Workforce - About You, Your Job, and Your Changing Work Environment*, which received nationwide attention and made Tom one of the nation's most sought after TV and Radio talk show guests.

In addition to a love of tennis and baseball, Tom is an avid amateur sailboat racing skipper and was appointed an "On Water Advisor" for America's Cup® XXVII held in his home San Diego waters. In beginning the Henry Lunt series, Tom is fulfilling a lifelong dream of bringing the adventure and romance of America's early sailing history to the attention of the world.

Henry Lunt & The Spymaster

Tom McNamara

NUVENTURES
PUBLISHING
La Jolla, California 92038-2489

NUVENTURES Titles

Look for NUVENTURES current and planned titles at your local bookstore:

America's Changing Workforce - About You, Your Job, and Your Changing Work Environment **ISBN 0-9625632-1-8**	Non-Fiction Trade Paper	$12.95
Henry Lunt & The Ranger **ISBN 0-9625632-3-4**	Fiction Hard Cover	$18.95
Widowmaker - A Thriller (To be released in late 1991) **ISBN 0-9625632-4-2**	Fiction Hard Cover	$18.95
Henry Lunt & The Spymaster (To be released early 1992) **ISBN 0-9625632-5-0**	Fiction Hard Cover	$18.95